MW01200757

BOOKS BY FRITZ PETERS

AVAILABLE THROUGH
HIRSCH GIOVANNI PUBLISHING

NOVELS
The World Next Door
Finistère
The Descent

~~~~~

MEMOIRS
Boyhood with Gurdjieff
Gurdjieff Remembered

THE WORLD NEXT DOOR

BY FRITZ PETERS

HIRSCH GIOVANNI PUBLISHING
LOS ANGELES

HIRSCH GIOVANNI PUBLISHING
LOS ANGELES, CALIFORNIA
6300 Canoga Avenue, Suite 1330 | Woodland Hills, CA 91367
www.hirschgiovanni.com

The Fritz Peters Collection
Managing Editor: Alexandra Carbone
Cover Design: Mathieu Carratier
Typesetting: Stewart A. Williams

First Published: New York: Farrar and Straus, 1949

ISBN 978-1-957241-12-8 / 1-957241-12-8
ISBN COLLECTION 978-1-957241-00-5

LCCN 2023916484

THE
WORLD
NEXT
DOOR

Originally Dedicated To:

Mary Lou, without whom this book
would not have been written...
And
the veterans, of war and society, in all psychiatric
institutions.

ONE

THE SHADOWS ARE THE FIRST to go. The movement is so slow, so
easy, you do not watch it; but now the pattern of the lawn, the sharp
trace of tree and house tremble and blend, lifting slowly from the earth
to meet the approach of darkness. And still you do not know. The
warning in the trees, their branches twisting against the coming of the
night, reaching out for the last light, is already too late. It is only when
you hear the silence, feel the tremor in your shoulders, that you know
this giant melancholy; then already the ground shadows are joining
the twilight, the ascending and descending night obliterating the tree
trunks, the corner of a house.

Fear comes suddenly, chilling and shocking. But in this there is
no bold stroke, only the slow preparation of terror. What child has
looked upon his first complete day and not felt the slow agony of
nightfall wresting it from him? With it come uncertainty and new
shadows—shadows with movement and hidden life, the life of the
small nighttime enemies: rodents, insects, marauders, and...and what?
The sounds and movements of people are contained and stifled, the
cry of alarm dies in the throat of a victim, the child looks quickly over
a shoulder for what is not there, and the gesture is stealthy, ill.

The houses protest: windows and doors snap into rectangles of
weak and angry light; radios chatter and laugh. Dogs whine at doors,
children on the road break into frenzied running, and everything they

have not seen pursues them as far as the slamming of a door, when their breath comes free and hard and safe again.

⌒

Rooted to my post outside the house, I drank my drink. Now there was no light left and yet my eyes were tied to the west. Only the liquor, a thin hot stream inside me, dripped like fuel to the last ember of warmth and light between my ribs, and fought the darkness.

But there is another light beginning now: a light that does not warm, but reveals and distorts. In this light, pallor becomes sickness, and sickness, death. As the darkness itself had spread like the moving blotch of blood upon bright cloth, so this light penetrated the darkness. It was only with this light of the moon, the false and treacherous substitute of nature, that I was driven inside to the small consolation of electricity, impertinently man-made. Still I could see out, could look upon the pale phosphorescent corpse of the world. There had been no promise in the setting of the sun, only a final, inevitable retreat; an end of light and no assurance of morning to end this siege of blackness.

The door whined and slammed. John, my stepfather. "It's such a beautiful night!"

"No. No! It's…" I shivered.

He looked at me, questioning. "Are you all right?"

"I'm cold. I'm going to bed. I'm all right."

But it was more than a preparation for bed or sleep. Rites of cleanliness and words of farewell, not of greeting. "Good night, John. Good night, Mother." Wishes, reassurances, a private readiness for a vigil. Tonight again I would lie awake, thwarting the surrender to the night, the threat of extinction implicit in the act of sleep. But surely I could not lie awake forever, even if tonight I must. I must, to keep that inner glow alive, that last link with the sun.

There is no escape from the moonlight. The blossoms on the apple trees outside my window cast their shadows and people the cover on the bed, the carpet. The bed itself is infected by the cold evil of this light. I glared up at the flat white disk, defying it; and then I watched and watched and watched. How it crawls and creeps around the room, staring into corners and crevices, leaving no escape from its path. Moon. Luna. Luna-tic. Moon-monamene-mens-menstrual-women. I could not close my eyes and yet to watch this was to absorb it. Women and madmen linked to the moon.

↬

How long had I watched? The lower rim of the sky through the trees changed slowly. Gray to pink. Pink to red. Again I looked for the moon, but the light was lighter, the light was real. This room faced the west. I rubbed my arms and put them under the covers without taking my eyes off the beginning light. It was terribly cold. Shivering, I got out of bed, found my bathrobe, and walked out of the bedroom into the living room. Through the glass and screen of the closed window, I found the bright orange-red glow in the sky. As it became larger, my excitement diminished slowly. And finally, there it was. What was the music, or did I just imagine it? No, I could hear it. Something was happening. Something important. Something I must not miss. The sun was moving, fighting its way to me through the trees, until at last I could see it completely: fiery and bright between two branches. Then and only then the fire inside me spread and reached out, meeting its maker.

"What are you doing up so early?"

Who was that?

Without moving, I said: "I couldn't sleep."

Was that my mother? Mother—mère—mare—*nightmare.*

"I had a nightmare."

But I didn't have a nightmare, did I? It was just the moon. Same thing? I turned and looked at my mother. Her face was mottled, yellow, ugly. Reflection of the sun? I looked again. It was yellow!

"I can look right into the sun," I said, astonished.

"I only knew one other person who could do that. Your uncle Oliver."

My uncle Oliver? What was she trying to tell me? Of course! I turned and faced her: still yellow. "Why didn't you tell me he was my father?"

I could see fear in her face, feel it as strongly as water rolling in and lapping against me. "David!" she said, her voice uncertain. "What do you mean?"

"Why didn't you tell me?"

"David! What are you saying?"

I looked back at the sun. That was better. "You know what I mean."

There were whispers in the room behind me. Then another voice: "Are you cold?"

I was cold, but I didn't mind as long as I could see the sun. "I want to go out in the sun," I said.

"But it's cold outside. Shall I make a fire?"

Who was that? I turned to look. Oh, John. He was shivering, but he was not afraid.

"It isn't cold in the sun. Look, I can look right at the sun!"

Silence.

"I'll put a chair out in the sunlight and you can sit out there if you want."

I nodded. "Isn't this Sunday?"

"Yes."

"I was born on Sunday, wasn't I?"

"Yes."

That was good. That was right.

"I'm going outside."

"But you're not dressed. You'll be cold."

"No." I shook my head. "I won't be cold in the sun. It's warm even in here, but the sun can't get in enough."

The grass was wet, but the air was warm as I had known it would be and the sun was almost to the tops of the pine trees now. What a wonderful day. The right day. And it was Sunday. I was born on Sunday. My father was my uncle. My uncle who was my father could look at the sun, too. But he was dead. Well, I had liked him, I had known. Even though I had thought he was my uncle and not my father.

"Here, David, sit down."

John again. He must have put the chair there. He handed me a blanket and then withdrew it. "Sit down and I'll wrap you up in the blanket."

John was a good man. Not afraid, but worried. I didn't need the blanket, but then I could always take it off. "All right."

Lying back in the canvas chair, I could still see the sun even with my eyes closed, and it was warm and comfortable. Why did people live in houses? Shivering in houses, manufacturing warmth and light. They were in the house now, she was afraid and he was not. Conflict, conflict, conflict. I was glad I was out of the house. Nothing but conflict all the time. Men and women, good and evil, positive and negative. Electricity, fire, explosions. Fighting all the time, and living in houses. If they would come out here and forget...forget in the sunlight. Should I go and tell them? But the house was cold. All that anyone needed was Sun, Air, Water, Earth. Why didn't they know? Well, no more trouble now. I knew at last. Thank God, I knew.

I looked intently at the sun. "Thank God," I said. "Now I know. Everything is all right." I closed my eyes again.

It felt so *good*. Good. God. Sun. Son of God. Created in the image of God. Was woman created in the image of God? What was there about that word? Wo-man. Woe to man. I sat up. Of course! Jesus Christ was a man. Buddha was a man. Mahomet was a man. They were all men. Joan of Arc. Had to burn her. Jesus. *Je sus*. I knew. He knew, and I know!

I opened my eyes and sat up. The sun was high and free above me now, no clouds, no trees, no nothing.

"Are you hungry? Don't you want some breakfast?"

It was my mother. Still yellow. I pulled the blanket open and then my bathrobe, exposing my chest to the sun. "I'm fine. It's warm in the sun."

"Don't you want to get dressed? Why don't you get dressed and then come out again?"

"All right." All right? Everything was all right. In fact, it was wonderful. Perhaps I'd better eat, I had a lot of work to do.

I followed her into the house and put on pants and a shirt. It was cold in the house.

"It's cold in here," I said.

"Shall I make a fire?"

"No, I'll go outside."

"But you have to eat. I'll make a fire. It won't take a minute." Why was she so anxious? What was the matter with her? I watched her obliquely as she rattled the stove. Back and forth, back and forth went the iron thing in her hand. And the look in her eye! First she looked at me, then at the stove, always shaking and shaking the iron thing. But the look! More than anxious. Scared. More than scared. I could feel it then, the way I had felt the fear, and it was more than fear. Angry fear. Determination.

She stopped shaking the iron thing and put some paper and wood into the stove. Fire. She lighted a match and touched it to the paper, leaving the door open and watching the flames. Fire? She smiled now. Such a smile! Fear, anger...cunning. Fire! Oh no. She wasn't going to burn the house down with me in it. I walked slowly to the door, frightened of the look in her eyes. Was she mad? Had she lost her mind? Look, she was blowing on the fire! I moved past her to the door.

"Where are you going?" Terror in her voice? She doesn't want me to go out. What would be the use of burning the house down if I'm out? Mother. Woman. Evil. But I was stronger than she, wasn't I? I opened the door.

"I'm going out," I said firmly.

"But I've built a fire for you!"

You're telling me you've built a fire for me. That's why I'm going out. But be careful, she doesn't know what she is doing.

"I know, but it isn't warm in here."

"Oh, David. What's the matter with you?"

What's the matter with me? That's a good one. You know I know. Woman's instinct. Now it's over. Now you're through, so you want to burn me up because I know about you. Because I found out.

"Nothing at all. I just want to be in the sunlight, that's all. The fire doesn't make it warm. The sun is warmer."

"But you have to have breakfast! It'll be warm in just a minute."

Warm? You mean it will be burning up in just a minute. Oh no. Not as easy as all that. I'm no fool.

"Why build a fire to make it warm inside, when it's warm outside? Isn't it easier to go out?"

Her body seemed to collapse. Of course. She was disappointed.

"All right then," she said.

I should hope to tell you!

It was so warm outside that I took off my shirt and the sun felt good on my chest and back. I stood in the middle of the lawn, turning and turning. Why did people wear clothes? Even when they were warm, when they went swimming, they always wore something. Not to protect. No, to hide. Hide what? Shame. That's all it was. If no one wore clothes, no one would be ashamed. Simple. Take off my clothes. Everybody take off their clothes. I took off my pants. Warm all over now. No clothes. Naked. The only thing they wanted to hide was sex. Why? All the men were the same, all the women were the same. What was there to hide? Nothing hidden, no secrets; no secrets, no excitement, no suspicion. No excitement and suspicion, no fear. *Very* simple.

Up and down, up and down. Warm wet grass, warm warm sun.

"David! *David!* Put your pants on!"

"What for? I haven't got anything to be ashamed of!"

"Someone will see you! Hurry! What will people think?"

"Who cares what people will think? What will they think? What *can* they think? Who hasn't seen a naked man? I'm no different than anyone else. Look. What have I got to hide?"

"David! You must put your pants on."

"I won't!"

"Oh, David, *please!*"

Oh what the hell! And it was colder with my pants on. What a business! No wonder everyone was mixed up. It was warm in the sun. You wanted to be warm. So you put on pants and got cold. Just to hide your sex. Who was fooled? Did somebody think I was different with pants on? No wonder sex was so complicated. Everybody was afraid of it. Everybody pretended they didn't have any sex by hiding it.

The first thing to do was change that. Everybody had to start all over again. Take off your pants and let the world look at you. They'd get used to it soon enough, and that would be the end of the trouble. Nothing to hide anymore. Say what you mean, be what you are. Live in the open. Walk in the sun. Houses, clothes. Lies, lies, lies. Everything made to hide something. Get dressed. Get in a house. Nobody can see you. Safety. Obscurity. Let there be light. Light. Sunlight. It might take a long time.

Up and down again. The lawn felt good under my feet. Earth. Stay close to the earth. Walk on the ground. Breathe the air. Feel the sun. Drink water. Drink the rain. Wouldn't need food. I wasn't hungry. I hadn't eaten.

Now what could be more natural? Cold inside. Go out. Warm outside. Take off your clothes. But no. Stay inside. Make a fire. Wrap up. *Why?* Civilization? Habits. That's what you were supposed to do. That's the way people lived. *Why?* Why so complicated? Cold in winter? Follow the sun. Hot in summer? Go in the water. Take off clothes. Simple. Too simple. Make everything difficult. Machines.

Machines. Machines. Progress. *Progress!* Start all over again. Progress a fight against nature. Nature: natural, logical, right, simple. Why was everyone against it? People want to be unhappy? No, not natural. Nobody understands.

Have to work while the sun is still up. The moon will come out tonight. Look out for the moon. Evil. Bad. Start with the sun. *Everybody* likes the sun. Beautiful sun. Look at it. Perfectly simple to look at it. Warm. Friendly. Everybody should look at it. Everybody could, but they're afraid of it. Have to conquer fear. Kill fear the first thing. Simple. I knew. I was happy. People look at the sun. Live in the sun. Feel like this. Simple, simple, simple. Everybody happy. No fights. No war. No bloodshed. No killing. First mistake to kill Christ. Ever since then wars. Even before. Was Buddha killed too? Was he before Christ, after Christ? All the same. Buddha, Mahomet, Christ. Messengers from God. God? Good. Dieu? Jehovah? Lord. Man is God. God is man. The light is warm. The light is the sun. The Good son. Good God. Son of God. Jesus Christ. Christ died to save you. Got killed, did not die. No good. Mistake. Tried to tell people. Can't tell them in words. Resistance to words in all people. Have to understand with eyes, hearts. Inside. It is all inside everybody. Babies know. Babies don't put on clothes, babies not afraid of light. Children know everything. To eat, breathe, sleep, stay in light, keep off clothes. Babies learn everything wrong after birth. Conditioning all wrong. Learn shame, fear. And a little child shall lead them. Everybody become babies again? Did babies fight? Learn to fight. Babies can't fight. Children fight. Children already conditioned by people. Civilization. All wrong. Get back to elementals. Babies elemental. Good. Elements. Earth, Air, Fire and Water.

What was that? A car. Men. People in the bushes looking at me? I walked over to them. John and two men. Hats, suits. Papers in their hands. "How do you do?"

"Will you come with me?"

They stayed in the bushes. Were they hiding from someone? Cold in the shade. Back on the lawn in the sun. Come with them where? Lie down. Feel the earth, the air, the sun. Good. Close your eyes. See the sun through them. Everything fine, everything wonderful, everything beautiful. I feel so *good*. I wish everybody felt so good, not like the men in the bushes, or my mother. Hiding in the house, hiding in the bushes, hiding in clothes. Just lie in the sun.

Another man in the bushes? I stood up and looked. Coming through the bushes. Bending over. Stand up and take off your shirt! Feel the sun!

"Hello, David."

"Hello."

Another man. Who were they? What difference? All people are the same. I turned my back on them. What was that noise? They had both come through the bushes. What was the matter with them? They didn't stand quite straight. Watching me? The sun seemed very low in the sky. Redder. What time was it?

Clink. Clink. What's that? They grabbed my arms.

"Let me go! What's the matter with you?"

"Now come on, David. No one's going to hurt you."

"What do you want?"

"We want you to come with us."

"Where?"

"Now come on, David."

"But where?"

Clink. Clink. "There."

There what? What was on my wrists? Metal? Handcuffs? *Handcuffs!*

"What are you doing to me?"

I saw John. "Where are we going?"

"It's all right, David. It's all right."

Is it? I looked at the handcuffs.

"Get in the car, David."

"*Where* are we going?"

Looks and silence. What were they hiding?

"We're your friends, David."

Handcuffs. Friends. Two and two make five? I held out my hands to them.

"Look at that. *You* are my friends?"

Another voice: "Will you come with me?"

Who was that? Carl. My brother! No, my brother-in-law. Same thing.

"Are you going, too?"

Why did he look uncertain? Why did they all? Where were we going?

"Yes, David, I'll come with you. John and I will come with you. Get in the car."

"Are we going for a ride?"

"Yes. We're taking you for a ride."

Gangsters? No, John and Carl were getting in the car, too. John on one side, Carl on the other. They were all right. Everything was all right. "I'm glad you came with me."

Who are the men in front of the car? Blue shirts. Caps.

"Who are they?"

No answer.

"Who are you?"

The one on the right turned around, only to look. Badge on his blue shirt. P-O-L-I-C-E. Police? Handcuffs. Criminal?

Where could we be going? But it was nice in the car. Friendly. John and Carl, smiling, smiling. Outside the sun, but warm even in here. Grass, trees, blossoms. Nice quiet car. Up a hill, over a bridge. Whoops! like a roller coaster. I stared at my hands. Handcuffs. Police. What had I done? Going to jail? Execution? Man is fated to die. Death is the logical end of life.

The car turned into a side road between two brick pillars. Beautiful grass, trees, bushes, and then buildings. To the left, the biggest building and in front of it a flagpole with the American flag at the very top. I watched the flagpole and the flag, and the car turned again driving directly towards them. I lowered my head to peer out of the window of the car. The flag was out of sight, above me, but I knew it was still there. The car drove past groups of people in front of the building and then came to a stop. Not a jail. Positively not a jail. Must be an execution. But why? John and Carl sad. Police sad. It's all right. I don't mind dying.

We got out. People on the steps leading into the building. People on the porch. People on the sidewalks. People around the flag. And there it was, waving in the wind, way up high. I smiled at the people. It's all right. Everybody has to die sometime. Please don't mind. I searched for the gallows. Would it be close to the flagpole? No, it would be a burning. Then wouldn't there be a stake? But not near the flagpole. It was made of wood. Mustn't burn the flag. How did I know it was to be a burning? I knew. The men who had been in the bushes and then in the front of the car were on each side of me, and we started up the steps between the people. I recognized one of them. The Chief of Police. How did I know him? Anyway he was very nice. Nice and sad, too. He said: "Now just take it easy and come along with us," and we went into the building.

It was very dark and cool inside. Was the stake in here, perhaps? Couldn't burn me in a building. Oh well, it was up to them, not to me. Would it take very long? I was tired and after I was dead I could sleep all the time. Let's go.

We walked along an endless hall, almost completely dark. How did they know where they were going? What had happened to John and Carl? Relatives weren't allowed to follow you to the stake, at least not all the way. The Chief of Police looked so unhappy. Was he sorry for me? I don't mind dying. Really I don't. He was kind, I could feel that. Probably he was sorry.

It was so dark that I could hardly see anything now. What I did see was not clear, but as if I was looking through a film of gelatin. We had stopped walking and were in a small room. There seemed to be several people, at least shapes, but only one of them was positively identifiable as a person. It was a man sitting behind a table, dressed in white. I could feel him more than I could see him, like the emanation I had felt from my mother. But I could see his eyes and something of his face. It was a cruel feeling that came from him. Hard and evil. Reptilian. I wasn't afraid of him but I knew he was evil. I could smell it as well as feel it. It made the air in the room seem very close.

His face became even clearer when he fixed his eyes on me: small black beads floating in soft pink sweating flesh. He had only glanced at me up to now, during a conversation he was having with someone. He said, directly to me:

"Well, son, how do you feel?"

I knew that he could not be addressing me since he was not my father. I looked around the room and finally turned to look in back of me. No one in back. No one next to me. Where was the Chief of Police? He had vanished, the other man had vanished, even the handcuffs were gone! I shook my free wrists, pleased. But what about the man's son? What was he, anyway, this man in white? I looked back at his face. A nurse. Why a nurse? I smiled, regretting my inability to find his son for him. He drummed his fingers on the table top and then fixed my eyes with his again.

"Come on, son, you can talk to me. How do you feel?"

He must be talking to me. Perhaps it was a form of kindness, calling me "son," like an old man calls any young man "son." But he was a person with absolutely no kindness, and not much older than I. Surely it didn't make any difference about him since I was already convicted and only waiting to go to the stake. Or would it be a death chamber here?

I leaned towards him. "Are you by any chance talking to me?" He smiled and looked away and then looked back at me again, straightening his face with effort. "Yes, my boy. I'm talking to you."

"My boy?" Was he laboring under some delusion? Or was he really my father? I thought for a moment, remembered the face of my own father clearly, and then smiled at him again. No, my father was my uncle! Well he wasn't my uncle either. But if he thought so, then I should be gentle with him.

"I don't see how I can help you. I'm not your son. But, of course, all men are brothers."

I hoped this was all right. It would have been unfair to him to allow him to believe that he was really my father.

I was glad to see that he was not disappointed, but surprised that he seemed amused. Was there something funny about this? How could you tell? To have a face like that, he must have had a terrible life. Everyone was basically good, and yet the good was all gone from him. How could anyone have a face so twisted that it radiated evil through the tight, thin mouth, the bullet-like eyes, so inappropriate in that fleshy face?

"What's your name?" he asked me—at any rate I assumed that he was asking me.

"I was christened..." I started to say and then remembered that, as far as I knew, I had not been christened at all. "I was named David Mitchell. People call me Mitch sometimes, too."

He nodded and began to write on a large sheet of paper which had mysteriously appeared before him, out of nowhere. When he had finished writing, he looked up at me again. "Now, David," he asked, "how do you feel?"

"I'm fine," I said. "Who are you anyway?"

"I'm Mr. Neider," he said. "Nurse Neider."

"How do *you* feel?" I had been right about his being a nurse then. I was glad to have him confirm it. It made me feel that he was not entirely suspect, since he had not tried to conceal his profession from me.

He did not answer my question but asked me my address, my telephone number, and then my mother's name.

"Which one?" I asked him.

"Which what?" Once more he seemed surprised...looking at me craftily. I contemplated the labor of having to explain about all her names and took a deep breath.

"What I mean is, which name do you want? She has several."

He looked unnecessarily puzzled and stopped writing. "Suppose you tell me all of them," he said with exaggerated patience.

"Her name was Clara Allen and then she married my father and became Mrs. Mitchell, and then she married my sister's father and became Mrs. Barnes, and then she married my stepfather, that is my present stepfather, and became Mrs. Lasky. I know it's complicated but I can't help that. Also, Mr. Mitchell, my father, is dead. Mr. Barnes, my sister's father—she's not really my sister, she's my half-sister—well, he's an alcoholic, I think; and Mr. Lasky, John that is, has disappeared. At least he was here, but he isn't any longer. Now which of those names did you want?"

He smiled a very unpleasant smile. "I think that's enough," he said. "You seem to have a good memory."

"Well, you have to remember things like that, don't you? I can't understand why people are always surprised when they find out that I have a different name from my mother. Haven't they ever heard of divorce?"

He did not answer this, but said something in a low voice to someone whom I could not see. Then I heard my mother's voice. Where had she come from? What was she doing here? John and Carl had disappeared. She had appeared. How did they come and go? Maybe I was blind, or almost blind. Oh well, if I was going to die, it surely didn't matter whether I could see or not. I looked at the face before me and it seemed a little clearer now. A male nurse. What did I need a nurse for? I looked around the room, but could see only walls and shapes. The face of the nurse was the one face I could distinguish. He was looking away from me and still talking. I heard my mother's voice but still could not see her. Was it a telephone conversation? But if so, where was the telephone? Or was it just that I couldn't see it?

The next thing I knew I was in another room, or perhaps it was the same room, although the desk and most of the people had disappeared, and another man said to me: "Take off your clothes." This man was not the nurse, not unhappy, not unkind, just gentle. Put on your clothes. Take off your clothes. Why didn't they make up their minds?

Probably they had a rule about not executing you in your own clothes. Would they burn me naked, was that it? Joan of Arc had worn something hadn't she? A kind of gray robe, I thought. Or was that only in the movies or in pictures? Anyway there were no other clothes in the room.

The man touched my shoulder and handed me a small bundle of clothing. "You can put these on," he said kindly.

I thanked him and he looked away from me as I undressed. While I would not have minded if he had looked at me, I thought this was both sensitive and polite and hurried to get out of my clothes and into the ones he had handed me: a pair of white pajamas of the same material as BVD's, clean but unironed, and a pair of rather heavy blue trousers and a jacket. Overalls, or more pajamas? I put them on anyway. Now, where was the stake?

Then he handed me a pair of slippers made of plaid flannel with open heels, and I put them on. When I walked, they made a shuffling sound and the heels clopped gently on the linoleum floor.

"Now what?" I asked him.

"Are you tired?"

"No." I had been tired, but I didn't feel tired now. I wanted to get it over with. Besides, the execution had to be in daylight, and it seemed to me that the room was already getting dark. Or was it just my eyes?

"You just come along with me," he said.

I had liked him at once and was glad to go with him. He led me into the hall and we stopped before a wide door. It opened and I saw that it was an elevator. We got in and he operated it himself. After a short ride, during which the elevator made a frightful loud buzzing, it came to a stop, the doors opened and we got out. He led me down another long corridor to a door which he unlocked with one of a large bunch of keys hanging from his belt. We were in another corridor, not so long, and turned to our left to face another door. He unlocked this door and opened it. Here was a large, wide room, filled with people in the same costume as mine, and my attendant smiled and said: "Well, here you are. Make yourself at home." Was it going to be a mass execution?

He gave me a little push as if to propel me into the room and away from him, so I said goodbye to him and walked into the center of the room. Several of the inhabitants of the room had looked at me as I came in and one of them came up to me.

"Hello," he said without offering to shake hands with me. "Want a cigarette?"

I shook my head and looked at his face. He was also very kind.

"No, thank you very much." I smiled to indicate my appreciation.

"Who are you?" he asked, and without waiting for an answer continued: "Where did you come from?"

I knew that he did not mean where had I just come from, but beyond the nurse whose image was already fading in my mind, and the small room where he had talked to me, I did not know, except for the car. Where had I come from? And what would my name mean to him? The question puzzled me, so I walked away from him, continuing to smile, hoping that he would not misunderstand. I was pleased to see that he did not take offense but followed me.

I had walked to a window and now looked out of it, through the bars, one of which I gripped in one hand. On the stubby grass—curious, my eyesight seemed to have returned—under the window, was a great flock of black birds. Beyond them, at a considerable distance, across a great expanse of lawn and field, I saw the large building in front of which stood the flagpole. If I had been there, how had I arrived here? Were there several buildings like that? I looked around the room, out of the windows on the opposite wall, through which I could see the entrance to this building. No flagpole. In any case, the entrance was not the same. I would have had to walk, or perhaps ride, to get here. I could not have forgotten that, could I?

Sensing my distress, the man who had offered me the cigarette said: "What's the matter?"

In a loud voice, I said to him: "Where am I?"

"This is Ward 8," he answered smiling, and while the words made no sense to me, I was reassured by his smile and the gentle affirmation of his nodding head. Apparently it was all right, whatever it was. I looked out again at the birds on the grass, struggling to find an adequate answer for his question about who I was and where I had come from. For some reason, I was unable to take my eyes off the birds. And then it came to me suddenly. Ravens! Something from the Bible about ravens: "Who provideth for the raven his food?" I asked him.

He shrugged his shoulders. "I don't know," he said. "What's your name?"

"I am the second coming of Christ," I said suddenly. As soon as I had said this, I understood why I had not been put to death yet. I had forgotten, of course, that my mission (even though I did not know exactly what it was) was not yet completed. Something to do with these men in blue?

I was so pleased and relieved with the discovery of who I was, and the obvious understanding of where I had come from, that I did not notice the man in white who had edged up to stand behind me. It was only when I felt his hand on my shoulder, knowing positively that he had not been there before, that I realized someone had come up behind me. "Now just take it easy, son," he said.

I turned to face him and the look on his face startled me. He belonged to the same company as that nurse. I recognized the basic evil in the face, the fear that is only in the eyes of an attacker. I moved my shoulder sharply away from him; even his touch was bad.

"Who are you?"

He reached out for my shoulder and took another firm grip on it. "Now don't you worry about that," he said. "You just take it easy."

There had been an undercurrent of sound and conversation in the room, but now there was only silence and all eyes were upon our group of three. My friend in blue stood firmly at my side, facing the man in white.

"Take it easy yourself," I said. "And let go of my shoulder. What are you afraid of, anyway?"

His tone deepened, menacing me. "Now look, son," he said, "we don't want any trouble around here, now do we?"

Was he mad? Who was making trouble besides this man himself?

"Why don't you go away then," I said, "and we won't have any trouble."

I had to pull myself away from his grip this time and could feel my face reddening with the struggle. He called out something which I could not understand, and seized me with both hands, locking them on my arms above the elbows. Before I could protest, two other men in white ran up to us, and now there were six pairs of hands on me. The two new men held my arms from behind, having pushed my blue-clad friend away, and the one who had started this was doing something with my hands which were held powerfully, outstretched towards him, by the men behind me. To my amazement I found that my hands were strapped in a leather contraption which was also belted around my waist. Simply another kind of handcuffs. What was this preoccupation with tying up my hands? The anger drained out of me, giving way to surprise at finding myself bound. I looked in amazement at the three men.

"What on earth are these for?"

Still menacing, the first man glared at me while the other two half dragged me to a nearby wooden chair and forced me into it. Then the first one leaned his face very close to mine and said: "I told you we didn't want any trouble from you."

"What was I doing?" I asked, even more puzzled.

"Don't you worry about that," he said. "Let this be a lesson to you. You gotta behave when you're in here."

Behave? Behave how? "If I don't worry about it, who will? How do you want me to behave?"

"Right now you just shut up," he growled.

He seemed seriously frightened for all his menace and his angry tones. What had I done to alarm him? Should I reassure him?

"I certainly don't want to make any trouble," I said calmly. "I didn't mean to frighten you. That was the last thing I wanted to do."

These words seemed to alarm him even more, but he did not say anything. He walked away with his companions and leaned against the wall near the door, glaring in my direction.

I contemplated my handcuffs, reflecting (with sudden understanding) that since I was the second coming of Christ, this was simply an act of fate. There was no point in objecting to it. But how was I supposed to accomplish my mission with my hands tied up? I strained my head to look again at the ravens, obviously in need of food, but there was nothing I could do for them now. They would have to survive until I could get food for them.

Since I was not tied to the chair, I stood up. Immediately the three men started in my direction so I sat down again. All of the people in the room (four men in white and perhaps sixty in blue) continued either to stare frankly in my direction or to glance at me from time to time. My friend, the offerer of cigarettes, had disappeared into the other blue men and I could not find him. Also, my eyes were getting bad again, or behaving oddly. I could see the ravens perfectly clearly, but the room and the men in it were vague.

I felt someone approaching me and was happy to see that my friend had returned. He smiled his warm friendly smile and said: "Don't worry, they'll let you out pretty soon."

Would he still remember about the cigarette?

"Could I have that cigarette now?" I asked. He was smoking. He glanced around the room and then put a cigarette in my mouth and held his own to it until I had lighted mine. "Thank you very much," I said.

He nodded and walked away from me. I saw him talking to the evil man in white and then he returned to me. "You can stand up if you want," he said, "but be quiet."

While I had no wish to stand up, I thought perhaps I had better do whatever he told me. He seemed to know this place pretty well.

"Would it be all right if I looked out of the window?"

He laughed. "Sure. Just don't make any noise."

I laid my cuffed hands on the window sill and the belt pulled against my back. I could just touch the bars of the window with my fingertips. "What do I have to wear these for?" I asked him.

He held his finger to his lips. "Watch out," he said. "Here he comes."

It was the same one. I managed a smile. "Are you going to take these off now?"

"Now look," he said. "Are you going to give me trouble again?"

"No," I said. He was really preposterous. Wasn't I allowed to ask him questions?

"All right then," he said. "How do you feel now?"

"I feel perfectly fine," I said. "Do you feel better?"

"Don't you worry about me," he said. "You just worry about yourself."

Don't worry. Do worry. He *was* confused.

"But there is nothing to worry about," I said. "I've felt fine all along, except for these things." I indicated my hands. "But you still look frightened. What are you afraid of?"

"Are you gonna take it easy?"

I must have said too much; probably he didn't like anyone to know he was afraid. I nodded quietly and he walked away from me again. I turned to my friend, still standing at my side. 'What's the matter with him? Is he nuts?"

My friend laughed. "You're okay," he said. Then he started away from me. "Just take it easy," he said.

I realized that I had, at least in someone's mind, created a disturbance. I continued to look at the ravens on the grass, thinking about their food problem. The conversation in the room had begun again and I was no longer the center of attention. My only real problem was to get out of the handcuffs. By bending my head over my hands and raising them as much as the belt would permit, I managed to extract the cigarette from my lips and hold it between the thumb and index finger of my left hand. It seemed to me that since there was no way to get the handcuffs off, the only solution was to burn my hands off. I applied the burning end to the back of my right hand and held it there. I could smell the burning flesh and hair but I could not feel anything, so I pressed down harder. After some time, I lifted the cigarette and found that I had made almost no progress. I shifted the cigarette to my right hand and performed the same operation on my left. When I had burned a small hole in the back of each hand, I put the cigarette— hardly more than a butt now—back between my lips and surveyed my hands. I was struck by a sudden memory of the nails that had been driven through Christ's hands on the cross, and realized at once that it was the disbelief of this man in white that had forced him, through his own fear, to put me in handcuffs. When he saw the scars he would of course realize who I was and deliver me from the handcuffs. I spit the cigarette end out of the window and turned away from it. There he was. I walked over to him and stopped in front of him with my hands spread out in front of me.

"Now will you believe me?"

"Jesus Christ!" he exclaimed and called out to someone.

I was very pleased. "That's right! Will you please take these off now? I can't burn them off."

The other men in white had materialized next to us and they were all in consultation, whispering to each other.

One of them looked at me. I did not remember his face, but I could see pain in his eyes. "Look," he said, "I'm going to take these off you, but you'll be quiet, won't you? You won't do anything wrong, will you?"

I did not remind him that I hadn't done anything wrong in the first place. "Of course I won't," I said.

He unfastened the belt behind my back and then lifted my arms. Very gently, he undid the leather cuffs around my wrists and lifted my hands slowly out of the contraption. His eyes were filled with sorrow.

"Please don't be unhappy," I said and put my hand on his shoulder. "I'm all right. Really I am."

He took my hand from his shoulder. "You sure are, kid," he said. The suffering was in his voice, too. It was painful to look at him, so I turned away and started back towards the window. I felt him following me and stopped. "What is it?"

"Wouldn't you like to get some rest?" he asked.

I realized that I was really very tired and the prospect of rest seemed very appealing. Of course I would not sleep (some stirring recollection about not sleeping trickled through my mind), but it would be nice to lie down. "Yes," I said. "I certainly would."

"Well, you come along with me," he said. "I'll take you to your room."

"My room?" Did they have a room for me? Had they expected me? He nodded. "Yeah, sure. Your room."

"You mean you knew I was coming?"

"Of course we knew."

Well, for heaven's sake! They knew and I hadn't even known myself!

I followed him to the door and waited for him to unlock it. Then down the corridor to another door, and then down the long wide corridor, apparently the entire length of the building. This was the way I had come in. At the end of the hall we stopped before another door and then went into another small corridor, just like the one we had left. Instead of going to the end, he stopped before a doorway at the side and unlocked the door and held it open for me. I entered a small room with a barred window and a bed. Nothing else. There was a bright light in the center of the ceiling. I sat on the edge of the bed which seemed very comfortable and inviting. He looked at me from the doorway.

"Think you can sleep here all right?"

"I'm sure I can rest," I said. "But I don't think I'll sleep. I haven't slept for a long time."

"Do you want me to get you something? Do you want a sleeping pill?" He was really awfully nice.

A sleeping pill? I knew that no sleeping pill would put me to sleep. Also, I had a faint memory of having been offered a sleeping pill once before, in the same words.

"Will you tell me something?" I asked.

He smiled. "If I can."

"What, exactly, is this place?"

"This is Ward 8," he said. "You were over on B, but I've brought you to A to sleep. There are no private rooms over there."

A? B? What was he talking about? "What do you mean A and B? Ward 8? Of what?"

"The Veterans Administration Hospital," he said.

"Hospital?" I repeated the word. Not a prison. Not a death house. "What am I here for? Are they going to operate on me?"

He shook his head. "Don't worry. No one is going to do anything to you. All you have to do is go to sleep."

Again the memory of someone offering me a sleeping pill fluttered through my mind, but too quickly for me to grasp it. What was I doing in the hospital now? "Am I sick?" I asked him.

The look of pain returned to his eyes, and he nodded his head slowly. "Yes."

I laughed. "But what's the matter with me?"

He made a gesture with his hands, a gesture of helplessness, but the look in his eyes betrayed a knowledge that he seemed unable to communicate. I had an idea, an inspiration really, and I began to laugh.

"Is this a mental hospital?"

His head nodded slowly.

Of course, this was 1947! What else would anyone do with Christ if he suddenly appeared on earth? What could they do with him except throw him in a mental hospital...an insane asylum? I was perfectly satisfied to be Christ, particularly since there did not seem to be anything I could do about it. But why hadn't it been arranged for me to reappear somewhere else? Who was it that was always predicting the return of Christ? The Theosophists? Well, where the hell were they? Or was this a test of some kind, to find out if I really was Christ? As far as I knew, all he had done the first time (or was it I who had done it?) was simply to say who he was and people had believed him, at least for a while. What had gone wrong then? If he hadn't made some mistake (or if I hadn't?) the first time, then all this wouldn't be necessary now. Well, whatever had gone wrong, here we were again, and it wasn't going so well this time either. Whoever had forced this destiny upon me probably knew what they were doing. Or did they? Perhaps they were not so all-knowing after all; perhaps their power didn't extend very far, actually, and the rest of it was up to me. The man was still waiting in the doorway, so I said:

"Well, you probably aren't responsible anyway. I guess it has to be like this. It isn't your fault. But how do I get out?"

He shrugged his shoulders. "Don't think about that now. What you need is some sleep. I'll get you that pill. You lie down now."

Although he was friendly, he didn't have any authority, so I decided not to argue with him. They'd have to let me see the people in charge sometime. I nodded to him and lay down on the bed. He closed the door and I listened to his footsteps going down the hall. Although I had heard them distinctly enough, there was considerable other noise in the hallway now. People talking in loud voices, lights being turned on and off. So this was a mental hospital. I remembered that before I had been Christ, when I was in the Army, I had been in a hospital. That was where they had offered me a sleeping pill! But why? I could see the Army hospital in my mind: the bed, the faces of the nurse and doctor, and my own face—the surprise I had felt when I realized I was not wounded. How had I come there, and if I was unhurt, why? I must have been wounded! The shells, the silence, and then the machine-gun fire. I felt my chest and stomach and then my legs. No. My head perhaps? No.

Then I laughed. That was a long time ago. This was a different hospital even. But had I really not been wounded? I could remember blood...

When he returned and unlocked the door, he was accompanied by another man: the one who had put the handcuffs on me earlier. Whether it was because of this man or for some other reason, both of them now seemed fearful and menacing. The one who had been so friendly extended a pill (it seemed very large to me) in the open palm of one hand but did not look into my eyes. I had always been suspicious of people who would not look into my eyes. Was it because of the other man? Or did he regret his friendliness? Were they supposed to be unfriendly? Was he Judas? The other man held a small paper cup filled with, probably, water and stood over me.

I looked at the pill and then at the two men. 'What is that?"

"Sodium amytal," said the man with the water. His voice was blank and hard.

"That won't put me to sleep," I said. "There's no point in wasting it."

"Now come on, sonny," that same voice again. "You just take that pill. It'll put you to sleep all right."

I was tired and bored with the need to explain why it wouldn't put me to sleep, but there was nothing else to do. "Do you have any cognac?" I asked.

"Any what?"

"Cognac. Or whiskey will probably be all right."

"Look, son, we don't serve liquor here. You just take this pill." He took the pill from the other man's hand and shoved it up to my face.

I turned my head away. "I don't want a drink. I want to go to sleep. I was in a hospital in the Army and I couldn't sleep so they gave me one sodium amytal and a full glass of cognac...that's brandy...and I went to sleep. They had tried plain sodium amytal and other things... phenobarbital, for instance, but they didn't work. After all, I *want* to go to sleep, you know."

"Now look, I don't want any more trouble with you tonight," he said. "I can't hang around here forever. You take this and shut up. Remember what happened last time."

I nodded wearily. "That's what I'm telling you. Last time they gave me brandy. I just told you. After all, I know, I was there." I looked into his face. "Where were you in the Army? Did you work in a hospital?"

"None of your business," he said. "Are you going to take this pill?"

I shrugged my shoulders. "If it'll make you feel any better, certainly. I wish I knew why you get so upset all the time." I took the pill and swallowed it. "There, do you feel better now?"

"I sure do. Here, drink some water." He handed me the paper cup and I drank a sip of water and handed it back to him. "Well, I'm glad you feel better, but it isn't going to do anything to me, I can guarantee that."

He started away from me and motioned to the other man to follow him. "Now you just lie down and go to sleep," he said.

"I'll lie down, but I certainly won't go to sleep. I'll try, but it's no use. If you had listened to me in the first place, you..."

He was at the doorway and he turned quickly, pointing his finger at me. "Are you going to lie down and shut up?"

The conversation seemed completely senseless to me, and I was ready to do whatever he asked just to have him leave, but it was they who wanted me to go to sleep and it seemed ridiculous to lie on the bed and not sleep. "What good is it going to do you or me if I lie here and don't sleep?" I asked impatiently.

"A lot! And you will go to sleep, if I have to knock you out. Know what I mean?"

There was no mistaking the meaning, since he was shaking his fist at me. "All right, all right. Anything you say. But I can't see what you want to do that for. If you'd just give me..."

He interrupted me by coming back to stand over the bed and shake his fist into my face. "Did you hear me?"

"Did *I* hear you? The whole hospital heard you!" I pushed his hand away from my face. "What's the matter with you, anyway? You want me to go to sleep, I want to go to sleep, and I've told you how to put me to sleep. And don't look so angry. I didn't invent cognac, the doctor gave it to me. If you..."

He leaned over, pushing me down on the bed, his fist on my chest.

"Dammit!" he shouted. "Will you shut up? What do you think this is, a bar?"

I looked at his fist on my chest until he removed it and then said as slowly and patiently as possible: "No. This is a hospital. If you don't have brandy or whiskey, then you must have alcohol. I don't think I'd like the taste of it, but I could swallow it if I had to, and it would certainly put me to sleep." I rose up on my elbows. "They explained to me about alcohol. After a certain point alcohol knocks you out, and that's exactly what it did. Isn't that what you want?"

The fist began shaking at me again. "Look, one more crack out of you and you're gonna get this right in your kisser."

I lay back on the bed and said nothing until he had left my bedside and backed to the door. The other man had disappeared. As he was about to go through the door, I said: "Well there isn't any sense to this, anyway. You'll have to admit that."

He shook his fist at me again and then backed out of the door. When he closed it and locked it, I realized that he had not turned out the light. To expect me to go to sleep with the light on was even more incredible. I got up out of the bed and went to the door, looking for a light switch, but there was none. I searched the other walls, but there was no way of turning off the light.

Reluctantly I went to the door and pounded on it, peering through the small rectangle of wired glass, into the darkened hall. I stopped pounding and listened, but could hear nothing except voices which seemed to come from some distance down the hallway. I could not hear what they were saying, but it was impossible that they could not hear me. I pounded again, hard, and this time I heard footsteps coming down the hall. A face appeared in the square of glass, looking at me, startled. I motioned in the direction of the light fixture and shouted:

"The light's on. How can I sleep with the light on?"

I had never seen this face before, of that I was certain. It smiled briefly and then the lips curled into a look of cunning. He had probably known the light was on all the time. He shook his head.

"Go to sleep," he said loudly and disappeared.

I waited until the sound of his footsteps in the hall had ceased and then started pounding on the door again. This time I heard several footsteps and finally the door opened suddenly. Three men burst into the room. "You hold him," said one of them, and once again two of them held my arms from behind me and the third fastened another leather contraption around my waist and circled my wrists with the leather cuffs.

"What good is this going to do?" I demanded when they had finished.

"Now look, bud," said the man who had fastened the cuffs, "once and for all, are you going to shut up?"

Why was it impossible to convey anything to these people? I determined to try once again. "Look," I said very slowly, enunciating clearly, "I want to go to sleep. You want me to go to sleep. I will be quiet if I go to sleep. Is that right?"

He nodded.

"Well how can I sleep with this thing on," I indicated the cuffs and belt with my head, "the light on, and the wrong medicine?"

"You just better, that's all."

I spoke even more slowly: "I will be glad to try. But you seem to be making it more difficult all the time. Why don't you turn the light off?"

He did not answer this, but said to the other two men who were still behind me: "Put him on the bed, boys."

I was lifted from the floor and tossed onto the bed, with the leather belt pressing into my back. There was certainly no convincing them. The two men then produced a sheet which they tied tightly around my chest and around the whole bed. The first one leaned over me and also shook his fist in my face. "Now look," he said. "We're going to leave the door open this time, and if there's one move out of you, we'll really put you to sleep. Understand?"

"You mean you'll knock me out?"

"You got it right the first time, buddy."

"Why?"

No one answered this question, but all three of them filed out of the room, leaving the door open. I closed my eyes and tried to find a comfortable position. After tossing and turning, I slipped out from under the sheet across my chest and tried to reconstruct the strap in my mind. There was certainly no point in staying tied up if there was any way out of it. By sitting on the bed and raising my hands as high as possible and bending over them, I was able to unfasten the buckle on one of the cuffs with my teeth. Then with one free hand, I reached around to my back and undid the belt. Both of my hands were bleeding now, but I felt no pain in them, only distaste for the sight of the blood.

I undid the buckle on the other cuff and was free of the strap. Now all I had to do was turn off the light. If the switch was not inside the room, then it must be outside. After all, they had to turn it on. I walked to the door, still carrying the strap, and peered out into the hall. I could see two men sitting on a bench at some distance from my room. The hall was almost entirely dark except for this light.

I reached around the opening and found a light switch. I pulled it up. Wrong one. The light in the hall went on. I turned it off at once and heard footsteps. I opened the door wide and went out into the hall to look on the other side of the door. Another switch. I clicked this switch and sure enough, the light went off. The footsteps were getting nearer now. I turned towards them and with the light off could barely distinguish the approaching white figures.

"I'm sorry to have disturbed you," I said, "but I really can't sleep with a light in my eyes." Then I held out the leather strap to them. "And you might want this," I said. "I certainly can't sleep in it."

"Well Jesus H. Christ!" one of them exclaimed, and the other one said: "I'll be damned!"

"Not H," I said. "Just Jesus Christ. And why will you be damned?"

"How the hell," said one of them, "did you ever get out of this?"

I started to explain, but I heard more footsteps, running down the hall towards us, and stopped. Someone put on the light again. The man who had threatened to knock me out.

"Hang on to him, boys," he said. I saw that threatening look in his eyes again and then he hit me on the chin and knocked me out as he had promised.

TWO

HAD I BEEN ASLEEP, HAD I lost consciousness? It was still night, or it was night again; the light was still on. Sodium amytal? Knockout? How long had they lasted? Gradually I pounded and shuddered into wakefulness. I was unable to move my hands, or even to move at all. The light was less bright and directly over me, but the room was completely different, and very large. By turning my head in every direction, I could see a great many beds in addition to my own. It was a long rectangle of a room and both side walls were lined with beds, small islands jutting into the room. In the center were three more beds, one of them mine. By craning my neck (I was apparently strapped to the bed and wrapped in some sort of mummy case), I could see the entire room, as my bed was at one end under two windows. All of the beds were occupied. Were they bundles or people?

My eyesight now seemed better than it had been, but it was still difficult to make out details. There was another light at the far end of the room, and by straining my back I could make out a desk or table and what appeared to be figures moving near it. Along with this, as if 1 had acquired double vision, came a series of confused memories of the room in which I had been previously, the men in white, the men in blue, the flagpole, the steps leading into the building. These images, for they were not memories that I could place in time, merged into each other without order, sequence or reason, and the room in which

I was now was no more distinct than the other images. Was I actually in it? Was it a dream? Was I still near the flagpole? It was only the recurring awareness of physical restraint which gave this bed and this room an occasional startling reality. The people I had encountered, the nurse, the attendants, had no physical reality. The physical details of their faces were absent, and I recalled them by feeling, associating a name or an event only with the feeling or sensation I had had from the person. When I recalled the nurse, it was a re-evocation of evil, but without a face, as a blind person might remember someone by smell or emanation, without ever having seen him. I was alternately certain that I had been here for a day, for infinity, and that I was not *here* at all. The transferences from place to place were accompanied by a sensation of pounding but without any lapse from consciousness to unconsciousness or vice-versa. I recognized momentarily that only on this day had I come to this place, but the recognition was neither actual nor real; it was a belief.

The conviction was immediately replaced by the knowledge that I was actually participating in a parade of coffins. Although I was in one of the coffins, I could see the entire parade, myself included, as from a height. The coffins passed in a circle around the flagpole in a ceremony connected with the flag. But no, I was participating in an examination, still in a coffin. The board of judges, looming indistinctly above me, were determined to have me talk incessantly. In fact, the entire purpose of the examination was to prevent me from ever ceasing to speak. Time, and with it sequence, order, purpose, and logic, had completely ceased to exist, leaving no limited or defined reality by which to judge anything. For the most part my mind seemed to have escaped my body and like a freed spirit roamed at will in its own sphere, observing the identity of my physical self with as much—but no more—interest than it did anything else.

The room was gradually making another transformation, now becoming the basement of a London building. I saw the street lamp outside the window in a steady downpour of rain. How had we arrived in England? The room itself had not changed physically; there were the same number of beds, but many of them were now empty. I was bound in what seemed to be layers of hot, damp cloth. I had a sensation of sharp, intermittent pain in my hands. On the bed next to mine was another bound figure, and I recognized him slowly as a German spy. But why was I, an American spy, wrapped and tied to this bed next to him? I had been captured by the Germans? But then why had he not been released? He had been captured by the Americans? Why had I not been released?

There was considerable movement in the room, people walking and talking, someone sweeping. By the feel of their presences I knew that some of them were on my side, some of them were against me. Obviously, the battle was still taking place, nothing had yet been decided, an important military victory was still at stake. One man I recognized at once as the butler of President Truman and also a member of the Congressional committee which had gathered at the far end of the room. The butler-member, to give me courage, approached my bed and offered me a cigarette, a definite indication that the tide was turning in our favor, perhaps the committee had captured the place at last. I accepted the cigarette and a light, greatly moved to know that my mission was at last accomplished and grateful for this acknowledgment of all that I had done. I thanked him. He moved away from me and during his absence, I smoked the cigarette down to a small butt. I could feel that it was going to burn my lips, so I spit it out of my mouth. To my consternation he returned immediately to my bedside and said: "What did you do with the cigarette?"

I knew that I would be punished for having spit it to the floor, so I lied: "I swallowed it, of course," certain that he had expected me to do that. He seemed startled but only said "oh" and walked away again.

The Congressional committee which had been huddled in a group at the end of the room had disappeared, and I realized that I had failed to reveal, or that they had failed to understand, that this was a Nazi hideout, and had left. There was terrible irony in this situation since I knew also that the real clue to the entire war, the complete solution, was in this room, in the conflict between myself and the German spy who lay bound next to me. They had absolutely failed to grasp it. It would have been impossible for me to tell them about it, even to tell the President's butler, since the German next to me would also have heard whatever I said.

The room was then invaded by the Germans again, those evil people of the night. To my surprise, a group of them came over to my bed and unbound me. Their presence emanated evil so strongly that I was nauseated. I lay, naked and defenseless, on the bed, confused and apprehensive, waiting for their next move. One of them, attempting a vocal kindness belied by his face, said: "Would you like to go to the latrine?"

Although I felt no physical need, I was convinced that the only way to handle these enemies (perhaps they did not know who I was, or had mistaken me for their ally) was to agree to whatever they suggested. This maneuver would at least give me time for observation. "Yes, I would," I said, attempting to appear both grateful and pleased.

I sat up on the bed. As I did so, I was aware of an immense weakness; it seemed to me that I could not possibly walk to any latrine and I also realized that I did not have the remotest idea where it was anyway. My weakness did not perturb them, in fact they were prepared for it, for one of them helped me to the floor and led me along the entire length of the room to the latrine. In it, there were several doorless stalls containing toilets, a urinal, and two or three sinks. The man led me to the urinal before which I stood weakly, barely able to hold myself up, until he, with a degree of sympathy surprising in anyone so disagreeable, led me without speaking to one of the stalls and I collapsed thankfully on the seat. I sat there for some time (he seemed to have disappeared) with my head in my hands. When I found enough strength to look up, I was surprised to find that I was not alone. An old man was seated on a toilet next to me, bent over and looking in my direction. He was obviously as weak, or weaker, than I was. He attempted to come to his feet, but seemed to lack the strength. As I watched him, I realized that he was, of course, my father. This gave me a strength which I had not felt up to then and I stood up, extending my hand.

"May I help you?" I asked him formally.

It occurred to me that he might not remember that he was my father and that it would be best not to mention it until he knew it himself. He smiled at me and gripped my arm just above the wrist. "Thank you, son," he murmured (at least he knew he was my father!) pulling himself up on my arm. When he was on his feet, I supported him with one arm around his back and the other under his arm. We started to stagger, balancing one against the other, towards the open doorway. "Just go slowly, Father," I said, and again he smiled.

One of the Nazis appeared in the doorway, looked at us, and then walked up to us quickly. His face was the first to imprint itself, as a physical image, on my mind. Now I saw him for the first time. His head was the shape of an up-ended flatiron, an enormous heavy, square jaw from which the face seemed to grow, ending finally almost in a point. There was a mouth with liver-colored lips set in the lower part of the flatiron, a great purple gash; and the eyes above a sharp, crooked nose were small and close together. He stared, like a rattlesnake poised to strike. Not only did I know that he was a Nazi, but also that he was one of the hierarchy, a power in the party.

"What do you think you're doing?" he asked. "Let go of him."

I was not sure which one of us he had addressed. There was a flatness in his eyes which made it impossible to tell whether he was looking at me or my father. Since my father seemed unaware of him, it was obviously up to me to speak. Although filled with fear, I knew that my father would most certainly fall to the ground if I should release my grip for even an instant, so I protested meekly (probably this was a prison camp!): "I'm only helping him." Then added quickly: "He's my father."

"Let go of him," he said again, his voice even lower and more threatening.

I stared in terror at the small black eyes (very like the eyes of that nurse) and said: "He'll fall down if I let him go."

Whether he moved or not, I did not know, but his frame suddenly increased in size, swelling up over me. "Will you let go of him?"

Nazi or no Nazi, prison camp or not, I knew that it was necessary to take a stand then. Whatever the consequences, it was inconceivable that I should let my father go. "No, I won't."

The face became black with fury (it had been only green before) and he seized me, pulling me away from my father who, as I had foreseen, crumpled and fell to the floor. Watching this thin, naked bundle collapse on the cement floor made me instantly furious, erasing my terror of the man who stood before me gripping my upper arm.

"Do you see what you've done, you fool?" I shouted at him, and once again in what seemed a relatively short space of time, I felt a blow on my chin. I saw it more than I felt it, as if I had severed my spirit from my body so that from a distant corner of the room I observed myself being struck and melting into a heap upon the floor next to my father.

I woke up, sudden and clear, in a bed. The sheets were dry and cool, and I was not bound in any way. I moved my hands tentatively to make sure of this. I raised myself up on the bed. It was daylight. I had come almost to a sitting position, when I collapsed again, not from weakness but in a memory of terror. I decided that it would be best to ascertain, by lifting my head, whether or not the Nazis were still there.

Inexplicably, the beds were all filled again, and with the one exception of myself, all the occupants were bound as I had been. The fact that I was in a perfectly comfortable bed, on which the sheets were clean and dry; that I was free and could even get up if I wanted to, convinced me that there had been an Allied attack during the night and that the prison had been captured. Obviously, the Congressional committee had known what they were doing. How stupid of me not to have realized that at the time. It seemed to me that it would have been easier for me if they had let me know, but possibly they had not known then who I was.

Perhaps it would be best to go over all the possibilities before making any move. I lay quietly in the bed, trying to remember everything I knew. I was an Allied (perhaps not American after all) spy, mistakenly incarcerated in this prison, a former concentration camp of the Nazis. The only evidence that the Allies had actually captured the place was that I was no longer bound. On the other hand, perhaps that was not conclusive. Perhaps the Nazis, who were certain to want information from me, were giving me a reprieve before questioning or torturing me. If only President Truman's butler would reappear, I could send for the President himself. Truman. I repeated the word over and over. Of its own accord, the word divided itself into two syllables: "TrueMan." The true man. The real man, the honest man, the man of faith! I was not certain that he was either present or available to me, but I did know that he was President of the United States, that he had been wisely, very wisely, appointed by destiny to lead us. Being a man of faith, a true man, he could not fail to win the final victory. Cheered by this realization, this conviction of victory, I sat up in bed (whatever the danger, my eventual salvation was now guaranteed and I was protected from every evil) and looked around the room. For the first time, it seemed light and cheerful. Several Allied guards (perhaps it was a medical ward and I was sick? In any case the guards, or whatever they were, were dressed in white) moved from bed to bed, talking to or handling the wrapped figures. I decided, since no one of them had noticed that I was sitting up, that it would be best to lie down again and wait for them to come to me.

The guard who finally appeared (his head looming out of space over mine, his face upside down) was—I knew instantly—an in-between. What I understood of his character from this sight of him was only that he was innocuous, although I had assumed that I would know immediately whether he was an Ally or still another Nazi. But now I did not. The actual physical face seemed to fit the description "Aryan" and perhaps I could only have been sure had he been a Negro or obviously Jewish. I remembered then that President Truman's butler had been a Negro. Of course: it was only the oppressed minorities who revealed automatically their sympathies in any struggle between Titans.

Under the circumstances it seemed best to wait until he, purposely or accidentally, disclosed, if not his identity, then at least his political tendencies. Conceivably the hospital or prison was shorthanded and forced to employ enemy prisoners? He looked at me for an extremely long time before smiling, carefully noncommittal, and saying:

"Well, good morning, how are you?"

If he was a clever Nazi, it might be disastrous for me to tell him that I was feeling well, for that might precipitate my torture, but if he was an Ally it would be unfair not to be honest with him. My conviction that all was well in any case came back to give me courage. "I feel fine," I said.

To my surprise, he said: "How would you like something to eat? Are you hungry?"

It seemed unlikely that the Germans would waste any food on an Allied spy, still it was possible. Even if my future safety was guaranteed by President Truman, it also seemed unjust to assume that I should not at least co-operate with him by being tactful and careful and not getting myself into any more trouble. Also, I was hungry. When had I eaten last? Not since I had been incarcerated in this room, however long that was.

Tentatively, I said: "Yes, I think I could eat," but I tried not to show anxiety, although the thought of food had given birth to a real pang of hunger which centered in my stomach.

"Can you get up by yourself?" he asked. His voice was still non-committal and cold, but not cold enough to seem unfriendly. After what had happened when I had last risen from my bed, I hesitated to get up again, but there did not seem to be anything else to do. Without replying, I sat up on the bed and swung my feet over the side. He took my arm and helped me to the floor, and once more I was led down the length of the room, this time to a table. I supported myself by leaning on it, assuming that this was where I would eat if I were going to be fed.

He had released my arm and now said: "Do you want to go to the latrine?"

That old trick again! I shook my head. "No, thank you."

"Do you want to take a shower?"

I stared at his face. So they were not going to feed me after all! I remembered from somewhere that water was life-giving, that it was possible to continue life by the absorption of water through the pores. If they would not feed me, perhaps I would find sustenance by taking a shower. In any case, he was waiting for a reply.

"Why, yes," I said. I did not take my eyes off him, watching for any false move that would reveal his position and stamp him as friend or enemy.

He led me around the table to a stall which I had not noticed. It stood about six feet from the far end of the table, isolated in the room. A shower, I knew perfectly well, was always in a bathroom, or a latrine, or if not, then in a shower room. This contraption, however, with three metal sides and a curtain at the front, was most certainly not a shower. What was it? Was this, after all, the place of execution? I had read somewhere that the Germans had made prisoners take showers before they were sent to the gas chamber. He was holding the curtain open, and I could distinguish a drain in the floor of the boxlike booth and, sure enough, a shower fixture in the open top. Perhaps it was a refinement about which I had not read? A combination shower and gas chamber?

"Go on," he said, pushing me towards it.

There was nothing to do then but trust myself to fate. I felt unable to resist, and my weakness was exaggerated by hunger. I stepped into the stall and the curtain was pulled across the front. I was reassured when I saw a soap dish containing a small piece of soap. Had the Nazis given soap to the condemned? Not probable since there had been a shortage of soap. Or had they done so in order to lull their victims into a false sense of security, postponing the knowledge of certain death?

I was shocked by a sudden stream of icy water falling on me in a flood and an immediate physical reaction of great interior heat. This warmth seemed entirely centered in me and was so great that the water turned hot almost immediately upon touching me. Great clouds of steam were rising all around me now, and I could barely see. This heat was an indication of strength which pleased me, and along with it I could feel my body drinking in the water, dissipating my weakness. I was so concerned with the flood of water that I no longer cared whether I was to be led to an execution chamber, but seized the soap and started to wash. Cleanliness, I recalled, was next to godliness...not below, but alongside it. It could do no harm to be clean.

I had about finished soaping myself (difficult to do since the soap was instantly washed off me by the torrent of water which varied, with my fluctuating emotions, from hot to cold) when a head appeared through the side of the curtain. "Had enough?"

I shrieked "yes" over the roar of the waters, and the flow ceased. I stood in the stall, dripping, until the curtain was ripped to one side and the man who had put me into the shower reappeared and handed me a towel. Well, that was some indication. The prisoners of the Nazis had not been allowed to dry themselves. "Come on out," he said.

I stepped out of the shower and dried myself vigorously, feeling no weakness at all now. When I had finished, the guard took the towel from me and, still more surprising, handed me a pair of white pajama trousers. I had assumed that I would remain naked, perhaps forever.

I put on the trousers and was handed a pajama top which I also put on. Quite gently, but without any commitment of feeling or show of kindness, I was led to a chair next to the large table. "Sit down and I'll bring you some food."

Either during the shower or while I was drying myself or dressing, several more of the guards had appeared, and from the way in which they glanced at me and the whispered tones in which they consulted each other, including the one who had taken charge of me, I judged that I was the subject of their conversation. I felt that I should not watch them openly, but it was difficult to take my eyes off them since I was still hopeful of being able to determine by observation who and what they were.

The conversation came to an end and I gathered that the promise of food had been forgotten or else that some other decision had been made as to my disposal. Two of them approached me and took positions on either side of me. A third then appeared carrying another leather contraption. I knew at once that I was to be handcuffed again but could think of no reason to protest since there was no visible means of escape from this place (there were far too many of them to make a rush for the door which was probably locked anyway). The only thing to do was to humor them. When they had looked at me and whispered together, they had been surrounded by an aura of doubt which was almost tangible, and I could think of several reasons for this doubt on their part although none of them seemed immediately final or conclusive. If they were Germans, then it was logical that if they knew who I was they would handcuff me. If they were Americans or Allies, spies like myself, perhaps they only held this room of the building in a kind of siege, and would bring suspicion upon me and themselves if they did not handcuff me. In any case, I would let them have their way.

I smiled approvingly at them and at the cuffs and extended my hands. This was the first time that I had looked at them and I was surprised to notice the scars, which were not yet healed and which gave the appearance of a kind of gray mucous mildew growing in two large spots, one on the back of each hand. I felt no pain, and had only a vague memory of how they had come to be there. Something to do with burning, but I was not sure what.

The three of them smiled tentatively and inserted my hands without force, and without resistance from me, into the cuffs and attached the leather belt rather loosely about my waist. I seemed to have grown considerably thinner (how long had I been here, after all?) and felt that I could easily slip out of this loose belt. But perhaps it was loose because they did not want to restrain me but only to give the appearance of restraint. I attempted a look of complicity towards the one who had brought the leather cuffs to the table and received in return a half-smile which I was unable to interpret as anything but an effort not to commit himself. That was probably because he was a friend in disguise but could not reveal himself to me in the presence of someone (one of the two who continued to stand beside me perhaps?) who was undoubtedly an enemy.

I was distracted by the reappearance of the one who had first spoken to me carrying, as he had promised, a tray of food. Whatever was to happen after this feeding (was it by any chance the last meal before death?), I was not concerned. The important thing was that he had not forgotten the food but had, of course, had to go and get it somewhere, probably from a kitchen.

Unfortunately, as soon as the tray was laid before me, I realized that it was most unpalatable; obviously prison fare. Well, at least I knew that this was a prison. There was a glass of some kind of fruit juice, a dish of gray porridge, a hard-boiled egg, and some thick, hard bacon, cold and greasy, and a cup of what looked like weak coffee diluted with milk. The smell of this food, in spite of my hunger, was so strong and so nauseating that I looked away from it. The men had gathered in a group around me and were intent upon both the plate of food and me. If they were friends, it was apparently important that I eat the food, and if they were not, it seemed equally important...I did not know what to do. I smelled it again and it was then that I realized that it was poison which accounted for the smell. They must be enemies. Perhaps the Allies actually were in control of the entire building and this was a German spy who had brought me the food, determined to get rid of me in spite of the fact that I was no longer in his power. It seemed to me that it would have been much simpler if the Allies had removed me as soon as they captured the place.

Since I could not eat the food and the problem of finding out where I was and who they were had become overwhelmingly important, I decided to try a shot in the dark.

"When am I going to get out of here?" I asked bluntly, in a loud voice. I had taken special pains to formulate this sentence exactly, avoiding such words as "released," which would have indicated that I knew this was a prison, or "executed," which would have given away my knowledge of their intent.

"Come on now, try and eat," someone said.

The maneuver, of which I was heartily sick by this time, of never replying to a question directly, made me still more certain that I was in a divided, mutually hostile camp.

"I'm not hungry," I said, thinking by this to force an answer to my question.

"But you said you were."

Of course, he was right. I had said I was. I could see myself getting into difficulties again.

I lifted my hands, which barely reached the table, restrained by the cuffs. "How can I eat with these things on?" I asked.

For answer, a hand seized the glass of vile-smelling juice (it smelled strongly of tin) and held it to my lips. "Drink this." Since this was an order and I was certain to encounter furious resistance should I refuse, I drank, swallowing all of it as rapidly as possible. If I was going to die, what matter if it was by poison; if I was not, then I wouldn't. It was simple, after all, but it was no help in determining the position or sympathies of these men.

I was then fed with a spoon, and consumed, by dint of not breathing and therefore not smelling, the entire bowl of porridge which fell heavily upon my uneasy stomach. Then the bacon was forced into my mouth and finally the egg. The egg was too much. I spit it out firmly and watched it roll around on the plate. I had gagged on the smell of it alone. There was a pause but, to my relief, no punitive action and the coffee was held to my lips. It was only lukewarm so that it was possible to swallow it, but it was strongly sugared (I hate sugar) and had a familiar unpleasant taste reminding me not of other coffee, but of some experience. I swallowed several times until I had drained the cup, and with each swallow the insistent but unclear recollection kept coming closer and closer. The Army! This was the coffee which they served in the Army! I had finished drinking it and took a rapid look around the room and at the men beside me. It didn't *look* like the Army. Had they captured a stock of Army coffee? But would they know how to make it so that it would taste the same? Or was it impossible to make it taste differently? It must be the Army. What could I really remember about this place?

I recalled a series of unconnected pictures, no time sequence, no logical connection between them. The flagpole, the main building, the nurse, the large crowded room, the small room where I had been told to sleep and hadn't, some judges, the London basement...but hadn't this been the basement? Weren't the judges here? Not a basement, no judges. Had it been this room? It resembled, as I looked at it now, nothing so much as a stage set. Perhaps that would explain the changes, the transformations from night to day, the changes in personnel (or actors), the complete lack of any plan. If it was not a stage set, still there was a basic identity between this room and the basement, the room where I had seen the judges. Or had I been moved, without my knowledge, from room to room? In any case, I had spent a period of time (long, short? I didn't know) *somewhere,* a place or places that sometimes resembled this place with all its beds.

My attention was suddenly absorbed by the unexpected emergence from the shower (I had not even been aware that anyone had been in the shower) of a dripping naked figure, frightfully thin. I was reminded at once of pictures I had seen of Buchenwald, except that this body seemed able to move of its own accord, whereas all the bodies I had seen in the—was it a newsreel?—picture had been dead, although no thinner. I watched him drying himself with a towel. Perhaps I would be able to determine something from whatever treatment he would receive.

The guards were much rougher with him than they had been with me and, significantly, gave him only pajama pants to wear, no shirt. This indicated a difference in our status, and I could only assume that I belonged to a higher, in some way superior, order of prisoner, if we were prisoners. He was forced quite roughly, and with loud shouted orders, into a chair opposite mine and not only was he handcuffed, but his feet were attached to the legs of his chair. I looked down instantly. Mine were definitely not attached. Another difference.

In addition to the fact that he looked starved and extremely weak, his hair was badly rumpled, and his whole appearance was one of dishevelment. Since I could not see a mirror in the room anywhere, I assumed that perhaps I looked as bad, or worse, than he did. Certainly I had not shaved during the entire time I had been wherever I had been, nor had I combed my hair or brushed my teeth. I was unable to reach my head with my hands to feel my beard or attempt to straighten my hair, so I contented myself with running my tongue over my teeth and feeling the layer of soft film on them. It was obvious that our conditions were alike, but I hoped I did not resemble him in any other way. I had no memory of my physical self, no consciousness of the color of my hair, and I could not evoke any image of what my face might look like. But as I looked at this thin skeletal figure opposite me, cramming the food into his mouth in spite of the restraining cuffs on his hands—his chair bent in towards the table and he himself crumpled over the plate—he reminded me of a chicken. A particular kind of chicken. His hair was red and I thought of a Rhode Island red, already plucked, which accounted for the nakedness. His nose protruded from the bony, shrunken face in much the same way as a beak and since his head was almost entirely in the plate as his hands shoveled the food into his mouth, the total appearance was one of pecking. When he had finished, he looked wildly around and then jumped to his feet. He was unable to stretch his arms but he hopped around, taking the chair with him, a giant tethered plucked fowl. Immediately, several of the guards forced him back to a sitting position. Cigarettes were then unexpectedly thrust into both of our mouths and we sat smoking, observed by the other men and scrutinizing each other in fear and doubt.

During this entire period, I identified everything by its feeling. While I hoped to gather information by observation of the faces or gestures or words of the people around me, information as to my whereabouts or their intentions, the people themselves were identified for me only by the sensation or feeling of their presences. Not their physical presence, but something which was communicated with great force, as fear is communicated silently to an animal. Instantaneously with my first vision of another person would come the conviction through the senses that he was good or evil, frightened or to be feared, kind or cruel, cunning, trustworthy, false, angry, pleased, or any one of dozens of other categories. I seemed particularly sensitive to any manifestations of kindness or cruelty, active hostility or fear. As I stared at this man opposite me (I knew only that he was a man from having seen him naked—he could have been and perhaps was a rooster), I sensed his fear and consequent hostility towards me and was shocked and frightened to realize that not only the guards, but probably all of those who were or had been similarly in the power of these guards, were also divided and mutually at odds with each other. It seemed impossible that two persons such as this man and myself were not allied simply by the situation in which, with minor differences, we found ourselves. He was as much a Nazi in temperament and feeling, although not in power, as the man who had attacked me the night before (or whenever that had been), and I was consequently still further confused. Conceivably this was hell or purgatory. I had no proof that these places did or did not exist and only assumed that if they did, this particular place could be one of them or perhaps a combination of both.

The only earthly organization that I could remember which grouped together such mutually hostile elements in a common mass of antagonism and fear was the Army, but I was fairly certain that this was not the Army. And yet I had no logical basis for such an assumption. Why wasn't it the Army? Perhaps the Army had finally taken control of the world. If they had, there was surely no reason for them to wear uniforms or otherwise identify themselves to the world which they had conquered. Had I done anything while I had been in the Army that would require this present treatment? Had I been subversive, or had I not performed whatever duties had been assigned to me? As far as I knew I had, but I reflected that the standards of the Army on its highest level were things about which I knew nothing, therefore anything was possible. Life, death...anything. Even a continuation of this present regime...forever.

The Army. What was it about the Army? And the Army hospital? Blood, blood—but no wound, and still a hospital. Should I have been wounded? Was there a connection between this place and that Army hospital?

I looked around for the guards again. Whenever I took my eyes off them, they disappeared. In fact, everything at which I did not direct my entire attention seemed not to exist. There was some curious inconsistency in the working of my eyes. Instead of being able to focus on one object and retain a visual awareness of being in a room, a visual consciousness of the number of objects and people in that room, all that existed was what was directly in my line of vision. My other senses were similarly affected in that I ceased to hear or smell that which I did not see in front of me, and I had also lost the power of moving my eyes independently of my head. In order to see anything, to look for anyone, it was necessary to move my entire head. Now, looking for the guards, the process was as always one that made me dizzy. I would turn my head and the objects in the room would sweep before me in a cluttered, unidentifiable mass. I had learned, instinctively, not to move my head quickly for if I had, I would have become ill from making the dizzying sweep. I located first one, then two and finally three of the guards— these independent, powerful beings who continued to baffle me. They had taken seats around the table and seemed only vaguely interested in us. One of them, however, seated on the table, took a sudden interest in me, apparently as a result of my having looked at him, and with a suspicious twisting of his lips into what might conceivably have been a smile, said: "Feeling better?"

"Yes."

Rather playfully, he licked his lips and said then: "Who are you?"

I gave him my name at once and asked: "Do you want my serial number?" If it was the Army he might be pleased, and if it was not then perhaps it would not matter. He seemed surprised and interested at this and said: "Why should I?"

Why did they answer questions with questions? He could have said, if he had nothing to hide, simply "yes" or "no," but I knew of no way to determine why he would or would not want to know it.

"Do you mean you don't want it?"

"What is it?"

So he did want it after all! "32301174," I said.

This pleased him, and he continued: "What's your rank?"

"I was a sergeant, a technical sergeant when I had that number," I said quickly, having remembered that I had been promoted to second lieutenant and, of course, my serial number had changed. This seemed a great deal to explain, but I went on as rapidly as I could. "I was made an officer later," I said, "and then my number was 0-202..." I couldn't remember it. "I don't remember the rest of it."

"Oh you don't?" I was not sure that this was a question but it seemed to be. Was it very bad not to have remembered the number?

"Oh," I went on, "it doesn't matter. I'm not in the Army anymore, I was discharged. Now all I have is a social security number and I can tell you what that is."

"What is it?"

"119-09-1938," I said.

"And what do you do?"

What did I do? I did not know what he could possibly mean by this. Did he mean what did I do here, or what?

I moved my head again and my eyes swept the room once more. I raised my hands as much as I could, also bending my head in the direction of one of the beds which I hoped I had spotted correctly as mine. At least it was empty. "I belong over there," I said, "but I don't do anything."

This did not seem to be satisfactory. He shook his head. "No, I mean what are you, what kind of work do you do?"

Work? What did I do? "Oh," I said, "I can do almost anything." For some reason, this remark brought forth a burst of laughter from the man who was questioning me and from the others as well. Was I wrong? I had done a lot of things, hadn't I?

"What did you do before you came here?"

"I was in the Army."

"And before that?"

"I did personnel work. I was a personnel manager."

More laughter.

"What are you doing here?" he asked.

"That's what I'd like to know." As soon as I had said this, I was afraid again. Had I revealed the fact that I not only did not know why I was here, but perhaps even that I didn't know what "here" was?

"Do you remember how you got here?"

Did I? Were all those unconnected visions dreams or reality?

"I remember a flagpole and a man, a nurse, Mr. Neider." The man exchanged a quick knowing look with someone behind me, and I could feel the sweat beginning to pour out of me. Perhaps that man, that flagpole, that building, had nothing to do with this place. "Did he send me here?" I asked, and then finally and uncontrollably: "What is this place anyway?"

"Don't you know?"

Might as well admit it. "No, I don't."

"Didn't they tell you?"

"They? Who?"

"Anyone?"

Had anyone told me? Should anyone have told me? "No. I woke up here and I was all wrapped up."

More and more laughter.

"Yeah? In what?"

"Hot sheets, I think."

A great wave of laughter greeted that. "Hot sheets! That's a good one."

I was beginning to enjoy this conversation. The laughter, although I was apparently the cause of it, was not unfriendly.

"Look, David," (had I told them my name? I must have...) "how do you feel, pretty good?"

"Oh, yes," I assured them, "I feel fine."

"Do you want to get out of here?"

"Yes." I nodded my head vigorously. "Yes, I do."

"Okay then. You just do what we say and we'll see about it. Maybe you can get out tomorrow."

Did they mean it? "All right, I will."

I felt happy and reassured by the conversation and was even more pleased when they took the cuffs off my hands and undid the belt around my waist. "Gee," one of them said, "we ought to do something about those hands." As soon as he said it I remembered burning them with the cigarette. "I burned those holes," I said, pleased with my sudden sharp memory.

"What for, boy?"

"I had to," I said. "They wouldn't take the cuffs off me. But they did after that."

The man continued to lean over me looking at my hands and shaking his head. "Boy, that's one way out, I guess."

I laughed. "Yes, it is."

"You better go back to bed now," he said, standing erect again.

I had been in bed for such a long time that the suggestion seemed senseless, and I was sorry to leave this jolly company. But I had promised to do whatever they told me.

The guard accompanied me to the bed which I had indicated earlier (I had been right!) and told me to lie down. As I started to get onto the bed, he stopped me suddenly with his hand on my arm. "Better take those pajamas off."

"Why?"

A stern look came into his face, so I took them off quickly without waiting for an answer.

He took them from me and said: "That's better, now lie down."

I lay on the bed and he called out: "Okay, boys!"

Almost immediately the bed was surrounded by men, more guards. Some of them carried wet twisted ropes of cloth over their arms and one of them, like the one who had accompanied me, was empty-handed. These two, to my astonishment, lifted me clear of the bed for a moment and when they let me down on it again, my body jerked involuntarily at the shocking touch of cold, wet cloth.

"What are you doing?" I cried out.

I received no answer, but the men sprang into action, the several heads which surrounded me leaned intently over my body. They tossed me in every direction, wrapping me tightly in more and more of these cold wet cloths. My teeth began to chatter uncontrollably, making it impossible for me to speak, and my body shivered violently inside the wrapping of icy wetness. When they had finished, they tied another sheet (or was it a rope?) under my arms and around the entire bed, so that I could no longer raise my body, and then another around my legs. When I was finally able to quiet the chattering of my teeth, I said: "What are you doing this for?"

"Sorry, son," said one of them, the same one who had looked so carefully at my hands, "doctor's orders."

"Doctor's orders? I haven't seen any doctor. What is this place, anyway? Who are you?"

"Now listen," he said. "Remember what I told you. You just do as we say and we'll get you out of here."

"Well, this is certainly some way to do it. What did I do to you?"

"I told you it's the doctor's orders."

"But I haven't seen the doctor. Where is he?"

"You will."

"When?"

If there was a doctor, which I certainly did not believe, then I wanted to see him at once.

"Is this a hospital?" I demanded.

"Yes, of course it is, what did you think it was?"

"Never mind what I thought. It's a damned funny hospital, that's all I can say. I want to see the doctor, and I want to see him now."

He laughed. "What are you gonna do, get tough with me?"

"This is a free country, isn't it?" Until I had said that, I had not been sure even of what country I was in. The words had sprung automatically to my lips, but when he nodded, I had a great sensation of joy. A free country must mean that I was in America.

"All right then," I said, "I demand to see a doctor, and that's my right. If you don't get me a doctor, I'll make so much noise that you'll have to get me a doctor. I won't stop shouting," my voice was near shouting by this time, "until you do!"

"Now look, sonny," he said threateningly, "if you know what's good for you, you won't shout. I told you you'd see the doctor when he gets ready to see you, and you will."

"How do I know you aren't lying?" I shouted at him.

He laughed: "Brother, you're just gonna have to take my word for that."

"The hell I will!" I began to shout, in a violent wild chanting rhythm: "I want to see the doctor! I want to see the doctor! I want to see the doctor!"

He clapped his hand over my mouth and held it there. "Look, you're gonna wake up all the guys in here," he said, indicating the other beds with his head. "Do you want me to get tough with you?"

He released my mouth and I shouted. "You wouldn't dare get tough with me. If I'm in a hospital, I'm here because I'm sick, and if I'm sick, I have a right to see the doctor."

He shrugged his shoulders and started away from the bed. I began my chant again at once, and through it I heard his voice: "I can't do anything with him, Mac."

And then another voice. "Christ, they're all the same. Give 'em a break and you get this."

Several angry faces appeared over the bed then, glaring down at me. The light—or was it the sun?—went out.

THREE

I AWOKE AGAIN, REVERBERATING TO THE intermittently deafening noise of a radio blaring into my ears. My eyesight had undergone another transformation and seemed linked in some way to my hearing. As great waves of blaring music poured into me, my vision became steadily clearer only to fade almost to blindness as the music descended into near silence. As far as I was able to judge in moments of visual clarity, the sound came from behind a screen which surrounded part of the bed next to me, concealing all but the lower half of a body. The sound was so loud, or suddenly so soft, that it was impossible to identify exactly what it was but it seemed to be the playing and singing of various popular songs simultaneously, accompanied by continuous static. After some moments of listening, I contributed to the din in the room by beginning to scream at regular intervals: "Quiet! Quiet! Can't we please have some quiet?" I remembered, indignantly, that someone had accused me of disturbing the other bodies (were they really alive?) on these beds, but I would never have been able to create any commotion to compare with this.

My screams did not precipitate any sudden quiet but only the appearance of several of my captors. They surrounded the bed and gazed down upon me, receding into a dim fog and then suddenly focusing into sharp threatening reality, frighteningly clear and close. Finally one of them spoke, his voice beginning in a whisper and ending in a great shout: "Are you going to give us trouble again?"

I was sure that I had never seen any of these men before, and the question seemed utterly meaningless. How could they stand the noise? All I had done was to ask for quiet. I was even surprised that they had heard my screams over the roar around me. "Why don't you turn off that radio?" I shouted.

"What radio?"

Was it possible that they were pretending not to hear the noise which had not only not abated but seemed now at the peak of its volume? "Can't you hear it?" I asked angrily.

"You mean that guy singing?"

"Singing!" It was impossible. "It's the loudest noise I've ever heard. Can't you stop him? You only seem to worry about me. What about him?"

They had stopped looking at me and were exchanging understanding glances among each other. At some secret signal, all but two of them disappeared. They put their hands on me, one of them felt my head, and then I was rolled over and tossed around by them on the bed until once more I lay free and stripped. I was startled by the sudden sound as of gunfire behind me and looked up. Two men were shaking open sheets with a sharp jerking movement which, because the sheets were obviously wet, made a loud report. Wet sheets again! I felt my body with my hands and my skin was wrinkled and soft as if I had been (and apparently I had) soaking in water for several hours, or perhaps days.

"I want to go to the bathroom," I said. I didn't, but I thought perhaps this would postpone the sheet-wrapping. No one replied.

Once more I was lifted from the bed, laid onto the cold, wet sheets, and securely bound in them. How many times had this happened? I had no idea.

"I'm hungry," I said.

Someone answered: "Shut up."

At some time, with someone, I had agreed to do whatever I was told to do. Had it been here, had it been with these people, that I had made such an agreement? Was it still binding? Would these people release me, or had the guard been changed? Perhaps they knew nothing about any promise. What actually was the promise? Ah, the doctor! "I want to see the doctor," I said sharply.

"That's exactly what you're going to do."

What had happened? Was I really going to see the doctor, or had they decided to tell me this only to pacify me? When, in time, was this? Hadn't they said something about "tomorrow"? Was this tomorrow? "When?" I asked.

"Any time now."

Perhaps they were not lying. I determined to stay awake to find out whether the doctor would actually appear. Had there perhaps been a doctor here when I had been asleep? Had I even been asleep? And if so, for how long? No use asking questions, I knew. I had tried that and always with disastrous results. There was nothing to do but wait, silent, and try to believe them again. But who were *they*? Captors, guards, attendants...*men,* anyway. Men in white. But always different. If I could only see their faces clearly for long enough to know them. I looked up but they had all disappeared, vanished. Where had they gone now?

I fastened my eyes upon a dark-black speck on the ceiling. If I could hold my vision there, perhaps the room would not transform itself and I would actually not go to sleep but retain this reality (or was *this* a dream?) until the doctor arrived. If it was not reality but a dream, however, then possibly a dream doctor would be perfectly real? But how could anything be real in a dream? Yes, but what was real? Was there such a thing as reality? Was it something you could touch? I moved my hands inside the tight binding of the wet sheets and pinched my leg. I could feel that, but did the physical sensation indicate reality? Was I dreaming that I had pinched myself, and if I was, would I not have felt the pinch? Perhaps I was dead. This was a frightening thought. Not death itself, but not knowing. Would you know if you were dead? How? Death. Death? What was death? No one knew, did they? Would a ghost know? Was it any different from life? What was life? Some association with the word "death" whirled rapidly around in my mind and I raced after it, reaching to stop it. Ah! I remembered something:

Death be not proud, though some have called thee
Mighty and dreadfull, for, thou art not soe,

What was that? Wasn't there more of it? Where had I heard it before? Was it written somewhere? What was the rest of it? I had a picture of words on a page:

One short sleepe past, wee wake eternally,
And death shall...something...death, thou shalt die.

"Wee wake eternally"? Then what was the difference between life and death? And "wee"? What was that? I could see the word spelt out before me: w-e-e. Meaning *small, tiny.* "Tiny wake eternally"? What about "wake"? People drank at a wake, drank what? A wee drappie? Eternal drunkenness? Where had I read this? I tried to see the book in my mind, but the picture was faint now. A name...some words...were printed on the top of the page but the letters wavered. I concentrated on them, wrinkling my brow. "Holy Sonnets" I finally made out. The letters had ceased moving and become sharply defined on the page. Ah-ha! Some churchman had written that. Of course it wouldn't make any sense. Death, death, death. I had read a story...when, where? On a bus, was it? A man in a coma had been buried alive and awakened in his tomb under the earth. Well, I was in no coma. Or was I? I shook my head vigorously from side to side, looked again at the spot on the ceiling. No coma. Good. No doctor either. I looked around again, angrily.

The noise had ceased. Had it ever existed? I had not heard it stop. Good God, I was in a bad way. My lips began to move of their own accord:

Move him into the sun—
Gently its touch awoke him once,
At home, whispering of fields unsown.
Always it woke him, even in France,
Until this morning and this snow.
If anything might rouse him now
The kind old sun will know.

Think how it wakes the seeds,—
Woke, once, the clays of a cold star.
Are limbs...

A head appeared over mine, eyes peering into my face. I had seen it somewhere before. Where? The mouth opened, exposing a great moist deep-red cavern: "What were you saying?
    I smiled. "There's more," I said. "Where was I?"
    "'Are limbs,'" he quoted.
    "'Are limbs'?" I paused. "Oh, yes."

Are limbs, so dear-achieved, are sides,
Full-nerved—still warm—too hard to stir?
Was it for this the clay grew tall?
—O what made fatuous sunbeams toil
To break earth's sleep at all?

The face had continued to lean over me as I recited. I stared meaningfully into the eyes above me (where had I seen them?) and quoted angrily:
    "Was it for *this* the clay grew tall?"

The man laid his hand on my shoulder and smiled. I still could not remember who he was, but the touch of his hand, even through the binding of sheets, was repulsive. I hated him, but who was he?

"Who are you?"

His eyes peered at me through thick glasses. Those eyes! "I'm Dr. Bowles," he said. Then I remembered.

"You son-of-a-bitch," I cried out. "You're Mr. Neider. I knew I knew you. You're no doctor, you're a goddam nurse! You told me so yourself!" This was really too much. "Is this or is this not a hospital?" I demanded.

"Now quiet, David," he said (so he remembered me, too?). "Yes, of course, this is a hospital."

"Then where are the doctors, or don't they have any?"

"Of course they do."

I was shouting by this time. "Then where are they?"

"You weren't awake when the doctor came around."

"Don't lie to me! Why did you tell me you were a doctor?"

He smiled again, radiating his grinning evil. "I wanted to see if you remembered me."

"Very clever. You sure thought that one up fast." At the top of my lungs I shouted: "I want to see the goddam doctor!"

The face disappeared, but by craning my neck and pressing my head against what seemed to be an iron bar at the head of the bed, I found it again. He had moved to the head of the next bed, in which there was another bound creature. "Don't pay any attention to that bastard," I hissed at him. "He's a lousy lying nurse. Don't tell him anything."

The great glasses turned to me. "Now, David, you know I'm your friend." The voice oozed out of him, hanging thickly in the air.

"Shove it up your ass, you phony."

He did not reply but moved again, the thick face fading into the thicker airy fog. And then more faces appeared over me. One of them seemed very sympathetic. "Just quiet down, will you, boy? You'll see the doctor. Honest. Wanna cigarette now?"

It was impossible to be angry with this face or this voice. The concentrated mass of hatred for the nurse, centered in my chest, ached its way through a painful transformation as I looked into the two bright liquid eyes above me. Again my vision was blurring, this time with pain. My body began to tremble into an overflow, falling in love with the sound of this voice, the look in these eyes.

I nodded, unable to speak.

He put the cigarette, already lighted, into my mouth. The end of it was damp and I tasted it violently, wanting to know the taste and feel of those lips. "Will I really see the doctor?"

"Yes, you will." I shuddered with ecstasy at the sound of his voice.

"But I never do. If he comes when I'm asleep, will you wake me up?" I knew I could believe him, but I could not bear to have him go.

"Yes, I promise I will."

"Will you be here?"

He smiled and nodded. "Yes." Then he put his hand...if I was dead, this was surely heaven! ...on my forehead.

I took a long drag on the cigarette and could feel the smoke moving nauseatingly down into my stomach. I was hungry and I was thirsty, too. "Can I have a drink of water?" The cigarette wobbled back and forth in my mouth and he took his hand away and removed the cigarette. I blew out the smoke and he put it back between my lips. "In a little while," he said.

"What's your name?" I asked.

"Mac," he said. "Just call me Mac."

Mac? Mac? Where had I heard that before? "Are you here all the time?"

"I'm on the day shift," he said. Whatever that meant.

"Have I seen you before?"

"Yes." He smiled again. Could he be an angel?

"I don't remember you," I said. "Are you sure I've seen you?"

He nodded. "Will you remember me next time?"

"I'll remember you forever," I said. But I couldn't have forgotten that face, that voice. Or had I lost my memory? I must have...I knew he was telling me the truth. He had said I would see a doctor and so perhaps this really was a hospital after all. Was I sick? What was the matter with me? How had I come here? Was I very sick?

"Am I very sick?" I asked.

"I've seen worse," he said. "You're not so bad. Just noisy."

"Noisy?" This I could not believe. Was he lying? No, he couldn't lie. I knew that. Even if he wanted to. He couldn't want to.

"What do I do?" I asked.

"You shout a lot." He continued to take the cigarette from my mouth at regular intervals and then put it back again. The touch of his fingers against my lips was wonderfully painful. "You're better today," he said. "Do you know who you are?"

"Yes," I said. "I'm David Mitchell."

"That's right."

"Did you know?"

"Yes."

"Then why did you ask me if you already knew?"

"I wanted to see if you knew, yourself."

"Why? Don't you trust me?"

He looked away for a moment...one horrible moment...as if I had caused him pain. "Oh, please," I said. "I'm sorry. I didn't want to hurt you."

He laughed, a low, beautiful laugh. "You're all right, David," he said. "You're getting along fine. Keep it up." He took the cigarette from my mouth for the last time, and patted my cheek. At this unexpected, unhoped for demonstration of kindness, understanding, affection, love, brotherhood, I began to cry. More painful, more wonderful even than the fact that I loved him was the knowledge that I had found an ally. He patted my cheek again. "Take it easy, boy," he said, and the words, framed in the sound of that beautiful voice, hung suspended, so that I heard them again and again.

"Please don't leave me," I said.

He smiled again. "I won't be far away," he said, but his image tore away from my eyes.

I looked and looked at the spot where he had been, re-creating the smile, the sound, the eyes, everything about him. I was safe now and happy. I had a friend, a protector. I could even go to sleep in safety now. I saw the spot on the ceiling again and fixed it with my eyes automatically. But I wouldn't have to watch it anymore. The smile grew on my face and I closed my eyes.

I had no time to go to sleep. Instantly the board of judges appeared. I could not see them clearly and was unable to identify any of them since there were no features on any of the faces...hardly faces at all, just blank oval spaces, poised on shoulders. They were seated behind a raised wooden platform, peering over at me. How could they peer without eyes? Perhaps they had eyes but I could not see them? Of course, I didn't have my glasses. In any case, they were definitely peering. One of them pointed his finger at me, extending his arm directly towards my face. "Sun," he said in a loud, commanding voice.

Was this going to begin again? Dully I repeated after him: "Sun."

He jerked his arm at me. "Go on," he ordered.

I was tired but there was no resisting this command.

"Sun," I intoned. "From Sun to Son to Son of God. Son of God to Jesus Christ. From Christ to Christmas. Christmas to Mass. Mass to solid mass. Solid mass to earth. Earth to element. Element to four elements. Four elements to earth, air, water, fire, the four elements. Four elements to Universe. Universe to everything. Everything to nothing. Nothing to space. Space to sky. Sky to sun. Sun to light. Light to fire. Fire to burn. Burn to stake. Stake to meat. Meat to broil. Broil to burn. Burn to fire. Fire to fireman. Fireman to red. Red to read. Read to scriptures. Scriptures to Bible. Bible to Church. Church to Service.

Service to serve. Serve to Serve God. God to Heaven. Heaven to hell. Hell to Devil. Devil to Satan. Satan to burn. Burn to fire. Fire to Sun. Sun to light. Light to white. White to pure. Pure to heart. Heart to blood. Blood to wound. Wound to hands. Hands to cross. Cross to crucifix. Crucifix to..." I hesitated and the judge immediately pointed his finger at me again... "To what?"

I was sweating now. "Crucifix to Nun. Nun to none. None to no one. No one to one. One to won. Won to war. War to battle. Battle to fight. Fight to kill. Kill to death. Death to life. Life to strife. Strife to strive. Strive to be. Be to not to be. No. Be to Être. Être to Est. Est to East. East to Sun. Sun to sky. Sky to blue. Blue to Heaven. Heaven to angel. Angel to wings. Wings to fly. Fly to up. Up to Sun. Sun to Son. Son to Jesus Christ. Christ to Earth and Christ to Heaven. Christ on the Cross. Cross to double cross. Double cross to Cross of Lorraine to France. France to frank. Frank to honest. Honest to the best policy. Policy to insurance. Insurance to security. Security to safety. Safety to save. Save to Jesus. Jesus to death. Death to Heaven. Heaven to God. God to Sky. Sky to Sun. Sun to Light. Light to see. See to Sea. Sea to Ocean. Ocean to water. Water to salt. Salt, sunshine and soda." What was wrong?

I stopped again. The judges were glaring at me from their eyeless vacuums. "Salt," I began again quickly, "to salt of the earth. Salt of the earth to ye. Ye to Je. Je to Jesus. Jesus to Je suis." Then I knew I had it. "Je suis and Jesus are the same. God in his own image is Man. Je suis—Jesus. Tu es—Tuer, to kill. Il est—île, island. Nous sommes—new sum. Vous êtes—you are. Ils sont—they are. Understand?"

The judges shook their heads, but they were not impatient or stern now, only waiting.

I recapitulated for them: "Jesus is killed—dead, leaving him alone on an island, but no man is an island, we are a new sum, you are, they are Jesus. But this time you must not kill him. Je suis tué, but I will live again, and you and they will be. See?"

They began to disappear slowly. I had passed the examination.

I opened my eyes. The room was dark except for a light in the center of the ceiling. I was no longer directly below it. The panel of judges had disappeared and I could not see where they had been. Had I been asleep? Had I been moved? Was this reality? How about the examination? A great warm happiness spread inside me. Mac! Where was Mac? "Mac!" I called out.

I heard footsteps and a dim face leaned over me. "Shhhh." A finger was held to a mouth.

"Where's Mac?"

"He's not here. Go to sleep."

"I want to see Mac!" I shouted, writhing on the bed.

Two hands were on my shoulders. "Take it easy."

Where had I heard that voice before? I looked at his face, straining to see it in the dark. My God, the Flatiron! The Nazis again. The happiness gave way to a wave of pain. Mac had been a dream...Love was only a dream. I shut my eyes hard and then opened them again. It was no use. I was awake and the face was still there.

"What are you doing here?"

The face was joined by several others and one of them said: "Is he off again? What does he want now?"

The Flatiron shook his head. I looked at the other faces. Sure enough, all Nazis. Weren't we strong enough to hold this place? Not even with all those planes? But Mac had said it was a hospital, hadn't he? It couldn't have been a dream. "I want to see the doctor," I said loudly.

The Flatiron spoke again: "You can't see the doctor now. It's nighttime."

Another face, much older and wrinkled, bent close to my head. "What's the matter, sonny?"

I tried to move away from the face. "Go away," I said, but he did not move. I shouted, hard into his ear: "I want to see the doctor!" He winced and jerked his head back. He looked at the Flatiron. "Think he wants to blow his top?" he asked him, and the Flatiron shrugged his shoulders. Finally they both looked at me. "Wanna blow your top, kid?"

"What do you mean by that?" Did they want me to shoot something out of the top of my head?

They exchanged a smile and the old one said: "Aw you know what we mean. How about it?"

"How about what?"

"Blowing your top? Wanna blow it?"

I could not understand the meaning of the words, but the look which they exchanged seemed so confident of my understanding that I searched my memory for some association with them. I recognized the phrase from the Army, but it meant having a fit of anger, beyond that there was no meaning in it. Since I was already having a fit of anger, how could I further blow my top? I was about to question them again, but they had disappeared. I craned my head to try and find them and found myself looking into...and being stared at by...the eyes in another face. The face of someone bound in the bed next to me. The sheets had become unbearably hot and damp. As soon as the eyes were aware of mine, the mouth opened and said: "Go ahead, blow it."

I thought I recognized this face. Wasn't it the head of the overgrown rooster I had seen across the table somewhere in the dim, dark past? Hadn't I seen that face eating and smoking?

"Blow what?" I was becoming increasingly impatient with this strange language.

"Your top," he insisted, staring at my incomprehension. Then he said: "Jerk it off."

"Jerk it off? You mean...?" I did not finish the sentence, but this time I understood him.

He nodded his head. "Sure," he said, "it's good for you. If you don't, you'll just get in hot water again. You really been raising hell around here."

"I have?" What had I been doing?

"You been raving all night. Was you out?"

"Raving?" What had I been raving about? "What was I doing?" He snickered. "You shoulda heard yourself. You didn't stop for twelve hours straight."

"What was I raving about?" This was serious.

"Christ, I don't know. Didn't make any sense, most of it. Stuff about Christ and the Army and the Nazis. I don't know."

The word Christ struck some chord of memory. But Nazis? The Nazis were here? Was one thing a dream, another thing reality? What was what?

"Better jerk it off," he said again, quietly.

I tried to think this through clearly. I knew that "jerk off" meant masturbate, but what did he mean by adding the word *it*? Did he mean to pull it off? I moved my right hand slowly under the tight binding until it was free in the crevice between my legs. It was there all right, every bit of it. I gave a long pull downwards. He couldn't mean that, it would be impossible. I looked at him again but he was only smiling. "Go ahead, kid," he said. I didn't think he was advising dismemberment. But what good would it do to masturbate? I had little enough energy anyway. Did they want me to have less? Was it just part of some plot of theirs? I looked at the face next to me again. Why would he be on their side? After all, he was tied up the same way I was. Something was way off here.

Suddenly the other men reappeared: the old wrinkled one and the Flatiron. "Did you blow it?"

I tried to raise myself up in the bed, but the restraining sheet around my chest held me down. "Look," I said. "What are you talking about?"

They both laughed and then the Flatiron fixed me with his eyes. "Wanna piss, kid?"

Hadn't the man next to me said I'd been raving for twelve hours? I certainly should need to piss whether I wanted to or not, but I didn't.

Had I wet the bed? When had I last seen a bathroom anyway? I hoped I hadn't wet the bed. That would be embarrassing. As for the offer, I wasn't sure what to make of it. Hadn't I been in a latrine? ...Yes, and it was there I'd first really seen Flatiron. When he'd knocked me and the old man down. Is that what would happen? I was about to say "no" ...but what would they think if I did? Wouldn't that mean that either I had or was going to wet the bed? And what kind of punishment would I get for that?

"Yes, please," I said.

This pleased them enormously. They roared with laughter and proceeded to untie the sheets that bound me to the bed. Then they turned me from side to side again, unwrapping the many damp hot sheets which had been bound around me. Without my having made the slightest effort, I found myself standing, shivering but breathing, between them, my right hand still clenched over my genitals. They were looking at me and I removed it hastily. After laughing again, they both guided me between the two rows of beds (had the room changed after all? the beds in the center had disappeared) towards the end of the room. Once again I was led into the latrine and propelled to the urinal. "I'll take care of him, Joe," said the Flatiron and the old man left us alone. I stood there for some minutes without result. I was embarrassed to have him watching me. Still smiling, he asked: "Wanna sit down?" and I nodded. Hadn't all this happened before? He led me to one of the stalls and I lowered my body onto the toilet seat. I sat there, thankful to be in a sitting position at last, and heard his voice again:

"Wanna blow it now?" he asked.

I looked up sharply, astonished. "Do you mean...?"

"Don't kid me, buddy," he laughed. "You know what I mean. Go ahead."

If he meant what I thought he meant, I certainly wasn't going to go ahead. I shook my head and looked down at the floor again. Even sitting was very tiring.

After what seemed a long pause, during which I raised my hands to rest my head in them, I felt my head pulled up, held by the hair. Instinctively I moved away and his body seemed to follow me. He still had a firm grip on my hair and pulled my head closer to him, rubbing himself against my face. "Come on, kid," he said. There was no doubt of what he wanted.

I held my lips firmly closed and tried hard to think of what to do. My position seemed to me only partly humiliating. More than that it was ludicrous. If this really was a hospital, what earthly purpose could this serve, anyway? I could remember that the doctor was supposed to see me (or was that a dream too?) and the condition was that I should do what I was told. Did that mean this? Was this one of the men who had told me that? I tried to lift my head to see his face, but he had such a firm grip on my hair that I could barely move. Could I identify him by smell perhaps? I smelled his body, inhaling deeply, but it smelled like any body, slightly musky, hot, giving me no clue to his identity. When he spoke, I remembered his face...Flatiron, of course. "Come on," he urged me in a quiet voice.

I began to laugh but without opening my mouth. What should I do? Was it some kind of a test? Was it really necessary to my eventual release? Was he the doctor? I pulled my head back sufficiently to be able to speak safely. "Are you the doctor?" I asked.

He pulled my head back with a jerk and looked down into my face. "I've got what you need, kid," he said. "Doesn't that make me the doctor? Come on..." and once again my head was pressed against him.

I wondered if he would knock me out if I didn't. Although my head was pressed so close to him that I could barely see, I retained the image I had had when he had looked into my face, seeing him standing before me, half-angry, half-pleading, with his pants crazily open. The whole picture was one of a small, frightened boy, fearful and ridiculous. He could never knock me out. I felt a sudden surge of strength and with it a kind of joy. My memory was also returning. While the sequence of events was something of which I was not at all sure, it seemed to me that first of all I had been interviewed by Mr. Neider. I could remember him very well. Then I had been in a large room filled with men in blue. In that room I had been handcuffed and I had burned my hands. From there I had been taken to a small room and had been told to go to sleep. After having been knocked out there, I had been transferred to a large room which apparently adjoined this latrine. The large room was a treatment room of some kind, and I was in a hospital. I had seen a lot of faces and among them, Mac. I was sure of it now. But where was he? What had he said? Day shift? This was nighttime. Of course, he wouldn't be here now.

As for this man, still leaning against me, the last time I'd seen him, I had been knocked out for the second time. I flexed the muscles in my arms, feeling stronger. Could I knock him out? Certainly not in this position.

What about him anyway? He was not the man who had told me that I could see the doctor if I did what I was told. It was a lot of other men. Anyway, he had said I couldn't see the doctor *now.* But that meant there must be a doctor, and that this must be a hospital. Every hospital had a doctor in attendance all the time. So there must be a doctor somewhere in this building now. If there was and if I made enough racket, wouldn't he be able to hear me wherever he was? Weren't the windows open?

I breathed air and heavy man-smell into my lungs through my nose, expanding my chest to straining point and then I let out a frightful blood-curdling yell. Not only did it frighten the man before me into recoiling, but it even frightened me so that I fell back against the wall of the toilet. My arm hit the metal handle projecting from the wall and the toilet flushed. It took me a moment to realize that it was I who had produced the wild sound which still reverberated over the gurgling toilet, and I was very pleased. Most important, I was free of Flatiron. He made a move in my direction and I stood up, feeling no weakness at all, and let out another shriek, marveling at the hugeness of my own voice. He recoiled again and motioned to me with his hands. But now I could see the fear in his eyes and it filled me with confidence. Wherever it might lead me, this was an advantage I would press.

I started for him, shrieking at the top of my lungs, feeling constantly warmer inside. The fear in his face was extreme and my confidence swelled. I had some power, God-given perhaps, to terrify this man. Whatever it was and wherever it came from, I knew I had it. I continued to advance towards him. Buttoning his fly, he backed away from me, out of the latrine into the large room. There he was met and surrounded by at least five other men. The feeling of power which had by this time filled me left me also completely undaunted. Five men? I would have advanced into a room of a hundred men. Raising my hands and glaring at them I walked towards them, still emitting violent hair-raising howls of anger. To my joy and astonishment (I could not quite believe this yet), all of them backed away from me. As I made my way through the doorway, I was careful to keep my back against the wall so that none of them could get behind me. Although still gesticulating and howling, I realized that it was not the sound or the gestures that terrified them. It was the look in my eyes. It was most important to continue to stare at them. When one of them made a move to separate himself from the group, I stared into his eyes and motioned him back. He remained in the group. When I had backed them into the center of the room so that they stood in a frightened huddle between the two rows of beds, I moved carefully in front of what I knew to be the shower stall. The curtain was open and it was empty. Also, it was protected on three sides.

I lowered my hands once I was in this safe vantage point and said sternly: "Now get the doctor." It was not a request but a command.

One of them made a move towards me, extending his arm in my direction. "Now look," he said, "we've sent for the doctor. You just take it easy."

I continued to glare at him and motioned him back. "If any one of you makes a move, I'll kill him," I said. I was not surprised at my conviction that I could have killed them and not even at the fact that they also seemed convinced of this.

"Don't lie," I went on. "You have not sent for any doctor. You," I pointed at one of them, "go and get him."

He started directly towards me again. "No," I said firmly, "that way," motioning to my right and around the shower stall. "Go on, but don't come near me."

He made a wide circle around me and disappeared behind the shower. Thinking that he might possibly attempt an attack from the side, I stepped back into the shower itself so that he would be forced to face me through the opening. As soon as I had done this, the entire group moved in my direction, and I knew that they thought I had trapped myself, but I simply glared at them without moving and they halted.

Finally the man I had sent for the doctor reappeared, and with him came a small grotesque man clothed in black. I knew at once that he was not a medical doctor but a clergyman. His tight red face radiated manufactured holiness. They had made a wide circle together and while the attendant rejoined the group he came to stand before me, at a safe distance, looking at me angrily and shaking his finger in my direction. His face became even redder and his expression combined petulance and irritation.

"Now you come right out of there!" he commanded. His voice was like the cluck of a chicken. The second person I had seen here who strongly resembled a fowl. Funny.

"Fuck you," I said. 'Who the hell do you think you are? Some lousy stinking priest telling me what to do."

He was taken aback. "Now, now," he said. 'Who said I was a priest?"

"You stink like a priest!" I shouted at him. "Get out of here." The small pinched face reddened even more at this and the finger shook more furiously. He appeared to be attempting to stare me down. We'd see about that! As if I were lowering the sights on a naval gun, I directed not only my eyes but the full force of strength and power which I felt rising within me, at him. He backed away slowly, his finger shaking still but without force. "Now don't get excited," he said tremulously.

"Who's excited?" I shrieked. "You goddam son-of-a-bitch trying to pass yourself off as a doctor. This is a hospital and I've been pushed around long enough. If I have to murder every last one of you bastards, I'm going to see the doctor. Now goddammit, go and get the son-of-a-bitch."

By this time I knew that he also was frightened, but in addition he had been insulted by something that I had said, for he said, his voice still wavering: "You'll certainly pay for this, young man!"

"Blow it out your ass!" I shouted back at him. "What the hell have I done? I've listened to a line of bullshit from these bastards and what the hell do they do? They won't even let me see a goddam doctor, that's what. As for you, you shrimp, I'll make you pay for this, not me!"

He nodded his head as if to pacify me but his eyes still blazed with insult and righteous anger. He gripped the black cloth of his coat with one fist and stared at me. "The doctor is on his way. If you just won't get excited."

"Says who?" My voice was as offensive as I could make it. *"You?"*

He nodded again. "Yes. Yes. You can trust me, my boy. On my honor, the doctor is on his way. Now just take it easy."

"Your honor, shit!" Because of the way in which he gripped his coat, however, I did believe him. Angry and insulted as he was, I did not feel that he was lying. His anger was not suppressed, at least, but openly hostile since I could see it exposed in his eyes.

We stood silently glaring at each other and finally he said, still without moving in my direction: "You think you're Jesus Christ, don't you?"

In a flash of memory, brilliant and clear, the entire scene in the big room came back to me. The ravens, my own declaration that I was the second coming of Christ, the burning of my hands, all of it. I glanced briefly at my hands, the scars were still there. "What do you mean *think,*" I said sarcastically. "I know I am."

"Now, my boy," he said. "You know that's impossible. How could you be Jesus Christ?"

His head had turned gradually to the side and his hands were extended before him in a questioning attitude. Of course, I was Jesus Christ, although I had forgotten it temporarily. The manifestation of power, the fact that I had held them off, all of them, was proof enough.

"Would you know just because you're a lying priest if I was or not?" I demanded angrily. "If you think I'm not, then move over here and I'll break your goddam neck. You prove to me that I'm not!"

"Be reasonable," he said gently, but I noticed that he made no move in my direction. "If you were, you certainly wouldn't threaten anyone!"

I laughed scornfully. "Oh no? That was the mistake Jesus made the first time. You think you're going to get me too?" I shook my head. "No such luck, you bastard. Why should I die this time? You can die, but not me."

"But, my boy," he said, still keeping his voice gentle but only with effort. "If you were the son of our Lord, we would have known it, it would have been revealed to us."

"Revealed! Ha! Since when would you recognize a revelation? What are the rules for it?"

"Now, my boy…"

I waved my hand at him, focusing my eyes on him again. "My boy, shit. Shut up."

He did.

Silent, the five or six men in white, with the small cleric huddled in front of them, stood in their little group, flickering their eyes at me and looking away again. I was increasingly conscious of my ability to hold them in place by merely directing the beam which emanated from my eyes at them. Was I perhaps outfitted with radar? Whatever it was, I was perfectly happy with it.

My pleasure was interrupted by an enormous cascade of water, very cold, falling upon me with great force. I realized at once that I was in the shower stall and that someone had turned the shower on from the outside. Again the water seemed to become hot as soon as it touched my body. In spite of my surprise when I first felt it, the water did not diminish my sense of power nor did I feel in any way endangered. I reached for the soap and lathered myself as best I could under the mountain of water that was raining down over me. It was refreshing and relaxing. Just what I needed. The curtain had not been drawn and I could still see the group which had not moved. A voice from behind the shower called out:

"Ready to come out?"

"Thank you very much," I replied, loudly courteous.

The water ceased.

A man, also dressed in white, but with a bearing of much more authority and importance than the others, stood before me. Also, his tunic was different. It buttoned on the side of his neck and then across his shoulder. Could it be that he was really the doctor after all? The upper garment he was wearing seemed to be the kind of jacket worn by doctors I had seen somewhere...in the movies? We peered at each other and I said pleasantly: "Are you the doctor?"

He glared at me sternly. "I'm Dr. Matthews. Now get out of there."

I laughed. "Oh no. Not so fast. How do I know you're a doctor?"

"I'm afraid you'll have to take my word for it." He reached for me with his hand, but I struck it quickly and with force. "Who says I will?"

He backed away. "All right then, come out by yourself. I don't want to force you out. But I am the doctor."

His voice seemed pleasant enough and I wanted to believe him. "Move away then," I said.

To my astonishment, he did. He moved back to join the group still facing me. "Come on out," he said, smiling.

Although I was confident of the power of the beam in my eyes, I was not certain that the doctor was also susceptible to it. Summoning force from the interior warmth which I could still feel, I directed my stare at him and to my satisfaction, he moved slightly, his face paling. "Keep those men out of the way," I ordered.

He did not answer me, but turned to them and said something that I could not hear. Four of them started moving in my direction, two to each side. So he was going to try a trick? I let them come and they stopped at a little distance from the shower stall, two of them on each side of the entrance, just beyond my reach. At a command from the doctor they started to move again, and I backed into the shower, simultaneously letting out another hair-raising shriek. I glared at the four of them rapidly and in turn. "One more move and I'll kill all of you!" I shouted.

They backed away and looked at the doctor. His face had become less stern. "No one is going to harm you," he said to me. "We only want you to go to bed."

I laughed. "Don't give me that! I know where my bed is, I don't need four men to drag me to it."

"They won't do anything to you, they'll only help you to your bed. Go on, boys."

"So help me!" I screamed at them. "I'll murder you!"

They had barely moved and now they stopped again.

"What do you intend to do," asked the doctor, "stay in there all night?"

"What do you want me to do?"

"I want you to go to bed."

I laughed again. "Get those men out of the way and I will."

"How do I know you'll keep your word?"

"How do I know you're a doctor?"

"Because I've told you I am."

I shrugged my shoulders. "I told you I'll go to bed."

"Do you promise me that you will?"

I laughed again. "Do you promise me that you're a doctor?"

"Of course, I do. I am a doctor."

"Prove it."

He shook his head. "Will you come out?"

"Get rid of them." I nodded at the men.

"All right, boys," he said. "Get away from him, come on back here."

I shook my head. "No good," I said. "Make them go to the end of the room."

"Now look here," he said, raising his hand and shaking his finger at me. "I've had just about enough out of you. Are you going to come out?"

I glared at him again. Perhaps it was radar after all, or atomic energy maybe? I seemed to be able to turn the beam on and off at will. Once again he paled and I said: "Are you going to make them go?"

"Move down to the end of the room, boys."

They backed away from him towards the opposite end of the room. He stood alone now, except for the priest.

I stepped out of the shower and looked quickly around the sides. There was no one there. Perhaps he was not going to play any tricks after all. To get to bed, I had to pass a few feet in front of the doctor and the priest. As I came near them, the priest looked at me, shaking his head. "That's much better," he said. "Much better."

I glared at him and he backed away. "Shut up, you lying prick," I said to him. I continued to watch the doctor with an occasional rapid glance at the group of men. When I reached my bed, it was empty except for a damp brown rubber sheet.

"I'm not going to go to bed on that," I said firmly.

The doctor moved past the priest in my direction. "That's far enough," I said.

He stopped. "Now you listen to me," he said. "You wanted to see me. In fact you sent for me. What do you want?"

"All in good time, Doc," I said to him. "First things first. You wanted *me* to go to bed." I pointed at the bed. "No sheets."

"Don't you worry, I'll take care of that. What do you want to see me about?"

I pointed at the bed again. "Sheets!" I screamed.

He put his hands to his ears. "All right!" he shouted back at me. He summoned the group of men and I made my way to the foot of the bed, next to the wall. They made no attempt to come near me, and I watched two of them as they brought clean sheets and made up the bed. I had no idea what season it was, but it seemed very warm. It must be summer, I decided. The windows were all open, and the air from the one behind me was pleasantly cool.

When the bed was made, the doctor said: "All right now, get in." I walked to the bed and sat on the end of it, facing him. He did not move, but to my astonishment said: "Would you like some pajamas?"

"Why, yes. I would. Thank you very much."

He smiled. "That's better." Then to one of the men: "Get him a pair of pajamas."

The pajamas were laid on the bed and I stood up to put them on, still watching for any false moves. As I dressed, the doctor came closer. I gave him a warning glance and he stopped just short of the head of the bed.

"All right, son," he said kindly. "What is it?"

I thought for a moment. "This is..." (what was the name?) "...this is a Veterans' Hospital. Right?"

He nodded. "That's right."

"Who are they?" I pointed to the group of men in white.

"Attendants."

"And this room?"

"It's called the pack room."

"And you're Dr. Matthews?"

"That's right."

"Why haven't you come to see me before?"

"I'm only the duty doctor. This is not my ward. Your own doctor comes to see you every day."

I laughed. "He does not."

"I know he does, son."

"If this is not your ward, how do you know? Did you see him come?"

"No," he shook his head, looking perplexed. "I didn't see him, but your ward doctor always visits this room every day. Perhaps you were asleep. Maybe you don't remember him."

"What's his name?"

"Dr. Bowles."

This time I roared with laughter. "You mean Mr. Neider!" I cried out.

He shook his head again. "No," he said. "Mr. Neider is the nurse. He probably comes here with Dr. Bowles."

"That's where you're wrong," I said. "He comes here alone and says he's Dr. Bowles. That's what he did today."

He shrugged his shoulders. "I don't know about that," he said. "Anyway, you sent for a doctor and here I am. What do you want?"

"Not so fast. When I asked for a doctor, *he* came in," I pointed at the priest, "and said he was a doctor. That's two people. But it's no Dr. Bowles. Why did he do that?"

The doctor turned to the priest, who said to me: "I'm Dr. Perrin. I only wanted to help you."

"By lying to me...?"

"My boy, you..."

"Oh shut up." I turned to the doctor again. "How do I know that you are really a doctor?"

"You don't," he said. "But Dr. Perrin here or any of these men can tell you I am. Besides, if I wasn't a doctor, I wouldn't be here listening to you."

"Okay then." I sat on the end of the bed once more. "Tell me something."

"What is it?"

"Since this is a hospital and you're a doctor, then I must be sick."

"Yes. Go on."

"Why don't I get treatment?"

"But you do. You are being treated here now. Later you will be moved to another ward. When you get better."

"What's the matter with me?"

"You're just nervous and over-excited. As soon as you calm down, you will be transferred from here."

"You said I was getting treated now. But if I haven't seen a doctor, who treats me? What do they do?"

He gestured towards the group of men behind him. "These men do. They do whatever the doctor tells them."

"You mean the doctor told them to knock me down?"

"Now, now, my boy," he said, "you know that no one has knocked you down."

I laughed. "Nuts to you," I said. "They do it regularly." Looking at the group of men, I pointed at the one on the end, the one with the flatiron face. "Ask him about that," I ordered the doctor, and then to the man: "Come here, you."

He stepped out of the group (I really was in command now, I could see that) and stopped to the right of the doctor. "Okay, tell him," I said, "and don't try any funny tricks."

"Well," he said in a low voice, "he was foolin' around with one of the guys in the latrine last night" (*last night?* I couldn't believe that!) "and he wouldn't let go of him so I had to force him a little. I didn't hurt him."

I could feel the fury rising inside me again. "Don't lie, you bastard," I shouted at him. "I wasn't fooling around with him. I was helping him. He couldn't walk." I glared at him with my radar beam. "How about tonight? Tell him why I started yelling tonight."

He looked innocently at the doctor and raised his shoulders. "I was in the latrine with him and he was just sitting there and all of a sudden he started to yell."

"Tell him the truth, you son-of-a-bitch!"

He leaned over to the doctor and whispered something into his ear and the doctor nodded.

I felt as if I were losing my advantage, that it was slipping out of my control. "He tried to fuck me!" I shouted. "Is that part of the treatment?"

The man gestured with his hands. "See what I mean?"

I rose to my feet and stood on the bed, staring down at them in rage. I could feel the heat rising to my eyes and head again and I pointed at the man. "You dirty lousy bastard," I shouted. "I'll kill you. If it takes the rest of my life, I'll murder you. I'll never forget your ugly face. I swear to God..." I looked at the priest. "You're supposed to be a holy man, listen to this. By all that's holy, by Jesus Christ himself, that son-of-a-bitch is lying. If I die trying, I'll kill him. I'll kill him." I turned to the doctor. "And if you're a doctor, you'll do something about this. Look at the face on that bastard. Can't you tell he's lying? Don't you know a prick when you see one?"

"If it's true," he said quietly, "it will be reported."

"Oh yeah? Like hell it will. You're like all the rest of them. How are you going to find out *if* it's true? It's my word against his, isn't it? Who are you going to believe? You already believe him."

He shook his head. "Not necessarily, but at least I know that he's not hysterical, and you are."

"Oh, so that's it!" I sat down on the bed again. There must be some way out. "Who's in charge of this hospital? Who's the head of it?" I asked him.

The doctor looked at me. "Dr. Crouse," he said.

"All right, get him."

The exasperation burst out in his eyes. "Now look here! I..."

"Look here yourself! All that any of you want is for me to shut up. I'm not going to stop until everybody knows about this. If you don't believe me, then get Dr. Crouse. If he doesn't believe me, then I'll tell General Bradley!"

"General Bradley?" He sounded astonished.

I nodded. "Sure. He's the head of the Veterans Administration, isn't he? I'll tell him, I'll tell Eisenhower, I'll tell Marshall, I'll tell the President. Try and stop me!"

"I didn't say I didn't believe you, I said that if..."

"Nuts to you! I heard what you said, and I know what you think. I *know* General Bradley, I worked for him in the Army. He'll hear about this, don't kid yourself."

"That won't be necessary," he said suddenly. "I believe you." I stared at him in surprise. "You believe *me?* How come?"

He shook his head as if he didn't know himself, and he looked as if he really did believe me. "I don't think you have any reason to lie," he said finally. "You must have had some reason to call me."

Although I did not trust him, this seemed reasonable. But his position was doubtful; he gave an impression of cleverness which I did not feel in any of the other men. I was not convinced. What reason could he have for believing me? What had I said that had made him change?

"Didn't you say I was being treated here? That these men were treating me?"

"Yes."

"How do you know what they do when you aren't here?"

"I don't always." That sounded honest.

"Don't you think something should be done about it then?"

"If there is anything wrong, I'm sure that something will be done about it."

If? Then he didn't believe me after all. "If you knock a man down, couldn't you kill him?"

"Possibly," he said, "but I'm sure that none of these men would mistreat a patient unnecessarily or purposely."

"You're *sure?* You said yourself that you couldn't know what they did when you weren't here. They can do anything they want to do." I had another thought, suddenly. "This is a mental hospital, isn't it? I'm not here for an operation am I?"

"Yes," he said, "this is a mental hospital, if you like. It's a psychiatric ward. This room is in the acute building. You have been very sick, you know."

"If this is a mental hospital," I continued, pressing my point, "then the patients are supposed to be insane, aren't they?"

"No," he said. "Not insane. Temporarily unbalanced perhaps, or disturbed. Not insane."

"But even if they're unbalanced or disturbed, that means they aren't quite right in the head doesn't it?"

He smiled. "Possibly."

"And," I continued, "it's very easy then to prove that what they say is also unbalanced..." I searched for a word, "...or distorted, isn't it? Why should anyone believe somebody who is nuts? Is that why you don't believe me?"

"I said I did believe you."

I stared at him. "Will you make up your mind?"

"I believe you." He sounded serious, he even looked serious. "Then what are you going to do about it?"

"I'm going to have this reported and investigated. I promise."

Well, at last! "Are you going to stay here now?"

"No."

I was frightened again. "You mean you're going to leave me alone with these men, *now?*"

"You don't have to worry," he said. "They won't do anything to you. It's gone too far for that."

I wondered exactly when it had gone too far and what had caused it. I also wondered just what that meant. I looked at his face again. He did look both serious and honest. Anyway, there wasn't much to do except to believe him. I put my hand to my chest and could still feel the warmth inside. As long as that was still there I knew I could kill them if necessary, but only if I didn't go to sleep, and if they didn't tie me up again. I patted the place between my ribs, happy because of it. My atomic battery.

"Are they going to wrap me up again?" I asked him.

"If you will promise to lie down in this bed and stay quiet, it will not be necessary. Will you promise?"

I nodded slowly. "Will you hear me if I yell?"

"Yes," he laughed. "I sure will. I'm just upstairs. If I hear anything I will come down again."

"Do you promise?"

"Yes."

I got into the bed then and lay down slowly, trying to keep my eyes on the men still huddled in a group in the center of the room.

The doctor put his hand on my forehead and held it there. "Don't forget your promise to be quiet," he said, "and don't worry. You have nothing to fear."

This verbal reassurance was not very comforting, but I could not think of anything to say. I watched him leave and then fastened my eyes on the men. They moved out of the group and walked towards the end of the room, but none of them came near me. As I continued to watch them, I heard a voice from the bed next to mine. "That's telling 'em, kid. You're okay. That Matthews is a good guy." I turned quickly in my bed to look at the head emerging from the bundle of wet sheets. "What do you know about Matthews?" I asked in a whisper.

The face smiled. "Plenty. I was on his ward before I came here."

"Then he really is a doctor?"

"Sure he is. If he says he'll do something, he'll do it. That bastard Arnold is finished now."

"Who's Arnold?"

He raised his eyebrows. "That pig that was after you. Didn't you know his name?"

I shook my head, and he said suddenly. "Sh-h-h. Here they come."

He closed his eyes and I lay back on the bed waiting for them, but they did not come near me. I was even beginning to be sure that I was actually safe from them now. Dr. Matthews was really a doctor, and I did not doubt the man in the bed next to mine. I did not know why and took another look at him. Of course! He was a Negro. I watched him, waiting until there was no movement in the room. "Psst," I whispered to him. "What's your name?"

His eyes opened and he smiled, showing his bright white teeth. It was not only the dim light in the room. He really was a Negro! I knew I could believe him. First Mac, then the doctor and now this man! Friends, allies! "What's your name?" I asked again.

"Andy," he said. "Just call me Andy."

I smiled at him. "Thanks."

"No need to thank me," he mumbled. "We all depending on you now."

"On me?" What for, I wondered.

"Yessir," he said with a low laugh. "You just keep up the good work, boy."

He smiled and closed his eyes again, and I lay back on the bed, staring at the ceiling. It was a wonderful day after all. I knew where I was, I had friends, and I had done something good, although I did not yet know what it was. I glanced at the brown head again, something stirring inside me. For the second time in a few hours, I fell in love.

FOUR

THE FIGURE EIGHT HAD GROWN increasingly on the ceiling and now while it had ceased growing in size, the outlines were becoming much sharper, so that the figure itself seemed to illuminate until it was glaring at me like a bright neon sign. As I looked at it I realized that it was not really a figure eight but a circle which had been twisted upon itself in such a way as to form an eight. The judges, their faces still indistinct, leaned down over me from their panel. "What is the formula?" one of them asked.

I stared at the figure eight, unable to take my eyes off it.

"It is not a formula in words," I replied, "but there is a way to do it."

"And that is?" This was not one voice but a chorus of voices, probably all of the judges speaking at once.

"You will notice," I said, pointing directly above me at the illuminated figure, "that the area surrounding the eight is an absolute square of black and that the inner portions of the eight are also black?"

"Yes," came the chorus.

"It is necessary," I said, "by force of will first of all to unloop the figure eight so that it will form the original perfect circle which it used to be."

No reply from the judges, but I could sense them waiting. "When this is done," I continued, "the light from the outline itself must be extended, again by force of will, to the center of the circle. When all of the light has been removed from the outline, you will finally have nothing but a concentrated point of light in the absolute center of the black square."

No remark from the judges.

"This is the difficult part," I said. "Using only the light from that concentrated point, the square is to be outlined with light, and no black must extend beyond the edges of that outline. When that has been done, the entire square, simultaneously from the outside and the inside...I think...must be illuminated so that there will be no black at all. This is the part that I do not know how to do."

"You will know only when you get to that part," said the voices. "Proceed."

I found that by moving my head it was not difficult to change the form of the figure eight, and I proceeded to outline the figure itself, thus bringing it into my body. Then, with a quick jerking motion, I threw it out of myself into space and, as I had predicted, it was now a perfect circle, a sun in eclipse. To remove the light from the outline and thus eradicate the circle was more difficult. It was first of all necessary to absorb the entire outline, or rather the light which was in the outline, and hold it in myself until there was none left. The only way in which I could do this was again to trace the form of the outline, this time a circle, with my head as I breathed in the light. I tried this several times unsuccessfully because my breath would not be contained and I felt a severe pain in my chest. I braced myself for one last mighty effort and this time all of the light disappeared. I then exhaled in a long careful breath which left my body as a beam of light and, again as I had told the judges, settled itself into an extremely bright, almost blinding pinpoint of light in the center of complete blackness.

I rested, breathing heavily, but not allowing my eyes to stray from the point above me. I was afraid the judges were becoming anxious, but I knew that the next step would require all my energy. This time it was necessary to absorb only half the light, sufficient to make the outline of the black square, leaving an exact half of light in the center for the filling-in which would come later. This was very difficult to do since I had no way of judging what half was. I inhaled what I hoped was sufficient light to make the outline of the square and it was then necessary to hold the light inside myself until such time as I could maneuver my head into line with one side of the square. I tried this several times, but I was either unable to complete the square or else I had inhaled too much light. At the conclusion of each of these failures, it was necessary again to inhale all of the outline and re-introduce it (always with complicated maneuverings of my head) into the central point of light.

"I don't think I can do it," I said finally.

"We're all counting on you now," said a voice.

Of course, I had forgotten. I had to do it.

I inhaled again and this time completed the formula successfully. I was exhausted, but apparently I was not to be allowed to rest. Someone, was it one of the judges? I could not be sure, asked: "And now?"

"Red, Yellow, Blue and then White," I said.

"Proceed. Hurry." The voice was urgent.

The frame of light and the small bright center remained motionless on the ceiling above me, and I stared at them. The colors, of course, were to be extracted from the white and then re-introduced into it to become white again, but I did not know how to begin.

"Red?" I asked.

"You must start with Blue," I answered myself.

As I began, I realized that this was going to be not only difficult but painful. By breathing in, without opening my mouth, it was possible to extract the blue from the white outline and the central point, but it was then necessary to exhale it completely, holding it in space above my head until all of it hung there suspended, a ball of glowing blue light. I then had to re-introduce the blue into my body by extracting a thread of blue from the ball and working it in to myself through the top of my head; then force it through myself down to my feet, bring it back up to the level of my arms and extend it out, in the form of a cross, to the tips of my fingers. With no breath left in me, but without breathing further (since this would absorb some of the blue in the wrong way), I introduced the thread of blue, like an illuminated electric wire, into my brain. I felt a sharp sensation of pain but continued to force it into me, the pain spreading along the line, until it seemed that I was forcing a giant cold needle through my flesh. It seemed to be bearable, however, so I continued and managed to complete the entire operation. The outline above me was now a square of black outlined in white light, with a white light in the center and a cross of blue which divided the square into four equal sections. It was now necessary to repeat this with yellow.

When I had finished the inhaling and controlled exhaling of the yellow, I started to introduce it into my head but as I began to do this, I heard a terrible cry of pain. My body moved violently in the bed, the judges disappeared from the elevated bench, the bench itself curled and melted like burning celluloid, the outline wavered and collapsed, and I was lying on a bed in a violent sweat. I could feel a sharp pain in my shoulder and at the base of my spine. Something in the bed? I moved but the pain followed me. Not in the bed, then. In me. It was only with enormous effort that I could reach the jabbing spot in my shoulder and when I did I took hold of something metallic. I pulled it up in front of my face and found that I was holding two loose wires, twisted together with their ends exposed. The rest of the wire seemed to be wrapped in rubber.

I then reached down to the base of my spine and touched a small flat disk but I was unable to move it without causing myself further pain. Finally, by lifting my body away from the disk, I was able to extricate it from my body and bring it up to the level of my eyes. It appeared to be a small disk with three sharp prongs sticking from it, rather like fine nails or perhaps heavy needles, and these had apparently been stuck into my spine. The disk was attached to a long black rubber tube. I looked around for the first time and found that the bed in which I was lying was surrounded by cloths...some sort of screen. The hospital again? But what was happening?

"I want to see the doctor!" I screamed at the top of my lungs, and then listened intently.

At first I heard voices whispering and then a scuffling of feet. A face appeared around the corner of the screen and I held up the wires and the disk.

"What are you doing to me?" I demanded.

The face did not say anything but blanched and disappeared. I heard a voice from outside the screen: "Jesus Christ! He's pulled it out!"

There was real terror in the words, but I was still completely in the dark.

"What is going on here?" I shouted and then I heard another voice. "Oh my God! Get the doctor!"

And then a third voice: "I've had so much trouble with that bastard, I hope he dies! He hasn't got anything in him except..." I could not hear the rest of his words, for they were lost in other voices and the sound of running.

The commotion died down slowly and the wires disappeared from my hands. Once more I heard the voices of the judges in chorus. "You will have to begin again," they shouted at me.

"I can't," I said, shaking my head. I knew I was much too tired for that.

"But there isn't any one else," said the chorus.

I breathed deeply and looked at the ceiling. "There is nothing there," I said.

A single voice—was it my own?—called out: "Concentrate! It will come."

I concentrated on the ceiling and gradually the figure eight appeared once more. I was aghast. "Do I have to begin from the beginning?"

There was no answer. I started all over again. When I came to the blue light, I hesitated, fearing the pain, but I knew that it was inescapable. I had to go through with it. It was not so painful this time. I started to breathe in the yellow, extracting it from the outline on the ceiling. When I introduced it into my head, the pain was sharp but not unbearable, and I completed the second cross successfully. The outline on the ceiling had changed again: the cross in the center was now green as a result of combining the yellow and blue. Only the red remained, beyond that I did not know what to do.

Breathing in and re-exhaling the red was not difficult, but the moment I attempted to insert the red into my head, the pain was more acute than ever. "You will have to go through pain," a very soft voice said to me, "you can stand it. Go ahead."

I plunged the wire of red into my head and felt it ripping down through my body to my feet, turning up again and finally reaching the center of my chest. Painfully and slowly it moved first to the right and then to the left, finally forming the cross. I was trembling, although the pain had ceased. "Now the white," the same voice said to me. There seemed to me to be infinite sadness in this voice, as if I was being asked to undertake the impossible, and asked regretfully.

This time I took a deep breath, inhaling all of the light in the formation above me, excepting the cross of light which remained distinctly above my head. The patch of white light which I had inhaled formed into a brilliant ball of light as I let it out slowly, holding it in place, and then a voice said: "Now!"

With tremendous effort and in excruciating pain, I traced the line of liquid white fire through my body, feeling it in my backbone and again as it divided itself to travel in separate flaming strands down my legs, then back again to my chest and out into my arms. When it was completed, the shining white cross blazed down on me as I lay almost dead below it. I was beyond the point of feeling pain now. I did not care what happened next. I knew that it was necessary to force the

expansion of this light from all directions of the cross at once until
the entire space above me was filled with white. I took a deep breath
and let it out gradually, concentrating with all the force of my being.
The light increased and increased until the form of the cross was no
longer visible. Finally the entire square was completely white, and I
stopped breathing. This was the end. But before my eyes, gradually, a
thin line of black crawled across the white space, dividing the square
into two separate rectangles.

"Now what?" I asked faintly.

"A rocket bomb will be fired through you, from right to left," said
a voice. "You must stand it. You are our only hope."

I spread out my arms and waited. It no longer mattered. I did not
care what happened to them—the voices—and certainly not what
might happen to me. I heard a violent explosion and felt the rocket
bomb pass through my arms and chest and finally disappear through
the tips of the fingers of my left hand. I was certain that this had
been accompanied by great, almost unendurable pain, but I had felt
nothing.

Suddenly, four men in white were grappling with my body on a
table, or was it a bed?

"He's on our side!" one of them exclaimed, but I was not interested.
The shape above me had completely disappeared except that now in
the center of the blinding white which I had apparently created, there
was a small dot of black. I knew that something had gone wrong.
"What's the matter," I asked feebly.

"You'll see," said a voice.

I continued to watch and the black spot expanded gradually to
form a circle. It was not quite complete, there was a small break in the
perfect circle of black. I heard another voice, and I knew that whoever
was speaking pitied me greatly and that he had tears in his eyes, but I
was unable to distinguish his face. "This will be the most difficult of
all your tasks," he said sadly. I nodded. It was now necessary to remove

the white from the center of the black outline of an incomplete circle, force the black back into a point and then obliterate it. The most difficult part of this maneuver was that it must be done with great rapidity.

In one deep breath, I inhaled all of the white, making certain that it came out through the small space where the circle did not quite join, and the black immediately focused into a small dot in the center again. Then with all my remaining force, I exhaled until I could no longer breathe and the black had disappeared. There was nothing but shining white in every direction.

I became aware of a pain in the upper region of my spine, on the left side, directly connected with my backbone. The judges had disappeared (although I had hardly been aware of them) and suddenly I was struck by a bolt of jagged yellow lightning which pierced my skull. It exploded in the center of my head, and the room appeared. I was lying across the bed, staring through the window at the gray sky outside. I searched in vain for the sun. It *must* be there. I heard a voice speaking to me, but I could not make out what it was saying. "It is broken," I said. "I did it, and I will not forsake it now. I am committed." I was not sure what I had committed myself to, nor even what or whom I would not forsake, but I had taken a vow and I knew that I could not ever break it.

In some way, the room had changed again. At first, I thought that it had been painted, but I could detect no odor of paint. It was very light now, the beds seemed to have been freshly made, but most of all it was quiet. Except for one elderly man, thin and gray-haired, who paced continually up and down the room, wearing only a pair of ill-fitting white pajamas, there was no movement in the room. The war, the conflict, whatever had been going on since I had first been incarcerated here, was over; that much I knew. The pacing man, however, seemed a remnant of the pre-victory days. The movement of his body (it was a kind of loping, really) fascinated me and I turned my head to keep him in my range of vision. I was not surprised to find that once again I was wrapped tightly in wet sheets; with the exception of this old walking man, so was everyone else. As he passed to and fro, keeping always to one end of the room, I noticed that his head was shaking continually in negation. It was a well-shaped head, and I admired the superb bone structure, the outlines of his nose and jaw and cheekbones. It was not that he was handsome, but rather as if his head had been chiseled from very fine, transparent stone. Something about his appearance troubled me, however, as if he were some link with a forgotten and distant past. Piece by piece, a recollection of him at another time formed in my mind. I knew first of all that he was Irish, that he was a poet, and that he was troubled by the victory which had been so recently won. But why then was he here?

All the enemies who had formerly occupied the room had been removed and yet I was sure that he was not entirely a friend, an ally. Irish. Of course! They had been neutral during the war...neutral in name, but possibly against the Allies. There had been rumors of German agents in Ireland, even bases for German planes. The explanation was obvious, then. He had, of course, not been removed with the enemies because he was not one of them, but his status as a suspicious neutral left him in doubt. I could not understand how he would solve this dilemma by pacing and shaking his head. As I continued to watch him, I felt a presence near the head of my bed and shifted my gaze to see it. An attendant stood over my bed.

"How do you feel?" he asked me.

"All right," I nodded to him, speaking quietly in order not to break in upon the silence of the room.

He lighted a cigarette and put it into my mouth. "The doctor's coming to see you this morning," he said.

I looked again at the Irishman and was about to ask the attendant something about him, when I decided that I had better not. Was he perhaps just another patient? This was, I knew, a mental hospital, but the dreams...had they been dreams? they were filled with a terrible, intense reality...still had such a hold on me that I could not dismiss them. Even if they were only dreams or fancies or fantasies of my fevered brain, what had given birth to them? What was the cause of them? They were so interlinked with the physical reality of this place that it was impossible for me to draw any concrete dividing line between something I knew to be a dream world and what I now saw around me. What about Flatiron—no, Arnold? Was he real, in the sense that this man standing by my bed was real, or was he also a figment of my imagination? A strong sensation of happiness began to well up inside me. I looked up at the man and recognized him. "Your name is Mac," I said.

He smiled and nodded. "That's right. I'm glad you remembered me. You're looking pretty good today."

I was fascinated by the sound of his voice. And then my feeling changed suddenly to embarrassment. Did he sense what I felt, and misinterpret it? I was trapped between an overwhelming desire to tell him how much I loved him, and the fear that he would not understand me. I looked quickly to the bed on my left, and sure enough the head of a colored man protruded from the great wrapping of cloth. The eyes were closed and he appeared to be asleep. But I also recognized him. Andy. Andy and Mac. I loved and needed them both. But there was something else. Something I was supposed to do for them...or for one of them. What was it?

"Do you know somebody named Arnold?" I asked.

Mac looked at me intently. "Why?"

"I remember him," I said. "You do know him, don't you?"

He shook his head. "No, I don't know him but I know about him. He's on the graveyard shift."

Graveyard? What did he mean by that? "On the what?"

"The shift that comes on at night."

"Oh." So that was why I only saw him at night. "What time is it?"

He glanced at his watch: "About seven-thirty," he said.

I looked at the window at the foot of my bed. It was light, but I could not tell if it was morning or evening. As if he sensed my question, he said: "Seven-thirty in the morning."

Then I wouldn't have to tell him. He understood...that was the way love was, you didn't have to ask questions. I looked at him gratefully: "Thank you." I had finished smoking and he took the cigarette from my mouth.

"Would you like to get up?"

"Should I?"

He smiled. "You don't have to, but you can if you feel like it."

"All right." I was extremely tired, but so pleased by this rediscovery of Mac and the gentle treatment which I was receiving from him that I wanted to get up if only to show my gratitude.

He unbound me and helped me to a sitting position.

"How do you feel?" he asked.

I smiled at him. He was so friendly! "Weak," I said.

"Just take it easy," he said. "You'll feel better when you've had some food."

He helped me off the bed and led me down the room to the table, in front of the shower. "Wait here a minute," he said. "I'll get you some pajamas."

I stood there, holding myself up by leaning on the table, and waited until he returned. There were two or three other attendants sitting behind the shower stall. They did not say anything. When Mac returned, he helped me get into the pajamas and said: "Do you want to go to the latrine?"

"I don't think so," I said.

"Maybe you'd better anyway." He pointed to an open doorway in the side of the room. "It's over there. Can you make it all right?"

I thought I could and again I wanted to live up to his expectation. "Yes," I said. "I think so."

I walked unsteadily away from him, through the doorway into the latrine. It was exactly as I had remembered it. Standing in front of the urinal, I leaned against the wall and waited. After some time, I extracted a tiny painful trickle of urine from my bladder, and then staggered to the sink. I felt very weak. Above the sink was a mirror and I stared into it, looking at the not-quite-clear wavy image. It must be me. I touched my hand to my cheek and felt the heavy growth of beard. Then I touched the glass with my hand and it was immediately reflected. No doubt about it, that was me. The reflection seemed incredibly thin. It was as if I had never seen myself before. I remembered with a start that I had probably been here for some time, so I made my way out of the latrine and back to the table. "When you've had some food," he had said. It was at this table that I had eaten before, wasn't it?

Without waiting for anyone to tell me what to do, I sat down on a chair and leaned over the table to rest my head. I don't know how long I had been there when a hand touched my shoulder. It was not Mac this time, but another attendant. "Here," he said, "drink this."

I took the glass from his hand and drained it. Fruit juice again, and that same tinny taste. Probably canned...oh, well. He put a plate in front of me and handed me a spoon.

"Can you eat all right?"

I nodded vigorously and started to eat. My appetite increased with each mouthful and, confident that I was gathering strength, I could feel the food sliding into my stomach. It seemed a great effort to raise the spoon to my lips and then it took all my concentration to chew the food. Not only were my gums tender so that it was painful, but my jaw was stiff and weak as well. When I had finished the porridge, another plate was placed before me. A hardboiled egg, bacon, and a piece of bread. I ate the bacon (the hard edges cutting into my mouth) and the bread, but the sight of the egg gave me a sensation of nausea. When I had finished the bacon and bread, I bit into it with determination: eggs were supposed to give you strength, weren't they? I certainly needed strength. It was very dry and I almost choked on it, but I managed to eat it all. If only I could have something to drink! No sooner said than done. A cup of coffee appeared before me, and in spite of the weak watery sweet taste, I drank it down rapidly. It was not very hot. The man had stood by my chair all the time I was eating and he now offered me a cigarette and handed me a package of matches.

As I lighted the cigarette I was certain that allowing me to do it myself was a sign of great favor. "Thank you," I said, and looked at him. I began to feel good again. Was I going to fall in love with him, too?

"Okay," he said and smiled in return. "Will you be all right for a while?"

"I think so. Yes."

With another smile, he left me and I smoked the cigarette slowly and then began to examine myself. I felt my chest and stomach and was surprised again at how thin I was. I looked down at my right hand pressing the small warm knot of food inside me, and noticed the burn scar. I had forgotten about that. I blushed at the memory and looked at my left hand. No doubt about it at all. Now that I had seen them both, I could feel a throbbing pain in each hand. I finished the cigarette and pinched the burning end of it with my fingers, putting it out Army-fashion. Then I tore the paper and sprinkled the tobacco on the floor and wadded the paper into a tiny ball which I dropped under the table.

From behind the shower stall the attendants were watching me, and I wondered if I should not have disposed of the cigarette that way, but they did not say anything. Two of them came over to me, and I was grateful to see that one of them was Mac. "Feeling better now?"

"Yes, thank you, I am."

"Good. I'm going to get you some blues, and while I'm gone, Al will give you a shower. Okay?"

I smiled weakly. "Anything you say."

"Good boy." He smiled at me again.

Unexpectedly, I felt a knot of pain growing inside me. I did not understand it at first, but it was connected to the smile and the words "good boy." Was this going to last, or would I suddenly wake up again, bound in a bed, staring into the eyes of someone like Arnold? With the pain had come weakness and a sickening feeling that I might start to cry. The kindness, the looks, the soft words, were almost more painful than anything else. At least when they had been angry with me, I had been angry, too, and not pained. But it was the fluctuation which hurt now; hurt because I could not quite believe it, and at the same time here it was, making me feel it. No it had not been love that I had felt, but a strained and terrible gratitude for the gentleness in them, in Mac particularly. I was torn between my doubt and the absolute necessity to believe whatever he told me.

As I watched him, he walked away and disappeared behind the shower stall. I stood up and took off my pajamas and walked over to the shower. When I was in it, Al pulled the curtain and said: "Let me know if it's too hot," and the water came pouring down over me again. I did not have the strength to wash myself, but stood there, soaking in the water. It seemed as if every pore in my body was parched for water, and as I breathed it in, my strength began to revive. Finally the water stopped and the curtain was pulled back. The two men, Al and Mac, stood on either side of the shower. I was handed a towel and when I had dried myself, a pair of white pajamas, and finally a pair of blue overall pajamas like the ones I remembered from the other room. Mac led me to a bench when I had dressed. It was under the window, facing the table.

"Sit down here," he said, "and wait for the doctor."

All this seemed too good to be true. Was I only dreaming again? "What's going to happen?" I asked him.

"If the doc says so," he answered, "you're going upstairs, back on the ward."

"You mean I'm going to leave here?"

He nodded. "That's right."

I sat down and leaned my head back against the wall, to one side of the open window. I was very tired and the cool air through the window breathed gently against my face. To be dry, sitting, cool and neither thirsty nor hungry...all at the same time...was more than I could bear. The tears of self-pity which I had held back before now started to my eyes again. With a great effort, I stopped them and closed my eyes tightly. Maybe this was heaven at last.

I heard a rustling noise and opened my eyes. A man, dressed in blue like myself, was sitting at the opposite end of the bench, staring at me, but the noise came from the far end of the room where one of the figures on a bed was being wrapped in wet sheets. I watched the process, feeling the eyes of the man next to me all the time, and when they had finished, I turned to face him. The only defense I had against people, the only way in which I could repel anyone, was to stare them down, and as I examined him, I continued to look into his face at a point directly between his eyes. Gradually he lowered his gaze and I was able to inspect him carefully. Although his beard was not as heavy as mine, he was also unshaven. The color of his face was dark and swarthy, his hair was a mass of close curls, uncombed, and his nose was prominent. From the distance of a few feet which separated us I could see a large blackhead, distinct in the shiny flesh, and wondered if he knew it was there.

He slid along the bench until his body touched mine. Glancing carefully around the room, he said: "Getting out?"

His tone of voice suggested great intimacy and understanding between us, but his presence was repulsive, so I huddled away from him into the corner of the bench.

"I'm waiting for the doctor," I said quietly, anxious because of the implication of secrecy in his voice which I could not understand.

He nodded his head rapidly. "Dr. Palmer's coming down, I think," he said. "He's a good guy. You'll get along O.K. with him."

He looked into my eyes, leering.

"You've certainly been raising hell," he went on, "but you're okay now. All you have to do is watch me and do the way I do and you'll get out all right."

His manner was that of a spy or an accomplice in a crime. But whose accomplice? Judging from his dress, I assumed momentarily that he was *my* accomplice, but in what way were we related? Did I need an accomplice? Had he been sent here purposely? Was he disguised or was he really a patient? If we were both patients, which I had taken for granted when I first saw him, then was there any need for this duplicity? Was it duplicity? Was there actually something that we had to conceal from the attendants? I looked around the room again. Most of the attendants were moving about, making beds; not concerned with us. I heard his voice again:

"You gotta know how to handle these people," he said. "You gotta use psychology. Now if it was Dr. Bowles, it would be different. But with this Palmer" (how did he know what doctor would be coming to see me?) "just handle him right and he won't give you any trouble. When he comes in, stand up and say 'Good morning, Doctor,' and then maybe ask him 'how are you' or something. But don't say too much. Let him ask the questions, and you answer them polite-like. Let him know you want to co-operate with him, and you'll do all right."

I looked into his face again, vastly confused. It had not occurred to me that any special behavior was required for a doctor and I distrusted his advice. I knew that I was, for whatever reasons, a patient and that the doctor was coming to see me. That core of reality, that small fleck of knowledge, was something I must hang onto. I assumed that by looking at me, or perhaps by asking a few simple questions, the doctor would make his own judgment. I suspected some dishonesty in this craftiness, it seemed an undue or unfair attempt to influence the doctor which would surely be recognized at once.

"But I couldn't fool the doctor," I protested.

"Of course not, kid!" he exclaimed and then looked hastily around him and dropped his voice to a whisper. "That's not the idea. Nobody wants to fool the doc. Just kinda help him along, you know. Give him the idea that you're on his side. Don't resist him. If he tells you anything, agree with him."

I shook my head, feeling a knot of fear expanding inside me. I could not trust this man, I knew. Laboriously, I recapitulated the situation in my mind, struggling not to lose my little island of reality. To think logically, to remember sequentially and to place things in a relative order, took great effort. I was in a hospital, therefore, I was sick. If I was sick, I needed treatment. If I needed treatment, then it seemed important not to try to influence the doctor in any way. The word treatment rang a bell. This room was a treatment room, and what had been happening here was a form of treatment. The fear enlarged. What if the doctor decided that I should stay here? If I could persuade him by assuming a false behavior that I should be transferred from this place, then was he a good doctor? How could he be a good doctor if I could fool him? If in an attempt to persuade him, I failed, and he saw through my plan then he would certainly keep me here in order to punish me for my dishonesty and because he would know that I was not really any better but only wanted to get out of here. On the other hand, if I was perfectly honest and straightforward with him, was it not also possible that he would decide to leave me here? I admitted that, for all I knew, it was. But I wanted desperately now, not only to be removed from this room but to get out of the hospital, and I had no idea what that might involve. Surely, in the long run, even if it meant staying here, my own health would be better served by not attempting to disguise anything. And if I did have to stay here...I stared at the beds, the bundles on them...was it actually so bad? Now that I knew where I was, knew some of the people...if I could retain my clarity of this moment, wouldn't it be bearable? That was a big *if.* And what about the nights? What about Arnold? Had he, or his associates, perhaps kept me from this moment longer than was necessary? What had they been doing with those wires? And Dr. Matthews? Did I know that he had done anything? Did I actually know that there was no danger in staying here further? Couldn't they murder me in my sleep and get away with it? Surely in any hospital patients *died,* as they would die anywhere else. Wouldn't they be able, easily—with the facilities of an entire hospital at their disposal—to put me to death and simply say that I had died during the night? Hadn't one of them said he hoped I would die? And didn't they have a lot against me now, after all that business with the priest and Dr. Matthews? Had they seen Dr. Matthews and persuaded him that I was nothing but a lunatic—a raving madman—that there was no truth in anything that I had told him?

Until the man next to me had spoken, I had felt peaceful and untroubled. Now the sweat was pouring off my body, trickling down under my arms. I wiped my face with my hands and glared at the man. Whatever he was, patient, spy, fake attendant (was he possibly a doctor!) the effect he had produced marked him as an enemy.

"What's your name?" I demanded.

"Why, kid?"

So he didn't want to give his name. Then he was certainly no friend.

"What's the matter?" I asked. "Don't you know your name?"

I was pleased with myself for having remembered that. Surely he would be as confused and frightened by that question as I had been myself. When in Rome...I wondered if I would be able to pick up their technique. Maybe this man did not know his name and would now be confronted with his own non-identity.

"Just call me Ike," he said confidentially. "All the boys call me Ike."

"What do you mean 'all the boys'?"

"The guys," he insisted, smiling. "You know."

I did not know, but I nodded. I didn't want to give him the idea that

I was not perfectly sure of myself. But his presence was increasingly disturbing to me.

"Why don't you go away?" I asked.

He gave me a warning look, but it was too late. I knew that someone was standing next to me and had probably heard what I had said. I was sure that no one would interpret it as a normal remark. It was Mac.

"What's the trouble?" he asked.

I hesitated. Perhaps a great deal would depend on my answer. I wanted to give him an honest answer, but I did not know quite what that would be. Before I could speak, Ike had moved away from me and began to talk rapidly.

"Not a thing, not a thing," he said placatingly. "Everything's just fine. We were just talking while we were waiting for the doc, that's all. No trouble at all. No trouble."

I glared at him again. *"You* were just talking," I said. "All I want is for you to leave me alone."

Mac looked at me. "Don't you like him? What's the matter?"

"I don't know him," I said, "so I don't know whether I like him or not. But he keeps giving me advice. Who is he?"

Mac laughed. "Don't pay any attention to him. He's just an old hand. One of the regulars."

His voice was friendly, so I judged with relief that I was in no trouble. But what did he mean by regulars? I wanted to ask him but thought it best to keep silent and let him think that I knew. Would he think it was odd that I did not ask him what "regulars" meant? I looked at his face, trying to see what he was thinking, but it was open and friendly. He patted my shoulder with his hand and walked away from us. Immediately, Ike slid down the bench until he was next to me again.

"Shouldn't raise your voice, kid," he whispered into my ear. "What do you want to tell him that for? He knows I don't give no trouble. It'll make you look suspicious. Don't say anything like that when the doc comes in. Remember!"

He slid rapidly back to the other end of the bench, and I was so fascinated by this peculiar ability to glide along the bench that the words did not penetrate. He seemed to have some inner locomotive power which enabled him to propel his body along the bench without visible help from his hands or feet. Or perhaps I hadn't noticed? In any case I hoped he would stay at the other end of the bench now.

A man suddenly looked around the side of the shower stall. Who was he? He was looking first at me and then at Ike. His head was small and rather elongated. Dark hair and eyes and a small dark mustache. He looked exactly like someone I had seen in the movies.

After observing us with interest, he came out from behind the shower and walked over to us. Apparently he was a friend of Ike's for he smiled at him and said: "Hiya, Ike." His voice was very smooth and he spoke with a definite accent. Italian? I wasn't sure. Not French, though. I knew that much. "I'll take him first," he said to Ike, pointing to me.

Take me where? What was he? I lifted my feet to the bench and wrapped my arms around my upraised knees. It was going to be difficult for him to take me anywhere in that position.

He stood before me now. "Ready?"

I looked at him. Ready for what? "What do you mean, 'ready'?" He lifted his hand and held a safety razor in front of my eyes. It was not the usual type since the entire blade was visible. It was as if the top part of a single-edge razor had been removed. What was he going to do with that? Had I been right (the memory crowded back in upon me) that this was a place of execution? Was he going to cut my throat, or was he offering me the razor so that I could do it myself? I looked hastily around the room, but Mac was nowhere to be seen. I looked back at the man in front of me. He still held the razor in his hand before my face. Was I supposed to take it and do something with it? Razor. Shave. Was I supposed to shave myself with that razor? I felt my beard. It would be impossible and I had no mirror, no soap.

"Quite a growth," he said. "I'll bet you're glad to get rid of it."

I nodded, but I still was not sure what was going to happen next.

"Put your feet on the floor," he suggested, and I did. Then he wrapped a towel around my neck. Was he going to shave me? Was he a barber? Where had I seen him anyway? What movie?

He started to lather my face.

"Hold still," he said, "or I might cut you."

Was this a threat? I looked at his face. While his eyes were intent on me, there was no malice in them. I held myself as rigidly as possible and he started to shave me. It was painful, my beard was so long, but the prospect of being able to touch the smooth skin when he had finished was very pleasant.

When he was through, he took a comb from his pocket and combed my hair, pulling it through the knots and tangles.

"There," he said. "You can wash your face now."

I looked at him. "Where?"

He laughed, and then wiped off my face with a damp towel. "I guess that'll be all right," he said.

Then I remembered that there had been a sink in the latrine. I should have remembered it before. Was I losing my memory? Would he tell someone that I had not known where to wash my face? Would the doctor be influenced against me if he found out? It was done now, so there was no way to rectify the error, but I told myself that I must be more careful in the future and watch what I said. My voice seemed to have a way of speaking automatically without any direction from me, and I knew that I would have to regain control over it so that I would not make myself seem sicker than I was. After all I did know where the latrine was and that there was a sink in it. Would it be all right if, in future, I did not reply immediately; if I took time to think? Or would that seem odd?

The barber was now shaving Ike at the other end of the bench. As I watched him, I admired the sure and easy way in which he handled the razor. How wonderful to be so confident and graceful, knowing exactly what one was doing. I wondered if he had any doubts, or if he might accidentally cut someone while he was shaving them. Accidentally? There are no accidents, Freud said so. There is meaning in everything. Freud. Psychiatry. Mental hospital. No accidents? Had there been a meaning in everything that had happened to me? What about the judges? I looked involuntarily at the ceiling, but there was nothing there, only blank gray cement. Had there been no judges then? Was it all a dream? Hadn't I concluded some sort of victory which had led to the possibility of my release from here? Had I passed an examination and hadn't the judges recommended my transfer? *Had there been any judges?* I realized that I did not know, and once again reacted physically, automatically lifting my feet to the bench and clasping my arms around my knees. What if the doctor said something about the judges? Would that mean they were real, or would it mean that I had said something about them in a dream and he would want to find out whether I thought they were real? I knew that it was terribly important to know before he arrived.

I was sweating again, terrified by my inability to distinguish reality from delusion. I looked hastily towards Ike and the barber, but there was no barber. Had the barber been real? I touched my face with my hands. No beard. There must have been a barber. I leaned across the bench to look at Ike. He had had a beard, I remembered distinctly. By squinting my eyes, I could see that he had been shaved. In fact he had a small cut on his neck and the blood was fresh in it. Thank God for that. Then the barber had simply gone while I was thinking about the judges.

While I stared at Ike's face, I felt another presence behind me. I turned around slowly (this might be the doctor) anxious not to give any impression of hurry or nervousness. A strange man, wearing a suit, a perfectly ordinary gray suit (no uniform) was standing next to the bench.

"Good morning," he said.

Over his shoulder I could see Mac's face and he smiled rapidly, urgently, winking his eye at me and nodding. Was this the doctor? But Dr. Matthews had been wearing a white coat. All doctors wore white coats, didn't they? Hadn't he said something to me? Shouldn't I reply?

"Good morning," I said.

He did not reply but looked at Ike. Maybe he hadn't spoken to me at all. I looked at Mac and he smiled encouragingly. Was it all right after all? I kept my eyes fastened on Mac, sure that he would give me some clue to what my behavior should be, and I could hear the man talking to Ike, but I did not listen to what he was saying. At a glance from Mac, I looked back at the man in the suit.

"How do you feel this morning?" he asked.

"I feel fine," I said, and then added, "sir." Out of the corner of my eye I could see that Ike was standing, smiling at the doctor and also glancing rapidly at me and seeming to bow slightly in the direction of the doctor. I was aware that my expression was one of complete confusion.

I started to get up from the bench, but my movements were very slow. The man (the doctor?) raised his hand and put it on my shoulder. "You needn't get up," he said kindly, so I sat down again. "I'm Dr. Palmer," he continued.

"How do you do?"

He ignored my question. "So you're feeling better now?"

"Yes, sir," I assured him, nodding my head up and down.

"Would you like to go back on the ward?"

"Back on the ward?" I repeated before I could stop myself. What ward? What did he mean? Had I been on a ward? Did he mean the big room where there were a lot of people? The question, my question, still rang in my ears. I knew that I must say something at once, that I must not let him know that I did not know what he meant. But perhaps "going back on the ward" meant going back to wet sheets and one of these beds? Wasn't this a ward?

"Upstairs," he added suddenly.

Then it wasn't here. "I guess that depends on you," I answered him. As soon as I had said it, I felt that this had been an inspiration. If he was the doctor and I was sick, then of course it was up to him. Very good. I congratulated myself.

"It depends more on you," he said.

Nausea. I had been wrong. "Does it?"

He nodded.

"Oh," I said weakly.

He had a pencil in his hand now and started to tap his fingernail with it slowly. "I think we'll try it out," he said.

Try out what? Could I ask him what that meant? Something to do with the pencil?

"Whatever you say," I said promptly. The least I could do, surely, was to agree with him.

He sighed and shook his head. "Okay, Mac, get their slips ready."

He looked at me again. "Take it easy now," he said. "I think you're coming along all right."

"Thank you," I said.

I was very relieved to see him walk away from me, but I wished people wouldn't keep telling me to "take it easy." Take what easy? What had I been doing?

While I waited for whatever was going to happen next, I looked carefully around the room. I gathered that I was probably going to be taken out of here and I was trying to imprint the room on my memory so that I would recognize it if I should ever see it again. It was important, I was sure, to remember everything from now on. Some improvement in my status was definitely indicated and perhaps it would be like a new beginning. I counted the beds, judged the length of the table, counted the chairs around it, observed their color, the color of the walls, the number of windows. I tried to impress the image of this room indelibly upon my brain as if I were marking it with a hot iron, burning it into myself.

A man in white clothing and a black bow tie materialized in front of the bench.

"Isaacson," he said nodding at Ike as if he knew him, and then he turned to me: "Mitchell?"

"Yes."

"Let's go."

I became immediately anxious. Where was Mac, or the other one—what was his name?—Al. Where was anyone, and who was this? I stood up and he motioned for us to follow him. We walked past the shower towards a door and as we approached it, it opened and Mac appeared. He came directly up to me and laid his hand on my shoulder. "Everything okay, kid?"

I shrugged my shoulders. How should I know? I glanced tentatively at the man in the bow tie and Mac said: "He'll take you up on the ward."

"Oh."

He held out his hand. "Well, so long," he said.

I took his hand and he shook mine firmly. "Take care of yourself," he went on, "and you'll be all right. Just do what they tell you up there."

I nodded. "Will I see you again?" The feelings I had had for him expanded again inside me.

"I hope not, for your sake," he laughed.

I held onto his hand until he pulled it away from mine, his face reddening.

"Goodbye then," I said and the man in the bow tie motioned for me to go through the doorway. As I entered the hall, I turned quickly but the door was already closing. "Thank you!" I called out, but it was too late. Why hadn't I remembered before? What would he think after all he had done for me? I hesitated, wondering if it would be all right for me to go back in, but the man and Ike were waiting and staring at me. "Come on, guy," said the man. "We haven't got all day."

"I'm coming," I said and started after him down the hall.

After passing through several halls, we came to an elevator and went up. When it came to a stop, the man in the bow tie opened the door. "This is it," he said glumly and motioned us both out.

We were in another small hall, a kind of anteroom, and facing us was the open doorway of what appeared to be a small office. To our left was a glass door and beyond it, miles of green. No buildings, nothing but lawn and trees, and a cement walk leading to the road which passed in front of this building.

"Wait here," the man said and walked through the doorway into the office. When he reappeared, he said to me: "In there," and nodded towards the office. Then he took Ike by his arm and said: "Come on, Ike," and they disappeared out of the anteroom into what seemed to be another hall, on my right.

I walked as far as the opening of the office and leaned over to look in. There was no one there. I stepped inside and waited. There was another room beyond this, about the same size, and I heard a voice: "In here."

Did that mean me? I looked around the room and then back into the anteroom. I was alone. I looked back into the other room and a head appeared around the side of the door. "Well, come on!" I hurried through the doorway and saw a woman (had that been a woman's head? had it been a woman's voice?) sitting at a table looking at a piece of paper.

"David Mitchell?" she asked, looking into my face. I nodded my head slowly, unable to speak. She was the most beautiful woman I had ever seen. She wore a dress, or perhaps it was a uniform, of light blue striped material, a white belt, a white collar, and a large cap that looked like the sail on a boat. Pale gold hair seemed to flow out from under the sail and surround her soft pink face. I stared at her admiringly and she smiled, almost as if she were embarrassed.

"Let's see your hands," she said.

I held them out palms up and she looked at them. "Turn them over."

I turned them over and we both stared at the scars. She breathed noisily. "How did you do this?"

"Do what?"

She pointed at my hands. "This."

"Oh," I said. *"That!* With a cigarette."

"Ouch!" She moved her shoulders as if she were in pain. "Yes, but how? Did you do it yourself?"

"Yes," I said. "I just burned them with the end of a cigarette." I looked into her face and shook my head consolingly. "It wasn't difficult," I said and then added, "and it didn't hurt. Really it didn't."

She shook her head again. "What did you do it for?"

"To make them take the cuffs off," I said. "And they did!" My voice was triumphant.

She was still shaking her head, but now she stood up. "I'll have to bandage those for you," she said. "Wait a minute."

I watched her, holding my hands before me, as she opened a glass-doored cabinet and took out several things: scissors, bandages, a small porcelain jar, and some liquid in a bottle. She put all these things on the table at which she had been sitting and then looked at me again. "This may hurt," she said.

I smiled. "Oh that doesn't matter," I assured her cheerfully.

She twisted some cotton around the end of a thick stick and dipped it into the bottle. "Ready?"

"Sure."

She started on my left hand and I watched her, absorbed. The scars were still covered with a drying gelatinous substance, grayishyellow in color, and she was trying, very gently, to scrape this away. As she worked, she would look up at me anxiously and I smiled continually in an effort to reassure her. Several times she stopped to throw away the cotton and then wrap new cotton around the stick. When she had finished with my left hand, she started on my right after another anxious glance. "You certainly can take it," she said. "Isn't it painful?"

I shook my head. "I can feel it," I said, "but it doesn't hurt much. Go ahead. Go on."

She shook her head again and cleaned off my right hand. "I guess that's the best I can do now," she said. "I'll bandage these for you."

She wiped them off again with some cotton dipped in a red fluid and then applied ointment with a flat round-ended piece of wood. She then put a square of cotton over each scar and across these, in the shape of a cross, two pieces of adhesive tape.

When she had finished, she put the things away in the cabinet, and patted me on my upper arm. With a wink, she said: "Good boy," and glanced again at my hands, "keep up the good work." I smiled at her and then noticed a small pin on her dress just below her shoulder. "Miss Yaddo" it read. Odd name, I thought. Was it her name? "Wait here a minute," she said and walked through a door. I gazed at my hands and the bandages. What had she meant by keeping up the good work and that wink? I remembered a voice saying something about doing a good job. Job? Work? What was I supposed to be doing? We're counting on you, the voice had said. Or had it? I looked at my hands again. Was there some significance in the white crosses of tape? What did they mean? Where had I seen them before? The diagram on the ceiling. My body trembled as I stood there recalling the pain and effort. Obviously there was some connection, but it was something that no one could speak about openly. Did I belong to some secret league? Cross. Christ. Was it true? Was I the second coming of Christ? I had been sure of it once. Maybe I had not been wrong. How could anyone know where or how Christ would reappear? Or in what form? Maybe there was nothing I could do about it. Was I simply inhabited by Christ, or directed by him?

The nurse re-appeared with another man, also wearing a bow tie, only this time it was a Negro. He smiled at me and said: "Hello, there," and I smiled back at him. Their two smiles were fixed on me, and in both of their eyes I could see a deep inner happiness. I began to tremble inside again. A Negro. Why was it that I knew that all the Negroes were my friends? And the nurse, too. The feeling turned to pain and my knees were weak. Now what? Was I falling in love with the nurse, or with both of them? What was the matter with me anyway?

The nurse spoke to me. "You will have to have these bandages changed every day," she said. "Just tell the attendant."

I looked puzzled.

"Do you understand?"

"I will have to have the bandages changed every day," I repeated. "Just tell the attendant."

She stared at me for a moment. "All right, then," she said. "Don't forget. And now Joe will take you to the ward."

"Thank you," I said.

"That's quite all right, David," she said. "I hope they feel all right."

"Oh yes, they do," I assured her and walked out of the office with the colored man at my side.

FIVE

WAS THIS THE SAME ROOM? The floors, walls, windows and furniture, even the shape of the room itself, seemed only an extension of the corridors, offices and passages through which I had come here. Was this just one of many identical rooms? I had no way of knowing if I had ever been here before, no landmarks. Was it from here that I had seen the ravens? Was it in this room that I had burned my hands?

When the door had been locked behind me again, I found an empty chair by a window and sat in it, ready to give it up at a moment's notice. Were the chairs assigned, like beds? Was this someone's special seat?

There was great activity in the room: talking, shouting, and whispered conversations. With the exception of four attendants, gathered near the entrance through which I had come, all the rest of them—fifty or more men—were dressed as I was, in blue. Some of them wore only blue trousers and no coats, some wore shoes, some boots, but most only slippers of the kind that I was wearing. In order to keep them on it was necessary to keep my feet firmly on the ground. They were much too large for me and had no heels. Carpet slippers? Was that what they were called? There was no carpet here, but only endless linoleum: great squares of black and tan.

Wondering if it would be possible to identify the room by the people in it, I looked around, searching for a familiar face. But how would I know? I did not remember any faces here, nor were there any images in my memory from the time I had been here (if I had!) before. Someone had talked to me, perhaps more than one person, but I could not evoke any memories of their physical appearance. Three or four of the blue-clad men were walking around the two large tables in the center of the room, round and round and round, never-ceasing. Except for occasional brief glances at another patient or towards a window, they walked with their eyes on the floor, shuffling along in their slippers as if they had been delegated to polish the floor. One of them wore only a pair of white socks, the soles of which were almost black.

Sunlight streamed across the room, and the shadow of the bars made a bold pattern on the floor. I turned to look out the window, through the bars, and sure enough: ravens. Was this then the same room? At a distance I could see another building of red brick and a flagpole. It looked like the same view, but I was not sure. Even the flagpole did not convince me. Perhaps there were several flagpoles here.

I was distracted by the sound of loud voices and the hushed, breathless scurry of feet racing over the floor. The four attendants had left their post by the door to run the length of the room to the source of the voices. I watched a brief tangled struggle of blue and white figures and the sound ceased. What had happened? Slowly the attendants strolled back towards the door, their arms ready to attack, their shoulders menacing the room generally; there was an assumption of malicious, ready power in this easy sauntering. It was frightening to watch, and the room which had buzzed with the noise of the patients was now deathly quiet.

What kind of a world was this? In spite of my acute memories of struggle and noise in the room of cold, wet sheets, there had been, nonetheless, a kind of order about that place which did not exist here. This was a world of madness, surely. These men in blue, caged together in this prison-like room, wandering back and forth, round and round like animals in a zoo, talking to themselves or to nothing, muttering to their neighbors, gesturing silently in the air; and the power-possessing attendants, lording it over their charges, observing them out of their heavy-lidded eyes, talking amongst themselves...what could or could not happen in a place like this? Here I knew no one. No Mac, no Al, not even Ike and not even...Arnold. That, at least, was good.

There was an empty bench beside me and one of the men who had been walking around the tables suddenly broke out of the circle and came over to sit on it. He looked at me searchingly as he sat down and then leaned over: "Got a cigarette?" he asked.

I felt in my pockets. Did I have a cigarette? "No," I said.

He smiled. "Here. Have one of mine," and offered me a crumpled package. I took one of the cigarettes, straightened it, and put it in my mouth. He lighted it for me. "We aren't supposed to have matches," he said. "Don't say anything."

"No, I won't," I replied hastily.

"Where did you come from?" He asked this after looking me over thoroughly and searching my face again.

"Downstairs," I said, remembering that I had come up in an elevator.

"Oh." Did that mean something to him? "What's the matter with your hands?"

I looked at my hands. "Burns," I said.

"Who burned you?"

He seemed very inquisitive. After all, who was he? Was it all right to answer his questions? "It was an accident," I said, lying.

He smiled. "Okay, kid." After a pause, he added: "You'll like it here. It's all right here, you know."

As I talked to him, I was conscious that several other patients had gathered around us. Two or three of them had only moved in towards us, keeping at a distance, but several others had crowded close around us, as if to listen to what we were saying. We both stopped talking and one of them walked over to my chair and looked steadily into my face.

"Haven't seen you around here before," he said.

"No, I..."

"Pleased to meet you," he interrupted, "you look much more intelligent than the rest of these people," he made a gesture of distaste with one hand. "I'd like to have a talk with you."

"Pleased to..."

He waved his hand at me, cutting me off. "What's your college?"

"I didn't go to college," I said quickly.

He studied my face. "Too bad. I thought surely you had. I'm a Harvard man, myself."

"Oh?" I was surprised. Was he really a Harvard man? "What are you doing here?"

He looked angry. "I am a schizo with paranoid complications," he said loudly.

"You are?" I was amazed. I wondered what that meant.

He smiled. "I certainly am. A most difficult case. Of course, I've told them how to handle me, but they don't pay any attention." He leaned close to my ear. "You watch your step around here or you'll get in real trouble...that is..." he paused.

"That is...what?" I asked, increasingly perplexed.

He stood up again, laughing bitterly. "That is unless you behave like a pure animal," he half shouted at me. "To be robbed of man's estate..."

"Oh for Christ's sake, shut up!" shouted the man sitting on the bench next to me.

The Harvard man tossed his head imperiously and pointed at the one who had shouted at him. "All the signs of a manic," he said with a laugh and walked away from us, winking at me. "You'll see," he called over his shoulder to me.

The man next to me laughed. "Don't pay any attention to that fart," he said, "we call him Joe College, he's too good for the rest of us, he goes after every new guy that comes in here. Tells 'em how smart they are and all that bull."

We were interrupted by another man snarling at both of us. "Gimme a cigarette," he said.

"I haven't got any," I answered, and then pointed at the man next to me. "He has some."

He looked at me angrily and said sharply to the man who had demanded the cigarette. "Beat it, you bastard, I ain't got no cigarettes!"

I looked at him in surprise. I knew there were several more in the pack. He looked at me again.

"What the hell are you trying to do?" he asked. He took the cigarette from my mouth and started to smoke it himself, at the same time continuing to smoke his own. He glared at the men in front of us. "Lousy sponging bastards," he said and stood up and walked away quickly with two cigarettes in his mouth.

His place was immediately taken by another man who stretched out full length on the bench. He carried a pillow under his arm, very dirty, covered with striped greasy ticking and no pillowcase. He put it under his head and stared up at me. I recoiled at the sight of him, for his head was held at an angle to his shoulders, his mouth was gaping, and one of his eyes winked and twitched at me continually. What was the matter with him?

He seemed to sense my recoil and he began to laugh. "I don't belong here," he said. "I'm sick." He pointed at his head and began to stutter through the smile on his face. I could not understand what he was trying to say, in fact he only repeated the same sound over and over, no words came out. "I...I...I...I...I...I..." and then another burst of laughter and he stopped stuttering. "I've got neurosyphilis and epilepsy," he said. "That's why they give me this pillow. Dr. Palmer's a regular guy. I have to lie down every now and then 'cause my head hurts."

His speech, even without the stutter, was not very clear since he did not, and apparently could not, close his mouth. He uttered the sounds of words slowly and incoherently out of this open gash of a mouth in the side of his face. I could see several rotten stumps where there should have been teeth, and then wide gaps between the stumps. By listening very hard, I could make out what he was saying and as he seemed very friendly, I tried to quell my distaste for his face and look at him. He began to stutter again. "Ha-ha-hahave y-y-y-y-y-you g-g-g-g-g-got a cigarette?" he asked finally.

I shook my head. "I'm sorry," I said.

He smiled again, or at least it looked like a smile. "That's all right. Just hold my hand."

He reached above his head and I looked at his hand. The nails were bent and cracked and his entire hand was so rough and wrinkled that it looked as if it was covered with a rash. If I did hold his hand would I catch something from him? What did he have? Syphilis?

"Pl...pl...pl...pl...ease," he stammered. "Just for a little while. It makes me feel better."

I took his hand carefully in mine and held it and he seemed to become quieter. His head, which had been moving slightly all the time that he had been talking, now ceased to move and only his mouth shuddered open and then attempted to close. It was somewhat like the breathing of a fish and I could hear a painful gasping sound. His eyes also jumped around in his face alarmingly. "I'm Ned," he said. "I'm only here once in a while. I like you. You're a nice guy."

His hand lay in mine, contentedly, even though he had to stretch his arm over his head in order to reach my hand. Another one of the group, which was still formed around us, suddenly opened his blue coat and pulled up his white pajama top, exposing his torso.

"Did I tell you about my scars?" he asked me.

"No."

Holding the shirt under his chin, which was pressed against his chest, he pointed at two scars on either side of his navel.

"They did it to me with bayonets," he said, eyeing me and managing to shake his bushy red hair violently even while holding up the shirt with his chin. "I was at Tarawa," he said. "I was gonna get married and have a baby, but she didn't want one, so I joined the Marines where I was gonna become an officer except that they stuck the bayonets in me.

If I'd been an officer I would have been all right." He forced my eyes down with his own to the scars again. "That's where they did it," he said, "and now I can't get married, because I can't have a baby. Gee, she was beautiful, though, but she doesn't wanna marry me now anymore because she's under age and because I can't have a baby now since the Marines and because I'm not an officer."

Someone else, a very tall bright-eyed colored man, pushed him to one side, and pointed his arm and hand, one finger extended stiffly, into my face.

"It's in your eyes," he said. "I can see it! It's in your eyes."

"What is?" Was there something in my eyes? What about what had happened downstairs? Was there something in my eyes that he could see? Was the power I knew I had had visible...did I still have it? What did he mean?

"You've been there, my boy," he said, "you've been there. It's in your eyes." He shook his head sadly. "If you only had it in your hands instead of your eyes. You have to get it into your hands." He stopped pointing at me and held his hands out. "Put it in your hands," he said.

I looked at my one free hand. Put what in my hands? What was he talking about? I looked up at him confused.

"Ah-ha!" he said. "It's gone, but you can't hide it from me. You can't hide it from me! Put it in your hands. Your hands." He wandered away, holding his hands before him and muttering to himself.

From the end of the room came a strongly accented voice, shouting out: "Seexteen years I been in this goddam place. Seexteen years! You think you got sometheeng weeth your Roosevelt! They take my money and keep me here. Seex thousand dollars, I got. I geeve it to Staleen, with seexteen eenches cock. You theenk your Roosevelt a man! Ha! You know Staleen? I seen it, I seen heem, seexteen eenches cock, beeger than Roosevelt. You want a bocket of sheet from Staleen? Ha?"

I looked around for the owner of this voice, but the sound seemed to have come through an open door at the end of the room. There had been general laughter at this outburst and a few men in the group before us had walked away, two of them to start again the interminable round of walking in the center of the room. The red-headed man who had talked about the Marines let his shirt down slowly and stood staring at me. The one who had said I had it in my eyes was walking around again, looking at me from time to time and shaking his head sadly. The two that remained standing before me, simply stared, and one of them, a very thin small boy with a crew haircut, said: "Let's play a game of ball. Here."

He made as if to throw something at me and then looked into my eyes expectantly. "You missed it," he said.

I watched him.

"Pick it up and throw it back," he urged.

I looked at the floor. Did he have a ball? Had he really thrown me a ball? I could not see one on the floor or in my lap. I had not felt a ball. "Go on," he continued. "Pick it up. Throw it."

"Where is it?"

With an expression of disgust, he leaned to the floor, picked up nothing and started to throw it in the air and catch it again.

"Just hold it a little longer," came the voice from my side. The man who continued to stand in front of me had not moved, but was staring and staring and I was beginning to have a prickling sensation in my spine. Maybe I could drive him away by staring back at him? I looked full into his eyes and concentrated on him, summoning the heat inside myself and directing it upon him. His eyes began to shift and the lids closed and opened rapidly. After a moment, he turned and walked away from me, looking over his shoulder. Perhaps the man had been right. I did have something in my eyes. I could drive people away with it, but it made me feel hot all over, and I felt that my face was getting red. I closed my eyes and tried to relax.

Someone shouted: "Anybody want their toenails cut?" and I opened my eyes again.

Several of the men were moving towards the door, gathering around a nurse who was seated in one of the chairs. Someone said: "Boy is she built! Get a load of that!" I craned my neck to see her.

"Turn on the radio," said the man lying next to me.

"What radio?"

He looked into my face. "There," he pointed with his free hand. "Behind you on the window sill."

I looked around, but I could not find anything. "There's no radio there," I said.

He let go of my hand and stood up. When he stared at the blank window sill he laughed again. "They must have taken it away," he said. "Let's get our fingernails cut."

Hadn't they called out "toenails"? Or was it fingernails? Could I get mine cut, too?

"The nurse," he said. "Come on!"

I stood up beside him and we waited in the group standing in front of the nurse. When it was his turn—what was his name, Ned?—he sat in the chair directly facing her and held up his foot. She took off the slipper and then the sock and started to cut his nails. He reached for my hand again and then said to the nurse. "Cut his, too," he glanced at me. "He's my friend." He held up our clasped hands. "See?"

The nurse looked briefly, and coldly, at me. "Yes, so I see," she said.

I was beginning to feel hot again.

When she had finished with him, he got out of the chair and she said: "Sit down," without looking at me. He pushed me into the chair and I took off my slipper and held up my foot. I was glad that I had had a bath that morning.

"Where are your socks?" she asked.

I shrugged my shoulders. "They didn't give me any."

She glanced at me again and then fastened her eyes on my hands.

"I haven't seen you before," she said.

I shook my head. "No. I just got here."

She turned to the attendant standing next to her chair. "Got any socks?" she asked him. "This boy needs socks."

There was no reply and she started to cut my toenails, holding my foot in one hand. "I'll paint your feet, too," she said.

"Thank you."

She smiled for the first time and looked at me. As she did, I felt myself growing hot again, and I stared at her. "Wow," she said and looked away. What was it? I wished I could see myself in a mirror. She seemed to be getting hot herself, as if I was making her face turn red by the sheer force of my own heat.

When she had cut the nails on my feet, she painted the spaces between my toes with something red and then said: "Let's see your hands."

As she cut my fingernails, she kept looking at the bandages but did not say anything about them. I wondered what she was thinking and continued to look at her head. I could see the beads of perspiration on her forehead. As I got up from the chair, she said to the attendant: "Boy, he's certainly hot. Don't forget the socks."

I walked away from her and looked for another place to sit down but all the chairs and benches seemed to be occupied. Ned had disappeared somewhere and I started to walk slowly around the room. Someone came up behind me and took my arm.

"Come with me," he said.

He led me to a corner of the room and sat down on the floor and looked up at me.

"Well, sit down," he said.

I sat down next to him and he reached inside his blue jacket, pulling out a small book. "Here," he said, handing it to me, "read to me."

"Read what?" I asked, looking at the cover of the book. On it, in gold, were the words "Holy Bible" and then in smaller letters, "self-pronouncing."

"Read it!" he said sharply. "You can read, can't you?"

I opened the book and squinted at it. The print was not easy to read. "'Great and manifold were the blessings, most dread Sovereign,'" I started and he interrupted me: "Not that! Open it up!"

I opened the book at random and started to read again:

"'And it came to pass, when King Hezekiah heard it, that he rent his clothes, and covered himself with sackcloth, and went into the house of the Lord. And he sent Eliakim, who was over the household, and Shebna the scribe, and the elders of the priests covered with sackcloth, unto Isaiah the prophet, the son of Amoz.'"

He took the book out of my hand, scowling at me, and barely looking at the book himself, opened it to another page and handed it back to me. "Go on," he said, "read that."

"'And Saul, yet breathing out threatenings and slaughter against the disciples of the Lord, went unto the high priest, And desired of him letters to Damascus to the synagogues, that, if he found any of this way, whether they were men or women, he might bring them bound unto Jerusalem.'" Bound. *Bound!*

"Go on," he commanded urgently, "that's good!"

"'And as he journeyed, he came near Damascus: and suddenly there shined round about him a light from heaven: ...'"

A light from heaven...The Sun. What was it about the sun? I had stopped reading and he took the book away from me suddenly and closed it, putting it back under his jacket. He stood up. "You can't read," he said angrily. "Go away."

I got up and backed out of the corner. He glared at me and sat down again, taking the book out of his jacket and opening it himself. With one finger on the page, he started to mumble to himself. I was still concerned about the sun.

At the end of the room, on my left, where I had seen the open door before, I now looked out. The door led onto a screened porch and an attendant was standing in the doorway. I walked up to him hesitantly, wondering if I could go out. He looked at me vaguely but without interest and I decided to try it. As I walked through the doorway past him, he moved to let me by. Apparently that was all right. Here, with screening on three sides (it was heavy wire), I could see the out-of-doors, other buildings, trees, grass, a road, but most of all the sun. It was high in the sky and only by leaning against the wire and looking almost straight up, could I look full into it. It felt very warm and pleasant, even with the wire pressed against my face. When had I looked at it before? How long had it been?

I kept my eyes upon it, looking directly into the circle of bright light in the cloudless sky, and closed my ears to the sounds around me. Only faintly was I aware that people were walking behind me and talking to themselves or each other. It didn't matter. Instead, I began to hear music again (I had heard it before, I was sure) and it obliterated all the other sounds on the porch. I concentrated on the sound as if I were trying to decode a message, but I did not understand it. Even if I had heard it before, I did not recognize its meaning. But it made me remember something. In the bright ball of sunlight I began to discern some image: a lawn, trees in blossom, (always with the sound of music in my ears). I was very happy with the gradual clearing image and the sound. The fears, doubts, and anxieties which I had begun to feel, confronted by these strange men in blue whose actions and words I could not fully comprehend, dropped away from me, rowing out of my body. The image became quite clear—only space and the trees and grass. I could smell the earth and the blossoms on the trees. Gradually, through the music I thought I could discern words: "Earth, Water, Air, Fire. Fire, Air, Water, Earth." Was that my own voice? And then a figure appeared in the image, walking on the grass, looking up and up into the sun. More figures appeared in the fringes of the image. Two men, walking up behind the figure in the center, something in their hands. The music was louder now, and with it the images grew bolder. They moved slowly, getting closer and closer, extending their arms and hands towards the man who still looked up. He turned suddenly and saw them for the first time and said something to them. They dropped their hands at once, with a clinking sound. Or was that part of the music? He looked away again and they moved abruptly upon him. They held his arms and his body began to twist and struggle between them, until suddenly they forced his hands together. I heard a terrible cry and the words: "No! No! No!" I was sure I recognized that voice.

My arms were held in two viselike grips, but my hands clung relentlessly to the wire screening. I was being pulled away but I could not turn my head from the sun. The cry, the repeated "No!" was ringing in my ears. As if my fingers were being ripped from my hands, I felt the wire screen slipping away from me and then the light disappeared. With the sun gone I could not see anything. After some kind of struggle against which I fought blindly, aware only of dim figures at my side, my sight came slowly back. I was still on the porch, but sitting in a chair in the shadow from the roof. Two attendants were with me, holding my arms. I looked at them.

"What's the matter?"

They looked at each other and then at me. "You all right?" one of them asked.

"Of course," I answered, nodding.

They released my arms slowly and leaned back against the wall of the building but did not move away from me.

"What was all the noise?" I asked. They only smiled at each other.

It was from the smiles that I knew—knew that I had been somewhere, a place that I had been before. And this: attendants, patients, wire screening, blue uniforms, none of it existed there. But I was back now. Was it a place I could reach at will? Some area of happiness that was available only to me? Could I get back to it? I closed my eyes. Perhaps that way...

I heard a voice: "Seexteen years I been here." I had heard that before.

I looked up at the attendants with sudden interest. "Has he really been here sixteen years?" I asked.

After another shared glance, one of them looked at me again.

"As far as I know he has," he said.

"Gosh," I said. "The poor guy!"

There was a loud shout from the big room behind us.

"Chow!"

One of the attendants took my arm again: "Hungry?"

"Yes." I stood up. They walked inside with me and one of them called out: "Okay, Staleen, chow!"

I heard a muttering sound behind us as we joined the large group of men in the center of the room.

The line passed through the doorway, into the hall, through another doorway, and down the stairs into another hall, winding its way into a room that was, as far as I could judge, directly below the large room where we had been. When I came into the room, I was assaulted by the smells of food and grease and by a wave of great heat. I watched the man before me and in my turn took a plastic plate from a pile. As they had done, I held it out and the men behind the counter loaded it with food from steaming pans: meat, vegetables, salad. One of them had only one eye and he winked it at me hard. I winked back and he laughed.

Dozens of tables with white cloths, the sun striping them with bars.

"Sit down," shouted an attendant.

Where? I hesitated and then made for an empty seat at one of them. Someone rushed ahead of me and took it.

"Hiya, Joe!"

I saw another empty seat at a table farther up and hurried to it. As I sat down, the other men already seated there looked at me and one of them picked up his plate and moved to another table. What had I done? I looked at the faces around me and some of them turned away immediately, others looked back at me. I looked at the plate and could feel the eyes watching me, particularly the man seated directly across from me. Beets, lettuce, turnips, peas, meat. Everything smelled of tin, or was it something else? The man across from me prodded at his food with his spoon and pushed his beets onto the tablecloth. The red juice formed a dark spot on the cloth. What was the matter with the beets? The lettuce was fresh. I picked it up in my fingers and ate it all rapidly. With his eyes still on me, he did the same, not touching the rest of his food.

There was a small butter plate at each place with rolls and butter, but no knife, only that one spoon. Could I spread butter with a spoon? Why not? I was afraid to ask for a knife. I ate the rolls. Everyone at the table was watching me now. They had all eaten their rolls and lettuce, nothing else.

An attendant came around and poured coffee into plastic cups lying at one end of the table and someone put a cup of coffee before me. I tasted it: too much sugar. I put it down. Five other cups went down on the table. Said a voice: "The food's no good." I smelled my plate. Through the general unpleasant odor of the food, something smelled good, untainted. I tasted again with my spoon. The turnips. I ate them, and everyone else at the table ate them, too. Why were they watching me? Then their eyes turned away from me and mine followed. We all watched the man at the end of the table, beginning to eat his meat. "It's good," he said between mouthfuls. Someone laughed and then one of the others tasted his meat and looked doubtfully at me. I recognized him. He was the big colored man who had talked about my eyes.

"You gonna eat it?" he demanded.

I smelled it again and the smell repelled me. "No," I said and he put down his spoon.

I looked out of the window next to the table and I could see the ravens. They walked about the grass, pecking here and there, looking up at the windows and the building. No one had fed them yet. There was a plate of bread in the middle of the table and I took one piece and laid it next to my plate, covering it with one hand. Two other hands reached for bread too. Leaning over the table, I managed to slip the bread into my shirt and held it there with my hand. Then I sat back and waited. Apparently at a signal, although I had not heard anything, everyone in the room stood up. We started out of the room in a jagged, uneven line. At the doorway, one of the men was stopped. "Put that bread back. No food goes out of here!" I clenched my piece of bread and looked wildly to the window. Then I rushed over to it and broke the bread hastily, throwing the pieces out through the bars. With noisy cackling and a fluttering sound of wings, the birds gathered under the window, tearing at the hunks of bread with their beaks. "Who provideth for the raven his food? When his young ones cry...when his young ones cry...when his..." what was the rest of it? Where had I read it? "Who provideth..." sounded like the Bible. Anyway, I provideth. I rejoined the straggling line, shaking the crumbs from under my blue jacket. No one had seen me.

At the door an attendant stopped me and handed me three cigarettes. I looked at them and then said "Thank you," but I had already been pushed out of his way and he did not hear me. I looked at them again: "Camel" was printed on one of them and "Lucky Strike" in gold on the other two.

"You want yours?" someone asked me. My what? He pointed at the cigarettes and I stuffed them into my pocket, turning my back on him.

At the top of the stairs, one of the attendants held out a lighted match and the men were lighting their cigarettes. I put one of the Lucky Strikes into my mouth and he lighted it for me, and then I went on through the doorway, back into the hall and the big room. I saw an empty space on a bench and sat down to smoke my cigarette. Someone came up to me and asked me for a light and I held out my cigarette. He tried to take it from me but I held onto it and he glared angrily at me and leaned down to light his own from the glowing end of mine.

"Son-of-a-bitch," he said furiously. What had I done?

The man who had talked about my eyes came up and sat in front of me on the floor.

"Tell me about it," he said.

"Tell you about what?"

He laughed. "I saw you looking into the sun." He shook his finger in my face. "Tell me about it."

"I don't know," I said. "I like to look at the sun." I looked down at his feet. He was wearing a pair of Army boots. "Where did you get the shoes?" I asked.

"Just asked for 'em," he said, smiling. "You were wearing shoes when you first came in. Ask for yours. When you see the doctor, ask for yours. He'll give 'em to you. Just ask him and see."

A young man with dark hair came up and knelt beside him, putting his arm around his shoulder. It was the gesture of a lover for his beloved, filled with tenderness. The man on the floor looked up.

"Oh hello, Henry," he said casually and disengaged the man's arm. "Go on away now," he continued.

The man he had called Henry sat down on the floor next to him, but was careful not to touch him. He just stared at his face.

"Shall I sing for you?" he asked.

No one answered. He looked at me, at the men beside me on the bench, and then again at the man next to him on the floor. He stood up suddenly and thrust his arms out desperately, looking sadly at the man seated on the floor. His voice burst out on the room. "Love is the sweetest thing," he intoned sadly and then sat down again, looking first at us and then again at the man beside him.

Someone on the bench next to me said: "O Jesus Christ" and got up and walked away.

I heard a voice in my ear: "Read to me, read to me." Once again the black Bible was shoved in front of me, open this time. I threw my cigarette out the window behind me and took the book from him.

As I looked at it, my heart began to beat wildly. The words leaped up at me from the page: "'Who provideth for the raven his food? When his young ones cry unto God, they wander for lack of meat.'" I read the words aloud and glanced quickly at the top of the page. JOB 38. I didn't remember ever having read it before. How had he happened to open it to that page? Had he read my mind? Had it been something I had done? Did I have some kind of supernatural power that was visible to others, that communicated my thoughts to them? Did he? I handed the book back to him and he smiled.

"You don't have to read it," he said, "but I saw you."

"You saw me what?"

"I saw you."

Did he mean he had seen me feeding the ravens? I went to the window again and looked out. The place where I had dropped the bread must have been almost directly below this window. By pressing my head against the bars, I could look straight down, but I could not see any bread. Only grass and ravens.

"You give 'em a sign?" asked the man with the Bible.

"What do you mean?"

He pointed to my hands. "We know by your hands. Take off the bandages. No use to hide it."

"Hide what?" I was supposed to have the bandages changed. When was it? I walked away from the window and back to the door. I held my hands out before the attendant. "I'm supposed to have these changed," I said.

"Who said so? The doctor tell you that?"

"No. The nurse. Miss..." I couldn't remember her name.

"You'll have to wait. Go sit down and I'll call you. What's your name?"

"Mitchell. David Mitchell."

"Okay, go sit down."

I went back to the bench but it was occupied now, so I walked to the porch again. When I was on the porch, I could find no empty chairs, but some men were sitting on the cement floor and I sat down in an open space, alone. I was beginning to worry again, but I was not sure of the cause of anxiety. I had expected something to happen when I came up here, but I could not remember what it was. Simply that I had known something would take place, that I would find out something. I heard a familiar voice nearby. "I was gonna get married," it said, "but now I can't have a baby any more. They didn't make me an officer, they did this instead."

Someone came up to me suddenly and sat next to me. He was dressed like the rest of us except that he was wearing a straw hat, dark glasses, and a pair of shoes.

"Who are you?" he asked.

"David Mitchell," I said.

He began to laugh. "You can't fool me," he said. "I used to see you down on the Potomac River. You lived there. Your name's Mitchell, all right, but not David."

Potomac River? "Who are you?"

"My name's Mitchell," he said, "but not David either. I knew you as soon as you came in here. Mitchell! Phooey. You're a phony, and you know it." He paused. "Maybe Mitchell, but not David Mitchell. I *know*."

"It is so!"

He touched his hat and then his glasses. "Don't try and kid me," he said. "I don't wear this hat for nothing, or these. I'm getting out of here. David Mitchell, my foot! You can fool the rest of these jerks, but not me."

Wasn't my name David Mitchell? I had to remember. I looked around the porch and then into the room. It didn't matter what you called the place: insane asylum, mental hospital, institution. There was no question about what it was. But what was going on? What was being done about these people? Were we simply going to stay here forever? How had I come here in the first place? What for? What about my family? Where were they? Could I get in touch with them? Didn't all these men have families: wives, mothers, fathers, sisters, brothers, children...something? What had they done to get here? How long were we all going to stay? Had they all come through that room downstairs? Was I really mad? Was this a permanent place of confinement? Would I ever be able to get in touch with anyone? Would I ever get out of this porch, this room, this building? How did anyone know anything about the people here? Were the doctors really doctors? Wasn't there some way to find out something...what was true and what wasn't true? My name was David Mitchell, whatever he said. It was.

I turned my head and looked directly into the face of the sun, stared at it a moment, and then looked back at my hands. No doubt about it, I could look directly into the sun. In fact, I liked to look at it. Wasn't that unusual?

"Can you look directly into the sunlight?" I asked the man in the straw hat.

"What do you think I wear sunglasses for?" he asked. "Nobody can look at the sun without blinking or wearing glasses."

"I can," I said and looked into it again.

"You're nuts," he said.

"I know." I nodded at him. "So are you." I pointed at the men on the porch. "We're all nuts. All of us. That's what we're here for. They've locked us up because we're nuts. Bats. Cuckoo. We've got a screw loose." I stood up. I felt energized and pleased with myself although I could not understand why. "Goddammit, I want to get my hands bandaged!"

I walked straight through the room to the doorway at the opposite end and the man with the straw hat followed me, sticking close to my side. We stood together in front of the attendant and I held out my hands again. "When am I going to get my hands bandaged?" I demanded.

"Well, where the hell have you been?" he asked. "I been looking for you. I'll take you out now."

The man in the straw hat began to laugh. I looked at him and then back at the attendant. "Aren't we all nuts...crazy?" I asked him.

He stared at me for a moment. "Well...not exactly."

"Well I am. If I wasn't, I wouldn't be in this madhouse with all these other nuts," I insisted.

He raised his eyebrows. "You've got something there," he said slowly. "Maybe you're beginning to get un-nuts."

I liked that word. "Un-nuts," I repeated softly. "I like that." We both laughed and the man in the straw hat glared at us and walked away.

This time there were several people in the office, not only the nurse. But it was not the nurse that had bandaged my hands...it was the one that had cut my nails. When we entered the room, the attendant said: "He says he's supposed to get his bandages changed."

The people in the room, all dressed in white, had stopped talking and were looking at us. The nurse stood up and looked at my hands. "Do you want me to take those off, or would you rather do it yourself?"

"I can do it," I said, and ripped the adhesive tape. She looked at the scars and shook her head. "Wait a minute." She walked into the adjoining room and brought a man back with her. "I wanted you to look at these, Mr. Neider," she said.

Neider! Sure enough! A flood of memory came back over me at the sight of his face. He looked at my hands first and then looked at me. "Oh," he said smiling faintly, the color coming to his cheeks, "so it's you. Well, well. How do you feel?"

If it was up to him, and for all I knew it was, maybe I'd never get out of here. Was he in charge of this place? I remembered his question and said: "I'm all right."

He said something to the nurse and then walked back into the other room. As she started to bandage my hands again, first washing them off and then putting ointment on them, I looked at her. She looked friendly, which meant that she could not be a friend of Mr. Neider's. Also he had blushed when he had seen me. I knew he had not forgotten trying to pretend that he was a doctor. I wondered if she knew about him. "Is he in charge here?" I asked.

"He's the head nurse," she said. "Why?"

"Oh."

"What's the matter?"

Before I could answer, he had come back into the room.

"You're Mitchell, aren't you?"

"Yes," I said.

He sat down at the desk and wrote something out on a pad and then handed two sheets of paper to the nurse. "Take care of these, will you? He'd better go over tomorrow morning if they have anyone going over." He looked at me again. "So you feel all right, do you?"

I nodded and he smiled, his eyes wavering, enormous, through his heavy glasses. "We'll see about that," he said grimly.

The nurse looked at the papers he had given her and raised her eyebrows, but she did not say anything. What was wrong? What had he written on the papers?

She turned away to get something and I leaned in the direction of the table. On the top slip of paper I could see written: "Mitchell, David. Ward 8." Below that was some type that I did not read and then again in ink: "Electrocardiograph."

What did that mean? Electro? Electrocute? "We'll see about that." And the tone of his voice. He'd better go over tomorrow morning. That meant me, didn't it? Go where? Could he do anything he wanted? Could he send me anywhere? Wasn't there a doctor to see here?

"Can I see the doctor?"

"What for?"

What did I want to see the doctor for? What could I tell her? "Can't I see him? Isn't he here?"

"Your hands are all right," she said. "The doctor will see you on the ward in the morning."

But in the morning was when I was going to be sent over somewhere. Had he planned that just so that I would not be able to see the doctor? "But I want to see him *now,*" I insisted.

The nurse's voice grew hard. "Well he isn't here. I told you you'd see him on the ward in the morning." She stuck the adhesive tape firmly on my hands. "Take him back, will you, Harry?"

Harry? It was the man who had come in with me. "Okay," he turned to me. "Come on, you."

"But I want to see the doctor!"

His face was angry now. "Dammit! She told you the doctor wasn't here now. You'll see him on the ward. Now, come on." He pulled me out of the room after him and we started down the hall. I looked back and in the opening of a doorway opposite the room where I had been there was a man standing, a man in a business suit. He said something that I could not hear and then I heard the nurse's voice. "Right away, Dr. Palmer."

So she had lied to me! I stopped dead in my tracks, staring back. The man glared at me and tightened his hand on my arm. "Come on, dammit," he said.

It was still early in the afternoon, the sun was high above the big building and the flagpole, when the shout of "Chow" rang out again. Once more, the straggling bunches of men, the push at the door, the long winding line down the staircase. The man with one eye winked at me again. Did he wink at everybody? I smelled the food as I walked towards a table. Where had I eaten earlier? At which table? This one? No, there was no window next to it. I must remember these things. If

I didn't remember, then I might go back to the pack room. Was it this table? I thought so and there was an empty seat there, so I sat down. Once more I smelled the food and, if possible, it smelled even worse than it had before. I let the plate stand in front of me on the table and tried to remember consecutively and accurately. The man in the bow tie had brought me upstairs. The nurse had bandaged my hands. I had been taken to the big room with all those men. The man had held my hand. Someone had given me a cigarette. I had come down here to lunch. I had read the Bible. I had smoked cigarettes. I felt in my pocket. I still had one cigarette there. They had given me three. Why three? Did that mean anything? I had had my toenails and fingernails cut. Then I had had my hands bandaged again. Twice? Wasn't I supposed to have them bandaged only once a day? Would the other nurse find out? Mr. Neider had been there. Did he know that it was only supposed to be once? He had written out the slips. Electrocardiograph. I wondered what was written on the other one.

Most important, Dr. Palmer had been there, I had seen him, but when I asked for him they had said he wasn't there. Why? There must be a motive. Mr. Neider hated me. I was sure of that. He hated me because he knew that I knew he was evil. He knew that I remembered that he had said he was a nurse and then pretended that he was a doctor later. Was that why he wouldn't let me see the doctor? The woman said that he was the chief nurse. That meant he was in charge. It meant that he could keep you from ever seeing the doctor if he wanted to. I had no way of getting out of that room unless someone with a key let me out. And Mr. Neider was in charge of all those men with keys. Something was all wrong somewhere. I had known that something was going to happen when I got upstairs. But what? Nothing had changed, actually, except that we ate regularly and we weren't in cold sheets anymore. Wasn't it really possible that they could simply keep me locked in that room forever? I had no way to get in touch with anyone. Perhaps no one knew where I was.

I smelled the food again. Something was definitely wrong with it, too. It did not smell right. Was it poisoned? Had the man winked at me to warn me? How could I find the answer to any of these things? I smelled the bread. It smelled all right and I ate it, buttering it with the handle of my spoon. One of the attendants came around and put down six cartons of milk on the table. Someone handed one to me and I opened it and smelled it. It smelled all right, so I drank it. If the milk and bread smelled all right, then there was nothing wrong with my sense of smell. That meant there was something wrong with the food. Why would they want to poison it? Was it all poisoned or just mine? The rest of the people at the table were eating their food and they looked all right. But they were not the same men...were they? ... as the ones who had been here at lunch. Was I at the wrong table after all? No one had said anything.

Perhaps I had made too much noise, or said too much to Dr. Matthews. If Mr. Neider hated me, and if...what was his name? *Arnold*...If Arnold hated me, and that priest...What had the doctor said? It had gone too far now? Maybe they could not kill me outright, but they could poison me and pretend it was accidental. It must be easy in a hospital. Of course people died in hospitals. Probably more people died in hospitals than anywhere else, and no one would ever know if I had been killed by the hospital staff. Perhaps I would not know myself. The possibility of death was not especially terrifying. But that no one would ever know! No one...who? My family? I could remember my mother talking to Mr. Neider. What if she really did know where I was and came to the hospital and asked about me. "We're awfully sorry," Mr. Neider would say, grinning at her, "but David died. Something wrong with his heart." Anything! He could say anything at all! They could get away with any kind of murder here. Raise too much fuss, and poof...you're dead. Raise no fuss, and you're here for life! But what if my mother suspected them? What if she demanded an autopsy? They could have that right at the hospital and tell her that they didn't find anything. Cause of death: Coronary something or other. Anyway, natural. Nothing suspicious in the contents of the deceased's stomach. There was only one thing to do. Get out of here. But how? What weapon did I have against a whole hospital? My eyes. I wondered if I still had that beam in my eyes. Wherever it had come from, whatever it had been, I knew I had had it and that it had been effective. Did I still have it? Come on, radar, I said to myself, and put my hands on my chest. I could feel the warmth growing inside me again. That was good. All I had to do was to get it into my eyes. I began to glare at the man opposite me, and I could feel my face reddening. He stopped eating and put his hands on the table. "What are you looking at?" he asked.

I did not answer him, but continued to stare into his face. I could feel the fear coming out of him. It *was* still there. I looked away. I had nothing against him. Would it affect other things besides people? Doors for instance? Could I burn my way through a door with it? I'd have to try that. But then what? Escape? I looked down at my clothes. Anybody would know in a minute that I had escaped. That's why they dressed you in blue, of course. Where could I get some clothes? That seemed too complicated. Perhaps I would have to do it with people. After all, my radar beam (thank God for it!) had got me to see Dr. Matthews and then out of the pack room, and it had been powerful enough to keep those men away from me and get me out of wet sheets. Maybe all I had to do was to stare people into doing what I wanted.

After supper, I found an empty bench and sat in the corner of it, puzzling to find a way out. Although the radar beam was my only weapon, there was no point in using it up unnecessarily. I had better wait until the important people came along. I would use it on Mr. Neider or the doctor. These people, the attendants, were only doing what they were told to do.

Someone sat down on the bench and began to stare at me. He looked angry and I wondered if he also had radar? I stared back at him and his face paled. If he did have it, he didn't know how to use it. "Tra la la la la la la," he began in a singsong voice.

"What did you say?" I asked him.

He stared at me blankly. "Tra la la la la la," he said, not singing.

"What does that mean?"

"La la," he said and winked at me.

"Tra la la la la la la la la, yourself," I said rapidly.

He laughed. "Tra la!"

"Boom!" I said.

"Boom boom boom!" He gestured with his arms, very pleased with himself and with me.

A gray-haired man stood over us, scowling. He pointed his finger at me, his thumb standing vertically from his hand. Then he aimed his hand like a revolver. "Pfft. Pfft. Pfft." With each "pfft" he made a jerking motion as if shooting a pistol. "Get in line!" he commanded.

"Pfft. Pfft. Pfft. Tra la la la. Boom boom boom. Get in line yourself. You're all nuts."

He saluted and walked away. He really was nuts! Yes, but then so was I, wasn't I?

I stood up, facing the window. I had had enough of this. Maybe I had been nuts, but dammit I was not nuts now. I could say *Pfft* or *boom* and aim an imaginary pistol at somebody, but at least I knew damn well I was doing it. I didn't go around doing that all the time and there were no doubts in my mind about it. And as for this radar business, maybe that was sort of queer but I couldn't help it. I had it and I had seen it work. Someone touched my shoulder. I turned abruptly.

It was Harvard again. What did they call him, Joe College?

"What do you want?" I was irritated.

"Hello there," he said smiling. His voice had a slight British accent, I thought. "I've been looking for you. How do you like the mob you're in here with?"

I looked angrily around the room. "They're human beings," I said. "And the important point is that you are also in with them."

"What are you, a socialist?" he asked.

I looked at him, puzzled. "No."

"I'm surprised. You're so concerned with the proletariat."

"I am?"

He nodded. 'What's the matter with you anyway? What are you doing here?"

"I wish I knew," I said. "What I want to know is how I'm going to get out."

He laughed again. "No, no. You have to know what's wrong. Are you catatonic? Schizophrenic? Dementia praecox? Paranoid? And there are others you know. Just look around you, you'd be amazed at the different types we have here. Incredible. Really incredible. Fascinating place for research."

Was he kidding? Was he a doctor, maybe? "What are *you* doing here?"

"I told you. I'm a schizo."

"Are you a doctor also?"

He shook his head. "Nothing so pretentious. Just a student."

"Well maybe you know why I'm here? What is wrong with me?"

He cocked his head to one side and observed me. "I really don't know. I've been watching you, but you change. You're very clever. I had thought you were a catatonic, but now I'm not sure. Anyway it's nice you're here. You're quite a cut above the rest of them."

Was this just another form of madness? I wondered what catatonic meant. I continued to look out of the window and it seemed to me that there were some men on the roof of the large red building near the flag. I strained my eyes to see more clearly. There were men there and they were erecting something, a kind of metal framework.

I pointed to them. "What are they doing?"

He glanced briefly, squinting at them. "Oh that! That's the new treatment for this building. Radar, I think. They're going to beam it at this room, you know."

Did he know what he was talking about? And radar? I had only *called* my own power radar, but was it possible that I had been right, that it was really radar and that they were erecting it to counteract my force?

"What good will that do?" I asked him, trying not to betray my anxiety.

He looked at me in amazement. "How on earth should I know?" he asked and then drifted slowly away from me, smiling. Oh, hell! Just another nut, after all, with all his grandiose talk. Where was I? What had I been thinking about before he came along?

The thing was to straighten everything out and find out what was what. I knew where I was, I knew when I had come here, I knew what I had done since I had been here. It was troubling, obviously, not to be able to remember exactly what had happened when I had been in that other room, But what of it? The important thing was to stick to *now*. Here and now. If I could get to see the doctor, maybe I could find out what had happened. Perhaps I'd had a temporary loss of memory, but it was over with and why try to disguise it if I had? How could I get to see the doctor? Maybe he'd be there when I got my bandages changed again. At least I could get out of this room for that, and that place was a lot nearer the doctor than this. I'd seen him there and if I saw him the next time, I'd talk to him no matter what. That was settled. All I had to do was wait until tomorrow when I got my new bandages. Simple.

I looked around the room again. Where did we sleep? On the benches? Impossible, there weren't enough of them. *Did* we sleep? Downstairs we were in bed all the time, here we were up all the time. Maybe there were no other beds in the hospital. Did we sleep downstairs? Better wait and find out. I was sleepy now, and although the bench was hard, I leaned back against the wall and closed my eyes. Not very comfortable, but perhaps I would be able to sleep here.

"Piss call!" Who had shouted that? I opened my eyes and watched the men gathering near the door. I got up and joined the group. The door was opened and we filed out into the hall. Near the end, a door was being held open by an attendant and the men walked in through it. I followed them. On the left of this room were a row of sinks extending from the door almost as far as the window at the opposite end. On the right, stalls with toilets. Most of the men were standing in front of these, waiting in line. I walked around the line and saw a man standing in front of the single urinal in the room. "Get back in line," somebody said and I went back to the end of the line.

Back into the hall and back into the big room. As I passed the attendant standing in the doorway, he said: "Do you want to brush your teeth?"

I had forgotten about that, and I moved my tongue over them.

"I certainly do."

"Okay, go ahead."

Go ahead where? I saw another door and a small group of men were going through it. I looked in. A barber chair and two sinks. In front of the sinks were two men brushing their teeth. Where did they get the toothbrushes?

I went back to the attendant. "I haven't got a toothbrush."

He looked at me and I at him. I had never seen him before. How the people changed around here! "I never saw you before," he said. "What's your name?"

"David Mitchell. I never saw you before, either. I haven't got a toothbrush."

"You're new here, aren't you?"

"I came up today," I said.

He smiled. "You'll have to get a toothbrush tomorrow morning. Ask any of the attendants or the nurse, if you see a nurse come in. I can't give you one now."

Even though I had not seen him before, I liked this man. "You mean I can't brush my teeth?"

He shook his head. "No, I'm sorry. You won't miss it one night."

"One night! I haven't brushed my teeth for a long time."

His eyes narrowed. "Where did you come from?"

"The pack room."

"Oh. Well, I can't get one now. You'll have to wait. But don't forget to ask for a toothbrush in the morning, will you?"

"No."

He took out a package of cigarettes and offered it to me. I took one and put it in my mouth and he lighted it for me. "Thank you," I said. "What's your name?"

"Dick. What did you say yours was? Mitchell?"

I nodded. "David Mitchell."

"Better get ready for bed," he said.

Ready for bed? What was I supposed to do? I looked at him, perplexed.

"Oh, of course, this is your first night. Come with me."

He led me to an empty bench. "Take off your blues and leave them in a pile here. Take off your socks, too. When you're ready, I'll show you to your bed."

"Where is it?"

"I don't know, I'll have to find out. One of the small rooms, I guess, the ward's full."

"Not the pack room?"

"Hell, no!" he said. "Don't worry. Just get your blues off."

"Okay."

And it wasn't the pack room. It was a small room, off the main corridor, with four beds in it. The man called Dick pointed out one of the beds. "You'd better take that one."

Dry sheets. A blanket folded at the end of the bed. Even if I had not seen the doctor, this was an improvement. I spread the blanket over the bed, took off my slippers and got in between the sheets. The light was still on. I sat up in bed again. Maybe I would have to learn to sleep with the light on. But why did they leave it on all night? Better wait and see. Surely other people slept in here, too? Maybe they'd turn off the lights after they came in.

I closed my eyes, but opened them almost instantly at a sound in the room. A colored man was getting into the bed next to me, and that seemed like a good omen. Also, another man was getting into the bed at the other end of the room and there was one empty bed between his and mine. Dick was standing in the doorway. "Okay," he said to the man at the end of the room, "snap it up!" The man got into the bed and the light went off suddenly, leaving me with the image of Dick's broad grin in front of my eyes. I heard his voice. "Good night," he said and I called out "Good night" in reply.

There was a momentary silence, but I knew he had not moved from the doorway. I heard his voice again, and there was laughter buried in the tone. "Good night, Mitchell. I hope you like us well enough to stay with us," he said. I knew there was no threat in this, that he only meant that he hoped I wouldn't go back to the pack room. It was a terribly nice thing to have thought of and said, in fact it was almost the kindest thing anyone could have said to me. I sat up in bed, peering at the doorway, but there was no one there. I had begun to tremble again, and I lay back suddenly. What the hell was the matter with me? What was I going to do, tremble into love every few minutes? Men, white or black, women…anyone, anything. Still, there it was, shaking and shuddering inside me. It was the kindness, that was it. I couldn't stand the kindness.

SIX

MY RADAR BEAM WAS A source of delight to me. Not only did it not diminish, but I found that I could exercise a certain control over it; I was able to summon it at will or to extinguish it. It had become very useful to me on the ward. I could repel attendants or patients at will. All that was necessary was to recognize the central source of heat in my solar plexus and move it into my eyes, stare angrily at my enemy, and he would become pale, frightened, and usually leave. Since the source of the power was definitely located inside me, in my chest, it must obviously come from the sun. Solar power, Solar plexus. For this reason, whenever I was not engaged in some routine—eating, visiting the latrine, having my bandages changed—I gazed at the sun, absorbing its light and warmth. The skies were continually bright and cloudless.

I had not seen Dr. Palmer again, even though I had looked for him on my visits to the office to have my hands bandaged, but I had had the satisfaction of turning the beam fully on Mr. Neider with the usual results: his face had been gradually possessed by fear, the color had drained from it, and he had managed to leave the room on some pretext or other. Apparently it had been effective in thwarting whatever scheme he had formulated against me when he had handed the papers to the nurse. No further reference had been made to electrocardiograph, and I had not been moved from the ward. His power, whatever it was, was no greater than mine.

In the course of several days on this ward, I had acquired a bench to myself. The other patients, the men in blue, accepted this without question and not even the attendants made any move to dislodge me. Because of this, I was surprised when I heard a voice behind me saying: "Sit down here on this bench with him."

I turned away from the bright afternoon sun to find an attendant and an extremely thin man standing beside him. This man was obviously a patient, dressed in blue like the rest of us, but he looked like an impish bird. (Everybody seemed to look like a bird.) His head and face were pointed, his bones standing out under the sallow flesh, and his head moved jerkily from time to time, in a birdlike twitch.

The attendant, I recognized his face but did not know his name, laughed and said to me: "He's just up from pack. Take care of him." Then he lowered the man onto the opposite side of the bench. He seemed unable to stand by himself, sinking onto the seat as the attendant lowered his arm. He sat there, with only an occasional jerk of his head, staring at me.

"Just up from pack. Take care of him." I repeated the words to myself, wondering just what they meant. What was I supposed to do? I looked up at the attendant, lighting a cigarette. I felt in my pocket, found one of the cigarettes which they had given me in the dining room, and put it in my mouth.

"May I have a light, please?"

He lighted the cigarette for me and then offered his package to the little man at the end of the bench. The man looked at him and jerked his head again, but did not say anything, did not extend his hand towards the package. Was he dumb? I closed my eyes, trying to sense him, to feel what he was. I could feel very little emanation from him, but what I did feel was not good. "Take care of him." Did that mean to protect him, or to give him the works? What could I do either to or for him? I opened my eyes again and looked at him. Of itself, I felt the beginning of the beam coming into my eyes. Perhaps I was supposed to disintegrate him? Could I? I breathed deeply, increasing the heat inside me until I could feel it strongly, almost hearing it reverberate against my ribs. Then I looked steadily and directly into his face. His eyes blinked and then stood out, round white marbles in the sunken, stretched skin. He jerked his head, cocking it to one side. I continued to direct the beam against him, into him. I found that by inhaling the cigarette smoke, the heat inside me seemed to increase still more. If I swallowed the smoke, would that make it even more intense? I swallowed a mouthful of smoke, and then swallowed again, watching him. His face paled, as I had expected, and with it a look combining fear and nausea came into his eyes.

I continued to stare at him, swallowing smoke and taking care not to blink which might give him respite, and he drew himself further into the corner of the bench. When I had almost entirely consumed the cigarette, I felt in my pocket and found another. I had planned to keep it until bedtime, but I could not stop now. I lighted it from the end of the other one and threw the old butt out of the window. As he saw me lighting another cigarette, the look in his eyes turned gradually to horror, and he seemed not only to shrink into the bench, but to wither. His hands trembled and he brought them together over his stomach. His body bent slowly, accompanied always by the twitching movement of his head. He drew his feet up under him, off the floor.

The room had become quieter, and several people were watching us. I could not look away from him now to see who they were, but I felt them gathering around us in a group. Someone said: "Boy, look at that!" and I reached out with one hand. Still without turning my eyes, I said: "Who's got a cigarette?" and felt one being pushed into my hand. Without moving my eyes, I lighted the third cigarette and saw the terror increase until it spread through the man's entire body. Incredibly, he was getting smaller before my eyes; the jerking of his head seemed intensified and uncontrollable, his hands continued to tremble, and he was unable to take his eyes off me.

If he was going to disintegrate, I hoped that he would hurry. I had swallowed clouds of smoke and my throat was becoming dry. Also, there was a wad, apparently of smoke, in the center of my stomach which formed an unpleasant area of pressure, like a beginning sickness. I heard a voice:

"Come on boys, break it up," and then felt a hand on my shoulder. 'What the hell are you doing?" Damn! I looked up, still glaring, at the attendant. To my surprise, it was my friend Dick. I smiled at once, dispelling the radar, dropping it back inside me. "Smoking," I answered him.

He shook his head, and turned to the little bird-man. "What's the matter, Johnny, are you sick?"

Johnny jerked his head away from me, turning it this time, and gazed up at him uncomprehending. He did not say anything.

Dick turned to me again. "You'd better lay off him." He nodded to the man he had called Johnny, and added, with a laugh, to me: "Give the poor guy a break!"

As he walked away, I looked at the little man still huddled on the bench. I smiled and blinked my eyes. He did not jerk his head at me now, and the fear began to wash away slowly. Perhaps I could use the power in reverse and revive him back to where he had been. Perhaps I had not been supposed to disintegrate him after all. My smile became broader and he continued to look at me.

"Hello, Johnny," I said, and while he did not answer, the fear had almost completely disappeared from his face. His hands stopped trembling, and he let his feet down to the floor. I was even more astonished. Not only was this a weapon, but it had all sorts of uses. Not only could I knock people out, or at least terrify them, but I could make them feel good. That would probably be very useful.

I looked back at the sun again, nodding towards it, the source of my power. I must learn all its uses, develop and perfect them. There was no telling what I could do with it eventually.

In the few days on this ward, the hospital had begun to assume a shape of its own, a reality of repetition, if not of meaning, and with it I could distinguish a form in what was supposed to be my illness. I had been both pleased and amused at the idea that, probably, the very core of that illness was the power I felt inside myself. Even to me, it did not represent a usual or normal power...certainly no one else here had it. I had never had it before, myself, but in searching my memory for its origin, it seemed a logical, heightened extension of the force that is latent in the eyes of everyone. I did not know by what means it had come to a fuller expression in me: I was either chosen for it, or I had stumbled secretly upon the key to its release. Why or how I had it were not the important questions, only the fact of its possession was important to me. I did not yet know what to do with it except to preserve it. I would certainly have use for it some time soon. It was my only weapon, means, power. Only with this could I command attention. The very fact that it was not usual, that the others here did not possess it, was proof that it was or would be considered the primary manifestation of my illness. It was my—for want of a better word—*thing*. It was the outer expression of sickness in me in the same way as the continuous repetition about the Marines was for the red-haired boy, no doubt. I used, to myself, the words "illness" and "sickness." People in hospitals were there because there was something wrong with them, because they were ill. Unfortunately, in this kind of hospital, a mental hospital, it was because people assumed they were ill.

I was alternately amused and embittered when confronted with the actual fact of my own confinement. Whatever had or had not taken place in the pack room, in the short space of time since I had been here, I had already proved my ability to deal with the conditions and limits of this ward. Not only to myself, but even to the attendants. I knew most of them by sight, if not by name. I knew which ones were on the day shift, which on the afternoon and night shifts. I greeted them and said goodbye to them. I carried on conversations with them. I did what I was told to do. At night I brushed my teeth, went to bed, slept. In the morning I found my clothes, dressed, washed my face, went to the latrine, went to breakfast. I answered the chow and latrine calls during the day, without protest. I remembered to have my bandages changed and was careful not to get them wet. I did not ask to see the doctor, which had always caused such an uproar. And yet with all this, there was no change. There was no indication that this was not a permanent confinement. And for what? What had I done? I could remember that I had taken my clothes off on the lawn in front of my house, and I could recognize that socially, that was undesirable. (Undesirable or not, the theory which had led up to it seemed to me to make sense, although the method of carrying it out had obviously been too drastic.) But what else had I done? What had I done that had warranted confinement, being locked up in this place? I didn't know, but I was determined to find out. For the time being, the policy of doing what I was told to do, without question, had certain rewards. I was left alone, I could concentrate on the development of my own inner strength; the use of that strength, that storehouse of energy, would come later. For now the important thing was to determine what, *here,* would be considered a normal pattern of behavior. I must discover it and conform to it; however difficult it might be, I must adopt an averageness that would give the appearance of health and normality.

It was not going to be easy, I was sure of that. The basic and terrifying obstacle, which I recognized repeatedly, was that no one, once in this place, was observed or considered as conceivably normal. For that reason, I knew that I could not behave in what was, for me, a normal manner. The approximation of normality which I hoped to be able to act out for the doctors (if they ever saw me) and the attendants would, I knew, have to be an exaggerated, abnormal normality. I would have to become, somehow, so extraordinarily sane, so outstandingly average that it would be noticed; otherwise I would surely be buried and forgotten here.

THE WORLD NEXT DOOR

I looked around at the other patients and the attendants. Was it really possible to do such a thing? I wondered if I would ever be able to figure out what was normal to these people? Was it possible to know what to do that would please them? I was forced to admit at least the feeling of defeat; it really did not look as if they could be impressed, or as if I could fathom their conception of the average man sufficiently well to emulate it. I shuddered and looked away from the attendants, out the window.

The sun was going down now, in fact only the last rays were left in the sky, glowing over the big building which faced this ward. I could accept the night, once it had arrived, but there was unbearable loneliness in the twilight, the receding sun and the gathering night. I heard the first of the final calls of the evening...to the latrine, the brushing of teeth, getting ready for bed. I stood up to take off my blues, my eyes still on the ending day, feeling the beginning of the night swallowing this place up. How many nights would I be here?

That night was the first since I had come upstairs that I did not sleep. Lying in bed in the dark, I listened to the faint sounds of beds creaking in the other rooms; the doors of the bedrooms were never closed at night. In my own room, in the bed at the far end, I heard the repetitive creaking of lonely self-satisfaction and reassurance. For that man, and probably for many others that I did not know about, every night began with a period of waiting; waiting until silence had absorbed the ward and the building itself, until they could begin this sad and silent rite of love with themselves, driving themselves into temporary, sterile ecstasy and exhaustion. And then the beds would lapse into silence again, the breathing would slow down once more.

From then on, there would only be occasional footsteps in the hall, whispered conversations, or from some distance away (was that the pack room?) a piercing scream, turning into jumbled violent words, or a long low moaning sound. Tonight, there was more than one cry in the ward, and through them I heard the sound of footsteps running down the hall. What was happening? I began to sweat.

Whatever it was called, however it was disguised, there was no question about what this place was. Again and again, I said to myself: This is an insane asylum. I tried to reconstruct in my mind what I knew of the building in which I was confined: the pack room on the ground floor on one side, opposite it the dining room, with miles of halls between them. On this floor, the wardroom at one end, the shower room, the latrine, and a sleeping ward. Probably something similar at the other end of the building: Rooms like this one where I was supposed to be sleeping flanked the corridor, connecting these two ends, and at the center near the entrance, offices. Were they offices? There was the room where my hands were bandaged, the anteroom which opened onto another office, and the door leading out of the building. That central place, those offices...that was the heart of this place, it was from there, I was sure, that orders were issued. But what orders, and how did they affect me or any of the rest of these people? How did we get here in the first place, and, once here, what chance was there of getting out at all? People were...what was the word? ... confined, committed to asylums.

Committed. Had I been committed? I struggled to remember back to the beginning again, back beyond the pack room. It was difficult to bridge the gap. The memory of the lawn, the sunlight, the ride in the car, all that had form and sequence. But what troubled me was what had happened after I got here. How had I been taken to the pack room in the first place, and what had happened when I was down there? I could remember the room well enough, but the sequence, the actual reality of it in time was beyond recollection. The wet sheets, the shower, the food, the cigarettes, Arnold, Dr. Matthews, Mac...they were clear enough, but no clearer than the judges, the examination, the pain. Was I really *nuts?* If anything had gone wrong with my mind, then it had really happened in that room. Was insanity, or whatever they called it, a process by which reality lost its limits and merged into dreams or nightmares? Was it possible that I had lost the power to distinguish between what was real and what was not real? Had my imagination substituted itself for actuality?

What was reality? A form of behavior? A social code? Was it something invented by man, or some intangible code of limitations that was passed on from generation to generation, with no real understanding of its source? Saints, martyrs, holy men...hadn't all of them heard voices, witnessed or performed miracles? What was a miracle? Something beyond the conception of the average man, something that was outside the limitations of the normal mind? Wasn't it a form of insanity?

I tossed in the bed, closing my eyes. I hadn't slept before I came here. I could not remember for how long, but I hadn't slept for a long time. Was that the way it had begun? Wasn't it important to sleep? Was that the means to sanity: to sleep regularly? Whatever part sleep played, it was obviously desirable that I should sleep. They wanted me to sleep, that's why they put me in a bed.

More footsteps and voices in the hall...a light. They stopped in the hall just outside my room and then I heard them coming in. A light was flashed in my eyes and I opened them.

"What's the matter, can't you sleep?"

"You woke me up," I lied. They must not know that I hadn't been asleep. That would be a sign of something wrong. Sleep must be important. People bought pills to sleep, books were written about sleeping and the importance of being able to sleep.

"Go back to sleep."

"I can't sleep with a light in my eyes, for God's sake!"

"Quiet."

I closed my eyes again. What would happen if I didn't sleep?

I was still awake when someone put his head into the room.

"All right, you guys, let's go!"

In the latrine, I looked at myself in the mirror. Did I look well? Thin. Tired. More tired than yesterday? I couldn't remember. Probably. I looked away from the mirror. and there was a man standing by the window, thrusting his arms out to the front, to the side, above his head, counting under his breath. What was he doing? He looked at me. "No exercise here," he said. "Have to keep up my strength. One two three four. One two three four."

An attendant came into the room and went directly over to him. "All right, Tom," he said sharply. "That's enough of that. Get out of here."

"I'm only doing my exercises," the man replied. "Have to keep fit."

"I told you that was enough. Come on out of here!" He led him away and the man muttered to himself.

Why didn't they let him do exercises? What was wrong with that? People did exercises to the radio every morning, didn't they? Wasn't that perfectly normal?

I walked down the hall to the large room and over to the bench where I had left my clothes. Five or six patients were sitting or standing around the room, dressing. There were two bundles of clothing on the bench, but neither of them was mine. Had I put them somewhere else? What had happened to them? I looked on the chair beside the bench. No, I knew I had left them on a bench. I walked to the next bench. More blue clothes, but I was sure they were not mine. Had I forgotten? Had I really left them somewhere else? I felt a cold hardness in my stomach. I had to find them before anyone found out that I didn't know where they were. I had to!

"What's the matter? Can't you find your clothes?"

I whirled around. The attendant was smiling at me. He was one of the night ones...the bad ones. The day shift was not here yet. Why was he so pleased? Had he moved them?

"I left them on that bench," I said. "They're gone."

"They couldn't be gone if you left them there. No one has touched anything in here."

"But I know they were there."

"You *know?*" The smile increased. "You probably thought you left them there. Better look around the room. You must have forgotten."

Had I really forgotten? Was that because I hadn't slept? I had a good memory. I had always had a good memory. Was I losing it? I couldn't believe him...I could not accept this and let go of my small anchor of confidence. "Someone must have moved them," I insisted.

Bigger smile. "Why would anyone want to move your clothes?"

"I don't know."

More men were in the room now, and more coming through the doorway all the time. I looked at the attendant again, hating his smile.

"You'd better find them," he said, and walked away from me. I walked around the room, looking on all the benches and the chairs. How would I be able to identify them if I did find them? They were all blue. Everybody wore blue clothes. Had someone else put mine on? If I had forgotten where I had left them, how could I be expected to remember the difference between my blue clothes and someone else's blue clothes? There was no difference in any of them except in size.

As I walked around the room, the other men looked at me knowingly. They knew I had lost them, that I couldn't find my own clothes. I had forgotten, I was losing my memory. I went back to the bench where I was sure I had left them. Two men were sitting on it now, both dressed. If I waited here until everybody was dressed, would I find them then? Wouldn't there be one pair of blues left over after everyone else was dressed, and wouldn't those be mine?

"Why aren't you getting dressed?" Another attendant. What was his name? Monty. I liked him. He was one of the day men, a Negro.

"Somebody took my clothes."

"Where did you leave them last night?"

"Right here on this bench."

The other two men looked at me and then one of them walked away.

"Are you sure, David?"

I started to nod, but I could not lie to him. "I think so." It was a frightful admission, my stomach was cold and empty now.

"Have you looked on the other benches?"

"Yes."

"You must have forgotten where you put them last night."

Then it was true. He thought I had forgotten, too. I must have!

"What am I going to do?"

"If they don't turn up, I'll get you another pair." He looked at me and shook his head. "You'll have to remember them from now on."

This was really bad. I knew it was bad. I hadn't slept and now I couldn't remember where I had put my clothes. I was sick, then. Something was really wrong with me, so that I had to be here. But why did they make it so difficult? Did they have to come around in the middle of the night and flash a light in my eyes? Did everyone have to wear blue clothes that you couldn't tell apart?

When everyone was dressed, there were no clothes left over. Didn't that prove that someone had taken them, that I had not forgotten them? It was better than finding them in another place, wasn't it?

Monty took me down the hall to the shower room and gave me a pair of blues.

"They must have been moved," I said. "Somebody must have taken them, or they would have been left over, wouldn't they?"

He smiled. "That crummy night shift," he said. "You gotta watch those boys."

"Why?"

He didn't answer, but he seemed angry, although not with me. "Come on, get into these. It's almost chow time."

I got into my clothes quickly. Did he mean that they had moved them? Anyway he didn't seem to think that I had forgotten where they were. Maybe I wasn't so sick after all, but I must learn how to sleep somehow. It wasn't good not to sleep, I knew that.

After breakfast, the whole room had changed. The tables, benches, and chairs were all moved to one end, someone was sweeping the floor, someone else was washing it with a mop. When they had finished one end of the room, all the furniture was moved and the other end was swept and washed. I heard my name called. It was Monty again.

"Do you want to do some work?"

"Sure. What?"

"Polish the floor." He pointed at a machine with a long cord on it.

"What do I do?"

He smiled at me. "I'll show you." He flicked a button on the handle and the machine started to growl and whirl around. He grabbed the handle. "Just walk up and down with this."

I took it from him, but it seemed almost alive. The handle pulled itself away from me. I tried walking up and down with it, but I could not keep it in a straight line. Monty and the other attendants were watching me and so were the patients. One of them came up to me as I struggled with the machine, trying to keep it from flying out of my hand. "That's not the way to do it. Give it to me."

He took it out of my hand and started up and down the room with it. He didn't seem to have any trouble, but I could not understand the secret of it. Maybe I should try it again. I went up to him.

"Let me do it."

He pushed me away. "No. You don't do it right."

He was a patient. He could do it. Did that mean he was not as sick as I was? Hadn't he had to learn how to use that machine? Was it really easy? It looked easy. I had a sinking feeling in my stomach again. I couldn't even do that. What would they think? Would they make a note of it and write it down somewhere? I could see what they would write. First the date, whatever that was, and then: "Mitchell, David. Unable to find clothes. Unable to polish floor." Would they add: "Unable to sleep?" Did they know? I had been awake when they had flashed the light in my eyes.

"Want to help with the furniture?"

It was Monty again. Was he giving me another chance? Surely I could move furniture all right. Would that make up for the black marks against me already?

The benches were very heavy, but I helped move them until the room was the way it had been before: benches and chairs around the walls, tables in the center.

Someone called out: "No smoking now." The floor was very clean and shiny, and I could see the stripes of light reflecting the path that had been made by the polishing machine. Nice and straight. I would have to learn how to operate that thing.

"Okay, boys," someone said sharply, "here they come."

There was a sudden bustle at the doorway and then a crowd of people swept into the room. I recognized Mr. Neider and Dr. Palmer and Miss Yaddo. So the doctor was coming to see us!

I was sitting on the right side of the room and the group of people, there must have been nine or ten of them, started rapidly down the opposite side. I was fascinated by their movement, it was as if they were on a platform on wheels, they moved as one great mass. There was a small man I had never seen before in the center of the group, barricaded by the nurses and attendants around him, and he seemed to be the most important person in the group. Who was he? The head of this place? They moved very fast, stopping...only pausing, as if to take in breath, really...to speak to a patient. I heard the voice of the little man: "Well, well, Joseph, how are you this morning?" but before Joseph had time to say anything...whoosh...the group was off again. They paused at the door leading out to the porch, gave the porch a great mass glance, and then whirled on. If this was my doctor, I wondered if he would speak to me? Maybe he could tell me what I was doing here. Or what I had to do to get out. If he wasn't my doctor, at least I knew Dr. Palmer. I stood up, standing squarely in their path.

As they came nearer to me, Miss Yaddo looked at me and winked. Then she narrowed her eyes and nodded her head at the little man.

What did that mean? I squared my shoulders. Dr. Palmer looked at me and nodded, and then glanced briefly at the little man, blinking both his eyes. I did not understand what was going on but felt they were trying to tell me something.

When they got to me, they were forced to stop. I stood directly between the benches and the tables in the center of the room, blocking their passage. Mr. Neider looked at me and looked away, Dr. Palmer whispered something in the ear of the little man, and the barricade of attendants opened up enough so that I was facing him.

"Good morning," he said, smiling. More whispering, more glances. Even though he had smiled, he only glanced at my face, and then looked away again. Dr. Palmer motioned to me with his hand, as if to tell me to get out of the way. I shook my head.

"Good morning," I said. "Who are you?"

He looked surprised. "I'm Dr. Bowles."

He looked away again. "You're..." more whispering. "You're David Mitchell, aren't you? Oh yes." He consulted a paper which Mr. Neider held before his eyes. "Of course. How are you?"

"I'm fine. How are you?"

The group started to move again, as if they would run over me. I did not budge. "What am I doing here?" I asked.

He smiled again. "You've been upset," he said. "You're here for treatment."

Treatment? What kind of treatment? "I don't get any treatment."

There was a pause, and more whispering. "For the time being you're under observation."

"Observation for what? Who observes me?"

My voice had become louder, and someone said: "Shhhhh."

I looked at the group in surprise. "You're the doctor here, aren't you? The head of this place? Don't you know what's the matter with me? How long are you going to keep me here?"

"Well, David," he was getting impatient. His smile was strained.

"That will depend on you."

"What do you mean? What am I supposed to do?"

"You're not supposed to do anything. We'll know how you are getting along, simply by observing you for a while. What I want you to do is just to take it easy here and eat a lot and get a lot of sleep."

"Then what?"

"We'll see, David. We'll see when we've seen how you get along."

"When will that be?" I had never seen him before, and I did not know if he would ever be in here again. He was whispering with Mr. Neider and then with Dr. Palmer. He turned to me again.

"Vous parlez français, n'est-ce-pas?"

"Mais oui, pourquoi?" Why did he want to talk French to me? "What's the matter with English?"

He moved his hand placatingly. "Moi aussi, je parle français," he said. "Nous allons parler français ensemble."

"Pourquoi faire?"

"Pas si fort," and then continuing in French: "I wish to speak in French with you because I like to speak French. That's all."

"If it pleases you, what the hell. But what are you going to do with me? For how long am I going to be made to stay here?"

"But as I have said to you, David, that depends on you. If we see progress, then there will undoubtedly be a change."

"Well then, tell me what it is, the progress. What am I to do?"

More whispering. "We are going to make some tests this afternoon. After that, we will see. Dr. Palmer will speak with you later, also perhaps some others." He turned to Dr. Palmer and said to him in English: "Make a note of that, Dr. Palmer. See this boy when you have time." He turned to Mr. Neider and whispered something to him.

I continued in French: "You have said that you are the Dr. Bowles, is it not so?"

"But yes: I am the Dr. Bowles."

I pointed at Mr. Neider. "Then why is it that that one there came to me and represented himself as the Dr. Bowles?"

"Oh come now," he said, also in French. "Be reasonable. I am certain that he did not represent himself as myself. Why would he have done such a thing?"

"I know nothing of that. That is what I am asking. Why? What for? Why speak in French? To what end can that serve?"

They advanced on me again and Dr. Bowles took my arm. "We are already late," he said. "Dr. Palmer will see you this afternoon and if you have questions, ask them of him. For now, let us pass."

"Not until I know why Mr. Neider misrepresented himself, please."

"Shhhhh. Not so fast. I will talk that over with Mr. Neider. There must be a mistake."

"And how, I would like to know what it is."

The group swept by me and out of the door. That was certainly puzzling. Why talk in French? I could tell from his accent that he was not French. Did he want to hide something from someone else? From the rest of the men, from the attendants? Well, we would see this afternoon. I wondered if I would actually see Dr. Palmer, and what these other individuals and tests were going to be. A lot was going to happen in the après-midi. Nous verrons bien.

"Boy you can sure rattle off that lingo, can't you?" It was Monty again.

"I used to live in France," I said.

"You did fine. Dr. Bowles was pleased with you. I could tell. Whenever you see him, just stand right up and talk to him."

"Will I see him again? When does he come around here, anyway?"

"Once or twice a week. You'll see him all right. Come on, I'll take you down to get your hands bandaged."

After lunch, I sat on the porch in the sunlight, wondering if they would call me and what the tests were going to be. Or did *examens* mean examinations? Would the doctor see me, really? There was nothing to do but wait. In a corner of the porch, the man Tom was exercising again. Arms up, forward, to the sides, down. One two three four. His voice whispered the commands. Someone came to stand beside me and put his hand on the back of my chair. I looked at him and he looked at me questioningly. I had seen him before, but I had never talked to him. He squatted on the floor and stared up at me. "You talked to them," he said. Did he mean the doctor? He went on: "They don't talk to anyone else, but they talked to you."

I didn't know if he thought that was wrong, or even what he thought. I looked at his face. Pale, like all of us, thin bloodless lips, sharp bones (were we all so thin?) black hair curling hard in place on his head.

He shook his head. "It won't do any good to talk to them. I talked to them at first, but nothing ever happened. You'll see. They're like everybody else, they pretend they're going to help you, but they don't." The look in his face became crafty. "They spoke to me this morning, 'Good morning, Joseph' they said, and then they walked away. They don't give you time to say anything. They have to keep you here." He made a wide circle with his arm. "They'll keep us all here, to keep their jobs. If they let us go, there wouldn't be anything for them to do. That's why they keep us here. That's why we'll never get out."

Did he know what he was talking about? "How long have you been here?" I asked him.

"How should I know? They don't let anybody have a calendar. They don't tell you the date. I asked them once, and they said I had to remember myself. How can you remember how long if you don't know when it is now?"

He was beginning to frighten me. How long had I been here? When had I come? Was it a Sunday? Yes. I was born on a Sunday. But what date had it been? What was the date now? Was there a calendar in the office? But even if there was, even if I could see it, how would I know how long it had been if I didn't know the date I came? It was May, wasn't it? There had been apple blossoms. A Sunday in May. What was it now? May, June? Maybe I could tell by the sun.

"Look out for him, he's a bastard." It was Joseph's voice, but when I turned he had slipped away from me. He was standing with his back to me, looking out through the wire screening. Who did he mean? There was an attendant standing in the doorway. Is that who he meant? I looked at his face but he didn't notice me. He was looking at the boy, Tom, still counting and thrusting his arms up and out, and as he watched he played with the keys hanging from his belt, twirling them around his finger in a wide circle and then around again in the opposite direction. I could not see his face very well, except that it was contorted into what seemed to be a sneer.

He moved towards Tom, still spinning the keys. "Hey Jo-Jo, whatcha doing?" Under the tone of his voice was a suggestion of contained laughter. Tom glared at him. "Keeping up my strength," he said. "One two three four."

The man leaned over to him and felt his muscle, stopping his arm. "Pretty strong, aren't you? Go on."

Tom stopped moving his arms and stared at the attendant.

"Why don't you leave me alone?"

The laughter was closer to his words when the attendant spoke again: "I'm not bothering you. Go ahead. One two three four."

Tom stood motionless. "A man'll rot here," he said. "No exercise."

"I told you to go ahead." There was no laughter in the voice now.

The other patients on the porch had turned to watch them, and the attendant looked around at them and then back to Tom. "Go on," he said. "Look, they're all waiting for you. Come on, one two three four."

Tom didn't move and the man took his arm again. "What's the matter?"

Tom broke angrily away from him. "Why don't you leave me alone? What did I do to you? Go away." He was a big man and his voice had lowered in anger. The attendant moved back from him and watched him silently, the keys still twirling. "Nobody wants to bother you, Tommy," he said. "We just want to watch you exercise." His voice was oily, and the laughter seemed to crawl through the words without ever breaking into sound.

"Leave me alone, you bastard. What do you want to pick on me for?" Tom raised his arms, flexing his muscles.

The attendant gestured at him. "Watch your language, son. Nobody's bothering you. Just go ahead and exercise. Don't pay any attention to us."

"Son-of-a-bitch! If there weren't so many of you, I'd break your neck!" Tom advanced slowly towards the attendant, who backed away from him towards my chair. Why hadn't he left him alone in the first place? What had he done? Why didn't he leave him alone now? Was this a test of some kind? Were they going to do something like this to me, too?

The attendant's voice was raised. "Easy there, big boy. Watch your language. You know what you'll get if you're not careful." Tom stopped, his hands on his hips, glowering down into the attendant's face. "Son-of-a-bitch. Son-of-a-bitch!" he repeated.

Another attendant appeared in the doorway. "What's up, Jerry? Everything okay?"

Joseph had been right. Whoever this Jerry was, he *was* a bastard. I must remember his name. I would have to watch out for him. I heard his voice again:

"Big boy's getting a little tough here. Looks kinda excited!"

Tom's voice rose, and he laughed. "Excited! You son-of-a-bitch! What was I doing? Nothing! You had to come along. I could break your neck. I'd like to break your goddam neck, you bastard!" He moved towards him again.

Jerry flashed a look at the other attendant and the entire porch was suddenly filled with movement. As if by some telepathic signal four attendants appeared, one of them pushed me out of the chair, and the four of them forced Tom into it, holding him there, wrestling with him. When they stood up away from him, he was sitting, red-faced and furious, mumbling to himself. His hands were in the same kind of cuffs I had been in before. But he hadn't done anything!

Again without warning, as if by some telepathic prearrangement, a doctor appeared (one I had not seen before) with a syringe. While the other attendants held Tom, the doctor worked the needle up and down and then stabbed it into his arm. I watched, horrified and fascinated, as the needle plowed through the flesh of his upper arm. I could hear it cutting into him.

All of the patients on the porch were watching this in complete silence, and their cumulative anger began to surround me. I could feel it hammering through the air on the porch, a mass of concentrated hatred directed towards the attendants. And I could feel it in myself, the slow uncontrollable rising of anger inside me.

Was it because he had felt it, too? Whatever the reason, Jerry was now looking at me. I knew that the anger in my face must be visible to him, and I tried to erase it, although I could not bring myself to smile into this twisted cruel face. "That's what happens when you get in trouble around here," he said.

Was he talking to me? He wasn't looking at anyone else.

"But he didn't do anything!" I exclaimed, in spite of myself. One of the attendants, still standing by the chair, was Monty. He gave me a warning look, but it was too late. Jerry's face was closer to mine now, and when he spoke I could feel the warm unpleasant breath from his mouth. "You want cuffs, too?" he said. My own feelings were confused and outraged. I shook my head and pressed myself back against the wall, and at the same time, uncontrollably, I lashed out at him: "You sadistic bastard," I said, "what the hell have I done?"

A smile now spread over his face and he leaned even closer to me. "Plenty," he said. "Plenty. It would be a pleasure to take care of you right."

The fear of him had drained out of me, replaced by a burning, corrosive hatred of this face. "You dirty, lousy prick," I said venomously. "Go ahead and try it. He only *wanted* to kill you...I will!"

"Oh yeah?" He grabbed my arms with his two hands.

Before I could think of an answer, I heard a sudden fierce cry. "Leave him alone!"

Once again the porch was flooded with movement, too fast for me to follow. Like an arrow sprung from a bow, one of the men in blue collided against Jerry, and they both crashed to the floor. I watched them on the floor at my feet. The man in blue was on top of Jerry now, hammering at his face.

It was all over in a moment. The other attendants seized the man in blue, pulling him off, grappling with him. More cuffs. I looked first at the white-clad body lying on the stone floor and then at the boy in blue, held by four attendants, his hands writhing in the leather cuffs. Someone said: "Take him back to pack," and two of the attendants walked him off the porch and into the big room. The other two bent over Jerry and picked him up. His eyelids batted slowly and he looked at me, a look filled with hatred and cruelty. He rubbed his chin and cheek with one hand and they led him inside, too.

I waited, standing against the wall, wondering what would happen to me now. It had been my fault. The boy who had leaped on him was defending me. Why? I didn't even know who he was, did I?

Monty came back onto the porch and looked at me warningly. "Don't get into trouble with him," he whispered. "He's a mean guy."

"Who?"

"That attendant, Jerry."

"But who was the other man? What happened anyway? Are they really taking him back to pack?"

He nodded. "He was due for it, anyway. He only came up today. His name's Andy Collins."

Andy Collins. *Andy.* I broke away from the porch and ran into the big room. They were on either side of the door...Jerry in one chair, and Andy, restrained and attended in the other. I looked at his face and then I remembered him. He was the colored boy that had been next to me in the pack room. The hell with the attendants. I went over to him. "I'm sorry," I said. "You shouldn't have done it. You shouldn't!"

He glared at me: "Shut up!"

I backed away from him. Maybe he was right to be angry. Maybe I would only get him into more trouble. Indirectly or directly I seemed to have a genius for getting myself and everyone else into trouble. I walked away from him and back onto the porch. At the entrance, I met Monty again and he motioned me inside with him. When we were back in the big room he walked me to the far end.

"You've gotta calm down," he whispered to me. "Jerry's in charge of this room."

"Why don't you tell the doctor about him, if you think he's a bastard, what difference does it make whether he's in charge or what he is?"

"Shhhhh. Not so loud. I told you he's the charge attendant. I'm only new here."

"You mean he's in charge of you, too?"

He nodded. "Sure he is. He's been in this racket a long time. He used to be over at Holt."

"Holt? What's that?"

"The state institution."

I was frightened. Monty was one of the few friendly attendants on our ward and now I had learned that he himself was afraid of that man. The charge attendant. Was he the one who observed us? Was it up to him if I saw the doctor? Was that what Joseph meant? Was it people like Jerry who would keep us here forever?

"Monty, tell me something."

"What?"

"What's the date?"

"May 26th."

Could I ask him any more? How far could he be trusted? "How..."

I began and then stopped.

"What is it?" he asked.

"How long have I been here?"

"Don't you remember?"

"I know I came on a Sunday."

He shook his head. "No. You came here on Friday. Four days ago."

"No, before that. I was here once before. It was Sunday evening, before I was in the pack room."

He shrugged his shoulders. "I never saw you before last Friday. Sunday's my day off. How long were you in pack?"

"I don't know. I can't remember."

The door opened next to us. "Mitchell?" The man looked around the room, and I stepped forward. "David Mitchell?" he asked and I nodded. He handed a slip to Monty and then said to me: "Come with me." He was wearing a bow tie, like the man who had brought me here from pack. Was I going back there too, then? Had I made so much trouble with Jerry that I was going to be sent back there? The other men didn't wear bow ties. Was this the same man? I didn't know. I looked at Monty.

"Go ahead," he said. "Don't keep the man waiting."

"Where am I going?"

Monty looked at the slip in his hand. "Over to the main building. Electrocardiograph. Go on."

I followed the man out and the door closed behind us. So Mr. Neider was having his way after all! But wouldn't Monty have warned me if it was something I shouldn't do? But how could you tell about any of them? How could you know? Didn't they all work here together? After all, Monty worked for that man Jerry and for Mr. Neider. Why would he be a friend of mine? Why would he help me out, if it might get him in trouble? Of course, he had warned me against Jerry.

"Come on!" said the man in the bow tie.

I hurried after him. "Okay. Okay!"

It was all right after all. The man took me over to the main building in a bus, and waited while they made X-rays (no one had said anything to me about that) and then led me through more corridors in the main building to the Electrocardiograph room. I was nervous and hot, wondering what was going to happen, and it seemed stifling in the room. Another man made some marks on my chest with a red pencil and then attached some wires to my arms and legs. As he sat in front of me he fanned himself with his hand and great drops of perspiration rolled off his face. Something like a mechanical pen was writing vigorously on a machine attached to the wires, scratching back and forth rapidly from one side to the other of a moving strip of paper. The man shook his head. "Too hot," he said, and undid the wires.

And that was all. The man in the bow tie had watched all this and now he led me back through the corridors and outside to the bus and we drove back to the other building.

As soon as we were back on the ward, Monty came up to me. "Where have you been?"

He knew where I had been. He had told me himself. What did he think, that I'd run away? How could I? I didn't even have a key! Had he lost his memory? "You know where I've been," I said. "Electrocardiograph." Then I added: "And X-rays, too."

"Oh that's right. Well the claims man wants to see you. Come on."

He led me to the shower room. It was dark and I could not see very well, but I could make out a man sitting on the bench. He got up when I came in and extended his hand. "Mr. Mitchell?" he asked me.

"Yes." I shook his hand.

"I'm Mr. Lucas of the claims office," he said. "I just want to get some information from you."

"What about?"

He had a pencil and some papers in one hand and a briefcase under his arm. He sat down again and said: "Let's sit down, shall we?"

I sat on the far end of the bench, away from him, and waited.

"Now let's see," he said, looking at the paper. "Your mother has applied for compensation for you, and we need some information from you. By the way, how do you feel?"

"I feel fine. My mother has applied for what?"

"Compensation."

"I don't understand what you mean." I said. "Compensation for what?"

He smiled. "You know about the G.I. Bill of Rights, don't you?"

"Yes."

"Well, as a veteran, you are eligible to apply for disability compensation, or a member of your family can apply for it for you."

I looked at him questioning: "What do you mean disability compensation? What's wrong with me?"

He hesitated. "Well, of course, the doctors are the final judges of that. After all, you've been under treatment here at the hospital. If the staff decides that you have a disability that is service-connected, then you will get compensation. Or it may be that even if the disability is not service-connected, you will get a limited amount of compensation."

"You mean I'm in the hospital because of something that happened to me in the Army?"

"Perhaps."

"I wasn't wounded."

"No, I know that. Actually I only need a little information from you. The application has already been filled out by your mother."

I stared at him, there was something about this I could not understand. Perhaps I had tuberculosis—they had taken X-rays and my chest had always been bad, doctors had always suspected me of having T.B.—and maybe they weren't telling me about it. "There's nothing to worry about," he said kindly, laying his hand on my arm. "It's just a routine formality, that's all. If you had not been well enough to answer these questions, we would have put through the application anyway.

Since you are, we wanted to check with you first."

"What happens when you put the application through?"

"It is sent to the Veterans Administration and they decide, on the basis of the claim and the medical findings, whether or not you are eligible for compensation. It's very simple. Now, do you remember the dates of your Army service? What we have here..."

He also asked my mother's name, my father's name, my occupation, what illnesses and operations I had had, did I have any scars, and several other questions, all of which I answered.

"Well," he said finally, "that seems to be complete. That's fine. Now all you have to do is sign here." He held the paper out to me and then handed me a pen.

"But why do I have to sign it?"

He hesitated again. "Well, whenever possible, the application is to be made by the veteran himself. Only in cases where the veteran is unable to make the application, can it be made by his family."

I shook my head. "I'm sorry, I don't understand this very well. What am I applying for? I thought my mother was applying for it, not me. What do I get if I sign this? What happens?"

"If the application is approved," he said patiently, "you will receive compensation from the government."

"Yes, but what for?"

"For your disability."

"But what is my disability?"

He looked away from me and then at the paper. "Nervous condition," he said.

"What do they pay for that?"

He shrugged his shoulders. "It depends on the extent of the disability."

"Look," I said, "let's get this straight. I have a nervous condition as a result of the war..." he held up his hand and I shook my head. "Well," I continued, "I have a nervous condition *maybe* as a result of the war, or something. You send this application to the Veterans Administration, and then the doctor sends a report, too. If they decide there is something wrong with me, then I get paid for it by the government, is that right?"

He nodded. "That's about it. You have the idea. And there is nothing unusual about it, I assure you. Several of the patients here are collecting compensation from the government now."

I pricked up my ears. What was the catch in that? I had a suspicion that there was something wrong, but I did not know what it was. I had only had a warning signal inside, like a breath of cold wind.

"You mean the people who are in here, the patients *here* are collecting compensation?"

"That's right. Some of them are."

"Because they're in here?"

"Well, because they're ill...disabled."

"Isn't that the same thing? If they weren't ill, they wouldn't be here, would they?"

"Well...no."

Then I knew what it was. "What happens when they get out?"

"That depends," he said. "Some of them collect it only while they are in the hospital...for limited disability during the period of their hospitalization."

"What can they do with the money while they're in here?"

"Nothing. It's kept for them until they do get out, or in some cases it is paid to their families. It depends entirely on the individual case."

"Do I have to sign it?"

He hesitated again. "No, you don't *have* to, if you don't want to. But there is no reason why you shouldn't. The compensation, if you receive any, is something you are entitled to as a veteran because of your illness. It will be up to the Veterans Administration and the doctors anyway. It can't do you any harm to sign it."

I shook my head again. "But what will you do with that paper if I don't sign it?"

"Well, in this case, I'm not sure. It depends on several things. We might hold it up until later, until you've had time to think it over. It might go through anyway. I don't know. It would not be up to me."

"Do you think I should sign it?"

"I can't really advise you one way or the other. I only know that it won't hurt anything; it won't affect your case if you do sign it. I mean, it won't affect your health or your treatment. Do you understand that all right?"

I nodded. "All right." I took the pen and then hesitated again. "Have you talked to my mother?"

"No," he said, "but Mr. Beckwith has talked to her."

"Who's he?"

"He's in charge of the claims section here."

"Oh."

I signed the paper and handed it back to him.

When I got back to the ward, one of the patients came up to me. I had seen him before, but I had never spoken to him. "You been talking to Lucas?" he asked.

"Yes, why?"

"Getting out?"

"Getting out?" I shook my head. "All he did was talk to me about a claim. He didn't say anything about getting out."

"I'm getting out," he said.

"You are?"

He nodded. "Sure. I've been in here long enough. All you have to do is say 'no' to everything they ask you. You'll get out soon enough."

What had I done? What did he mean? "What do you mean, say 'no' to everything?"

"If you're a claim case, it takes a lot longer," he said. "The doctors have to submit a report. It makes a lot of difference. If you're not a claim case, boom, you're out as soon as the doctor thinks you're okay. No red tape. No complications."

"I signed it," I said. "My mother had already applied for it. That's what the man told me."

He winked at me. "It's no good without your signature, unless you can't sign it. I didn't sign mine. They aren't going to keep me in here. I've had enough of this place."

I walked away from him. What had I done now? Would they be able to keep me in here now? Was it a trick? Had I really signed myself in?

"Mitchell!"

It was Jerry, the charge attendant. "What is it?"

"Come on."

Where was I going now? What had happened today? Had it been only this morning that I had seen Dr. Bowles? Was this day never going to end?

Down the hall. Bandages? That was probably it. But no. He led me to the door of the room opposite the office and knocked on it. Someone said "come in," and we entered. Wasn't this Dr. Palmer's office? Who was this man?

"David Mitchell?" he asked me.

"Yes."

"Sit down." He indicated a chair across the desk from him and I sat down.

"I'm Mr. Newton," he said. How many people had I met today anyway? Lucas, Dr. Bowles, now Newton. What did he want?

"Have a cigarette?"

"Oh." I looked around the room. "May I?"

"Certainly. Go ahead." He laid the pack on the table together with a book of matches. I took a cigarette and lighted it.

"I'll leave them right there," he said. "We may need them."

We may need them? What for? Was this going to take a long time? What did he want? Who was he? He was reading from a file folder. Finally he looked up at me. Was I wrong or was he embarrassed? What *was* going on?

"Now, David," he said. "I want to ask you a few questions."

I became suddenly and uncontrollably angry.

"Everybody wants to ask me questions but nobody ever tells me anything. There are some questions I'd like to ask you or somebody around here. What's going on around this place?"

"Now, now," he said. "Don't get excited. If you have any questions, I'll try to answer them for you. What's the trouble?"

"Well for one thing, who are you?"

"I told you, I'm Mr. Newton."

I laughed. "What does that mean to me? I'm Mr. Jones, Mr. Smith, Mr. Beckwith, Mr. Neider, Mr. Lucas, Mr. Mitchell. Does that mean I know who you are? What do you do? What do you want? Who's in charge of this place? What is going to happen to me and the rest of the people like me? What's wrong with me? What am I doing here?"

He laughed apologetically. "Not so fast, please. I guess I should have explained a little more fully. My name is Newton, and I'm in Vocational Rehabilitation…"

"What's that?"

"Well…" he hesitated. Didn't he know what it was? "My job is to find out what the patients like to do, what they'd like to learn, what kind of interests they have, what kind of work they can do, so that we can give them an occupation while they're here. Instead of sitting on the ward all the time, they can study or work…occupy their time. It's a therapeutic measure."

"You want to give me a job? How long do you think I'm going to be here?"

"Well, that depends on the doctor, of course. But while you are here…"

"Depends on the doctor!" I stormed at him. "Who ever sees the doctor! I saw Dr. Palmer once in the pack room, and then Dr. Bowles came into the ward surrounded by a bunch of people and raced through it as if he was going to a fire. The only way he can ever see you is if you stop him and make him talk to you. And then he talked to me in French."

"I didn't know you talked French," he said.

I nodded, and then exclaimed: "Don't get off the subject. What's that got to do with anything? What difference does it make? If I could talk Chinese, what would that mean? What I want to know is how the doctor can give a report to anybody, or make up his mind about anything when he hardly sees anyone, and then when he does, he acts as if he was being held up and keeps trying to get away from you. Isn't he supposed to see the patients? Did you ever try to see a doctor around this place? Well, did you?"

I was leaning over the table, glaring furiously at him.

He smiled uncomfortably. "Have another cigarette," he said.

"No. I want an answer."

He sighed. "Look, David. I realize that things are a little difficult once in a while. We do the best we can, but there are a great many patients here and it is almost impossible for us to give them individual attention. I'm sure that if you ask to see Dr. Bowles, he will see you and answer your questions."

"You're sure?"

He nodded. "Yes, I am. I know Dr. Bowles is a fine man…"

"I don't care what kind of a man he is. If you're so sure he can see me, get him now. I'll be glad to see him."

He shook his head. "He isn't here now."

I laughed. "You see what I mean? He's *never* here!"

"Well, David, as I said, we do the best we can, and I'm sure that Dr. Bowles will see you when he has time. You must try to realize that this is a very large place and…"

"Look, Mr. Newton, what do I care about your troubles? I have enough troubles of my own. You want me to try and realize how hard everything is for you! I'm supposed to be the patient here, aren't I? Well, all I want to find out is what is wrong with me and what's going to be done about it. Somebody here must know!"

"Well, of course, David. Of course, they do."

"Sure. Sure. Oh, the hell with it. What do you want to know?"

He looked at the paper again. "Now, let's see. You came here on Sunday, May 11th, didn't you?"

Did I? I counted rapidly, was it May 11th? Was there a calendar around here someplace? I found a calendar on the wall, and counted back. Probably it was May 11th. Well, I had found out one thing! Still it was a chance. He might be fooling me. "Yes," I said.

"Good. And you were in the pack room until last Friday, right?"

I looked at the calendar again. It had been Friday, Monty had said so. That would make it the twenty-third and this would be the twenty-sixth.

"Yes," I said. "That's right."

"How do you feel?"

"I feel fine. Just fine. I want to get out of here."

He wiped his brow. It was beginning to get hot. "That's what we all want," he said.

I looked at him in surprise. "Are you kidding?"

"Of course not, David. We would like to see all the patients get well and go home. That's our job."

Well, well, well! That was the first time I'd heard that.

"I'll be glad to help you by going right now," I said.

He smiled. "That depends on the doctor, not on me, but I'd say you were coming along pretty well."

"You would?"

He nodded again. "Yes, I would, David." He meant it.

"And just how would you know? Have you seen me before?"

"No, but..."

"No buts about it. How do you know I was ever any different?"

He paused and looked at the paper. "Well, while you were in the pack room..."

"I didn't ask to go to the pack room. I know about that, even if I don't remember it all. How would you act if somebody wrapped you up in a lot of cold, wet sheets? What would you do, say 'thank you'?"

He shook his head wearily. "Perhaps we'd better wait until another day. There are some questions I have to ask you, but maybe you don't feel like answering them just now." He seemed tired and unhappy.

"This is as good a time as any. May I have another cigarette?"

"By all means," he said. "Here's a light."

I inhaled deeply and blew the smoke out. "Okay, shoot. What do you want to know?"

"How much do you remember about coming here?"

"All of it."

"Are you sure?"

I nodded. "Yep."

He kept looking at the paper. "Suppose you tell me about it."

"What's that paper?"

"Your file. Why?"

"Does it say there how and why I'm here?"

"Yes, it does."

"Good. Then you tell me what it says and I'll tell you if it's right."

He hesitated and lifted his shoulders. He looked embarrassed. "According to this report you took all your clothes off, you..."

I glared at him. "That's right. I took all my clothes off on the lawn in front of the house."

"Do you know why you did it?"

I hesitated. I knew why, I could remember what I had thought and felt at the time, but it did not seem quite so convincing now. "Yes." I said it slowly. "It seemed to me that there was a lot of unnecessary shame in the world, and that it was all caused by wearing clothes."

"Hmmmmm." He did not say anything and looked at the paper again. Why was he so embarrassed? '

"There's something else here I'd like to ask you about."

"Well, what is it?"

He took a deep drag on the cigarette and looked away from me.

"While you were in the pack room, I believe you had some difficulty with one of the attendants."

Oh so that was it. "Are you talking about Arnold?"

He looked back at the paper. "Why, yes. That was his name."

"Well, what about it? I've had difficulty with everybody. Not only with him."

"Well, uh..." He looked at me and then looked away again. Looking out of the window, he continued. "Have you ever had any homosexual experience, what I mean is..."

"I know what you mean. Yes."

"Do you..." he hesitated again. "Would you say that you are a homosexual?"

"No. I wouldn't."

"But you have had..."

I interrupted him. "Did you ever take a drink?"

"Yes, I..."

"Does that make you an alcoholic?"

"No."

"All right."

He looked at the file again. "Well, let's put it this way, then. Do you know what led up to it?"

"Yes, I do."

He looked away from me. "Would you mind talking to me about it? You've been very co-operative up to now, I..."

My voice was cold. "I don't mind. What do you want to know?"

"Well, I'd like to know why...since you admit, uh...why you say you are not homosexual."

"Look, Mr. Newton. Don't be so embarrassed. Tell me what a homosexual is first. What is the difference between a homosexual and someone who isn't homosexual?"

He continued to be embarrassed. "Well, perhaps we could say that a homosexual is a person who prefers to have sexual relations with his own sex...with other men."

"All right then, I'm not one."

"But you have had..."

"Yes, I've had an experience. I slept with another man."

"Well do you know why?"

I shrugged my shoulders. "I was in love with him, that's all."

"What happened?"

"I don't know. It just wasn't any good. It's very simple really, even if it's hard to explain. I didn't even want to go to bed with him at first, and then when I did, I simply thought what the hell, maybe that's the way I am. So what? So I went to bed with him. It was all right for a while, but it didn't last. It wasn't any good. I don't know *why*...it just wasn't. It wasn't right, somehow. So that was the end of it."

"And was that the only time?"

"Yes."

"When was that?"

"About ten years ago, I guess." I counted on my fingers. "Yes, ten years ago."

"And you've never had any similar experience since then?"

"No."

He looked at the file again. "It says here that while you were in the Army, there was a general..."

"Oh, *that!* You don't have to worry about *that!* There was a general who...it wasn't an experience. Nothing happened. He tried to get funny, that's all."

"You're sure nothing happened?"

"That depends on what you mean. Quite a lot happened, but not what you're thinking. I was locked up for a few days and the doctor wouldn't send me to a hospital because he was afraid I'd tell somebody about it and mention the general's name if I got a chance."

"He locked you up for that?"

I nodded. "Why? What's all this got to do with rehabilitation, or whatever you called it?"

"Well," he said, hesitating again. "There was a report in your file about that experience in the Army and then the other one you mentioned and then there was that...that business in the pack room."

"What exactly are you trying to find out? Are you trying to find out one way or the other if I am a homosexual?"

"Yes."

"Well, I told you. The answer is no."

He hesitated again. "Well..."

"Look," I said, "maybe I'm supposed to be nuts, but all you've got is a lot of information that doesn't prove anything. I know this much, that I know what has happened to me and that you don't. I told you honestly about one experience that I don't quite understand myself. I've asked myself all these questions. It is true that at that time, in the beginning, I was willing to be a fairy, or whatever you want to call it, if that's the way it was. But it wasn't any good...it didn't turn out to be that way. Maybe you think I'm lying, I don't know, I can't even find out. But as for the rest of this business, it's just Arnold's word against mine, and whatever you have in that file about the Army. I was there both times. I know what happened. I knew that son-of-a-bitch Matthews was a liar."

He motioned to me with his hand. "Now, David. Dr. Matthews hasn't accused you of anything. The incident was reported, and, naturally, we want to investigate it, to find out what the truth really is. It is not an accusation against you. We..."

"No, wait. It is an accusation against me. You believe me, so that's why you're asking me these questions, isn't it? Look, Mr. Newton, I don't give a damn what you think. But I do know that if there was no accusation against me, none of this would be necessary. And, as I said, I *know*. But who is asking Arnold questions? And if anyone is, what good will it do when both of us deny it? At some point, somebody is going to have to make up his mind about us...about which one is telling the truth and which one is not. Anybody with brains and guts would know by looking at Arnold, just by looking at him. He's cruel...but he's sane, he works here, he's okay. Why? Who says so? What do you know about him? What does anybody know about him? What does anyone know except what they hear? What do you want, witnesses? How are you going to know anything when you get finished with me? Who is lying? Me or Arnold? Who was lying before? Me or the general? Who gave you the information about the general anyway?"

"As a matter of fact, David, it was your mother."

"And what did she say about it?"

"Well," more hesitation, "she mentioned your early experience and then that...as a possible cause of your illness."

I was furious, and at the same time had a sudden curious flash of memory about my mother. During all the time I had been in the hospital, I had hardly thought of her at all, except to wonder what she was going to do about getting me out, and what she had done to get me in.

"Oh she did, did she? So where are we now? Did she also mention that the general was sent back to the states because he was psychoneurotic, or did she forget that?" I leaned back in my chair and smiled bitterly. "Did she by any chance tell you that she'd spent quite a good deal of time in the nut house herself?"

"Well," he said, "I didn't talk to your mother myself...I..."

"Oh nuts!" I said. "This isn't getting anyone anywhere. I've told you what I've told you and now you can go and report it to whoever the hell you have to report it to, and they'll believe what they goddam well want to believe anyway, so where does that leave me?"

He smiled. "That isn't quite right, David. As a matter of fact, you've cleared a lot of things up yourself. Right here and now."

"I have?"

"Yes, I think so, and I'm going to say I think so. If it is possible to tell an honest person by looking at them and listening to them, then I'd say you were honest. I think you're honest with yourself, which is a lot more important. You are right when you say we can't prove anything, there is no evidence. But I believe you and whatever comes up, I'm on your side. It was only natural, after reading this report and then after that incident in the pack room that the doctors wondered...but, unfortunately for men like you—and this is between you and me—I know that some of the attendants in these hospitals are...are..."

I didn't let him finish. "Well, I have nothing to hide," I said. "I've thought about all this. I've admitted to myself that I was attracted by a man once, and I've been afraid of it, I've worried about it, I've lived with it. But what does it make me? Abnormal? Is that why I'm locked up here? Is it especially unusual? Do you have any record on Arnold for instance? Do you have any record on me that makes you think that I'd force somebody to..."

He interrupted me quickly. "No, no, there's nothing like that. Nothing at all."

"Is Arnold still working here?"

"I don't really know, I..."

"Balls, you don't know! And you wouldn't tell me anyway. I'm only a goddam patient. I'm a patient and that lousy—is an attendant. Oh don't look so goddammed shocked...the lousy stinking bastard. Do you know what I thought? That if I didn't do what Arnold told me to do, that I'd never get out of the pack room. How many other patients does that happen to, and what can they do about it? Not a goddam thing except wait until by some miracle they get out of here, hoping that nobody knows anything about it. And are they right? I'll say they are. You'd know if Arnold wasn't working here, if you know this much about it. And is he? Of course, he is. You want me to prove what I did, or didn't do. But have you asked him? And while we're on this, how about the other things that go on around this dump? How about the people that get knocked out? Is that part of the treatment? Sure, beat up the patients, it's good for them! What's in the record about whoever knocked me out the first night I was here? What's in the record about Arnold knocking me down, or is there anything there? No, of course not. We're nuts, so nothing we say can be believed, can it? But Arnold and the rest of the attendants are all sane. They make the reports to the doctors about us. The hell with what we say. No, don't interrupt me. You might as well get it all. What about Jerry, the charge attendant on our ward? What about Mr. Neider? Did you ever take a good look at those faces? Now *there* are a couple of boys for you! One of them teases a patient into getting violent and then has him cuffed and gives him a shot. And Mr. Neider! Why does he pass himself off as a doctor?

"Look, Mr. Newton, don't expect me to believe too much. I'm a dope, or I wouldn't be here, but not that much of a dope. Sure, you're anxious to do everything you can for us, how could I possibly doubt it? Everything that happens here...everything that has happened to me has been for my own welfare, hasn't it? Sure. For all I know you're just one more Arnold or Mr. Neider. Vocational Rehabilitation, shit! Have you decided what work you're going to have me do now? What shall I study? Applied psychology from Mr. Neider, or maybe from Arnold? Could I learn how to mistreat the doctors, perhaps?"

I had grown angrier all the time, and the words had come across the table in a torrent.

"Now, now, David!" he said, trying to calm me down. "I do believe you, I do. I mean it."

"Now, now, my ass! I've heard enough bull shit around here. I'm supposed to shut up, I'm supposed to 'take it easy,' I'm supposed not to raise my voice, or get angry. And I'd like to know why the hell I should! How much crap am I supposed to take? You believe me! So where does that leave me? Right back where I was, brother, and I know it."

"No, dammit!" He stood up suddenly. "I think things are going to be a lot better for you from now on."

"I'll believe it when I see it."

He smiled at me. "Here, have another cigarette." He sat down again.

I took a cigarette from the package and he lighted it for me.

"Just one more thing," he said. "You really will be better off if you're not on the ward all the time. What kind of work would you like to do?"

I shrugged my shoulders. "I don't care."

"It says here," he tapped the file, "that you're a typist."

"Yes, I am."

"Well, I could give you a job in the typing section. You could practice typing if you wanted, or if you're good, we could give you some work to do there. I think you might like it. Mr. Sweetwater is in charge of the section and I know you'd like him."

That sounded reasonable enough. Now that my anger was cooling off, I had to admit that I liked this man and believed him.

"What can I lose?"

"Good," he said. "Shall we say Mondays, Wednesdays and Fridays... in the afternoons?" He looked at the calendar and hesitated. "Perhaps Mondays, Tuesdays and Fridays would be better. Wednesday is a visiting day."

"It is?" That was the first I had heard of that.

"Yes. Do you think you'll be having any visitors? Your family live near here?"

Did they? Where was here? We had driven here, I remembered. Maybe it wasn't so far. "Yes." Maybe I would have a visitor.

"We'd better not make it Wednesdays then. You can start on Friday of this week. I'll see that someone calls for you."

"Okay." I looked at him questioningly. "Is that all?"

"Yes, David, and thank you very much."

He really did seem to be a nice kind of a guy. "I'm sorry I got so mad," I said.

He smiled. "I think you had good reason to. Wait here a minute and I'll get someone to take you back to the ward." He put his hand on my shoulder. "You can have the rest of these cigarettes, if you like."

"Well! Thank you very much."

SEVEN

Friday, Saturday, Sunday, Monday, Tuesday, Wednesday... was it Sunday night that I had not slept? So much seemed to have happened in those few days, and yet with all of it, I was conscious mostly of the sense of waiting. As I lay in bed Tuesday night, the pack room was miles and years away from me, lying like a great hole in my mind, a timeless, sequenceless pit. And around it were the other memories: Dr. Bowles, X-ray, Electrocardiograph, Mr. Lucas, Mr. Newton, Jerry. Could all these things have happened in only a few days, or had I really been there for weeks and weeks?

For however long I had been there, I was exhausted. Not tired, but weighted down and weak. The only thing to do was to sleep and sleep. Whatever was to be figured out, whatever reality all these events would come to mean eventually, I could not fathom it now. But even as my eyes closed, the lids falling over them, the questions and anxieties beat their way around my head. What about the claims man? What would happen to me as a result of signing that paper? Why had my mother applied for compensation? The very fact that she had applied for it must mean that I was really sick. Had she been there to see me to know for herself? Was that why she had applied for compensation? The questions seemed to take a physical shape, spinning around in my brain...but the whirlpool in which they were contained was a separate and special compartment, not my mind...not the mind or heart which had been mine before I had ever come here. Now I had a second self, intruding upon whatever it was that had been me, contained in the terrible, chilling shadow of this illness—for it was that which ate into everything, corroding and rotting. Whatever you knew, whatever you felt, whatever you were...once you were here...was suspect, unreliable. Not to them, the doctors, attendants, nurses...but to me. It would never be the same again...never like the time before that passage through wherever it had been. At the bottom of this pit there was no sudden strong hard rock of confidence, no place where I said finally... this is me. This is what I am, what I believe, what I know. Instead there was only endlessness, deeper and deeper.

I insisted upon some base of reality, and curiously enough there was a projection, a shape which I could fasten upon. I had been frightened of it at first, and now I could hold to it and look at it, even finding some comfort in the fact that there was one thing I knew...the fact of my own fallibility. I knew that I knew nothing, and knowing nothing is part of the cement in the foundation.

I felt myself sinking into sleep as into a whirlpool of oblivion; sucked down and down by the force of my exhaustion. Still the frantic, endless questions would not stop: how would I ever get out of this place, and deeper than that, *would I?* The interminable questions I had been asked and the evasive answers. What was being done here? Did they try to knock you out with a round of incomprehensible activity? Better sleep. I hadn't slept one night already, and that was bad. I let go, and the whirlpool started spinning faster and faster, until I was sucked into the center of it, whirling with it, in the midst of papers and faces, bandages, bow ties, blue clothes, white clothes, sheets, needles, fists. Someone was talking in French. *Il faut parler en français. Pourquoi?* Are you getting out? Come on! Leering faces, grasping hands. This is what will happen to you. Bzzt. Bzzt. Was that the X-ray machine? One two three four. Leave me alone! Just say no to everything. Just a few questions. What *am* I doing here? That depends on the doctor. It depends on you.

Where is the doctor? He's not here. Don't sign that paper. Sign that paper. Don't sign that paper. Take off your shirt. Put on your shirt. Do you have any scars? What are those? How did they happen? What is your mother's name? Where do you live? Why am I here? Ask Dr. Bowles. But where is Dr. Bowles? I'm Dr. Bowles. No, I'm Dr. Bowles. He's Dr. Bowles. We are all Dr. Bowles. *Parlez-vous anglais?* Ask Dr. Bowles. *Parlezvous français? Je suis le Dr. Bowles.* Dr. Palmer will tell you. Shhhhh. He's not here. Do you want to go to the latrine? Are you tired? Do you want to get up? How do you feel? Stay here. In there. In here. Sit down. Stand up. No smoking. Have a cigarette. Polish the floor. Move the furniture. Don't get excited! I want you to rest. You're under observation! Lie down! Get up! What's the matter? Stop that noise. Shut up! Turn on the light! Turn off the light! Get up! Get up! Up and up and up to the sun. Warm in the sun. Cold inside. Don't light the fire! Please please don't light the fire. Don't burn me up! Do you want a pill? Do you want a sleeping pill? No more trouble out of you, or...boom! Fire! No. Sun...sun...sun. Wonderful, wonderful sun. It's all right, it's all right. It's wonderful-lovely-fine-all-right.

What's-the-matter-with-you-are-you-dreaming? Am I? Who said that? Take me out of these sheets. Let me go!

"David. David!"

I sat up in bed. "What is it?"

Time to get up? My head was spinning. Get up, find your clothes, who moved them? Where are they? Somebody took my clothes!

Spinning, spinning, slower, slower. Who was shaking me?

"What...is...it?"

"Get up, David. It's time to get up."

Oh. Bow tie. Where was I going now? I couldn't take my eyes off the bow tie. "Come on, get up!"

"Okay. Okay."

I sat on the edge of the bed. I must have been dreaming. What about the claims man? What day was it? Had I signed a paper that would keep me in here? Where was the man with the bow tie? Get up. The floor was cold.

I shuffled into the bathroom and held my head under the tap. Someone was looking at me. A man in blue. What did he want? "Get out of the way," he said. I stood back from the sink and he turned on all the faucets, one by one, and left them running. He flushed the urinal. He flushed each of the toilets in turn. Then he smiled.

"Cleanliness! Cleanliness! Cleanliness!" he shouted at me. "That's the whole answer. Water! Water! Water!" He shook his finger in my face and I gaped at him. "Tsk, tsk," he said, and turned away and flushed all the toilets again. What had happened? Had the patients taken over the hospital? Why did he want all the water to run? Why was he flushing the toilets?

I backed out of the bathroom and walked into the wardroom. Where had I left my clothes this time? I looked around the room. I could not even remember undressing. Maybe I had really lost my memory. Where was my bench? That one? I felt so tired that I could not see clearly without squinting hard. That *looked* like the bench. So did all the benches. Three sets of blues. Was one of them mine? I felt in the pockets. Didn't I have a package of cigarettes? They looked like my clothes. No cigarettes, though. What had happened? Were these the wrong clothes? No, I didn't think so. Wasn't there a spot on my pants? There had been. There it was. Must be mine. No cigarettes, though.

I put on the clothes. Some bastard had taken my cigarettes, a full package almost. Well, half a pack anyway. Son-of-a-bitch! I went to the door.

"I had a package of cigarettes in these last night. Somebody took them."

Shrug. Shrug. "Can't expect me to watch everybody's clothes. Shouldn't leave things in your clothes."

"Where am I supposed to put them, then?"

The face zoomed into mine. "You aren't supposed to have them!"

Oh? Then why had Mr. Newton given them to me? Had he been trying to get me into trouble? Other people had cigarettes, other patients. Did anybody know anything around here? Were there any rules?

"Other people have them."

"Well they aren't supposed to have them."

"Then why do they?"

"How should I know?"

Was that reasonable? If he didn't know why, who could?

"Don't you care?"

"Why should I?"

"Then if you don't, who does? Who makes the rules?"

"Oh, for Christ's sake. Shut up!"

After breakfast I lay down on my bench and closed my eyes. I was still exhausted. "Good morning, David." I sat up and opened my eyes. It was a woman. The nurse. What was she doing here?

"Do you want me to fix your bandages?"

I nodded dumbly.

"Didn't you sleep last night?"

"Yes."

"You've been sleeping all morning."

How did she know? Was she an attendant now? "Let's go to the office, shall we?"

In the office she took off my bandages and looked at the scars. "These are getting along pretty well," she said. "I think I'll leave them open. I'll just clean them off a little. You won't need bandages anymore."

"Are you a new attendant?"

"David!" She looked shocked. "You know me, don't you?"

"Of course. You're Miss Yaddo."

"That's right. Had you forgotten?"

I shook my head. "Of course not, I…"

"You were just sleepy, that's all. Don't worry about it. It's all right." She looked around the room and then whispered: "There's some good news this morning."

"There is? What?"

She started to say something and then didn't. Someone had come into the room. "Let's see how those hands look."

The man, I had never seen him before, took my hands and looked at them. "You're David Mitchell, aren't you?"

"Yes."

"Pleased to meet you. My name is Mitchell, too."

"It is?"

"Yes." He turned to the nurse. "I guess that's all," he said to her. He moved over to the window, and I went along with him. He had not let go of my hands. He continued to look at them. Suddenly, in a low voice, he said: "See that rat out there?"

What had happened to this place overnight? Everybody was nuts. Was there a rat somewhere? I looked out the window. I could see two men standing on the walk outside the building, talking. I could not see who they were. I looked around the lawn. "Rat?" I asked.

"There." He pointed at the two men.

I squinted hard. Mr. Neider was it? And who was the other one? Dr. Palmer?

"I think that's Mr. Neider and Dr. Palmer," I said.

He nodded and then whispered. "That's right. You got rid of that rat."

I looked at him. "Do you feel all right?" I asked him.

"Shhhhh. Of course. I thought you'd want to know. He's through, and he's not the only one, some of his pals are out, too."

I couldn't make head or tail of what he was talking about.

"What about the rat?" I asked in a whisper.

He nodded in the direction of Mr. Neider. "You really did a job on him," he said.

"I did? What did I do?"

"Shhhhh." Then in a loud voice, he said: "Well, these look fine." He released my hands and I dropped them to my side. "I'd better look at them again tomorrow," he said. "Will you remember that?" He gave me a conspiratorial look and walked out of the room. Miss Yaddo came in again. "Come on, David," she said cheerfully, "I'll take you back to the ward."

Everyone seemed very happy. Especially what was his name...Mr. Mitchell.

"Did he tell you?" Miss Yaddo asked me.

"Tell me what?"

She leaned over and whispered in my ear: "About Mr. Neider?"

"He called him a rat," I said.

"We all feel very good today, David," she said. Then she added: "Thanks to you."

"Thanks to me?"

She nodded and looked at me mysteriously. "That's right!"

Do you see that rat? You got rid of that guy. Some of his pals, too. Thanks to me, they were all happy? Everybody had gone crazy, surely. I wondered if it would be any easier to get out if the attendants and the nurses were really cuckoo? It must be catching. Probably it was a germ.

When my name was called that afternoon, I was taken for the first time to the opposite end of the building, into another large room, identical with our wardroom. Spotlessly clean, the floor highly polished, the room was almost empty. Only a few of the benches were occupied: small, individual groups of *civilians,* people from the outside world, dressed in ordinary clothes, and in each group, one man in blue. I stood in the doorway with the attendant who had led me down here, and only after she had risen and started towards us did I see my mother. Automatically I went towards her, without feeling much of anything at first. When I had been told that this was visiting day, that I might have a visitor, I had frozen up immediately, against the possibility that I would not have a visitor. And even now, as we sat on a bench together, after she had kissed me, I had not come alive. There were so many things crowding up inside me, questions to be asked, answers to be dreaded...

She looked at me. "I've brought you some things," she said.

She had a small package and a large paper bag. "This is a bag of fruit," she said. "I don't imagine you get any fresh fruit here, and this..." indicating the small package, "...is some cigarettes. I didn't know what kind you wanted, I hope these are all right."

"Oh they're fine, thanks so much." I looked into her face, but I did not know how to begin.

Almost as if to forestall me, as if she knew about the torrent that was forming inside me, she said: "Are you comfortable? The doctor says you're getting along well, that you've made very good progress." She looked around the room. "It seems to be very clean."

I could almost hear the snapping inside me. "How long am I going to be here?"

She blinked and looked away from me. "Well, I don't know. That depends on the doctor, David."

"Oh? He says it depends on me."

She looked at me briefly. "You look well but you're thin."

I nodded. "Yes, I know. But if I'm getting along all right...if the doctor says so, then when can I go home?"

"Oh, darling," she began and hesitated, "I don't know. He said something about a trial visit soon. I'll talk to him again. You can't go home definitely until you've been on a trial visit first."

"You mean I have to go home and then come back again?"

She nodded.

"But I couldn't do that!"

She did not look at me.

"But I couldn't! You don't know what it's like here! The doctor couldn't have told you; you can't imagine the things that have happened. I can't stay here! I couldn't come back. Can't you get me out?"

"Shhhhh, David," her voice was very low, "the attendant is looking at us. Don't talk so loudly. I know it must be awful for you, but there isn't anything I can do right away. I will see what I can do about the trial visit. I'll make it as soon as I can, really I will. Here now, don't you want a cigarette?"

"Oh yes, of course."

I opened a package of cigarettes and offered her one and then took one myself. As I lighted them both, I could feel myself getting hot inside. It seemed impossible to convey in any words why it was so important to get out. The other people in the room had stopped talking amongst each other and were looking at us. I looked around at them and recognized some of the patients. The people with them must be their families, I supposed. One of the men near us was sitting next to an older woman, holding her hand. The tears were streaming down his face. It was a ludicrous tableau because he was a big man, and on the ward very self-contained, very confident and self-assured. And now I saw him crumpled into another kind of being, a small defenseless child.

"I know I was sick," I said, "but I'm not now, really I'm not. But to be cooped up this way, to be..."

"Oh, David, I know. Really I do. I will do whatever I can, you know I will."

"They put me in handcuffs," I said, "they knocked me down...out. They tried to..." I couldn't finish the sentence.

She shook her head. "David, they couldn't have. They wouldn't. This is one of the best hospitals around here, they couldn't have..."

"But they did." I stared at her. "Don't you believe me?"

"Of course I do. Of course!"

"Then how can you say they couldn't have! How can you?"

"You mustn't talk so loudly, David. Really you mustn't. Look: I've brought some cards along. Let's play a game, shall we?"

I couldn't understand this. If only I could get away from this ward, these people, these attendants. This was like being visited in a prison. I couldn't tell her anything here, everybody seemed to be listening. And now she wanted to play cards. Well, maybe if I played cards with her that would prove something to her. That I was well, that I was really all right.

There were two chairs near a table in the center of the room and we moved to them and she laid the cards on the table. "What do you want to play?" she asked me.

"I don't care. Anything."

"Casino?"

"Okay."

I watched her as she dealt the cards, and a mass of desperation and frustration began to form inside my chest. There was something frightful about this. My family represented my only hope outside this place. My only means to get out of here, and what were we doing about it? Sitting at a table playing cards. This was really a kind of madness. I didn't know how to begin to tell her. I couldn't understand. Didn't she *know* how important, how significant this moment was?

"Did you bring my glasses? I can't see well without my glasses. I've had a terrible time with my eyes."

"The doctor has them," she said. "I wanted to give them to you, but the doctor said he would give them to you later. I did bring them, David."

We started to play.

"If the doctor has them, I'll never get them. It's almost impossible to see the doctor. Do you know that the first time I saw the doctor was last Friday! I never saw him before that."

She smiled. "He's probably very busy, David."

"Yes, but isn't he supposed to see us? How can he tell you if I'm getting along well or not if he doesn't see us? I've only seen him once. Once!"

"Oh, David, please don't talk so loudly. Please!"

But I would not be put off now.

"What about the claims man? Did you see the claims man? Are they going to keep me in here because of the claim that you applied for?"

She shook her head. "Of course not. I didn't know anything about it until they told me to apply for compensation for you. If you're entitled to it, why shouldn't you get it? You could get about a hundred and forty dollars a month, I think they said. Wouldn't that make you feel better? At least you'd have something for all this. You might as well get it if you can."

I nodded. "Well it's all right if you're sure it won't keep me in here any longer."

"It won't, David, really it won't. I've talked to the claims man and the doctor, and they both assure me that it won't."

"Oh. What else did they ask you? What else did you tell them?"

She stopped playing and looked at her cards. "They asked me a lot of questions, of course. I told them whatever I knew. They asked me if you drank a lot and I said you didn't; they wanted to know how much you smoked and I told them."

"What did you tell them?"

"About smoking? I said about a package a day. They wanted to know if you were nervous, and I said no more than anyone."

"Did you talk to Mr. Neider?"

"Yes. The first time. The day you came."

"Why did I come with the police? Why was I handcuffed?"

"You wouldn't come with us. We had Dr. Spencer up to see you, but you wouldn't go with him. We had to get the police."

She took my hand in hers. "Don't be so upset, darling. I've told you that I'll do what I can about getting you home as soon as I can. And I will. Really I will. But don't talk about it now, it can only upset you to think about it and talk about it now. John sent you his love, by the way."

"How is he?"

"He's fine." Then she added: "He's worried about you, though."

"He is? Why?"

"He was frightened that day."

"Frightened? Why? I wasn't violent."

She smiled. "You weren't so quiet about going to the hospital."

"Well who *would* be quiet in handcuffs?"

She smiled again. "I know, David. But that's all over now, and we had to do it that way. I'll explain it all to you sometime. Let's play. Come on."

We played for a while in silence, and then she said: "Are you really feeling better? You do look better. Is the food all right?"

"It's not bad. But I can never get off the ward. You don't know what it's like staying on the ward all day long with all those men."

"Yes, I do, David. I know it's hard. But after you've been home on your trial visit, you'll probably get a pass and then you'll be able to go outside, you'll be able to get off the ward."

"After I come back!"

She nodded. "I explained to you, David, that you'll have to come back. That's the rule."

I had an idea. "Can't you get Dr. Spencer to come and see me? Couldn't he get me out? After all he's my doctor. He's been my doctor for years."

"Yes, darling, but he's not a psychiatrist. I'll talk to him if you want me to, but I'm sure there's nothing he can do."

"Am I..." I hesitated.

"What, David?"

"Am I *committed?*"

"No."

"Then how can they keep me here?"

"They can't really. I can sign you out as soon as you're all right."

"But I'm all right now! Why don't you sign me out now?"

"Even if I did sign you out now, you couldn't go home right away. You'd have to wait about ten days."

"Then all the more reason! Sign me out today so that I can go home in ten days!"

She took my hand again. "Believe me, David, you aren't well enough to go home yet. You've got to sleep and rest and calm down more before you can go home. I'm sure they treat you well here, and if you will just be patient and not get excited, then it will all go very quickly. You've only been here a short time and you really are getting along awfully well. As soon as I possibly can, I'll sign you out. I won't keep you here. I don't want you to stay here, you know. But you must stay until you're really well enough. You don't want anything like this to happen again, do you?"

"But it won't! I know it won't. I'd never let it happen again. But can't you understand what it's like being here? Can't you..."

A hand was laid on my shoulder. It was Monty.

"How are you getting along? Isn't it nice to be having a visitor?"

"Yes, but..."

His voice was low and urgent. "Your mother can't stay very long, David. Have a good time while she's here, but don't talk too loud. You're disturbing the others, and besides Jerry's getting impatient."

Jerry! "You see," I said. "You heard him say Jerry. You should see him. He's terrible. You don't know what he does to the patients. What he tried to do to me. They're all afraid of him, even the attendants are afraid of him. I have to get away from here."

"Shhhhh. David." It was Monty again, and my mother looked at me and nodded, agreeing with him.

We played cards some more and then suddenly she looked at her watch. "I have to see the doctor again before I go, and it's getting late, David."

She stood up and put the cards in her purse. "Believe me, darling, I know how it is here. I'll talk to the doctor right away about your trial visit; just be patient until then. When you're home, we'll be able to talk everything over and if you're all right then, and if you're really feeling better, then I promise I'll sign you out while you're home and perhaps you won't have to come back at all, or maybe only for a few days at the most. But we can't talk about it all here. You understand that, don't you?"

"Yes, I guess so."

The ridiculous thing was that there was nothing to do. I knew there was nothing to say, nothing to do to change that. And, after all, perhaps she was right. If it had been possible up to now (I was still *alive!*) then maybe I could wait for the trial visit. At least, I had to admit that that was a hope, something to look forward to, to work for, to wait for.

"You don't feel too badly about it, do you?" she asked.

"No, I don't." I smiled as warmly as I could. "I guess you're right. It's just that..."

"I know, David. I know. Come on. I'll go back to the office with you."

For the first time, she looked directly at the scars on my hands.

"The doctor told me about that," she said.

I looked at them. "Did he tell you why? Did he tell you about the leather cuffs?"

"No."

"He wouldn't!"

We started out of the room, down the hall.

"You remember what I told you about the Army hospital? How they gave me cognac to put me to sleep?"

"Yes."

"Well they tried to give me sodium amytal the first night here. There was a lot of trouble about that. I told them that it wouldn't do me any good, but they insisted that it would."

"Oh. That was my fault, David. I was so upset that day, I forgot what you had told me. I told them to give you sodium amytal. I'm sorry. Anyway, I don't suppose they would have given you anything to drink here. But I am sorry."

"Oh, you told them? Well at least that explains that."

She stopped in the hall before we got to the office.

"I'm so glad to see you so much better, darling," she said. "You will promise to be good, won't you? Don't get into any trouble."

"Will you really try to get me home as soon as you can? Will you?"

"I promise I will, David. I promise. And I'll come back on Sunday to see you again. Then I'll know more. Maybe you can even go home then. We'll see."

"All right. I'll try. I will try."

She kissed me.

"Good, David. Now I must see the doctor. Goodbye, darling."

"Goodbye."

I watched her go into the doctor's office and then an attendant came up to me.

"What's in that bag?"

"Fruit...and cigarettes."

"You can't take those on the ward with you."

"But they're mine. My mother brought them to me."

"Doesn't matter. You can't take them on the ward. Give them to me and I'll keep them in the locker out here."

"No."

"Now come on, don't be unreasonable. You can get them whenever you want. You can keep one package of cigarettes, but no matches. And when you want more, you can get them. They'll be held in your name. Just ask the nurse."

"But the fruit will spoil."

"Well..." He looked into the bag. "If you want to, you can take this down to supper with you and share it with the other boys, but you can't take it on the ward. Do you want to do that?"

"Okay."

"All right, then. Give it to me now and I'll give it to you at suppertime."

"Okay."

The attendant did bring me the bag of fruit and I took it to supper with me. Although I could not understand it...was it the fruit? Was it the fact that I had had a visitor (most of the patients had not had anyone come to see them)...some strange change had come over the attendants and the other patients. Several of the patients whom I knew by sight or name seemed to make a point of sitting with me at the table, eyeing the bag of fruit, accepting it gratefully. Finally, one of them, a big husky colored man who had often looked at me, but who had never spoken to me before, looked up from his place across from me at the table.

"Your mother came to see you, didn't she?"

I nodded.

He bit into the apple I had given him. "Sure is wonderful to taste real fresh fruit," he said. "Is she going to take you home?"

I shook my head. "She says I'm not well enough yet, but that she's going to try and get me home on a trial visit soon."

"That's good," he said. "You're lucky. You haven't been here very long. You just wait until that visit, and then you can convince her. She'll get you out. Your family can get you out of here quick if they want. It's up to them. You won't have any trouble."

I liked him, and I was cheered by what he had said. The fact that I had been able to extract the promise from my mother...the promise to do what she could, was like a good omen, a goodluck piece that I could carry around in my pocket.

"It's the ones that don't get any visitors that are in a bad way," he went on. "Then it's up to the hospital, and they don't care if you never get home. But if you have someone waiting for you, it's easy. You don't have to worry, you'll be all right. You just take it easy until her next visit. She'll get you home all right."

"Haven't you got a family?"

He nodded. "Yeah, but they live in Springfield. They can't get up here very often. I was home already."

"You were? On a visit?"

"Yeah."

"Why didn't you get out? Why didn't they take you home with them?"

He shook his head and the smile disappeared. "I fucked up when I was home. I raised hell with them trying to get out, so they sent me back. I should have talked reasonably to them, but I didn't. I was too anxious." He looked into my eyes again. "When you do get home, just go slow. They'll see you're okay and they'll get you home. But if you start raising hell about it, they'll just send you back. People get afraid of us in here, you know. They get scared and think we're murderers, real lunatics. They don't understand what it's like. When you begin to act up even a little…or if you get mad, then they shove you right back in. Think you're gonna kill 'em. Nobody is afraid of anything so much as somebody who's supposed to be nuts. Other people can get mad, but you can't anymore. You have to be calm all the time."

"Yeah. I know what you mean. I started to get excited today, and it wasn't so good. My mother kept wanting me to shut up."

He nodded again. "Sure. If she visits you again, just be nice to her, don't say anything. Say everything's all right, and then she'll think you're really coming along fine."

"I guess you're right."

He nodded again and then looked straight into my face. "I like you," he said. "What's your name?"

"David Mitchell. What's yours?"

"David Everett," he said. "Funny we should have the same name David, isn't it?"

"I think it's nice."

"I'll call you Mitch," he said.

"Okay. Lots of people call me that. In the Army they called me Mitch a lot."

"Okay, Mitch." He looked away from me again. "You don't mind me being a nigger, do you?"

He said it as if he already knew that I didn't. It wasn't a question, it was a statement. "No, of course I don't."

"I know you don't," he said, "that's one thing I like about you. But it won't do you any good."

"What do you mean?"

"The other guys'll call you a nigger-lover," he said.

"The hell with them."

He shook his head. "It's not so easy. A lot of people say that, but they can make it tough."

"You don't have to worry about that, I don't care what they say." I smiled at him. "They can say whatever they want to...Dave."

One of the other patients sitting at the table had been listening to us. He spoke up suddenly: "Boy! Buddies already, huh?" We didn't say anything, but David looked at him hard.

"That's a good one," the man went on. "Buddies with a coon."

"Go to hell!" I said angrily.

He laughed. "Just a couple of the boys, that's what you are."

I was about to say something and David put his hand on mine.

"Take it easy, Mitch. Take it easy. Remember what I said. It won't be easy."

I looked away from the other man. "Okay. Okay. I'm sorry."

"Hell. Sorry nothing. I know what it's like. Come on, let's go."

EIGHT

It was the sudden sight of the lawn again that shocked my visit home into reality. From the time of my mother's first visit to the hospital until one short week later when I was suddenly informed that I would be going home that very day, I had lived in an insulated and protected world. I had almost ceased to think or feel or participate (beyond the physical routine of the hospital) in anything that I did. And now, seeing the grass, and then the trees and the house, something inside me slammed itself back into being, almost as if I had unwittingly struck the starter of a car, shocking the motor into life.

As I followed my mother across the lawn, walking slowly, surprised by the wetness of the grass (it had not been raining, I knew it had not been raining) I said:

"But the grass is wet!"

She turned. "Yes, it's been like this for a week. So damp, the dew never dries up." And then she went into the house, leaving me alone on the lawn.

Although I knew it was not a delusion, the last week in the hospital began at that moment inside me as an experience. What had happened to me, passively, only now at this moment took any emotional effect; and as I stood there, the week of routine, the moment of my departure, penetrated into my body, flowing through me as blood. The mysterious man with a bow tie who—only that morning—had appeared and taken me from the ward to the hitherto dream interview with Dr. Bowles and Mr. Mitchell in the ward office. Only the fact of the lawn, the wetness of my shoes prevented me from turning to search for them now...but this was not happening, it had happened.

Dr. Bowles shaking my hand and smiling.

"Well, well. You've been getting along fine. We have good news for you."

"You have? What is it?" My head cocking suspiciously towards him. What was it about him that I distrusted?

"You're going home today. I've decided to take a chance on you and give you a week's trial visit with your family. How does that sound?"

"What do you mean? Today? Now?" He did, he had, here I was!

And then the nodding of his head. "Yes. Your mother will be here in about an hour."

"What did you mean about taking a chance on me?"

"Just that. You've been here a very short time. I've never let a patient go home so soon, but I have confidence in you. I think you're coming along just fine, and I want you to know how I feel. I want you to know that I trust you...that I believe in you and that I think you'll do very well on this visit. If you do, we may be able to get you out very soon. Come back here for two weeks or so, and we'll transfer you to Ward 10 and from there you'll go home permanently." A warning hand, a change in the tone of voice: "Of course, that is if everything goes all right. I don't want you to count on it, but I do want you to know that now it's up to you. If we get a good report on you after your visit, and if all goes well when you come back, then you will really go home for good."

Could he be believed, ever? Everything sounded so smooth, so easy with that man. Liquid, immersing, flooding...I wondered. And then the attendant was there again, standing over me, looking at me, with Dr. Bowles's voice ringing in my ears, and then my own voice:

"You wouldn't kid me, would you?"

"I should say not. I wouldn't think of it. It means a great deal to me, too. We're counting on you to make a good showing for us."

"Oh?" Team spirit? Go out and make a touchdown? I looked at my clothes. "Am I going home in these?"

He shook his head then. "Certainly not. Your clothes will be here in a few minutes. The clothing man has gone to get them. You just sit out there in the hall on that bench and wait until they get here."

Waving me away with his hand and his smile; the attendant leaning over me and then leading me to the bench in the hall, for the waiting to begin. The face of the clock, I could see it from the bench: ten minutes past eleven then...and that immovable minute hand. Except when I looked away from it; and then it would leap ahead, only to stop when I looked back at it. The exercise of forcing time to move by not looking at the clock, and the terrible bending of my eyes towards it.

What had happened during that week? No more Mr. Neider. No more a lot of things. No more tests, no more questions. Mr. Newton had been swallowed up, too. What about the work I was to have done...? I had seen him only that one time, at that interview, and then nothing had happened. Something phony about him too. Too bad. I had liked him. Maybe he had gotten into trouble because of me, or because of what he'd done or said about me, or something.

And then the men had wandered into the hall on their way to lunch, and the waiting had gone on and on and on until they had come back again, with me still there. Movement, then, all of a sudden. The clothing man with my clothes...quick, into Dr. Palmer's office. Take off your clothes, give them to me. Looking at me all the time while I undressed, his eyes so searching that I was embarrassed and turned away from him. But he wouldn't give me my own clothes until I handed him the hospital clothes and stood before him naked and blushing. And then, even then, his hesitation and the long slow inspection of my body, missing nothing. And at last they were put into my hands with a laugh and more waiting and watching as I got dressed. And then the hall again.

Twelve o'clock it had been, now twelve-thirty, one o'clock. Interminable passing of attendants and nurses, even Dr. Bowles with a warning, preventive wave of his hand and nod of his head, keeping me silent. Almost two o'clock, and the ache of hunger in my stomach, the wanting to go to the bathroom, and then the voice in the anteroom. My mother's voice!

"David!"

I looked up, startled. I was on the lawn.

"David."

There she was, holding the door open.

"What is it?"

"Aren't you coming in? I've made some lunch for us."

She looked frightened, the way she had that morning. Frightened and threatening. Oh dear, was it going to be that way? I hurried across the lawn. Normal, normal, normal, normal! Oh God help me and make me normal, normal. Make me whatever will convince them, *please.*

"Good, I'm hungry."

But it was cold and tomblike in the house and I wanted...mustn't, *mustn't*...I so wanted to be back in the sunlight. But not that again, not that! The food trickled down inside me, sickening, and I breathed hard and ate and ate, aching against the fork and spoon, hating them.

"I imagine that tastes better than the hospital food, doesn't it?"

Keep cool. Keep cool. But the sweat forms anyway. "You bet!"

"How is the food there, David?"

Be reasonable, be good. "Well actually it's not bad at all. Not like this, of course..." smile, smile "...but really not bad."

Nod, nod, nod goes her head. "That's good. You know we just didn't know what to do. We can't afford a private place, and the state institution would cost *something*..."

Oh must you, must you! "Of course. No, I'm sure it's really very good as...as hospitals go. Mother..." the fork trembled wildly in my hand. "Mother..."

"What is it, David?"

"How long..." but see her face, you mustn't ask her now, it's too soon, it's no good asking her now... "how long will I have to stay there?" Hands hard, hard on the table.

Looking away, then looking too bright at me. "You must be patient, dear. You must. We'll see. Wait until John gets here. Wait a few days. We'll see. We'll talk about it."

My hands were so tight, gripping the wooden table top. Relax, relax. "Do you want to rest for a while?"

Anything. "Yes, I guess I do. I was up so early. I waited so long." Was that all right? Should I want to rest? Anyway it was better lying down, but I hated the house, the memory of the moon from this bed. And why was it so cold in here in the daytime?

"Look what I brought for supper!" It was John and he held them up for me to see: the pitiful naked bodies of the chickens, dyed here and there with their own blood, the useless stained beaks. Like that man in the pack room. Didn't he know how awful it was? How frightful they looked and were? Please, John, please take them away. Don't make me look at them. But don't say anything. "Oh my!" Had I ever said anything like that before? Insipid expression. "They look good."

And there they dangled and dangled from his hand. "Wait until you taste them...young, tender, delicious."

God! People are monsters! "I'll bet they're good. They look wonderful."

"I brought some beer. You want some beer, David?"

Too late the warning look, the whisper...I could hear everything, see everything, feel everything... "He's not supposed to drink. Dr. Bowles said he shouldn't drink." "Oh, hell, a glass of beer...?" "Well, whatever you say."

And then: "Do you want a glass of beer, David?"

Rise slowly from the bed, yawn, stretch your arms, easy, easy. "Why, I don't mind if I do. Just a glass."

"Let's sit outside. Under the trees. I'll get some glasses. It's good and cold."

It was good outside, much better. And the beer goes easily down and down, washing things gently along with it. John was nice without chickens. The apple blossoms were dead on the trees now. Little curled brown death on the branches and the twigs.

"Do you want some more?"

Take it easy, watch out. Exaggerated and slow, my voice said for me: "Well, perhaps a bit more. Very refreshing. Just a half."

Is it really all right? Watch them, watch them.

〜

If the traces of the blood had not been entirely fried away, it would have been impossible. As it was, the sound of my own teeth ripping through the tender chicken flesh was the sound of the needle in Tom's arm.

"Delicious. Delicious." "Aren't they good?" Grind, grind of teeth. "You're looking well, David." Oh yes, oh yes. "They come from a little farm down the road. He keeps them in cages and gets them very fat. No exercise at all. Just food, food. They eat and eat. These were only six weeks old. And so big already. You can eat the bones!" Crunch, crunch. Jesus Christ!

〜

How many days of looks and voices and meals was it? How many incredible terrible hours of not saying, not asking, not hurrying? Of just half a glass more of beer, of remembering not to forget? Good morning, and good night. Of whatever wasn't, being. Whatever happened I slept well, I was fine, I was wonderful. And how are you? Of course, I'm fine! But really are you all right? Seriously, I've never felt better. Simply wonderful. Why of course, I'd love to take a ride.

I'd love to go to the post office. Certainly I don't mind. No, I'm not tired. Yes, I'd love to rest for just a while. Nothing I'd like better than to listen to the radio. Isn't it beautiful? *Tum dada tum te tum tum tum! With independent tobacco experts it's Luckies two to one!* Something under the direction of someone. *Esquire Boot Pol-ISH! Snap back with Stanback! We now take you to the...* "I hate Dvorak!" "Really?" "Yes, don't you?" "Oh, I like any music. Leave it on."

⤙

"I brought home a bottle of sherry. Only eighty-nine cents. And good, too! No kidding. Why pay more when you can get this. And for eighty-nine cents. Here, have a glass."

"Do you really think he should, John? You know what the doctor said."

"Ah...the doctor! He doesn't drink too much. He's getting along fine. Aren't you, David?"

"I certainly feel fine. Whatever you say, though. Whatever you say."

"Sure, come on. How could this hurt you? Here."

"Well," raise the glass and smile, "here's how."

"Skoal!"

"Here's mud in your eye!"

"John..." put the glass down, don't tremble.

"What is it, Dave?"

Oh thank you, thank you. That's the first time you've called me *Dave.* Thank you!

"John, don't you think I could be signed out now? Don't you really?" Oh please don't look away like that. Please. We have to talk about it. We have to. The time is going. Days have passed already. I'll have to go back. I have to know first.

"Well, David..." David again right away, no more Dave now... "Why don't you wait a while?"

"But, John, I..." Oh for God's sake be reasonable! "Well," a deep,

deep cooling breath, don't get hot... "perhaps you're right. But I think you'll understand when I tell you this. Maybe I was a little over-excited about the hospital at first, but I don't want to go back...to have to go back not *knowing*, John. Don't you see? It's like being in prison. You can get me out. I'm not asking you to get me out right now, but just sign me out. I'll go back for a while, but if I can only know that you've signed me out and that I will be coming home for good. Don't you see?"

"Here, have some more sherry. Have a cigarette. Isn't this good sherry for only eighty-nine cents?"

"Yes, it's awfully..."

"Now boys, dinner's ready. Finish your drinks."

Plates knives forks spoons glasses. "I'll help you, Clara."

Oh John!!

"No, no, finish your drinks."

Silence.

"Do you understand, John? Do you?"

"Look, David. How about waiting for another visit? You'll come home again in a couple of weeks anyway, and maybe we'll know then. I don't want anything to...I don't want..."

"What?"

Red in the face, difficult smile now.

"Well..."

"Oh, John, I know what you mean. But it won't happen again. I know how it must have been for you. I do understand. But it's over. Really it's over now. It was sudden, it was violent in a way, and now it's over. Don't you think I'm all right?"

"I think you're getting along awfully well, David. I do think that."

"Then..."

"Come on now, finish up. Here's dinner."

"Mother..."

Unfold the napkins, hold the serving spoon over the steaming dish, look into my eyes, suspended, interrupted action... "What is it, David?"

But you know what it is, dammit! How can I tell you before the spoon touches the food?

"Oh, nothing."

Down goes the spoon. "What is it, David? Aren't you feeling well?"

"Of course, I'm feeling well. What about getting me out?"

"There's plenty of time to talk about that, David. You seem a little excited now. Perhaps you've had too much sherry. Let's wait until after dinner."

Good God! Don't give me so much food! "Gee, that's a lot of stew."

Exchange of looks between them. Then: "Aren't you hungry?"

A big silence. Big, waiting, unfriendly.

"Not very, actually."

"Oh."

What had happened? Everything's changed in the room. They've gone away.

"Do you want to wait awhile?"

"Yes."

"Hmmmmm." Looks and looks. I'm "him" in their minds now...I can see the words running around...keep him calm, say their eyes, humor him...

The hand on the bottle. "We might as well finish this bottle then."

"Oh, John, do you think...?"

"Of course. Stimulates the appetite. It's early yet. Come on, have a glass with us."

"Well, if you're sure."

"Sure I'm sure. We can heat dinner up. Can't hurt a stew. It's better when it's heated up. I'm not very hungry myself."

"Well..." look at them both, bring them back. "What about it?"

She squared her shoulders, drank her drink. "Well, David, let's at least wait until we've found out about the claim."

"The claim. What do you mean?"

"The claim for compensation."

"I know. What about it?"

"Let's wait until we've had a decision about it. If you left the hospital now, it might affect the doctor's opinion about it."

"So what?"

Another swallow. "Well look. Did you know that you might get one hundred and thirty-one dollars a month? After all you wouldn't..."

"One hundred and thirty-one dollars a month? For what?"

"Compensation from the government...for your illness. Why shouldn't you get it? You're entitled to it."

"Entitled to it? What do you mean 'entitled to it'?"

"Well you are. As a veteran, you're entitled to it."

"Only if I'm sick. Only if I've got a permanent disability."

"Well you've been sick. You can't know yourself how..."

"What do you mean *I* can't know? Of course, I know how sick I *was*."

"Then if you do know, what's your objection?"

"But that's all over with. They aren't going to pay me a pension for life for that!"

"Why aren't they? The doctor said it had a very good chance of going through. That this is very probably a service-connected illness."

"What difference does it make what it is, if it's over? Do you think I'm still sick?"

"Here," John again. "Have a little more. Last of the bottle."

"Okay. Thanks. Do you think I'm still sick?"

"Well..." Fingers on the glass, fingers rubbing the tablecloth. "I don't think you're completely well."

Boom.

"All right, maybe not. But it's like a wound. There's a scar, an effect, if you wish, but it's begun to heal over. I know I'm nervous, I'm tired, maybe I'm not completely myself. But who wouldn't be nervous with the hospital hanging over his head?"

"You said yourself that you thought it was a good hospital. After all, it's only a question of a few *weeks*. You know we want you out as soon as you are well enough. Really well enough."

"How will you know?"

"Well you've just said yourself that you were nervous and tired. You'll get over that after a few weeks in the hospital..." more hesitation and rubbing of fingers "...and, David, be sensible. Think of what it would mean to you to have an income like that...something you could rely on. You wouldn't have to worry about getting a job right away, you could do whatever you wanted to do for a while once you had that money. You could really take a good long rest, and you'll probably need it. Wouldn't that be worth it to you?"

"But you have to understand. I don't want to rook the government out of money. I'm not sick anymore. That's over with. The thing that will make me well is to be out of the hospital. You don't know, you'll never know what it was like there, what it *is* like!"

Laughter. Laughter? What about! "But you forget, David. I do know."

"Then all the more reason!" Thank God she had remembered herself.

"But it wasn't really so bad, David."

"Wasn't so bad?! Don't you remember when I saw you there myself? How terrible it was for you? The things they did to you!"

"Well...well, it always seems bad at the moment. But, David, if I'd had the chance to get an income for life...for *life*...a few weeks wouldn't have mattered one way or the other. Think of what it will mean to you to have that!"

"But I don't want it! Nothing could be worth staying in the hospital, don't you see that? Can't you remember! You wanted to die! You told me so. You said so!"

"David, don't you think we should eat now?"

"No. Dammit, no. Not until this is settled."

"It isn't good for you not to eat. You didn't eat much lunch."

"The hell with that! I can't eat while this is still unsettled."

"Well, it certainly isn't good for you not to eat."

"Oh, for Christ's sake, drop that! Since I don't want the pension, how about it? Will you or will you not sign me out?"

Huge silence. Enormous!

"David..." finally, "David, if you won't think of yourself, then think of me."

"All right, I'm thinking of you. What about you?"

"Yes, but you aren't. You only see your point of view. You haven't looked at it from my point of view at all."

"What is your point of view?"

"Did you know what was happening to you the day you went to the hospital?"

Did I? "Well, I..."

"You see, darling, of course you didn't. Don't you realize that something like that could easily happen again? You've always been nervous, and besides, remember that I had several recurrences. I know what I'm talking about. If something like that happened again, then there would be some money to...well, it isn't fair to ask John to..."

Ice Ice Ice...my blood was freezing. "The hospital is *free*."

"Yes, I know. But John had to pay the doctor that came to see you, he had to give some money to the Chief of Police. There have been extra expenses in connection with...David, where are you going?"

"I'll be right back. I'm going to get my checkbook."

"But, David! I don't want any money from you. You know I don't. Don't listen to her. You're like my own son to me, you know that."

"How much did it cost?"

Silence.

"Will fifty dollars cover it?"

"David, I don't want your money. You know..."

"Here. I don't want yours, either."

"David, darling, I'm sorry...I..."

"Mother. Are you going to sign me out?"

"When the decision about the claim has come through."

"Not before?"

"No. David. Listen to me. I shouldn't have said that about John. I know he's fond of you and that he doesn't want your money. But what if something happened to him? Then what? Suppose you had another attack and John wasn't here to...well, people do have accidents, you know."

"What if the claim is turned down?"

"But it hasn't been! If it is, naturally we'll sign you out right away. But what is the sense of refusing the money, or taking a chance of not getting it by getting out now? You have to go back for a while, anyway."

"Does he? I thought the doctor said that he could get out right away."

"What did you say?"

"Nothing, darling, John didn't talk to the doctor."

"What did she tell you, John? What did she tell you?"

Silence.

"What did you tell him?"

"Oh all right, David. I could sign you out right now. But I'm not going to. If you won't be sensible and think of all of us, then I will. John has done a great deal for you and if you continue to live with us that would be one way of helping to pay him back. After all, you won't be able to work for a while when you do get out."

"Do you mean that if you signed me out now, I could get out without having to go back?"

"Yes. Well, you might have to see the doctor."

"And you're not going to sign me out?"

She shook her head. "No, David. And I've told you why. John, don't you think I'm right?"

"Well..."

"Leave him out of this."

"Now, David..."

"Now David, shit!"

"David, don't use that tone with me."

"Oh? What is this, the victor and the vanquished? Are we going to be pure all of a sudden? I shouldn't think the word 'shit' would offend you. After all you've been around, you've led a pretty active life, you must have heard it before, along with all the..."

"David! I will not sit here and be insulted!"

"Okay. Get up then! Don't listen. But I'll sit here, I suppose, and have sentence pronounced on me."

"Sentence! You're so melodramatic. You're so *unreasonable*, David. For the sake of your own health, I wouldn't think of signing you out now. I didn't want to talk about all this, I knew you weren't well enough; but now I'm glad it has come out. It proves to me that you're still sick."

"There's just one thing I want to know. Just one thing."

"What is it?"

"Is this final? You will not sign me out? Just answer yes or no. Will you?"

"No, David. I won't."

I picked up the telephone and handed it to her. "Here, call the hospital and tell them to come and get me. I'm going back now. I won't stay in this house any longer..."

"David...! Oh, hello, operator. Sorry, it was a mistake."

Clunk.

"David, don't be a fool!"

It couldn't be. It wasn't possible! I stood up from the table.

"What are you doing?!"

"I'll go myself."

"*David!* You can't! You haven't had your dinner even!"

"Oh go to hell!" I started for the door.

"David. If you go out that door, I warn you..."

Bang. The hell with all of them.

It was dark on the lawn and I could hear them in the house behind me. They'd follow me and pick me up, sure thing. I ran across the lawn, into the bushes. I had to hide and think now. In the bushes, the air was free and cool around me. I wouldn't have to go back to the hospital at all! They'd come out, they wouldn't see me, they'd drive off down the road. I could go the other way. Damn! I didn't have any money. Maybe I could pick up a ride on the back highway.

"David! David! David!" John passed only a few feet from me. The dumbbell...he didn't even have a flashlight!

"I can't find him. I don't know where he's gone." Back in the house. What were they doing? Maybe now was the time to get away. If they came after me, I'd see the lights of the car...there were bushes along the road. I could hide in the bushes. Quickly and silently I made my way along the driveway, past the car, out on the road. Black, black... and alone. Away from them.

I saw the lights of a car and ducked into the bushes. It pulled past me and turned into the drive. I watched it through the bushes. Two men. They hurried across the lawn, into the house. As they closed the door, I stood up, and felt in my pockets. Why hadn't I gotten some money! Where could I possibly go? It really was insane to start off like this... someone would be sure to pick me up. I held my hands hard against my chest. If only I could stop feeling, not believe what I did feel. It couldn't be true...they couldn't have said what they had said. Maybe I had had another delusion. Surely I could convince them. They wouldn't send me back, now that they could really sign me out for good so I wouldn't have to go back. Maybe if I apologized...anything...anything...but I couldn't go back.

I made my way slowly across the lawn and stood before the door. I looked up at the moon, wishing the sun were out. I believe in the sun but not in this...not in this light. "Oh God...Oh Jesus Christ...if there is a God. No. I know I shouldn't say that, I know that if I don't believe in you you can't help me...but believe me, God, believe me, I can't go back. Make them see it! Make them see it! Oh God help me!"

I opened the door suddenly, quickly...eight eyes. Who was that? I walked in and closed the door behind me. Right up to the man.

"Hello. I know you. You're the Chief of Police."

"That's right, my boy. Where've you been?"

"I just went out for a walk." I looked anxiously at my mother and at John. What had they already said to him? "I got a little steamed up," I said. "So I had to go out and cool off."

No answer.

"I'm sorry they called you..."

I saw the handcuffs then, hanging from his hand. Don't move, don't look surprised. "I guess you got kind of worried," I said slowly.

"As a matter of fact, I did."

"Look, Mother, I'm sorry...I...Let's talk this thing over again. I'm sure we can work it out. I didn't mean to get so upset. I'm sorry, really I am."

She looked away.

"Mother...I..."

"I think you were very unreasonable, David."

"But, Mother, you can't expect me to want to go back!"

"David, I do expect you to realize what's best. A few weeks..."

"But you can't mean that!"

"But I do, David. You just won't understand."

"But it's like sending me back to prison!"

"Oh, David, you know it's not. You shouldn't talk that way. They've got good doctors there, they treat you well. Why, you hardly know what happened anyway. The doctor himself told me that you were in a delusion most of the time!"

I struck my chest hard with my clenched fist, but I couldn't keep it in. "But you have to believe me! You have to! I know what happened there!"

"David...You forget that I know about these things from my own experience. You couldn't have known."

"But you have to believe me!" I looked around at the faces in the room. "Doesn't anybody believe me?"

No answer.

I looked at the Chief of Police. "What are you doing here? Why don't you go home?"

"I came to take you back, son." He looked at the floor.

"Mother, tell him to go home."

"David," she looked at the floor too. "I think perhaps it's best if you do go back."

"But not like this! Do you realize what that will mean?"

"I've already phoned the hospital, David. After all, I didn't know where you'd gone. They may be out looking for you now."

"Well then, call them back!"

Silence.

"I guess we'd better take you along, son." It was the Chief of Police again.

"Are you serious? Are you going to let this happen?"

"You've made it happen, David."

"Here, son." I'd heard that clink before.

"No...but surely you aren't going to...Look, I'll go with you, but..."

A pause...look and looks. "I think we'd better, son."

"Stop calling me son! And you...yes, you. Tell him to put those handcuffs on me. Go on, tell him!"

"I don't have to tell him, David."

"Oh yes you do. Go on, tell him. Then it will be final. Don't worry, I'll go now. I'll go all right."

She nodded to him, but she didn't say anything, and I lifted my arms, holding my hands out to him. He looked away from me as he locked the cuffs on. "That didn't hurt, did it?"

"No." I shook my head and then held my hands up in front of her eyes. "Look at this," I said. "I'm your son. I'm your criminal son. Look at these...you may not have the chance again. How do you like it?"

"Oh, David! How can you?"

I smiled. Somehow it was all right. "I don't know how I can, but I can. I guess cruelty runs in the family. But don't worry, it's all right now. It's finished. It's really finished. Just one thing. I want you to know just one thing. I hate you. I am absolutely and perfectly sane. You're my mother. He's my stepfather, he's the Chief of Police, and he's...you're a policeman, aren't you? ...and he's a policeman. My name is David Mitchell and I'm handcuffed and I'm being taken back to the nut house. I want you to remember this moment as long as you live. I want you to remember when you wake up at night and you're cold that your son hates you and will always hate you. I want this moment to be burned into your memory forever. I want you to know that now they'll have to keep me in the hospital forever, because if I do get out... *and I will*...the first thing I will do is kill you. I'll get so well that I'll pass any board of doctors, and then I'll kill you. And I'll kill you with these two hands. In fact, I'll kill all of you. Unless...yes, unless there is one person in this room who has the guts, the nerve, the honesty, the courage, the belief, the faith...that's it...the faith in another human being, to let me out of these now. Is there any one here who believes in God? Who believes in himself? If there's anyone in this room who can look into himself and feel right about this, then take me away. But if you don't believe this...if you don't believe what you're doing now... if you have any faith at all, let me go. Let me go!"

No one looked at me.

"Okay, Chief, let's go. I don't need to know anything more."

"David..."

"Shut up. Don't ever try to see me again...ever. And remember, the day will come when these hands will take that throat..."

"David Mitchell! Don't you threaten me! If you do, maybe you won't get out!"

I laughed. "Oh but I will. You see, nothing could possibly stop me now. Now I have a real reason to get out. Something to live for! I have to get out now because I have something to do when I get out. Don't worry, I'll get out without any help from you or from anyone. And when I do, God help you!"

❧

The Chief got in the back of the car with me, and put his hand on my shoulder.

"I'm terribly sorry, son," he said. "I couldn't help it. I couldn't do anything else. Please don't be angry with me. I have a son of my own... just a little younger than you...I..."

"Oh Christ, take your hands off me! Don't call me son!"

NINE

CATACOMBS? NO, MONT-SAINT-MICHEL, THE VAULTED ceiling. Slowly, slowly, beautifully the camels as to music marched between the rows of kneeling, black-gowned people. The naked men were strapped to the camels' backs, arched over the humps, ropes around their legs and chests, lying back with their mouths open, unconscious. From time to time one of the women in the crowd would look up at a figure on a passing camel, the tears flooding from her eyes. The entire crowd was weeping, it was a mourning procession. Camels in Mont-Saint-Michel? And what and who were these stripped and strapped men?

The ceiling turned slowly to water, held above the corridor itself by some mysterious force. It was no longer vaulted, but yellow. If only the water would fall! There was a glow above me, the light of the moon through heavy fog, and I wrenched upwards towards it but was held back by the sudden horizontal pain across my chest. The ceiling wavered and wavered, the fog began to lift. Water, water, water! My throat was shriveling, my eyes were drying up in their sockets. My hands tore at my chest.

It was a restraining sheet! What was I doing in the hall? In the hall outside the wardroom? There would be a drinking fountain here if I could only get out of this bed! I pulled my body up and up, forcing it against the iron bars at the head of the bed, my feet wriggling out of their bonds. Free, I leaped and fell in one movement to the floor and the room began to spin again. I had to get to the water, but I could not see anything here, nothing at all. I got to my knees and pulled myself up on the bed until I stood beside it. Where would the water be? I felt along the wall, staring and staring. What had happened to my eyes?

Feeling along the wall, my right hand plunged into space. A hole in the wall? A doorway? My fingers touched metal. The drinking fountain. I pulled myself over to it, hanging onto the fountain, and my head fell on it, my cheekbone banging against the metal mouthpiece. I found the spigot and the water hit my face, my eyes, oh God my eyes! And then my mouth. Like fire at first and then cooling into my throat. I drank and drank and drank. "Hey! He's not supposed to be drinking! How did he get out of bed?"

Hands, arms, bodies. It was awful, I couldn't see anything. I bit the metal and my teeth squeaked away from it as the hands pulled me back.

"You're not supposed to drink after insulin!"

"Where am I?"

"Ward 6."

"Ward 6? That's not my ward. What's happened to my eyes?"

"Come on, come on. Lie down."

"Can't I have some more water? Please, please. I'm so thirsty."

"Back to bed."

"All right."

"Hell, don't tie him up, it's almost breakfast time anyway."

"Think he can get up?"

"Yeah, it's okay for breakfast."

Silence. If they'd go away I'd get the water again.

"Keep him away from that water fountain."

"Damn you. Damn you."

"All right, kid, shove it. No water, see?"

Silence.

People, people, people: around the bed, in the hall; but I can only feel them passing by, wandering around. I can't see them at all.

"Okay, Mitchell. You better get up now."

"I can't see anything."

"I'll help you. I've got your clothes here."

"Thanks."

I felt for the shirt and then the trousers and struggled into them.

"Wanna go to the latrine?"

"God, I want a drink."

"Wait until breakfast. Only a few minutes. You weren't supposed to have any water."

"Why not?"

"Search me."

Was he an attendant or what? I couldn't see him.

I felt in the pocket of my blues. They were there: my glasses. I put them on, and peered around me. Still I couldn't see anything. Something that looked like an opening, figures passing through the hall, somebody moving the bed in which I had been.

"Chow!"

"Can I wash my face?"

"Hurry up. I'll help you."

Hand on my arm, sink against my stomach. I cupped my hands and filled them with water, rinsing and drinking simultaneously.

"Okay, come on. That's enough."

Back into the hall.

"Can you get to the mess hall all right?"

"No. I can't go downstairs. I can't see well enough."

"It isn't downstairs. Right down the hall. There."

"I'll take him down, Joe. I know the guy. He was in the pack room with me."

"Okay, take him down."

"Come on, Mitch."

"Who are you?"

"You wouldn't know me. Just another patient. Another locked-up bastard, that's all."

"What's your name?"

"Walt. Just call me Walt. What have they been doing to you?"

"I don't know. I can't see anything at all. They gave me a shot last night. Something."

"Insulin shock, I'll bet."

"Yeah. Somebody said insulin this morning."

"I thought you were home on pass."

"How do you know so much?"

"We know everything up here. We look out of the windows all day long. We see everybody coming in, going out."

"What is this ward? Ward 6?"

"Yeah. The suicide ward. We're all in good shape up here. No psychotics, no maniacs. Kinda calm and nice. You'll like us. We all want to kill ourselves."

"You do? Why?"

"I don't know. It's our illness. Nice mild nuts bent on self-destruction."

"Do you want to kill yourself?"

"Not specially. Just sometimes."

"What am I doing here?"

"Don't know. Here...here we are. Come on, sit down. Can you see any better?"

"No."

He put my hands on the back of a chair.

"There. Sit down. I'll help you with your food."

I sat down and he put a spoon in my hand. "See the bowl?" He put my fingers on the edge of a plastic bowl.

"What's this stuff?"

"Cereal."

As I ate I began to see a little better. I could make out the form of the bowl in front of me on the white tablecloth. It was removed suddenly and replaced by a plate. A round object...a cup? ...was put next to the plate.

"Getting along all right?"

"Yes. Thanks. How did you know me?"

"We all know you. I think the whole hospital knows you, after the pack room. You're a character around here. We're glad you're back. Are you gonna raise some more hell for us?"

"My God, was it that bad?"

"Bad, my foot! You got 'em all worried. I hope you keep it up. How come you didn't stay home? Didn't they give you a week? It's always a week the first visit."

The pain began to form then, hard and bright inside me. I remembered the house, my mother, John, the policemen, the handcuffs, the car. And then back here. The little room, the office, and the colored nurse. Coming at me with the needle. "What are you going to do?" "I'm sorry," she had said, and then looked at the policeman standing next to me. Was it then that she had, unaccountably, begun to cry? She had, although I couldn't understand why, and when I looked at the policeman there were tears in his eyes, too. Only after she had given me the shot did he take off the handcuffs and then she had led me into another office and everything had begun to spin and whirl. That was when my eyes had gone bad. I had stood there in front of the desk and the man behind it, the man in white, sitting there looking at me had begun to melt and dissolve, like a piece of sugar in water.

I took a drink from the cup and stared, squinting at it through my glasses. It took a more definite form. Maybe I would get my eyesight back. What had happened?

I knew then that I didn't want to remember, but it was like the other times when I tried to hold it in my chest and it wouldn't stay in. Like a beam of light now it began to spread and spread until I could feel it in the back of my neck at the base of my skull, the flood of knowing coming over me. What had I done? I'd really alienated my family now!

The sweat began to leap out from my pores, all over my body at once. "I'll kill you, I'll kill you!" That's what I'd said. I'd told her never to come back, never to come to see me again. Well, that was that. But why the pain? Words, words, words. They poured down over me, submerging me in an avalanche of silent sound. "Won't somebody believe me? Won't somebody please believe me? You have to believe me." That was it. That was the whole thing. I had to have somebody believe me.

I swallowed hard. Nobody did. That was what had happened. Nobody believed me at all.

"Hey, Mitch. Come on. Let's go back on the ward." I felt his hand on my arm. "What is it, kid? What's the matter?"

I tried to laugh, but I couldn't. I stood up and felt his arm around my shoulder. "Hey...you can't do that! What the hell is it? What did they do to you?"

I couldn't stop them...the tears came faster and faster now, pouring in little channels down my cheeks.

"Aw gee, kid. Stop. Don't do that. Come on with me, I'll take you back to the ward. What is it? Tell me about it."

I shook my head and he led me out of the mess hall into the ward. "It isn't fair," I said. "It isn't fair!"

"Jesus, kid. Stop it. Don't go on like that. Nothing's that bad. You're in good shape. You were going great. What happened while you were home? What did they do to you?"

I shook my head again. "I'll be all right in a minute. I'll be all right. Thanks."

"Here, sit down here. How're your eyes now?"

"They're better, thanks."

"Want a cigarette?"

"Yes, please."

"Wait here, I'll get a light. I'll be right back."

"Here." He put a cigarette in my mouth. "Now come on, buck up. You're okay. You'll be okay. Just take it easy, calm down. That's better."

My eyesight came back fast. When the ward door opened and the group of people whirled in, I recognized the doctor right away. Dr. Bowles, Dr. Palmer, another man I'd never seen before, and then a bunch of attendants and Mr. Mitchell and a nurse. I didn't get up to see them, I didn't make any move beyond watching them whisk their way around the room. And then the whole group came to an abrupt halt in front of me. The man who called himself Walt was still sitting beside me. We both looked at the group and Walt said:

"Good morning, Doc."

"Good morning, my boy. How are you?"

"I'm okay." He looked at me and then back at the doctor. "What have you bastards been doing to this guy?"

The doctor looked at me.

"Good morning," I said.

"Well, David." He sat down on the bench next to me. On the other side I could feel Walt's hand on mine, he pressed my hand hard and then let go of it.

"Well, David," the doctor said again. "I'm certainly disappointed in you."

"You are? Why?"

"I didn't expect to see you back here. I certainly never expected that. Don't you remember our conversation? Why, I thought you were practically ready to go home...and then to come back like that. I *am* disappointed!"

The man I didn't know leaned over us. "What happened?" he asked.

I looked at him and Dr. Bowles said: "Oh, David, I don't think you know Dr. Russell, do you?"

I shook my head. "No, I don't. Hello."

"Hello, David," he said. "What happened?"

I shrugged my shoulders. How could I possibly tell him? "I had an argument with my family."

"What about?"

"I don't know how to explain it…about a lot of things. Mostly about getting out, and then about compensation. I wanted somebody to…" "Somebody to believe in me" was what I wanted to say, but I couldn't speak the words out loud.

"To what, David?"

I shrugged my shoulders again and then looked at Dr. Bowles.

"This is the suicide ward, isn't it? What am I doing here?"

He didn't answer at once, but looked at Dr. Russell and then back at me. "I don't think you'll have to stay here. The doctor on duty last night was a little worried when you came in. He thought it was best to put you up here. Would you like to go back to your own ward?"

I nodded. "I guess so. At least I'm not going to commit suicide. I don't want to. I don't think I should be here."

"Good. Then I'll have you transferred back today. Now, tell me, how do you feel?"

I didn't know what it was, maybe it was the word "feel" but I could feel the tears coming to my eyes again. "I feel…" and then my voice broke. "I feel all right."

"Let me take him back, Doctor. I'd like to talk to him for a minute." It was Dr. Russell.

"Would you? Fine." And then to me: "Dr. Russell will take you down, David. I'll see you later."

Off they went.

"Ready to go now, David?"

"Yes, I guess so."

"Hey, Mitch!"

"Yeah?" It was Walt.

"Good luck, kid. Keep your chin up!" He shook my hand.

"Gosh, thanks. Thanks for everything!"

"See you in church!"

We walked down the hall, Dr. Russell holding my arm in his hand.

"You don't mind walking down one flight, do you?"

"No." Why was everyone being so nice to me all of a sudden?

"Now, will you come in here for a minute? I want to talk to you."

"All right."

"Cigarette?"

"Please."

"Now, do you want to talk about what happened at home?"

He held the match out to me and I inhaled deeply on the cigarette, tasting the sulphur from the match.

"I don't know where to begin."

"Anywhere. It doesn't matter. Was it all right at first?"

I shook my head. "Not really. I had the feeling that I was being watched all the time. You know, as if they expected me to do something violent...as if they were afraid of me."

He nodded. "Yes, I know."

"And then...the time was going by, and my mother had promised that we would talk things over when I was home. The argument was about getting me out of the hospital."

"What did they say?"

"Well it finally came out that they could sign me out...Look, Doctor, tell me: can they sign me out? Could they right now, if they wanted to?"

He nodded. "Yes, they..." he hesitated. "They *could*."

"What do you mean?"

"Well, David, tell me something. Would it be the best thing for you if they did? Do *you* think you'd be better off at home?"

"Not now, I guess. I guess that's all washed up."

"Well, I don't know. Tell me a little more about it. As I said, they *could* sign you out, but apparently they didn't want to. Was that it? Did you have an argument because they didn't want to sign you out now?"

"Mostly."

"What else?"

"Well there was quite a lot of talk about compensation, too."

"What about it?"

I smoked hard. "My mother said she wouldn't sign me out until we knew about the claim. Whether I was going to get any money or not."

He shook his head. "The old familiar line..." he said softly. "Yes, that often happens. In a way it's reasonable enough, you know."

"Yes, I guess it is, but it's all wrong somehow. It's like keeping a person locked up...it *is* keeping a person locked up for the money that might be in it."

"Well, not quite. After all, it would be *your* money, not theirs."

"Yes."

"Was there anything else?"

"I don't think so. Except that I..." I took a deep breath. "...I threatened to kill my mother if I ever got out of here."

He laughed then. "That's not unheard of, David. How do you feel about it now?"

I shrugged my shoulders. "I guess I'll just take that much longer getting out now."

"And do you still want to kill her this morning?"

Did I? "I don't honestly know. I don't want to see her. I still think I was right and she was wrong. The thing is...I needed, I wanted..."

"What, David?"

Could I tell him? "Dr. Russell, I don't know if you can understand this, but..."

He waited, lighting another cigarette.

"You see, I know I was pretty sick. I admit that. And I don't know why. Maybe I'm wrong, but it seems to me that for this kind of sickness, when you begin to get well, you're worried, you're anxious, you're nervous...It's as if you'd lost something, lost yourself in a way."

He nodded. "Go on."

"Well, I don't know if a doctor can do a lot for you. I don't know what a hospital can do for you. But if somebody believes in you, really believes that you're getting well, if someone loves you enough to have real faith in you, then I think it can make all the difference. I tried to explain that to them. If they could only believe me, if they'd shown me that they really believed in me, I wouldn't have minded coming back for a while. But to come back, knowing that they didn't. That was what was so terrible about it. I couldn't stand that...even when I..." Oh Christ, was I going to start crying again? "I'm sorry, I can't help it. But it's unfair! It's so rotten of them somehow."

"All right, David, try and relax. It's a terrible situation and a very difficult one. Let's see if there's anything we can think of...anything we can do here to help out. Do you think you want to see them again?"

"Who? My mother you mean?"

"Yes."

"I don't know now. I told them I never wanted to see them again. I told them I'd kill them."

"I wouldn't worry too much about that. They may not have taken that so seriously. The thing that concerns me is what to do next. You don't have a very good opinion of the hospital, do you?"

I blushed. "It's not that. But to have to stay on the ward all day long...I know I'm nuts, too...but some of those men, some of the attendants..."

"Yes, I think I understand. But, since you do have to be in the hospital for a while anyway, perhaps we can do something about it. You remember Mr. Newton, don't you?"

"Yes, I was supposed to work for him as a typist but then nothing happened."

"I know. That was because you were scheduled to go home so soon, we didn't start you on anything then. But it's different now. He's asked about you, and you could start to work for him right away. Today if you want. If you feel all right. How do you feel?"

"My eyes are better now, but I feel kind of sick at my stomach."

"Too sick to work?"

"I don't think so."

"Good. Then I'll see him and perhaps you can start today."

"All right."

"And one other thing. Have you done any occupational therapy? I think not."

"I don't know. I don't think so. What is it?"

"Oh, shop work. I can put you down for the morning schedule for O.T. and at least three afternoons a week you'd be working for Mr. Sweetwater in typing. That would get you off the ward a bit. Would you like that?"

"Sure I would."

"Good, then I'll arrange it. Now if there's nothing else you want to talk about, I think Dr. Bowles wants to see you."

"He does? Well, first, will you tell me one more thing?"

"Certainly, what is it?"

"Who are you? I mean, are you my doctor now?"

"Not exactly. I'm Dr. Russell, as you know, and I'm the ward surgeon—that's what we're called—I'm a psychiatrist, actually. I've been on my vacation and I'll be in charge for the next two weeks while Dr. Bowles goes on his vacation."

"How do you know so much about me?"

"I'm interested in your case. I read your file and the doctors talked to me about you."

"Well why is everyone so nice all of a sudden? What happened?"

He smiled. "I didn't know we were so bad. We *try* to be nice all the time. Maybe we're not always successful, but we do try."

"You succeed."

"I'm glad to hear that, David," he said. "Shall we see if Dr. Bowles can see us now?"

"All right."

Dr. Bowles was sitting at his desk talking to Mr. Mitchell. He looked up as we came in and then motioned Mr. Mitchell away.

"Come in, come in. Well, have you and Dr. Russell had your little talk? What do you think of this boy, Russ?"

Dr. Russell nodded and smiled. "All right," he said.

"Sit down, David, sit down. Now..." he looked at me fixedly. "As I told you, I'm really disappointed in you. I had expected a lot from you, but I guess I was too hasty. But that's neither here nor there is it? Not now. Ha ha!"

There was a long pause, and he looked away from me.

"Did Dr. Russell tell you that I was going to be away for a while?"

"Yes, he did."

"Good. Good. You see, David, we doctors have to get a little rest, just like everyone else. But it's a little different. We can't afford to lose touch entirely. *Now*...I'm very much interested in your case, as you know."

"You are?"

He looked surprised. "Well, of course I am...sending you home so soon and everything. Anyway, Dr. Russell is going to be in charge here for the next couple of weeks and I wanted to talk to you before I left. I want you to co-operate with him in every way, just as if I were here myself. Just because I'm going to be away for a while doesn't mean that you won't get attention..." He looked at me and smiled..."I believe you have complained about our treatment of you from time to time."

This man irritated me. "You're mistaken, Doctor. Not about the treatment. Just about the lack of it."

"Well now...you realize we're very busy. You must know that we don't forget about our patients...but we are very busy."

I wished he'd get it over with. "Yes," I said. "I do realize that. You must need a rest."

"Now, David. Now, now, don't be sarcastic. You work with us and we'll work with you. *Now* about this trouble with your family. That's what I wanted to see you about. I've talked to your mother and I've had permission from her to start you on a different kind of treatment, but it won't begin until I've left so I wanted you to know that I knew about it."

"What is it?"

"Well, we've decided to give you a course of electric shock treatments. I think they will prove very beneficial."

Shock treatment? Wasn't that what they'd done to me in the pack room?

"What do you mean, you've decided to give me shock treatments? I already had one in the pack room."

He shook his head. "No you didn't, David."

"Well then, what was that?"

He sighed. "David, you must have confidence in us. We give whatever treatment is necessary and that is all. Now these shock treatments..."

"What are they?" I looked at Bowles and then up at Russell. He was frowning.

"Well, I can't explain all that now. Dr. Russell will talk to you before the first treatment." He glanced at Russell standing next to me. "Make a note of that, Russ, will you?"

"After you've had a partial series, we'll give you an examination and see how you're getting along. I'm a firm believer in shock therapy, very modern, right up-to-date, and very effective in almost all cases. We've had a great deal of success here with it."

Dr. Russell's voice: "When did you want him to start, Doctor?"

"I'd planned for tomorrow morning." His voice sounded unfriendly. "Any objections?"

"Well..." Dr. Russell's voice wavered. "I'm planning to start him on O.T. and with Sweetwater in the afternoons. Newton was talking to me about him."

Dr. Bowles frowned at him and then at me. "Well perhaps that will be all right, too. If he has the late session in O.T. and the first period in shock, there's no reason why it shouldn't work out. Pretty heavy schedule though, don't you think, Russ?"

"No. Not for him."

Dr. Bowles laughed. "Hmmmm. Well, you're in charge. You're the doctor until I get back, ha, ha!"

"Is that all you wanted to tell me, Doctor?"

"Yes, I think so."

"May I ask you something?"

"Certainly, my boy, certainly."

"I want my shoes."

"We'll think about that. We'll think about it."

"Where is the typing place?"

"Over in one of the other buildings, why?"

"That's why I want my shoes. If I'm going to be going outside, I want shoes."

"We'll see."

"When, when you get back?"

"Well..."

Dr. Russell cut in on him: "There isn't any reason why he shouldn't have his shoes, is there, Dr. Bowles?"

"Now, Russ, I know a lot about this case, I..."

"Doctor...Shall I take David back to the ward? We can talk about his shoes later."

"All right."

"Look, Dr. Bowles," I said, not getting up. "What's the trouble? A lot of men have their shoes. It's perfectly reasonable that I should have them, if I'm going to be going off the ward. Why shouldn't I have them?"

He shook his finger in my face. "David, I can see why you got yourself in trouble at home. You like to argue. Now we doctors know much more about these things than you do. When I think you should have your shoes, I'll see that you get them...I..."

"But you aren't going to be here to think about my shoes. I do not like to argue, but I get awfully tired of lame excuses. If I can't have my shoes, then say so. If I can, what's all the talk about? It's just a question of yes or no. You must know now how you feel about it. I don't want to argue, I just want you to make up your mind, or is that asking too much?"

I felt a restraining hand on my shoulder. Dr. Russell.

"Come on, David, let's go back to the ward."

I stood up. "All right, but I'd certainly like to know about my shoes first!"

"Now, David," Dr. Bowles's finger was pointing at me again. "We've made a good many exceptions in your case. We sent you home early, we gave you your glasses...I don't think you should expect everything to happen so quickly and just the way you want it. After all we know what we're doing."

"Look, Dr. Bowles. I would *love* to believe that, but when you hem and haw about a perfectly simple question, then I think you don't know what you're doing. You said you were taking a chance on me when you sent me home...well, obviously, you didn't know what you were doing if you were taking a chance. But what kind of chance are you taking about my shoes? And what kind of a chance were you taking about my glasses? If you do know what you're doing, just say yes or no and that will be that!"

"Come on, David. Let's go back to the ward."

"Oh all right. And you," I pointed at Dr. Bowles, "I hope you have a good vacation. When you make up your mind about giving me my shoes...if you do...send me a postcard. I'll be here."

"David...I..." He stopped, his mouth open, and then smiled abruptly. "Thanks. I will have a good vacation. I'll try not to think about you too much." He laughed then, and for the first time I liked him.

"Okay," I said, "but I hope I haunt your dreams. I'll bet that's one way out of here."

"All right, all right. Run along now."

As we went out of the room, the secretary sitting at the typewriter desk gave me a great big smile. I felt pretty good. In the hall Dr. Russell shook his head and then laughed loudly.

"What are you laughing at?"

"Nothing, David. Nothing. Well...you certainly don't let go, do you?"

"Should I?"

He laughed again. "Not for my money." Then his voice dropped. "I'll get your shoes for you all right, I think. And I'll see you tomorrow."

"Okay. Thanks, Doctor."

"Not at all."

TEN

WHEN THEY LET ME BACK onto the ward, I walked over to the window and looked out. This was the first gray day since I had been in the hospital. I had felt better when I had been talking to the doctors, but now the pain inside my chest, the memory of my visit home, the argument with my mother, settled and spread. It was not a day for sunlight...even the sun had deserted me now.

I felt a hand on my shoulder, and turned around. Six or seven patients stood in a group around me. The hand belonged to Dave Everett.

"Hi there, Mitch. How come you're back so soon?"

"Hello, David!" It was Joseph, who had said the doctors never talked to him anymore.

"David Mitchell!" That was Joe College. Harvard.

"Mitchell. Well." The man with the open mouth and the pillow. My lip began to tremble. And then more tears. It was a homecoming of a kind, they were glad to see me, and in a curious way, I was glad to see them, too. I resisted it...I didn't want to be glad to be here...

"Did you get any while you were gone?" The silent boy who had played ball with me.

"What?"

"Nookie. Did you grab yourself a piece while you were out?"

"No."

Tone of amazement. "What the hell else would anybody go out for? Jesus Christ! What are you, a nance?"

"Oh, I got screwed all right," I said, "but not the way you mean!"

"What happened, boy?" It was Dave.

"Golly, Dave, don't ask me now. I've been talking to the doctor. I guess I really screwed things up for sure. He says not, but it looks that way to me."

"Trouble with your family?"

"Yeah."

"Come on, let's go over and sit down. Wanna talk about it?"

I shook my head.

"Okay. Let me know when you do."

He walked away, smiling.

The Harvard man was staring at me. "Don't tell me your visit home was not a success," he said.

"All right," I said angrily. "I won't tell you."

"No point in getting offended, old boy. After all, I only asked. I'm sorry if it didn't work out."

"Oh forget it. I'm sorry. It sure didn't work out."

"And didn't you have any of the other consolations? Didn't you deprive any maiden of her maidenhead? Or are there no maidens left in the outer world?"

"Oh for God's sake!"

"But seriously, my boy. Don't you have a girl? Some lovely girl waiting for her mad love?"

"For God's sake, shut up!" Why did it sound so really filthy from him?

I walked away from them over to where Dave was sitting and sat down next to him. He didn't say anything to me, only smiled. When Harvard had spoken to me, I'd thought suddenly, and for the first time in a long time, for the first time since I'd come here, of Sarah. It was funny that I hadn't thought of her before...what was it? Had I repressed her, was that it? I hadn't thought of or even wanted a woman since I'd been here…at least not until now. And now all of a sudden, the pain was gone and replaced by something as urgent, as painful and demanding. I wanted her. I wanted any woman. In spite of the mounting desire inside me, the ache of it in the pit of my stomach, I was angry. Did sex have to be dirty always? Why was it that this terrible hunger was something we all repudiated and vilified? Vile words (and we all used them, I used them) and suggestive, ugly connotations. The desire, as I thought, underwent a sudden and complete transformation inside me. How could anything that was so essentially wonderful… beautiful really, if we weren't afraid to admit it, be so universally and completely dragged in filth all the time? I thought of Sarah again, of the last time I had slept with her…not so long before…not so long. And what had there been in us that had to be reduced…ever…to four-letter words? Why, incidentally, did they call it a "piece"? I'd be dammed if I knew. And there it was…I'd thought of it myself that time. I was just as bad as the rest of them. I wondered why it was so shameful… something to be laughed at? If people could be honest about that, a lot of things might be very different.

"Whatcha thinkin' about, Mitch?"

"Dave, I…" I felt my face redden. "I was thinking about a girl."

"Yeah, I know. It's tough."

"Oh not just *that*. It isn't only that, Dave. You know."

He smiled sadly. "I know how you feel, boy. Sometimes it isn't that piece you have to have…it's something else. I know what you mean. Did you see your girl? Do you have a girl?"

I shook my head. "In a way I have, but since the war…Besides I don't think she'd want to see me after this. I don't know. Anyway, I haven't seen her for a long time."

He laughed. "You know the chaplain's been asking after you."

"He has? What did he want?"

"He was cagey at first and then finally he came out with it. Didn't know your name. Just wanted to know about the guy who thought he was Jesus Christ. Asked me a lot of questions."

"He did? What were they?"

"Oh...about did you think you really were Jesus Christ and stuff like that. I told him I didn't know. Do you?"

"No." I shook my head. "That was just part of the business, I guess. I sure thought so at the time."

"For all of me, you could be!"

"*What?*"

"Why not? Whatever kind of religion you have, Jesus Christ wasn't much more than a good Joe. Maybe a little holy...more than most of us, but when you read all that Bible crap as if it was a book, he wasn't anything fancy. Just a hell of a good guy. Kind of a real man, I think, until those writers got hold of him. Yes sir, if Jesus Christ is going to come back, there's no reason why you couldn't be him. Better than a lot of people I know. Besides, where else would they put him? Right in a nut house. Only safe place. Guy going around preaching about love your enemies and stuff like that. Sure as hell he'd go into a nut factory, or else a hoosegow."

"I guess he would at that!"

"Sure thing. Besides, coming back to you. How about your eyes? Remember how you used to stare at everybody? You had something there. You really got them down. You burned people up as if you had fire in your eyes. The first time you said you were Jesus Christ, you really looked like him, I can tell you."

"Were you here?"

"Sure, I was here."

"But you never said anything to me for a long time."

"Brother, I should say not! You looked too convincing for me. I wasn't going to fool around with you if you were Jesus Christ. I believe in that man...and if he's gonna come back I'm not fooling around with him till I know who he is. And I still don't know. I'm not saying

I think you are Jesus Christ, but dammit, I'm not denying the possibility. The Lord moves in strange ways. Chaplain said so himself. You almost convinced him, telling him he wouldn't know a revelation if he saw one."

"Did he tell you that?"

"Sure he did. Damn good line, too. If I'd thought of that, maybe I could have been Jesus Christ myself. When he told me that I almost believed it all over again."

"You mean you did believe it at first?"

"Well, pretty much. Besides, you made a hell of a lot of sense."

"You don't believe it now, do you?"

"I don't think so. I don't know."

We both laughed. "We could sure do something with that," he said.

That afternoon they brought me my shoes and escorted me out of the building to a small building in the yard in back of Ward 8. Like a classroom, the room was lined with small tables (Army tables) on which stood typewriters. On the walls were charts of typewriter keyboards. I was introduced to Mr. Sweetwater...almost the first person there who looked at me with only cursory interest, as if I was perhaps just another human being, not a confined specialty to be observed and classified. He took me to a desk and asked me to try out a typewriter. When I had practiced typing for a few minutes, he came back to my desk, looked over my shoulder at what I had written and smiled.

"About how fast do you type?" he asked.

"Around sixty words a minute, I guess. I could do better than eighty at one time, but I haven't had much practice recently."

"Have you ever typed stencils?"

"Yes."

"Would you mind doing some for me?"

"Not at all."

As he went back to his desk, I watched him. Whatever the reasons, I felt immediately easy with this man. Funny name though, Sweetwater. He was smiling to himself as he looked at a paper on his desk and then opened a drawer and took out two blue stencils. Tall and thin, his body was bent over the desk (his carriage, even when he walked was never quite erect, as if he was carrying a heavy load on his shoulders) and the smile never completely disappeared from his face. Under the prominent cheekbones, his flesh made a sudden inward thrust to bulge again at the lips and jaw. There was a faint blue tinge of beard on his lower jaw and neck, and his hair looked as if it had not been combed.

When he came back to my desk, he handed me the stencils, a bottle of correction fluid, and some paper covered with closely spaced typewriting. He leaned over me and scratched his head.

"This thing should really be edited before it's typed," he said. He was like no one I had seen in the hospital, impersonal, disinterested, gentle. As he stood beside me, I thought of various people that I had worked for and how I would have welcomed a boss like this man. I wondered if there was another trick of some kind involved in this. Could it be that he didn't know he was dealing with a bunch of looneys? I took a quick glance around the room at the other people sitting behind their desks, typing. It looked, except for the blue uniforms, like a class in typing. Whatever it was, it was a great deal better than staying on the ward.

"Do you think you could go over it before you type it and correct the English? I think the idea is clear enough, but it is very poorly expressed."

"I guess so. What is it, actually?"

He smiled. "As you'll see when you read it, it's supposed to be an article on vocational rehabilitation by one of the patients who fancies himself a writer. The only thing you'll have to watch is that you don't exceed the columns on this page. It's for the weekly hospital newspaper."

"All right. I'll see what I can do with it."

I took a blank sheet of paper, lined up the columns on it roughly and put it into the typewriter. I read the article over...he was right about the English...and then typed a draft of it, correcting as I wrote. It fitted the columns fairly well. When I had finished, I took it over to him and asked him to read it.

"I can respace this paragraph a little," I said, "then I think it will fill out this last column all right. I only need one more line." He read it over and nodded. "That's fine. Fine."

When I had finished typing the stencils, I took them over to him and laid them on his desk.

"Is there anything else you want me to do now?"

He looked at his wrist watch. "I don't think so," he said. "It's almost time for you to go anyway." He looked at me. "Would you come outside for a minute? I'd like to talk to you."

"Sure."

We walked outside together and stopped in front of the building.

"How long have you been here?" he asked me.

I calculated rapidly. "I don't know exactly," I said. "About a month, I guess, including a few days at home."

"You've had quite a bit of experience, haven't you? I mean stencils and so on."

"Yes."

"My problem," he went on, "is to find people who already know something about this kind of work. There aren't many patients available to us who have had any real experience. Most of them are students. Do you think you'd like to work on the hospital newspaper regularly, or would you rather study something? What we need here is someone who can go over the copy and edit it a little and then set it up properly and type the stencils."

"I don't see why not. I think it would probably be good for me to have something like that to do."

"Fine. Then I'll tell you...I guess Dr. Russell told you, or perhaps it was Mr. Newton, that you'd come down here three times a week.

However, if you'd really like to work on this, I could arrange, I think, to have you come down every day. Of course, you wouldn't have to come down on visiting days."

"Why yes, that would be fine." Visiting days? I wondered if I would have any visitors anymore. Something in me began to tighten up.

"Good, then I'll fix it up. I'll try to see Mr. Newton this afternoon. And thank you for what you've done today. It was fine. Now, if you'll wait here a moment, I'll get someone to take you back to the ward."

He went back into the office and left me standing in front of the building. I looked up at the brick walls of the ward building, the barred windows. No sun yet. And out here, mostly bare earth between the small buildings in the walled yard. In a few places stubbly growth of grass, two small trees. I bent down suddenly and put my hand on the earth and then touched a small struggling clump of grass. It felt good to my hand. Strange that here it should mean so much to me, when at home I had accepted it easily, had not felt the grass with my hands. Funny that I hadn't thanked God for being able to touch it, after all those days of being cooped up. I hoped I would remember when I finally got out of here never to take the grass for granted again.

Shower night that night. After supper, we lined up in groups of six, standing by the wardroom door, waiting for our turn. As I waited in a group—Dave, Harvard, a young blond boy, the boy called Henry, another man I didn't know, and myself—I thought about the day and looked happily down at my shoes. Two people today I liked. Dr. Russell and Mr. Sweetwater. Maybe my luck had changed after all. The thought of my mother...home, lurked inside me somewhere, but I held it back successfully, not feeling anything. I was afraid of a moment that was bound to come, the moment when the fact of my confinement, without possibility of any outside help now, would bear in on me again. I could think of it now, but I didn't feel it, as if I were a spectator at the movie reel of my own mind, at a preview of what was to come. Along with the lurking, not-quite-present feeling was a premonition of something...something to be feared.

We filed into the shower room from the hall and undressed, throwing our dirty clothes into a large bin. As we took our clothes off, I felt a familiar process beginning, the not-so-faint, suppressed sexual interest that all men seem to have in other men. Like when you took a shower in school or in the Army, and yet it was not quite the same. Here there was more detachment, the glances were less repressed, more overt and in a sense less involving. It was not so much the feeling of being looked at as a person, but as a thing, an object without any specific individual identity, without humanity. Dave was standing next to me and I looked at his body: big and brown and shining...as if covered with a very faint film of oil. His muscles moved easily under their casing, he was beautifully built.

We were the first two in the showers and the others waited for us. In an unspoken agreement, he began suddenly and automatically to wash my back and when he had finished, I washed his, liking the feel of the smooth skin under my hands. I had never really touched the brown skin of a colored man before...it was exciting in a way. I wondered if it was anything more than that...I didn't think so. Just nice to look at and feel.

He looked at me and jerked his eyes towards the young blond boy standing near us waiting to get in the shower. "Watch that," he said in a low voice.

I looked at the boy and then back at Dave, puzzled. He jerked his head in the direction of the young boy again, and I looked at him. He was watching both of us intently as we stood rinsing our bodies, the shower beating down on us. There was a kind of hunger in his eyes and right along with it you could sense, and even see, the battle going on inside him. I looked away and stepped out of the shower. Did he do it on purpose? Just as I stepped out, he stepped forward, brushing my body with his own as he plunged himself into the warm current.

We dressed silently and walked back into the wardroom, to sit down on an empty bench.

"Why did you want me to watch him?" I asked.

"You may not know it," he said, "but you were seeing the beginning of something. I've seen it lots of times here. It's like being witness to a birth."

"What do you mean?"

"Didn't you see the look in his eyes, the way he was staring at us?"

"Yes, of course I did."

"Sex," he said. "Pure sex, plain and simple. That's what happens to them after a while in here. A man doesn't stop wanting sex just because he's locked up...anybody knows that...but that's not the bad part of it. The bad part is when you see it happening to a kid like that. A perfectly normal guy."

"You mean you think he's going to end up homo?"

"I don't know...yet. Probably though. Kids like that take it hard. They don't know how to fight it. With some of these other guys, it doesn't matter what they do. They run it off at night, or if they get a chance, they'll go after one of the other patients, but that's not the same thing...it's just gratification with them. Nothing more. But with him it's the works. He didn't want just any old thing, you could see that in his eyes. He wanted one of us, you or me, personally and specifically. It was happening to him inside. You could see it."

"Yeah, I guess you're right." I shook my head and then stared at him. "How come you know so much about all this? How long have you been here? What *are* you, anyway? I mean when you're not in here."

He laughed. "You won't believe it, Mitch. You won't believe it. I was going to be an attendant in one of these joints. I was in one of the other V.A. hospitals taking training when I cracked up."

"What happened?"

"I couldn't take it. It was a hell of a place. It was before the clean-up that Bradley did on these places. You should have seen them then. Boy, the attendants were really bastards. I couldn't take it. I began to dream about it at night and then pretty soon I'd had it. I was in the pack room here for almost three months...off and on."

"My God! How did you survive?"

He smiled and shrugged his shoulders. "We have a lot of means to survive." I knew he meant the colored people. "It's like having nine lives when we come into a place like this. Not so different from life on the outside, actually. Almost as if we'd done it all before. You can get used to anything. Sometimes I think it's just fated that way. Us Negroes have to put up with that...it's destiny for us. Funny thing though the more you get so you can stand it yourself, the harder it is to look at the others: like when I saw you the first time, for instance. Maybe what was happening to you, what you were feeling, was no worse than it had been with me, but you couldn't cover it up the way I can. Your skin is still thin, so that when you're hurt, it's all open and exposed. Like the look in your eyes this morning. I'll never forget it."

"I can't understand how you see so much."

He looked at me and smiled. "Guess you think I talk a lot, but I don't. You're about the only one I ever talk to here. And when you've been in this place for a long time, and you watch and watch, you begin to understand things. You look at these men and you'll see everything one time or another. Everything that can happen to them happens here. And you see the real trouble with these places, too. You see why they aren't successful, why so many guys end up in here for life."

"Why?"

"Understanding. Nobody really understands them, everyone is afraid of them here, so they never see them as people, just ordinary people. The way you'd look at a guy who'd lost his leg or something. The doctors, the attendants, the nurses, the families...They can't project over to us. To them it's an *experience.* That's all. Like if somebody gets knocked down, one of them'll think, 'What the hell is so awful about that?' They never see that maybe for that guy being knocked down is the most terrible thing in the world. Like with you this morning: I've been home, I've been sent back. Hell, I was prepared for it before I even went home. I expected it. It wasn't much of anything for me. But for you...it was all over you, like you'd been given a death blow. I don't know what happened, Mitch, but it hit your guts. Different things hit different people different ways. What you got at home hit you in the center, right in the middle, they got you where you live. That's what happens to all the guys...people don't know where they live, inside, so they're bound to hit it sometime. Especially the bastards that work in these places."

He shook his head thoughtfully. "It's a hell of a thing to say about other men, but look at these attendants for instance. They're men like the rest of us. Nothing wrong with them, and yet after they've been in here for a while, they change. You can see them come in...it's what was happening to me that finally got me. You see a new guy come in and he's all steamed up. He's come to work here because he wants to do something for the nuts, he wants to *help,* and for a while he's a house on fire, can't do enough, and then it happens to him, too. You see him losing his heart or the thing that makes him tick. One day he'll kick a patient and if he goes through that one all right, then he's an attendant good and proper. It's like getting a degree. Guess it's just that too much misery is something you can't take and look at. You get so that you have to beat it up and strike at it. That's what I did. I hit a poor bastard and I liked it. It made me feel good when I'd done it, and then it knocked me for a loop. I couldn't sleep, I couldn't live with myself. I'd hit myself really. I sure did. Here's where I ended up, and I sure found out. You learn to be sadistic after a while, almost like you had to be to stay here. I hate these guys, but I can't always blame them. I know what it's like."

Patients and attendants. Funny how words had strange, new meanings for you when they went over and over in your mind. How apt the word patient. The one sustaining quality of any confined man: infinite patience, patience beyond hell and heaven, patience bigger than martyrdom, something that goes through and beyond it. Martyrdom is something else. You have to want to be a martyr; it's a form of masochism, but patience goes still further. It's not masochistic because it's never personal. Just a terrible final waiting. And odd, then, that the word attendant...it must come from the French...should be applied to these other men. Attendant. Waiting. Waiting and waiting forever and for God knows what.

"David Mitchell!"

I had been almost in a trance and I was brought suddenly out of it by the sound of my name being called.

I stood up. "What is it?"

"Come here!"

It was Mr. Harris, the night charge attendant. "Yes, what is it?"

"Come with me."

He took me out of the ward and into the office. There he handed me a file folder and a pencil.

"Hear you've been working in Typing."

"Yes. Why?"

"You did all right. You're going great. Want to make out a chart for me?"

"Sure...what?"

"We got three more patients in today. Have to add three beds. In the big room in back. Will you make a plan of the room and space the beds out on it, draw them in? Thirty-two instead of twenty-nine. Here's the old one, the way we had them spaced. See how many we have to put against each wall."

I looked at the chart he had given me. Little rectangles to indicate the beds: thirteen on each side and three lengthways in the center of the room.

"That's simple," I said. "Just add one more bed to either side and put an extra one here." I pointed to the chart.

"I know that, but will you draw it and space it out?"

"Okay."

I wondered why he had picked me. Never could tell anything about an attendant.

I sat at the desk, measuring and ruling and drawing in the little rectangles to indicate the beds. Each rectangle had the name of a man in it and I copied them in again, leaving the three new ones blank. Then I waited for Mr. Harris to come back. Funny thing about him, he looked exactly like General...what was his name? The one who had been in charge of the Atomic Bomb project. I couldn't remember. I remembered my radar beam...I had thought it was atomic power at one time. Hell! Just another association, another one of those link-ups that my mind seemed to like to make by itself. Don't pay any attention to it. And yet, why had he picked me? Was he, perhaps, General...whoosis? And there was all that business about the Army in the pack room. I tried to dismiss my thoughts, but you never could tell about the people around here, or why they did things.

When he came back another man came with him. The man who brought the milk around. He was carrying a big wooden box, filled with dozens of small paper cartons of milk.

I handed the chart to Mr. Harris and he glanced at it briefly. "That's fine," he said. "Now, look here."

I watched them as they unloaded the cartons of milk from the box. Then they opened six of them and Mr. Harris undid some capsules and poured some blue powder into each one of the open cartons of milk. He threw the cellophane shells of the capsules into the wastebasket.

"What's that?" I asked.

"Sodium amytal," he said.

"Oh." Why on earth was he showing me this? I began to feel like a spy or his accomplice in something that wasn't quite aboveboard.

"You know...what's his name...you know the guy they call Joe College, don't you?"

"Oh, you mean Harvard?"

He seemed amused. "Is that what you call him?"

"That's what I call him. I don't know what his name is."

"He talks to you a lot, doesn't he?"

"Sometimes. Why?"

He winked at me. "Don't worry, you'll see."

Down the hall again, the three of us this time. They had put all the milk back into the box, with the six cartons they had opened at the very bottom.

When we were on the ward, Mr. Harris shouted "Milk!" and the patients gathered around the table as they handed it out. Harvard was there from the first, but they kept avoiding him, as if he wasn't there at all. Finally when they got to the bottom of the box, they handed one to him; one of the cartons with sodium amytal in it. They had already given me one that was untouched. Or was it? Did it have something in it that someone else had put in? The top didn't look as if it had ever been opened. But why had they shown me what they had done and what did it have to do with Harvard? I looked at him and he looked back at me suspiciously.

He opened the container of milk and smelled it. Then he tasted it tentatively. "Hey, Mitch," he said.

"What is it?"

Mr. Harris and the man who had brought the milk were watching me, but not openly.

"Is your milk all right?"

I opened my container and tasted it. "Sure it is, why?"

"Mine isn't."

"What's the matter with it?" They were still watching us both. I wondered what I was supposed to do.

"It's got something in it."

Mr. Harris looked up at him. "Maybe it's sour. Here's another one."

Harvard shook his head. "Oh, no," he said angrily. "It's not sour. It's got something in it."

"Don't be silly. It's like all the other milk."

What was this all about?

Harvard looked at me again: "Here, you taste it."

"What for? My milk is all right. I don't want yours."

"Taste it. Tell me if it tastes funny to you."

Well, what the hell. I didn't know what I was supposed to do. If they didn't want me to taste it, they'd have to say so. I was angry with them now. I couldn't understand what they were trying to do.

I took it from him and tasted it.

"It does have a funny taste," I said.

He looked triumphantly at Mr. Harris. "See?"

Mr. Harris looked at me. "It's just sour, isn't it David?"

"No. It's got sodium amytal in it. I could taste it."

Mr. Harris looked angrily at me. "Sodium amytal? What do you mean?"

"Oh for God's sake," I said. "What are you trying to do? Of course it has sodium amytal in it. I saw you put it in!"

Harvard looked at Mr. Harris even more triumphantly then. He took the carton and threw it out of the window, between the bars. Mr. Harris looked furiously at me, and the man who had brought in the milk began to laugh. "I told you it wouldn't work, John," he said. They both glared at me then and walked out of the ward, taking the box with them. Harvard came back to stand next to me. "Thanks, David," he said.

"Oh, that's all right," I said. I still wondered why they had let me see them...shown me what they were doing. Was I supposed to have pretended the milk was all right? If so, why hadn't they told me to? At least I could have said yes or no.

"It's a good thing you're an honest man," Harvard said to me.

I shrugged my shoulders. "I'll never understand these guys," I said.

"Ha! I could tell you about them. They want to put me to sleep. That's what sodium amytal is for, to put you to sleep. The doctor says

I'm supposed to take it, but I won't."

He seemed very excited to me.

"Don't you sleep?"

"No, I certainly don't."

"Well then why don't you take it?"

"You dope!" he sneered at me. "And let them get away with murder around here?"

"What do you mean?"

"I know what kind of thing goes on here at night! Don't think I don't keep my eyes open. Sure, they want to put me to sleep, that way I won't be able to see what goes on."

"Don't you ever sleep?"

"Nope. Never."

I shook my head. "You'll end up in the pack room."

"That's what you think! Come here."

He led me over to the window. It was still very light although there was no sun. "See that radio tower? Remember when they started to build it?"

I had forgotten it, but I could see it clearly against the evening sky now. "Yes, what about it?"

"They finished it today."

"So?"

"God you're a dope! Tonight is when they'll start using it. Tonight! You think I'm going to go to sleep with that thing beamed at us?"

Could they really do whatever they wanted around here? Was there something in what he said? I'd heard about experiments in remote control...and I remembered that he had said it was radar.

"What will they do with it?"

"How should I know? That's what I'm going to find out tonight. Put me to sleep! The hell they will."

Dave walked over to us and put his hand on my shoulder. "What's up, boys?"

Harvard gave him a threatening look and then looked at me. He held his finger to his lips. "Shhhhh," he said and walked rapidly away from us.

"What's up, Mitch?"

"Oh, Harvard was trying to tell me something about that radio tower. Says they're going to beam it at us and use it to do something to the patients tonight."

He laughed.

"Something else, Dave." I told him about Mr. Harris and the chart and then about the sodium amytal in the milk.

He laughed again. "Don't worry about that," he said. "They knew Harvard likes you...he never talks to anyone else so they wanted you to say the milk was okay."

"But why didn't they tell me that, then?"

"God knows!"

We continued to look out the window. The flag was still flying and two nurses were walking along the path in front of the main building. When they had disappeared from sight, we saw a man come out of the main building.

"Look at him," I said. "He's in an Army uniform. I wonder what he's doing here?"

"I don't know."

The man walked a short ways up the path and stopped, looking fixedly at our building. It was difficult to see him clearly at this distance, but it was almost as if he were looking directly at me. He made a sudden gesture with his right arm, pointing directly at the flag. Then he did it twice more, dropped his arm and walked on up the path.

"Hey, Dave, did you see that?"

"Yeah. I wonder what goes on?"

We continued to watch him and once more he stopped, stared at our building and repeated the gesture three times. We looked at each other and then back at him. Again the same thing. A few steps up the path, stop, and the same gestures three times. Then he turned and walked rapidly back to the main building and in through the door.

"Well, I'll be damned!" I said.

"Boy, maybe everyone's got it. They don't let the nuts out at this hour of the night!"

"What do you suppose it means, Dave?"

"Damned if I know."

I began to wonder. Mr. Harris who looked like General...Groves, that was it!...and the business about radar and atomic power and what Harvard had said about the radio tower. And then my dream... or was it a dream? ...about being in the Army, being a spy. Was there something to all this? I clenched one of the bars with my right hand. Surely I wasn't going to go back into a delusion of the kind I'd been in, was I? I felt depressed then. The almost-gaiety that I had felt inside me because of Dr. Russell, Mr. Sweetwater, getting my shoes...began to fold and disappear, replaced now more fully by the sensation of something impending and threatening. I looked slowly around the room at the men, seated on the chairs and benches or walking around. Was this really a kind of dream world, was I perhaps only dreaming all this? A feeling of exhaustion began to spread through me. I was so tired of this...all of it. It took so much energy to get through these interminable days, never knowing what was really happening.

For some reason, the idea of death came into my mind. Not a brutal or sudden death, but something quiet and beckoning. The faint memory of pain passed over me like a small cloud. If I could die, this would really be over with, forever. I looked out the window again. The hospital, and beyond it the hospital grounds, and from there spreading out, the roads leading to cities and towns, the masses of buildings where now people were huddling, worrying, loving, living... What did it all mean? What was my own struggle and questioning about anyway? To get out of the hospital, I had said to myself, and yet to get out for what? So that I could go back to huddle with other people who meant nothing to me…to work for things which were of no importance? To do things that I did not want to do? Was it really so different outside? What would I do there that I didn't do here? I would continue in the same way. I would have enemies outside as well as here. I would be as much and as little threatened, loved or hated; would love and hate there, too. What for? And for what reason had I threatened to kill my family? For revenge against them? For having behaved intolerably? For not believing me? But who believed anyone, anywhere? What was all this fantastic, insane struggle about? What was it in people that made them fight and fight and fight against life, against each other?

Not actively, not violently, I began to want to die. Looking out the window at the disappearing light, the cool wind of death brushed past me. Bedtime came and I lay back in my bed, silent and waiting. I wondered how much power I had. Would it be possible just to wish for death, really wish for it with all of myself and make it come true? How wonderful it would be never to wake up again. Death, looked at from one viewpoint, began the moment one was born. We were born to die!

Dick, the attendant, came into the room and stood by my bed. With his hand on the iron bedpost, he looked down at me. "Anything wrong, David?" Funny, he must have had a premonition about me. It was as if he knew what I was thinking.

He raised his hand and pointed out the window. I turned my head in the bed and looked out, following the direction of his arm and hand.

"See those lights over there?" Three green glowing lights. I had seen them before.

"Yes."

He stared and stared at them.

"That's where I'm going to be at eleven o'clock."

"You mean you live there?"

He laughed, but his laughter was not gay. "No." He shook his head. "But there's where I'm going to be. Can you see them?"

"Yes, sure." What was the matter with him?

"Good. Well, I'd better be going. Good night, David."

"Good night, Dick."

He went out and I stared through the open, dark doorway after him, listening to his footsteps going down the hall. Something odd was certainly going on here tonight. Maybe Harvard had been right after all. But it wasn't only tonight. Everything had changed. Dr. Russell...everyone had been nice to me. And then that business with Mr. Harris and the other man. It was too confusing, and besides I had something else to do.

If I thought really hard could I bring it about? I closed my eyes and tried to picture nothing but deep, deep black. Blacker and blacker, so black that it began to penetrate into my body, obliterating it bit by bit. With the spreading blackness, I relaxed, sinking down and down into the bed, into a wonderful softness. I dared not think about the possibility too much, it might not happen, but maybe this way I could die. I was so tired.

ELEVEN

THERE WAS A SMALL SPACE, a widening of the corridor near the central offices, a projection in which there were benches, a few chairs, and a table. Several men in blue were seated on the benches and chairs and in the center of them a lady in gray, seated by the table laden with food and coffee, handing it out to them, one by one.

He sat in the middle of one bench, his head lying back against the bench, his mouth open. Slowly, his eyelids moved, his eyes opened, his head jerked forward. Blinking, blinking, his eyes saw the woman, looking at the cross in red on her little gray cap.

"Would you like an egg?" she said.

He blinked several more times and stared at her.

Finally: "What?"

"Would you like an egg? A cracker? A cup of coffee?"

"Who are you?" His head backed away from the egg. poised in her hand before him.

"Have an egg."

"No." Then again, intently: "Who are you?"

"Mrs. Dawson. I'm a gray lady."

"Gray lady," he said slowly after her.

His head moved from one side to the other, he put his hands in back of his neck, feeling the knot of pressure, like a golf ball in the back of his head. He looked at the men on either side of him, then down at himself. His hand moved warily, touching his leg, he felt the material of the pants between his fingers. He looked at the pattern on the floor...

"What...where...who...?"

"A cup of coffee?" She put it in his hand, held the hand for a moment, then released it. The hand, his hand, balanced the cup of coffee and he stared at it.

"I..."

Silence.

"Are you sure you don't want an egg?"

"I don't know."

"Here, have one. Salt?"

Have an egg. Coffee, cracker...salt...blue material, the floor, pattern on the floor. *I. What was, who am I?*

He drank from the paper cup of coffee. *Paper. Hot.*

"What has happened to...to...*me.* To me?"

"Have a cracker. An egg?"

"Who am I?"

"Don't you know who you are? Don't you know, David?"

Who said that? Man at my...his...right? Look at him. David? Heard that before...that, heard that before. David, david, david, david. He...I...me. Pain, knot tied in my head. Where..."Who are you, please?"

"You know me, David. This is the hospital. You've just come out of shock."

Shock. Shock. Something up above him. Something below me. I, you...you belong to me. Lower, lower, lower, in and in, inside him. I, we. *They.* Belong to...him?

Breathing hard, I was breathing hard. Hands, arms, legs, stomach. Touch my head. Hands on face. I...*David Mitchell.* Hospital? Hospital? Shock? *Shock!!*

Egg. Spit it out. No. Somewhere else that. Rolling around on a plate...spinning. They didn't do anything to me. What's that? Man in white walking behind the bench. Look...he smiles. You smile. Who?

"Hello, David."

Me? That's right. *David.* "Hello?"

"How do you feel?"

I looked at my hand. I...feel...with...touch the material again. Thing in my head at the back. Hand on my chest. How do I feel? "I feel all right."

"Good."

Who? Doctor, doctor, doctor? Right this way, David. No, in here. Right there. But the thing in the middle, my back, I...? That's all right. Now here...gauze, wood...open your mouth. Swish, swish on my head. Salt. Have an egg, salt? No, not that. On my head. *Here!* And then? Then nothing, nothing. Before? More before?

We are going to give you...Dr. Russell. I'm the doctor, I've got what you need. Let go...No, not that, that wasn't it.

"David?"

"Yes?"

"Are you all right? Do you want an egg?"

You, too? Doctor...Palmer? No, Doctor...Russell? *Russell.*

"Dr. Russell?"

"Yes, David."

"But you...I...I can't, I...I can't remember!!!! I can't remember. What's happened?"

"You'll be all right. You're coming along fine. I'll see you later."

Goodbye, goodbye, goodbye. Pad, pad, pad down the hall, littler and littler, down the hall to the...I don't know. Look down again: me, in the pants me. Shoes. They gave me back my shoes at the hospital. No, here. This is the...is it? ...the hospital. Sun. Son. No. No sun. But that's somewhere, too. This? Have an egg? Want a pill? Little boy? Mother, don't go away, don't leave me alone here. Take me with you! *Mother, take me with you!!* But...not little, big. You're coming along fine. I am? *I* am. Pocket. Glasses. My glasses. David's glasses. My David's glasses. Hello. How do you do? Who are you? David? Well. So am I? Oh, we are. Fine. Shall we put on our glasses? Would you like an egg? Madam will give you an egg...with salt...without salt. Or coffee, or perhaps a cracker? Did he say shock treatment? But...on a *bed?* Shock treatment on a *bed?* Bonjour. Je suis le Docteur Bowles. Ah, vous-êtes, êtes-vous. Je suis, suis-je? Beatrice Lillie? Gray lady? Hand, I mean hands. Oh, spots. No, burns. Burns, burns, burns. Ssssss! Cigarette, smell. Yes! Burning...funny, no feeling? Doesn't it hurt?

Like a storm breaking inside me, the knot at the back of my neck began to explode. Little bolts of lightning, violent flashes of unconnected memory. As if with my hands, I grabbed at them, putting them here...there...where does this one go? What is this one? No, wrong shape, wrong *thing,* not me. What am I doing? All these things mine? Go together? I can't remember. Ronald Colman can't remember. Shock, fell down. Greer Garson was it? Kilts? *Lost Horizon? NO.* Something...Hilton, Mr. Chips. Random...Random *Harvest.* Amnesia. David, do you have Ronald...amnesia, I mean? Shock treatment? No, he didn't have shock treatment, just fell down, on a bicycle was it? Forgot her, everything. Shock treatment. Shock therapy. Electric shock. What does it do?

Voulez-vous shock treatment? Voulez-vous un egg? Avec salt? Sel? Non? Oh come on. You've lost your...memory. I have not! I'm an...No, I'm David. Me, this, David. It's called that. On a bench in the hall with the gray lady. Old gray bonnet. Put on your old gray lady with the red cross on it. That's silly. I have too not lost my memory. Dr. Russell. Dr. Bowles. Dr. Palmer. Hospital. Me. David, me. Me Mitchell. I am David Mitchell and I am in a hospital and I am sitting on a bench and I am drinking a cup of coffee and the gray lady is giving me an egg with salt and the sun is not out and I am feeling fine and I...I burned my hands with a cigarette and then I...David. But no, not me. Black David. David and Goliath. No, *black.* Smile. David Everett. I'm glad we have the same name. I think it's nice. Buddies with a coon! Coon? They always wash their food before they eat it. My father had a pet raccoon once and he always washed his food before he ate it. He did? Black David in the room with white David. David and David. How do you do? Do you want to talk about it? Look what's happening to him, you can see it happening to him.

What are you doing here? You've come to take me back? Back? Back...back...back. House, trees, lawn, the sky of night night. Branches against the night, last of the sun, the sun. I'm not violent, not violent... don't need these. Take them off. Terrible having them on, having had them on, knowing I've had them on. Like prison, prison, prison. Prison, hospital, Army? Was any of it, all of it *true?* Too true, too good to be true, too true to be good. What is truth but the man...the man before you. This. Legs arms and stomach, eyes teeth nose hair, navel toes fingers nails, smells and sweat...inside things, thoughts feelings desires hungers thirsts, round and round inside things. Needs. I need thee, oh I need thee. Awful voice, ugly woman, I *neeeeeed thee ev'ry hour* oh gray-hay-hay-shus lorrrrr...d! Abide with *me*. Me, me, me, me, moi, I, je. I am the beginning and the end, Alpha and Omega. Birth and Death. And that isn't all, not by a long shot, that isn't all... the most modern of treatments, excellent results, a full course of the latest electric shock treatments by the courtesy of Dr. Bowles. No first name at all, just plain Bowles.

All right, David, that's enough of that. Put it together, don't let it get away, it all fits somewhere, somewhere, somehow. Sequence, order, like in the...the delusions. No sequence and no order. Make me have delusions with shock treatment? Lightning in my head in the ack-ack-pack room. Ack-ack-ack...in my battery in the Army they called me ack-ack mitchell, did they not, *n'est-ce pas. Oui,* they did. Come back. Like in the paaaaaack room, lightning in my head. Here without lightning but...delusions, take me back? Make me have delusions? On purpose. Have to fool them then. How many shock treatments make a round...a full course. A baker's dozen...one extra for the journey. No, no, no you don't, gently down the shock! Merrily, merrily. What the hell. I feel all right, I feel fine. Must have thought I was nuts. I feel with my hands. Joke when I was eight or was it six? Anyway, joke. Ha ha. Remember remember. When you and I were young, when you and I were sweet sixteen. Way back there...but there's a hole in it, lots of holes, big one right here, empty, empty, empty. Supposed to be like that? Delusions on purpose, make you have them? Everybody crazy. Dr. Russell...a patient maybe? Crafty, crafty...take over the hospital? shock-treat the doctors, attendants, drive everybody cuckoo, cuckoo?

Now I lay me down to...

"David Mitchell?"

That is I, that is me. A whole complete mixed-up individual (individuum?) that is appellated by the name of, designated with the tag of David and then Mitchell. At your service!

"Yes, yes. What is it?"

"Come with me."

Certainly, certainly, why not. Who cares? Come with me. Viens avec moi...viens avec moi pour fêter le printemps. Come with me to fest...*feast*...fester, accent circonflexe equals celebrate. Come with me to celebrate the spring. In the *woods?* Why, mister! Tsk tsk. Ah-ha, that's the ward. Can't fool me. And this is not the way to the ward. Who wants to go to the old ward anyhow? Down the stairs for what... lunch? No. Stop in front of the door. Knock. Frapper. Voulez-vous un oeuf? Pas du tout. Je *loathe* les oeufs. Cela pue. Come in, come in.

Well, what do you know? The sun is out. Good old sun, good old soleil...hi! Bonjour, buenos dias, Good morning, *day,* I mean. Good day.

"David Mitchell. From 8."

"How do you do?"

"How do *you* do?"

"I'm Mr. Saunders."

"I'm Mr. Mitchell." Shake hands, bow a little. "And what, Mr. Saunders, can I do for you?"

All right, go ahead and laugh. I feel good too.

"What would you like to do?"

"Do?"

"What is..." What the hell is this place?

"This is Occupational Therapy. Didn't you know you were coming here?"

"Yes! Of course! Well, so *this* is Occupational Therapy."

"That's right."

"And what are you going to do to me, here?"

"Nothing. Since this is your first time here, you don't have to do anything. You can just look around if you'd like."

"No, I'll do something."

"What, then? Would you like to weave something? Do you enjoy woodwork? Ever done anything with leather...or pottery?"

"Well..."

"Here. Come with me. I'll take you around and show you what the others are doing. Give you an idea."

"Okay."

Zoom...zoom. Back and forth. "See what a nice scarf Joel is making?" So his name was Joel...the little blond boy from...where? From the shower room. It was getting easier to remember now. The knot was gone from the back of my neck.

"Scarf?" I looked at it. It must have been twenty feet long.

Mr. Saunders caught the look in my eye and took my arm. "See, he's making a bowl, and this man..."

"Hi, Mitch!"

"Dave! Hello. I didn't know you were coming down here."

"Yep. We were assigned together."

"Good."

"What are you making?"

"A ring. A nice silver ring."

"Who for?"

He laughed. "For number one. For me and myself. I'm gonna put it on my finger and every time I look at it, I'm gonna say: Brother, you made that in the nut factory. Gonna keep me out of here for ever!" We both roared with laughter, and several of the other men looked up at us.

"Well, David, see anything that appeals to you?"

"No. Wood I think. I'll make something out of wood. All right?"

"Sure. What kind of thing are you thinking of? A box, a cigarette box? Or perhaps..."

"Bookends. A horrible pair of bookends."

"Horrible? Why do you say that?"

I laughed. "The first thing I ever made in school was just that, a horrible pair of bookends. You should have seen them. I want to go back and make some better ones so I can forget those. Besides, don't pay any attention to me, I've just come from shock."

He frowned. "Oh, I didn't know. How do you feel?"

"Kind of wild and wonderful," I said. "I don't know how long it will last. I thought I'd lost my memory at first. Worse than that even. It was like being born. I thought I was somebody else. In fact I don't think I knew who or what *I* was. But things keep coming back to me. Like those bookends for instance. I haven't thought of those for years, literally years."

"Let's pick out a good piece of wood, shall we? I think I have a piece of cedar over here that you might like to work with."

I looked back over my shoulder. "Did you say he was making a scarf?"

"Yes." He nodded. "He's been working on it for months." He lowered his voice. "Actually I hope he'll decide to finish it soon, he's got two good looms tied up with it now."

"Who's it for?"

"His mother."

"My God! What does he want to do, strangle her with it? It must be twenty feet long!"

Mr. Saunders shook with laughter and held his finger to his lips. "You *are* feeling good. Maybe he does, I don't know. Hadn't thought of that. Maybe he wants to make six scarves out of it." He opened the door of a cabinet and took out a piece of wood. "There, how do you like that?"

"Gee, that's fine."

"Good. I'll give you a saw and anything else you need and you can work right here. Does the radio bother you?"

"No." I listened to it for the first time and stopped still. What was the music? I had heard it before. I knew I had!

"Do you know that?"

"I think so...it's on the tip of my tongue...I think...No! I know! Scarlatti! Scarlatti Sonatas...Know who's playing them, too. Casadesus. I'll bet anything."

He looked at me and smiled.

"Well! Not many people would have known that. Are you a musician?"

I shook my head. "No, I studied once. But I love it even though I don't play myself. Gee, it's nice to hear those again. I haven't heard them for a long time. I have the records at home."

"How long have you been here, David?"

"About a...about a month, I think. Damn! I feel sort of funny in my mind about that shock treatment, I keep thinking I'm wrong or that I don't know what I do remember, although everything seems to have come back to me now. Yes. It's just about a month, I guess."

"Oh. Well it's not surprising that I've never seen you before. I hardly ever get a patient here in so short a time."

"Really? Then that's good, isn't it?"

He smiled again. "Why yes. I should say it was very good."

I worked automatically, sawing in rhythm to the music, but the light-headedness, the gaiety I had felt, was slowly and certainly displaced by a small gnawing fear. My mind seemed almost to have a life and direction of its own, sorting and rejecting, fitting bits and pieces of memory together, recalling names and people, groping for exact sequence, questioning and doubting. I wondered if there was any such thing as total recall, or were there gaps that I did not recognize as gaps, holes which I would never be able to refill if only because I did not know they were holes? Was it possible for any doctor, any scientist to conscientiously take upon himself the responsibility of attacking the mind of another human being in this way...firing volts of electricity into a man's brain without any positive and direct aim? What was the purpose? To make me forget something? But what, and how could anyone know that I would forget the right things and remember the right things? Was there some selective process in this bolt of electricity that had been shot through me by which only certain things would be obliterated?

Even as I worked, a growing, nameless dread...the fear of being forced to lose my memory, even my mind perhaps...took shape inside me. I remembered the men with whom I had waited in the wardroom before the treatment. Men whose faces were blank and dull, smileless and without life. They were in the middle of the course already, and some were even on their second course of shock treatments. Was that vacuum-like expression an inevitable result of the treatment? Would I too gradually develop a fixed stare, a slow and thoughtless manner of moving? Or would I become addicted to the treatment...like the one man, the one exception in the waiting group, who had been unable to stop talking, laughing and fidgeting. "Gonna get shock!" he had exclaimed over and over, smiling, licking his lips like an alcoholic or a dope fiend. And horrible as it had been to watch him, even that was better than the emptiness of the others. In him, at least, life still ebbed and flowed, there was something recoverable in that man, but the life of the others seemed to have been exploded out of them.

"I have gotten permission..." was that what Dr. Bowles had said? Had he secured a written statement? Was it necessary to do that? Was the treatment so serious a step that responsibility had to be defined beforehand so that the doctor, the hospital...officialdom...had to be absolved before it began? Would there be any way to avoid further treatments?

The prospect of increasing blankness stretched out before me. I believed, but belief is not knowledge, that I had remembered everything. But would I, after each successive treatment, delude myself into thinking that, and not know? However much I might be able to recall of my pre-shock existence, the barrier of shock...the moment of actual blacking out...rose up as an obstacle beyond which I could not really pass. I could reach over it and remember the past, without any knowledge of how much of it could be seen and remembered beyond that barrier. Was there some way to circumvent the effect of the treatment effectively? I remembered again the way in which my mind had seemed to circle above me as the woman offered me the egg... as if it had separated itself from my body, to wait in the corridor until it was safe to re-enter the physical casing of my head, its proper home. Anything seemed possible here...perhaps I could detach my mind consciously before the treatment and then re-attach it afterwards. I would have to try something like that before the next one, idiotic as the idea seemed to me now. And yet no one thing was idiotic in this place, this wild world of unbalance. The idea of being able to isolate my own mind and store it in space for future use seemed incongruous, mad even, but certainly not impossible. Here, there were no laws, no rules, no real guides. I knew that from the evasive questions and answers, the looks and glances of acute doubt and uncertainty on the faces of the doctors and nurses. They were experimenting with us... experimenting in the void. There was no definite and precise track upon which they could base their own course of action. Did they, for example, *know* when a patient was cured? There was no scar to heal, no wound to stop bleeding. You seem to be better, you look better, I think you are getting along all right, how do you feel, you're looking pretty good…but no absolute statement of knowledge. The wound has healed, the germ is dead, the virus has been eliminated, the leg has been cut off, the infection has been stopped. A fine thing I had done: repudiating my family, cutting myself off from them and putting myself automatically into the care of these people. When we think you are all right you will be discharged! What peculiar combination of events would bring them to the place of thinking or determining that I had arrived at a state of being which corresponded to "all right" in their judgment? Was I normal before I had come here? What was normal? Who could know? If I had been accidentally locked up and had behaved as a so-called "normal" human being in confinement, would I not have been considered insane? Would I have accepted the conditions of this hospital as either necessary or desirable? Was not the acceptance of this kind of world…and every patient had to come to accept it at least sufficiently in order to deal with it…a certain sign of abnormality? Was it not highly average, completely normal, to revolt and fight against confinement and restraint?

"Time's up!"

I laid down the wood and the saw and looked around. The man at the table next to me was working with a sheet of copper, cutting it with heavy shears. Without any reason, without knowing what I was doing or why, I covered two small pieces of copper cuttings with my hand and then picked them up, looking around to be sure that I had not been seen. I felt them with my fingers, fairly heavy sheeting, twisted by the shears and with a sharp cutting edge. I put them carefully into the pocket of my inner shirt, the white pajama top, and pressed my hand over them, feeling them against my chest.

"Well, you didn't do so badly this morning. I think you're coming along very well."

"Good."

"Hand me the saw and the square, will you please?"

"Certainly."

"Thank you. I'll see you tomorrow, and I'll keep these right here on top of this cabinet, so that you will know where they are. Oh...here's a pencil, you'd better write your name on them."

I took the pencil and wrote the word *Mitchell* on both pieces of wood and handed them back to him. "Could I keep the pencil?"

He hesitated. "I'd like to give it to you and I think it would be perfectly all right, but...well, ask one of your ward attendants, will you? I'm sure they will give you one."

"Oh, all right." He was perfectly right, of course. He probably had no authority to give me a pencil. Even so, it was disheartening always to meet with that look of uncertainty, that momentary hesitation; to see the question forming in their minds...Dare I...Could I? and then the excuse, the assurance that of course it was all right but that they... whoever it was...couldn't do it. It was always someone else who had the answer, the key, the power, the right. From the attendants to the nurses to the doctors and then where? Where was the end of the chain-of-command? Who was the final authority...the omnipotent force or person who *decided*...well, if I could have a pencil, if I was sane? Was it God, my family, the government? Or, and much more likely, was it just some fortuitous combination of circumstances labeled chance? Since there was no such thing as obvious normality, no ruler or scale by which to judge the mind of a man, then how was it ever done? By a combination of feelings and attitudes? Opinions, likes, dislikes, hopes, fears...God alone knew what it might be and he wasn't here very often, surely.

Back on the ward after lunch I asked for pencil and paper and to my surprise they were given to me immediately. Something had surely gone wrong with this place, everyone was becoming friendly, co-operative, helpful, acquiescent. Perhaps I had not done myself any harm after all, or perhaps I had simply misjudged the hospital before. Or...

probably it had something to do with Dr. Russell. He was in charge now, and it had only been since he had taken over from Dr. Bowles that everything had seemed to change.

After they gave me the paper and pencil, I sat down at the table in the center of the room. Again, in the same detached way that I had picked up the pieces of copper...almost without participation of *self,* as if I was an instrument, a tool of some sort I began to write, not quite sure of what was going to come out on the page. *Notebook,* I wrote carefully and neatly at the top of the page. I then made a list of the names of all the doctors, nurses and attendants that I knew, and next to each name I put a code mark. A circle for *good,* an "x" for *bad.* In shorthand, I then made a brief note about each one of them: why they were good or bad, and if bad, what they had done to me or to the other patients. When I had completed this I read it over with pleasure. What a good idea! How had I come to think of this? Again in shorthand, under the heading *Notebook* I wrote: *Record of the Behavior of the Personnel of this Institution.* They had better continue to behave from now on.

I folded up the piece of paper and put it in my inner pocket along with the little pieces of copper. From now on I would have to observe them very carefully and make notes of their actions, the things they said, whatever was wrong in their treatment of the patients. I'd have to get some more paper, certainly!

As the afternoon wore on—this was the most interminable day I had ever known—I became increasingly aware of the separate life of my own mind. Without informing me of its intentions, without thinking, which seemed to me the means by which the mind, my mind, allowed me to participate...to *do* consciously, I found myself doing things impulsively, thinking things (except that it was not thinking in the usual sense, there was no process of conscious deliberate thought nor was there one of traceable association), deciding and judging without precedent or logical basis, as if, independent of me, an autonomous mental process having its own laws and logic was taking place inside me simultaneously with whatever I happened to be doing. In the typing room I did the work which Mr. Sweetwater gave to me automatically, as a machine might do it. When I had finished, I inserted a piece of blank paper in the typewriter and again, in the same way that I had started my notebook earlier, I began to write, not knowing what was going to come out. I wondered if this was perhaps automatic writing.

This time I did not make any list of hospital personnel, but typed a long and detailed self-history, beginning with my earliest memories. I wrote it in a kind of typewritten shorthand, not for any purpose of disguise, but simply to save time and get down everything as rapidly as possible. I was still hard at work on it, on the third page, when the rehabilitation period was over. I folded the three typewritten sheets carefully and put them with the notebook and the copper in my pocket. It bulged noticeably now.

Had it been the electricity which had divorced me from my own mind? And what else had happened that I was not aware of? Was I filled with electricity now, or had it gone in and gone right out again? Maybe I was like a battery: if I held a light bulb in my hand, it might light just from contact. I wondered. I had been able to store up my radar energy at one time, perhaps now I would store up electricity from the shock treatments. I might even light up myself some day?

In the middle of this pleasant electrical reverie, some inner impulse halted my thoughts. What kind of direction was my mind taking now? This was like being driven by a car rather than driving it. What sort of idiotic reverie was this: light a bulb by holding it in my hand! My delusions, my own delusions, were not much sillier than that at their worst: in fact there had been a kind of logic to them that was still very real to me. Not a recognizable or usual logic perhaps, but the feeling of logic, the same feeling that I had had as a child when the anonymous meaningless figures of two and two making four had been suddenly and wonderfully transformed and illuminated by the simple expedient of combining two separate groups of two apples each into one group of four apples. Something inside me then had lighted up...this I *knew* and *understood*. The translation from the unknown to the actual, logical, believable world had been complete and satisfying. In the same way my so-called deluded logic had been happy and right and satisfying to me. And after all, were they really delusions? The board of judges, obviously...after all there had been no board of judges, at least not of earthly, tangible judges, and probably the diagram beginning with the figure eight was also a delusion. But the trial, the examination, even the symbolism of the light patterns and the colors had a meaning of some kind, I was certain. The physical form was what made all of it a delusion, the fact that I was in acute mental torment at the time...and yet was it not perfectly possible, perfectly *logical* even, that the judges and the examination were real in the sense that it was only a heightened process of self-examination, self-judgment, self-determination? Not everything could be defined in words or even in thoughts. Surely colors and sound were languages, meaningful and informative, in the same manner as words. Wasn't it only that we did not know the language as well...or perhaps not at all? The color red, for example, was certainly as pregnantly meaningful as the word "yes."

And then Jesus Christ. What about that? I had not *thought* I was Jesus Christ when I had burned my hands. I had *known* that I was. It had been more than a conviction or a belief, and far simpler than either of those things. It had been knowledge in the same sense that I now knew that this was my right hand. In a sense it was a surer and more complete knowledge than that, or than the fact that I *knew* that I was David Mitchell. I knew my name only because it had been told to me, it was knowledge from the outside, whereas the knowledge that I was Jesus Christ had come from the inside, from the starting point of all knowledge. Was it not from within that we observed and knew... everything? The final confirmation of understanding did not come to us from the outside, but only from within ourselves. Was it then not only possible, but probable, likely even, that an impulse arising from the world within ourselves was surer and more to be trusted than any other knowledge? I could not say to myself honestly that I was not Jesus Christ reincarnate. I had no knowledge or understanding with which to oppose that one-time certainty. It was only the conventional world, the outside world, other people and the manmade rules and values by which those people lived, that had made me dis-believe it. But again, disbelief was not knowledge, not certainty. It was only *doubt*.

Once again some warning impulse held me up. Was I now beginning to believe in my own delusions? Retreating into a world which did not really exist except as an escape from the real world, the tangible world of society which I hated, feared, distrusted, and condemned? Or was this a fight against that corrupt and seemingly insane society...a society in which wars, insane asylums, prisons, electric chairs, concentration camps, courts of law, were accepted as logically and humanly inevitable? Escape or not, I was certainly not wrong to object to it, fight against it. And yet where is the limit of compromise? Where is the barrier at which one can stop and conscientiously, honestly say to oneself: "I am against this but beyond here I will not fight it. There is nothing further I can do about it." Was not the world a world of individuals, no matter how loosely or tightly grouped into societies, political groups, countries, and little worlds? And if so, was it not the responsibility of the individual not to compromise? Not to stop there and say: I can go no further? Was it not up to the individual...to me ...to say, definitely and uncompromisingly: "This I will not do. This I cannot countenance. This is something I oppose" ...And what was there to lose? Life could be lost, yes. But life was lost. Was it better to be killed on a beach in Normandy than in a prison as a conscientious objector? Was it ever *good* to die for the lack of a principle? And for myself, would it not be better, perhaps, to die as Jesus Christ, believing in and behaving in accordance with his...my own...inner principles and understanding; better than to make what could not be other than an odious compromise, an attempt to make peace with a world which was essentially alien and hostile anyway?

Or was this very argument a form of evasion of the core of my own conflict? The core which I could not recognize perhaps...and which now, as a result of shock treatment, I might even have forgotten forever.

Whatever I had forgotten, there was a deeper fear of what I had never known, a fear of what had brought me here. It could have been *blood*... bullets...air raids...terror. Was it the death that I had seen around me, shaming me into wanting it for myself? Or was it, more simply, the soldier's necessary preparation for death, the obligation to die, that had caused me to seek it here?

Would I ever know?

TWELVE

DR. RUSSELL SENT FOR ME early the next morning. Whatever beginning doubts I had felt about him vanished when I saw him. I *knew* by his presence that he could be trusted, and yet, curiously, what he told me was alarming. He smiled and said good morning and then abruptly he announced that I was going to get a pass. I would have the freedom of the hospital grounds, would be able to go where I liked to go, do whatever I wanted to do, restricted only by my schedule of shock treatments, occupational therapy and vocational rehabilitation. My immediate reaction was one of alarm, serving only to increase the nameless premonition of disaster which I was sure hung over me. Next to a discharge, this was the most desirable thing that could happen to me...it was tantamount to a parole, to being put on my own feet...and yet it seemed like stretching the run of luck (for I could not quite believe that purpose or motive was behind this) which I had experienced since my return to the hospital.

He caught my surprised look, the momentary reluctance, and waited for me to explain it, but to express it to him would have been impossible; it would surely have been a manifestation of neuroticism to show or admit any fear about getting a pass, being liberated from the ward.

"Just remember," he said then, breaking the waiting silence between us, "that you have to report to O.T. at ten-thirty every morning and to

Typing at two. Then, of course, on Tuesdays and Fridays your shock treatments, but they will notify you about them anyway."

"Thank you very much, Dr. Russell," I said.

He smiled. "Not at all, Mitchell. I'm glad to see you coming along so well." He hesitated. "Of course, you may not want to use your pass today. It's almost time," he looked at his watch, "for O.T. now, and then, of course, this is visiting day."

Again that warning bell inside. Visiting day. Well, in a few hours I'd find out about that!

My nervousness and the sensation of impending disaster hung over me and enlarged during the O.T. period and through lunch. After eating, the doors were locked on us, no one was to be allowed out on pass until after the visiting period was over. I sat on the porch with Dave, waiting.

"Dr. Russell gave me a pass this morning," I said to him.

"That's *good!*" he exclaimed at once. "I think I'm going to get one myself. I talked to him this morning. Maybe the end of this week, he said."

"Gee, that's swell. That's really the next step before discharge, isn't it?"

He nodded, and then asked: "What's your status here?"

"What do you mean?"

"How were you signed in?"

I shrugged my shoulders. "I don't know. My family signed me in, I think."

"And you think they won't sign you out?"

I hesitated. "That's right...they *said* they wouldn't."

"Why don't you try for an A.M.A.?"

"What's that?"

"Discharge against medical advice."

"I don't know what you mean."

"It's easy," he said. "The hospital doesn't like it much, of course, but if you're not a committed patient, they can't hold you here legally, and you can sign yourself out against the advice of the doctors. All you have to do is to sign a statement relieving them of responsibility for your case. Of course, you sign away your hospitalization rights along with it."

"Why don't you?" I looked at him, feeling vaguely suspicious. "There's certainly nothing wrong with you," I said. "I can't understand why you haven't done it before."

"Well..." He hesitated. "I'm committed. I was committed after my first visit home."

"And you mean that once you're committed, you can't sign yourself out?"

"That's right. Maybe you'd better try it before they commit you."

"Do you think they would?"

"They'd sure try it if they thought you were going to try to get out on your own."

I wondered if I could really trust his information. After all, he must be in here for some reason. Was this conversation just an indication of his particular illness? Some comforting thought that it was possible to get out of here?

"How could I find out more about it?"

"Go over to claims and see Mr. Beckwith. You've got a pass now, you can go over there any time."

"Where is it?"

"In the main building. On the second floor. It's called the contact section. The doctors can't stop you from going over there, it's an administrative department of the government, really...they give you advice about claims and they have all the information about commitments, voluntary admissions, discharges and so on."

"Damn! I think I'll go over there this afternoon. I wonder if they'll let me out today."

"I think so. They usually let the pass patients out about an hour after visiting period begins."

Maybe that would be one more step...and what a step! Then I could show them!

The porch looked out over the road from the main building and the entrance to our ward building. Visitors were walking along the road, turning in on the cement sidewalk and up to the entrance by the offices. I watched them coming in, disappearing behind the glass doors. Usually, after a few minutes, a patient's name would be called and he would be led out to see them, in the other wardroom.

"Hey, Mitch."

"What is it?"

"Isn't that your mother?"

I looked in the direction in which he was pointing. Sure enough. My first impulse was to get off the porch, to hide, but I did not give in to it. I sat there staring at her, but she did not look up. She looked very well. A new dress, or one that I did not remember, and she had done something to her hair, probably had it waved.

"She's certainly a good-looking woman," David said.

I nodded absently. "Yes, she is."

As I watched her; the mixed feelings, the suspicions, the sensation of trouble ahead, seemed to join into one central emotion. Looking at her, walking slowly and thoughtfully up the cement walk now, a package under her arm, I felt a kind of impudence about this action she was taking. Remembering that scene at home, the policemen, John, the definite statement: "No, I will not sign you out" ...I began to boil slowly inside. She wouldn't sign me out, no, but she'd come to see me here. Come to visit me with a little package of candy or cigarettes, or a book maybe, just to make sure with some small bribe of something— cigarettes for instance—of which I could never get enough from the hospital; yes, to make sure that I'd manage to stay happily here until such time as the claim came through. And, of course, my good will would be important...without that monthly check I wasn't of much use to her, and with it (if I got it) it was of no use to her unless she had my good will to make sure of her cut. Now, for the first time since I'd been sent back to the hospital, the feelings, the anger, the rage, the self-pity (I could recognize it now as self-pity) bubbled up in me, causing me to sweat again. I knew now what had been wrong, why my mind seemed to have separated itself from me…it was because I hadn't allowed myself to feel any of these things up to now. But now, now, the heat inside me, like a welding iron, was fusing my mind, my feeling, my whole self, into one again: a solid, quivering mass of hatred, anger, and righteousness, directed against the woman…my mother (I said the words to myself contemptuously) who had just disappeared into the main entrance of the building.

A.M.A. The perfect solution!

"David Mitchell!"

I walked slowly, arrogantly into the wardroom. "Yes?"

"Visitor," said the attendant.

I shook my head. "My mother you mean?"

"Yes."

"Tell her I don't want to see her."

A moment's silence, a look of alarm on his face.

"Hey, are you kidding? Come on."

I shook my head again firmly. "Oh no, I'm not. Tell her I don't want to see her. I told her myself and I meant it."

He looked at me piercingly. "It's your funeral, brother. You're sure you know what you're doing?"

I nodded. "Yep." Then I turned and walked away from him, back on to the porch. I sat down next to Dave again.

"Hey. What's up?"

Although I was trembling inside, and covered with sweat outside, I tried to be calm. "Nothing. I just don't want to see her, that's all."

He gave me a long look, taking in his breath and holding it. He shook his head slowly but did not say anything.

I waited, watching, for what seemed an interminable length of time, and then she appeared in the door, on the steps, starting slowly down the walk. She no longer had the package, and suddenly she put her hands to her face. I could tell that she was crying. She stopped for a moment on the walk, took a handkerchief from her bag, and then started walking towards the road. I could not see her face, but from the movement of her shoulders, I knew that she could not stop crying. I felt a terrible wracking sharp pain inside me. I had wanted this to happen, I had wanted to do whatever I could to pay her back for that evening, to throw a knife into her insides and twist it around, stabbing the vital spot in her, and yet now that I had done it, it was almost unbearably painful to me. I was gripped by alternating feelings of revenge and satisfaction; and by the horror of having caused real pain. Now I was doing what had been done to me...which made me as bad as I had made her, reducing me to the same level of viciousness. And yet, with equal force, I felt a sensation of power and happiness...I could do this, I was not ineffective just because I was locked up. This way, she would know. Through her own pain now, she would be able to sense and understand what she had done to me. This way was the only way; by striking back I could reduce her, render her ineffective, too. Whatever power she had had, whatever confidence in the rightness of what she had done, what she had thought, would be destroyed by this. Now she knew what she had done to me, now she was paying for it.

But I felt sick and empty inside...I wanted to vomit. I got up suddenly, walked rapidly across the wardroom to the door. "Can I go to the latrine, please? I'm sick."

The attendant unlocked the door. "Go ahead."

When I was in the hall, he called after me: "Hey, Mitchell, you can go out if you want. All men with passes can go out now."

In the latrine, I knelt by one of the toilets, half-sick. If I stuck my finger down my throat, maybe I'd be sick and that would end the nausea, but I didn't try. The sickness enlarged and then receded. I guessed that I would be all right and stood up tentatively. Yes, it was better now. The hall door was open and I walked down to the office. "May I have my pass, please. David Mitchell," I said to the nurse.

"Just a minute, please." She got up from the desk and crossed the anteroom into the other office. I watched her go in and stop in front of the desk where Dr. Russell was sitting. She said something to him in a low voice and then came back to me. "All right." There was a strange look on her face. I wondered what was wrong.

Out of the door, down the steps...I had expected something from this moment, something important, symbolic, vital: it was the first time, the very first time, that I walked freely and alone down the steps, onto the walk away from that building. Even the day itself was perfect for it. All morning the sun had battled with the clouds, shooting a ray through them here or there and then being momentarily defeated again. And now, symbolically certainly...I could not dismiss it as coincidence...the sun blazed down on the hospital, having suddenly broken through the clouds. I looked up at the small space of blue surrounding the sun and in all directions, as if the four winds emanated from the sun itself, the clouds seemed to be fleeing from it in disordered defeat. I could almost *hear* it, like the triumphant, exciting swell of a symphony orchestra...the first great climax of music involving every instrument. A small thrill of pleasure shot through me and then died abruptly. The day was right, the elements were with me, and yet it was myself, something in me, that was unable to participate in this. Somehow, it didn't matter, it didn't matter at all.

I looked at the walk, the lawn, the road, the trees and fields, and finally beyond them...the fence. Whatever this was, however I might have expected it to be...the fence killed it finally for me. For this was only an enlargement of the cage, an extension of its limits. As I reached the foot of the steps, someone started up the walk, someone I knew... Dr. Palmer! We met halfway down the walk and he smiled at me.

"Well, Mitchell! So you've got a pass."

"Yes, I have."

"Good." And then his eyes ran over me quickly, examining. "Hope it won't give you any ideas," he said.

"Ideas? What do you mean?" As I said the words, I wondered how many millions of times I had said them. I seemed always to be asking people what they meant, almost as if I was destined never to know what was behind the words they were saying. Or was I looking for a motive?

He laughed and turned to look across the grounds towards the highway beyond the gate and the fence.

"Some of our patients," he said, "try to escape from here. In fact, some of them succeed." He turned back to face me. "We've had a few who have gotten away successfully and even found themselves jobs."

"Why are you telling me this?" His whole manner seemed to me to be studied and over-careful...it seemed impossible that he was not saying these things to me for a purpose. Doctors, I reflected, like all other human "mechanisms" must have unconscious (or was the word subconscious?) minds. Did he want me to try to escape without knowing, consciously, that he had any such wish?

His smile seemed self-conscious when he replied: "I want you to promise me that you won't try to escape."

"As far as I'm concerned there is only one way out of here," I said, looking down at my blue clothes. "Out the front door, in my own clothes. You won't have to worry about me."

Did I detect a look of disappointment on his face? Or was it my imagination again? Not only that, but deeper and more troubling: would I ever really know, except through words which I could pin to people, quote back to them, the difference between what really took place inside a person and what was going on in my own imagination?

I continued on down the walk to the road. As I turned down the road, in the direction of the main building, I looked up at the building I had left, the ward. Behind the heavy screening on the porch, several men stood, looking out, watching me. So that was what I looked like

THE WORLD NEXT DOOR

in my cage! Whatever dignity man might have intrinsically, he had none here. Well, I was going to remedy that, at least for myself. I looked away from the building and its staring inmates and continued down the road.

Past the flagpole, up the steps, my fingers holding tightly on to the pass in my right-hand pocket. Attendants, nurses, other people, standing around the halls. I tried not to notice them and hoped they were not watching me as I walked through the doorway. I wondered where the stairs were. I looked down the long hall that ran across the building, first to the left and then to the right. I could see no stairs, but decided to take a chance. Down to the right, past several open doorways, small offices, and just before the corridor ended, a staircase. I went up slowly and stopped on the second floor, at the head of the stairs and looked down the hall. The contact section was almost opposite me. Well! What was the name of the man? Mr. Lucas had seen me, but he had told me the name of the head man. Mr. ...Mr. Beckwith! I walked across the hall and into the office. A large, fat man with a pleasant round face, dark hair, bushy eyebrows, was sitting behind a big desk, and near him (I could only see his back) someone typing. I hesitated in the doorway and the fat man looked up.

"Mr. Beckwith?"

"Yes. What is it?"

I moved into the room and stopped before his desk. "I want some information."

"Yes?" His forehead wrinkled and he looked at me, puzzled. "What's your name?"

"David Mitchell."

A flash of recognition seemed to cross his face, but I could not be sure.

"Where are you from?"

"Ward 8."

"Oh." The man stopped typing and looked at me, then he and Mr.

Beckwith exchanged a glance. I had the feeling that things were not going quite as they should.

Mr. Beckwith again. Studied now, like Dr. Palmer. "What is it that you want to know?"

"I want to find out what my status is."

They both hesitated, exchanging another look. "Does your ward doctor know you're here?"

I shrugged my shoulders. "I don't know. Why?"

"You're supposed to have permission to come over here. They usually notify us when a patient is coming to see us."

Suddenly bold, I sat down in an empty chair by his desk. "Well, I have a pass. No one told me that I couldn't come here, and since I'm here..."

"Well..." He didn't seem anxious to get rid of me, actually.

"What is my status? Am I a voluntary admission, a temporary commitment...I mean am I temporarily committed, or what? Am I permanently committed, for example?"

"Well...I..." He turned to the typist, who had continued not to type and was listening to us. "Will you see if the records on David Mitchell are in the file, John?"

We waited silently while he looked through the file. "No, I don't have anything on him here."

He looked at me wide-eyed. "Your file is not here."

"Not here?" That was difficult to believe. "Don't you have files on all the patients?"

"Yes..." He looked at the man called John again. "Do you think it might be downstairs?" he asked him.

The typist hesitated too long before finally saying: "Why, yes."

Mr. Beckwith turned to me, and now he was wearing that same placating look, as if to say "I know you're mad and I'm terrified of you, but just be calm until I can get help..." What he did say was: "I'll have to go downstairs and see if I can get your file, if you don't mind waiting here a moment." As an afterthought, he took a package of cigarettes from his pocket and offered it to me. "Have a cigarette, won't you?" I took one, wearily recognizing the pacification routine.

"Thank you," I said, and watched him go out the door. I looked at the other man and he began to type immediately.

Mr. Beckwith was gone for about ten minutes and when he returned he seemed nervous and excited. "Well," he said, as if embarrassed, "I had a look at your file, but it's not complete. I really don't know what your status is. However, if you'll go back to the ward, I'm sure either Dr. Russell or Dr. Palmer will be glad to tell you. They know, you know."

"Is that what they just told you?" I asked bluntly.

His eyes opened wider, and the red of his face darkened still more. "What do you mean?"

I laughed. "Nobody in this place will be glad to tell me anything. You've obviously called them up. If you have a file on me, and I'm sure you do, it's here, not downstairs. However, it doesn't matter. I'll ask Dr. Russell or Dr. Palmer, if you insist."

"Well I assure you, we..." he stopped.

"Well? Go on."

"Ah...it really would be better if you talked to one of the doctors, you know. I don't have authorization to...to..."

"Oh God," I said. "You, too. All right, all right. If you can't or won't answer that question, I have a couple of others." I glanced at his chair. "Why don't you sit down?"

He laughed. "Well, yes. I guess I will. Now what is it?"

"May I have another one of your cigarettes? I don't get many on the ward."

He offered me the package again. "By all means. Of course."

I took one and he lighted it for me. I blew the smoke across the desk at him. "What do I have to do to get an A.M.A. discharge?"

He looked shocked. "A.M.A.?"

"Yes. You've heard of it, haven't you?"

"Oh, of course, of course. But...well, only some patients can be discharged against medical advice, you know."

"For instance?"

"Well, a committed patient cannot get an A.M.A. discharge."

"Not even if they are only committed temporarily?"

"Not until the end of the temporary commitment."

"In other words," I said, "I have to find out my status first, is that right?"

He nodded. "But in any case," he said, "it's a very serious step. I don't think it's advisable, really."

"Why?"

"It means that you forfeit your right to be treated in a Veterans Administration Hospital and what's more any claim you have made is automatically denied. You cannot collect any compensation."

"Oh, I don't mind about that. I don't want compensation anyway."

"You don't?" He looked at his desk and then back at me. "I happen to know something about your case, Mitchell, and actually I think it would be very foolish of you to apply for an A.M.A. discharge now. We should have a decision on your claim fairly soon and it may very well be that it will be favorable, you know."

"Favorable?"

"Yes. It may be awarded. You may get a pension."

"Is that favorable?"

He shrugged his shoulders. "I don't know why not. It means that the government looks upon your application favorably."

"In other words, you think that to be awarded a pension...or compensation...is a good thing. That it is a good thing to have a disability?"

He rubbed his head, looking nervous again. "Well, I wouldn't put it that way, of course, but since you applied for compensation and it is available to you if the decision is favorable..."

I struck the desk with my right hand. "But I did not apply for compensation, my family did."

He spread his hands out on the desk. "Well, in any case, it was applied for..."

"Mr. Beckwith," I cut in on him, "who is going to pay for all this?"

"The government, naturally."

"It costs quite a lot, doesn't it? And, when you say the government, you mean the taxpayers, do you not?"

"Yes."

"Does that mean you?"

"Well..."

"And me?"

He nodded, smiling. "Yes."

"Well, I don't think I can afford it."

He looked puzzled. "I'm afraid I don't quite understand what you mean."

"Oh, it's not so difficult as all that. The government can't afford it. There has to be some stopping place. After all, if every soldier gets a pension just because he's entitled to it, we're going to build up a dandy little public debt, or so it seems to me. But actually, that's beside the point. I don't want it for other reasons."

He shook his head. "That's the first time I ever heard anyone wanting to refuse money."

"I wouldn't refuse money, Mr. Beckwith. But compensation is something else. After all, I couldn't get it—at least I wouldn't get it—unless I was disabled, would I?"

"No. Naturally not."

"But I don't consider myself disabled."

"Well, perhaps the doctors do."

"I don't care what they say. They don't know what they're talking about if they say I'm disabled. In any case, did you ever think of the psychological effect on me if I accept compensation for mental disability? It's all very well if I'd lost my leg or something, okay. But just what have I lost and who determines its worth? Have I lost my mind? And if I have, what is the market value of the human mind these days? Fifty cents a month for the cerebrum? Seventy-five for something else? You tell me."

He looked away. "Well, of course, when you put it that way...You see, Mitchell, the government isn't paying you that way...they are simply making up, or trying to make up, for your inability to work."

I laughed. "The only inability to work that I have is disinclination. If I had enough money so that I wouldn't have to work, then I wouldn't work. But what happens to me? Is that supposed to increase my desire to work? Build up my initiative?"

He paused for a moment. "Well," he said finally, "that is one way to look at it, I must admit. But surely, just having a monthly check from the government wouldn't keep you from doing something you wanted to do, would it?"

"No, I don't think it would. But who says that I want to work? And besides, does having that monthly check come in, does so much money a month build up my confidence in myself...when it's paid me because there's something wrong with me? I should think that the only way ever to get well, after this kind of an illness, is to be able to know that there is nothing wrong with me. This way, the first of every month or so, I'd have a definite reminder that there was a screw loose somewhere." I shook my head. "I haven't got it figured out all the way, but there's something definitely backwards in this system of compensation."

"Well, perhaps there is. Perhaps there is. Anyway, we don't know that you will get a pension yet."

I had an idea. "If I do," I said, "what says I have to cash the checks?"

"Why nothing. And, as I say, you don't even know you'll get any. However, if this claim is turned down, you can apply for limited disability...for the time you were in the hospital."

"Well, that would be all right. I wouldn't mind getting paid for that." I scratched my head. "In fact, I think I should get paid for that. It's certainly the roughest work I've ever had to do."

"Good, then. We'll notify you about this other claim and if it's turned down, you can apply for limited disability."

"What about applying for that now?"

He shook his head. "You *could* apply for it," he said, "but it would nullify the original application. I suggest you wait until we've heard from this one."

I stood up. "Okay. And thanks. I'm still sorry that you won't tell me about my status, though."

He also stood up. "It isn't that we won't tell you...it's..."

"Oh, look," I said, "come off it. Authorization, responsibility. I still say if you have a file, and you admit you do, then you know. Let it go at that, okay?"

I walked to the door. "So long, and thanks."

"Goodbye, Mr. Mitchell. Oh, and don't forget to get the doctor's permission if you want to see us again."

"Don't worry, I won't."

Across the fields again, on the road. I looked at the grass and the trees, and was irritated that I could not simply enjoy my freedom and accept it. But now I knew that something funny was going on. I was determined to find out about my status. At the door of the building which housed Ward 8, I rang the bell, and the nurse who came to open it seemed surprised. "You don't have to come back yet," she said, "you have another hour or so, you know."

"I know. I want to see the doctor. I don't care who. Either Dr. Russell or Dr. Palmer."

She hesitated. "Well, they're both very busy now. This is the only day that some of the parents and visitors can see them you know. Wait here a minute, will you? and I'll find out if one of them can see you."

I sat on the bench in the anteroom next to a colored woman who was apparently waiting to see the doctor. Her fingers moved nervously on her handbag, opening and closing the clasp. She looked at me and then said suddenly:

"Are you on Ward 8?"

I nodded. "Yes, why?"

She smiled and shook her head. "Two of my boys are on Ward 8. Maybe you know them?"

"I don't know. What are their names?"

"Collins," she said. "Andrew and Harold Collins."

"Of course! I know Andy. I don't think I know Harold, though."

She sighed. "I come every visiting day, and it just seems I can never get to see them. The doctor tells me they're both in the pack room now and that I can't possibly see them. I wish I knew what the pack room..."

"Anything you want to know. I can tell you all about it."

"What's it like? Have you been there?"

"Sure," I said. "I was there the same time with Andy. He was in the bed next to mine."

"What's it like?"

I raised my eyebrows. "Not much fun," I said. "They keep everyone wrapped up in cold, wet sheets and tied to a bed."

"Oh." She looked away from me. "I just wish I could get a look at them."

I hesitated and then touched her arm. "Look," I said and pointed out through the glass door. "See that room over there, downstairs... there...where all those windows are?"

"Yes."

"Well, when you go out, just walk over and look in those windows. That's the pack room. Maybe you'll see one of them."

She looked at me and then squeezed my hand. "What's your name, son?"

"Mitchell," I said. "David Mitchell."

"Well," she said. "I'm happy to know you. And I truly thank you.

I'll do that if the doctor won't let me see them. I'll do that."

"Good. Don't tell anybody I told you, though."

"Oh, I won't! I wouldn't think of that. I know how they are around here. I get nervous every time I come here." She laughed a high, thin laugh and leaned over to me. "You know, every time I come here I just get so nervous...well, I get the diarrhea something terrible. Every single time. I sometimes wonder how it's possible for a person to get well in a place like this, I really do."

I looked at her hard. "Boy, am I glad to hear you say that! Listen, Mrs. Collins, you just said something. If there's anything you can do, once those boys of yours get out of the pack room, get them out of here. No matter what the doctors tell you...get them out. If they stay here, they'll never get well. If you knew..."

"David Mitchell?"

I looked up angrily. I was remembering the day they had taken Andy Collins back to the pack room for jumping that bastard Jerry when he had started in on me. "What is it?" I said roughly. "The doctors can't see you today."

I stood up. "You mean they won't!"

"Now, David." It was the nurse. "You mustn't be like that. Surely you know that Dr. Russell or Dr. Palmer would see you if they had the time. Today is an especially busy day, I told you that."

"Oh nuts to you," I said. "Every day is a busy day if somebody around here wants it to be. If they only had to say 'no' to you, then why did it take so long? Did they give you instructions as to what you should say to me and how to refuse, because they knew I'd suspect that they simply didn't want to see me?"

The nurse made a sad mouth. "David," she said reprovingly. "I'm certainly sorry to hear you say things like that...I'm really disappointed in you."

"You and Dr. Bowles," I said. "It sure doesn't take much to disappoint you two. But if you are, it really doesn't cut any ice with me, so you might as well get over it." I turned to Mrs. Collins. "You see what I mean, Mrs. Collins? This is typical of the way they do things around here. It's like an obstacle course in the Army, except that here they have a special runaround that nobody seems to be able to figure out. Don't forget what I told you, for God's sake."

She smiled. "I surely won't, and I can't thank you enough, Mr. Mitchell."

I smiled back. "Don't mention it."

"David! You're not supposed to talk to visitors!"

"Oh all right, all right! Goodbye Mrs. Collins."

"Goodbye."

THIRTEEN

"**MITCHELL, DAVID. ADMITTED 5:40 PM** Sunday May 11. Assigned directly to Ward 8. *Mitchell is a committed patient...*"

I handed the file back across the desk to Dr. Palmer, and took a deep breath. "It doesn't say whether I'm temporarily or..." I hesitated and took another breath "...or permanently committed. Which is it?"

He closed the cover of the file and looked at me. "Permanent," he said. "I'm sorry to be the one to tell you this, but you wanted to know, so..."

"So you told me. What does it mean exactly?"

He opened his fingers and spread his hands and then clenched them both into fists again. "It means that you will be here until we feel that you are well enough to be discharged. If, at the end of one year, you are still here, you will go before a board of doctors and they will review the case to decide whether the commitment should stand for another year. Of course, if we decide that you are getting along all right before then, we will release you in the custody of your parents."

I looked away from him. "Mitchell is a committed patient." Underlined. Mitchell is a dead duck!

"When was I committed?"

"I don't know the exact date."

"But I wasn't committed when I first came in, was I?"

"No, I don't believe you were."

"Then when was it?"

"As I said, I don't know."

"Oh all right, you don't know. But who decides when somebody is going to be committed? What happens to get me committed all of a sudden, if I haven't been committed from the very beginning?"

"There are different reasons," he answered slowly. "In your case, it was probably on the advice of the doctors."

"Probably? Aren't you one of the doctors? Don't you know any of the answers to these things?"

"Well, I'm not in charge. Dr. Bowles would make the final decision."

"You mean Dr. Bowles committed me...or had me committed?"

"No. You were probably actually committed by your parents on the advice of Dr. Bowles. The hospital would not normally commit a patient without consulting the patient's family and recommending that they do it."

"How is it done?"

"Usually the family goes before a court...a state court...and initiates commitment proceedings."

"But why?"

"Well, as I told you, it's usually on the advice of the doctors."

"All right...*usually*...but why in this case?"

"I don't honestly know, David. I imagine that it was done in your case only as a protective measure."

"A protective measure!?"

He nodded. "Yes. Then while you are on a visit, if anything happens, if you get into any trouble, you are not responsible. You would not be criminally liable, for example, if you got into any trouble with another person, or were in an accident. In fact, sometimes some patients are committed as a matter of routine before they go on a visit home for the first time."

I shook my head. "People are certainly watching out for me, aren't they?"

He hesitated. "I imagine it must be a shock, David, but try not to be upset about it. It doesn't mean that we are going to keep you here. In fact, the worst of it is the word itself. Many people simply have an unpleasant association with that word. I'm sure it was only a routine commitment in your case, and will not prevent your release in custody of your parents."

I stood up. Custody, commitment, release...strange, final words. But it was not just the words. It was a taking away of your hands...in a final sense. Whatever my destiny, my physical destiny in relation to this place, it was entirely out of my hands. It was up to the doctors now, and to my parents. Custody. And that could mean only one thing. The custody would last as long as they, my mother really, felt that I was all right. If she changed her mind...back I'd come. That was out. But if I couldn't be released in her custody, then what? Would I have to stay here a full year? Well...

"Okay, Dr. Palmer. Thanks."

"I'm sorry, David, I don't like to give you this kind of news, but as I say, you wanted to know and it isn't bad news really, it's..."

"Oh, that's all right. That's all right. I don't care anymore. I'm getting used to it. Things were going so well for a while, I knew something like this was going to happen. Back to the mines for me. Thanks again."

I opened the door and walked down the hall towards the ward. No wonder he hadn't wanted to see me yesterday. And even as I had lain in bed the night before, I had known this. In fact, I'd known it as soon as Mr. Beckwith had gone downstairs out of his office. As if he hadn't known. He just hadn't wanted to tell me himself. That was all. Well...this would be a day to remember. The day I found out that I was committed to the nut factory! I revisualized the calendar on the wall of Dr. Palmer's office: Thursday, June 12. One of my historic dates. Right next to Sunday, May 11.

"Time," "sequence," "reality," "order," "sanity," "insanity" ...all of these, like any other combinations of the twenty-six letters of the alphabet of the English language, are first of all words. They are endowed with meaning by individuals and probably by groups of individuals and societies. But whether or not there is a basic meaning, comprehensible to every man...whether or not the word "time" for example is identical in meaning to every single individual is at least questionable. The same is true of the word "commitment." For me, *myself,* an individual named, by some accident of preference or choice, David Mitchell, the word contained at least the suggestion of several meanings beyond that which had first leaped into my mind. Other words suggested themselves: helplessness, emasculation, powerlessness. And beyond that one word, the actual treachery of words themselves extended throughout the language. What was the force behind language that gave it meaning? What did a commitment mean to my mother, to Mr. Beckwith, to Dr. Russell, to Dr. Palmer? ...surely not what it meant to me.

With the distrust of language, the sudden (and to me, terrible) shift in my position, and therefore in my course, acquired a special meaning for me. Whatever else the commitment might represent... legally, or medically...it was basically the final attack of society upon an individual who has in some way attacked that society. And attack can presuppose only two (perhaps three?) courses of action: defeat—or the acceptance of defeat (which is not really a course of action at all, but only the result of attack); a counterattack on the part of the person attacked; or, the possible third, a contributory attack upon himself of the victim, a joining of forces with his attackers for the purpose of his own self-destruction. Whatever else had happened to me, I had been attacked by the society, the world, the *group,* or whatever it was that up to now, in any extremes of circumstance, I had considered as my society, world or social group. First of all, what were the reasons?

Outwardly and legally, to protect me. But basically it was not my protection, but the protection of that society, which was at stake. And now, as a possible co-attacker, what was my position in that society? How far could I go with it, to how much of society and the world as I knew it, did I honestly subscribe?

The days following the twelfth of June ceased to exist as days. Once more I lost my sense of time, order, sequence and logic, not through having mislaid them in a delusion of my own, but through a more purposeful, and to me, more logical procedure. The society that invented and subscribed to the theoretically general meanings of these words, the accepted definitions, was now a society from which I was separated. Since it had cast me out, I was no longer a part of it. Of what value was it to me, and of what value was it *period?* Presumably I would be invited back into that society, and the general, and apparently natural, assumption was that I would, of course, accept. That I would accept not only with humility, but with conditions, their conditions. But does a man, one man, one individual, have no conditions regarding the society in which he chooses to live? I was amused, in this sudden timelessness in which I now found myself, to realize that here suddenly I was faced with a choice. The world had, quite without intention, offered me a choice. By putting me beyond its boundary temporarily, its boundary was for the first time visible to me. Was the world—which now seemed only an enormous extension of the grounds and eventually the fences of this institution—something that a person would *choose* to live in? Of the invitation which I was sure to get someday...I had doubts. Was it not, rather, up to the world to make me an offer? Perhaps they would extend me an invitation..."The world invites you to participate in its life. We have automobiles, museums, radios, movies, stainless-steel sinks, garbage-disposal units, dishwashers, automatic laundries, hotels, cafés, wars, storms, mental hospitals, prisons, railroad stations, lunch counters, nightclubs, books, women, children, men, dogs, cats, birds, doctors, psychiatrists, attendants, nurses, universities, trains, political systems, cocktail parties, theatres, motor boats, airplanes...and so on. We hope that you will share this world with us, or that you will want to."

But given the choice, would I? Would anyone? You, he, she, they, not only me? What were the alternatives? The first one that occurred to me was the world beyond the barrier which I had crossed, the world of my own delusions. The world where "no" had meant only "no" and not *maybe, perhaps,* or even *yes.* The world where no one ever said: "I'm not sure," "Don't you think?" "What do you mean?" and where there was no uncertainty. The other immediate alternative which came automatically to my mind was death. Suicide. I did not think of it with any feeling, in fact I was devoid of any feeling at all now. I thought of it only as an alternative...the world of the unknown, unfelt, unexperienced. It did not seem to me that it could be anything less than preferable. With the recognition of my lack of feeling, came several questions. Is it not feeling, really, which gives us meaning as individuals and which gives to the things of the world a meaning which can be shared among people? Was it not my lack of feeling (which is perhaps another word for belief, faith...it is imperative to feel belief and faith in order to have them, to approximate the states of "mind" implied by the words) which made even my daily routine now *senseless*? I woke up at a time of day called morning, simply because I had formed that habit. The word morning itself was meaningless, as was any word, except by its association. Could such a word ever convey properly—to everyone—that first waking moment? The first glimpse of gray or sunny sky? The first smell of rain, the first breath of wind, the arrival at the final destination of whatever night-journey had been made?

Being away from, detached from, outside of the world, makes you see it for the first time without identification and therefore without feeling. I had loved the world, or I had at least deluded myself for years into thinking I loved it. I knew now, and I knew *forever,* that there was much that I had never loved and would certainly never love again (or for the first time). As for people, I had loved them once. Really loved them. And that was only when all of this had begun. On the 11th of May I had been so separated from the world (I remembered the happiness of that day so well, longing to feel it again) that for once I had not needed it, had not wanted anything from it, had not desired anything in relation to it, had not (in the ordinary sense) loved, feared, hated it. And from that place, in that happiness, I had loved everybody, because I had for the first time, then, nothing against them. No reason not to love them. Everything, everyone, including myself, was forgotten and consequently forgiven...which is simply another way of saying "forgotten." But now, not so. Now it was up to me. Now, and this had never been true before, I could see as I had never seen; observe, look, judge and choose. And there was a great deal I did not like...too much.

In bed one night...I do not know *what* night...the days had gone on, passing by and over me without interest and with only mechanical participation on my part...I made my decision. It seemed wonderful and even miraculous that only now could I recognize that I, myself, not my outward mind, had known that this moment was to come. Had I not, already, had a strong premonition of disaster? Had I not, without realization of what I was actually doing, picked up the small pieces of copper, sharp as razors, in the O.T. room and kept them without knowing why? And now I knew. I had looked, watched, listened, examined for...how long? days? nights? ...a period, in any case, and there was no question. The logical end of man is death. There was nothing, nothing that attracted me back into the world (whether or not I was invited). For what conceivable reasons could I postpone...or want to postpone my own death? Only one...some inner prejudice against suicide. And yet, was that prejudice actually a prejudice of nature? Was it valid? Could it be that one should, for some cosmic reason, choose or want to stay in a world of apartments, motor cars, and gas stoves—fearing death and hating life? And fearing death? What was there to be afraid of? How could anyone not *long* for it? Life was identical with this institution...it was simply a larger insane asylum, with an atom bomb for shock treatment.

I determined, without any feeling, any reaction, to kill myself. I would give God (or whoever was the boss of all this madness) one final chance. This night I would wish, with all my being, simply to die quietly, non-participating, passively. But should I awaken in the morning, then I would take matters into my own hands. The tools for suicide seemed to me incredibly available. If one should wish a spectacular and quick death...a dramatic demise...there was always O.T. Saws, knives, blowtorches, chisels, scissors...the possibilities were fascinating. Or the wardroom? Glass in every window. All you had to do was break it to acquire a wonderful weapon. If I should wish to do it quietly, I could beat my head to a pulp on the head of the bed, the floor, rush against the wall, or...use my little copper cutting edges. In any event, it would not be difficult. I wondered momentarily whether, in the event I would have to commit suicide, it would not be a service to the patients to take a more complicated way out. If I killed a few of the attendants first, would that not alleviate their lot? And would I not then be electrocuted or hanged? The process, the means to death, was unimportant to me. I had felt absolutely no pain when I had burned my hands, and it seemed probable that I would not feel any pain from hanging, burning, beating, electrocution, or cutting. In any case, it couldn't last long even if I did.

I closed my eyes and drew my forces together, concentrating them into the middle of myself. Surely it was possible this way...and this was the right way. I began to sense myself drifting off into something...was it sleep...? It seemed different to me. Different, chosen and welcome. It was too bad that there was nothing, no one, to say goodbye to. There wasn't.

To my astonishment, I awoke next morning in a place which I identified instantly as bedroom 7 of Ward 8 of the Veterans Administration Hospital. For a brief moment I wondered if I had died and this was actually another world, but I decided that no other world could possibly duplicate the conditions of the earth so perfectly. Well, it hadn't worked. The only remaining thing now was to determine the manner of suicide.

I thought about this problem through breakfast, examining the various possibilities (still without feeling or personal reaction to the fact of my own death—such a departure from the world seemed in no way tragic or sentimental) and coming only to the conclusion that I was not suited by nature to a violent form of death. It seemed logical to fall back on my bits of copper. In bed that night I would (and it would be easy) cut one or two vital arteries and quietly bleed to death. The only problem which remained for me, when I was sitting on my bench on the ward after breakfast, was whether or not the act of suicide—which was a responsible and definite act against society—was something which I could naturally take upon myself. Since, from the point of view of nature I was perturbed (I could find no precedent in nature for suicide: trees, birds, animals did not, as far as I knew, take their own lives) about taking my own life, it seemed necessary to find some human justification for an act that was essentially the act of a human being, not a natural being. If, for example, I could inform the hospital—the world—of my reasons for this act, that of itself would justify the violence inherent in it. After thinking it over, I sat down at the table and took out the papers from my pocket. I looked over the "notebook," my record of the performance of the attendants and nurses and doctors, and laughed. It seemed a petty sort of thing to have done. I had two blank sheets of paper and in a careful hand, I began to write:

In consequence of the manifold blessings of this earth, I am forced to an unnatural act which will have been committed before this document will be read. I have been forced, by the separation of my own values from the values which are apparently normal to society in general, to take my own life. My reasons for this follow:

For the sake of society, and the peace of mind of its members, I have been confined in a mental institution. Confinement, which should be obvious to anyone reading this, is an impossible condition for any reasonable human being. Since there seems no way out of it, for too long a period of time, I find that death—the only alternative—is preferable. I have a few comments to make on the underlying reasons which have brought me to such a decision:

I am in a hospital, and therefore sick.

It is the assumption of society that I am sick, since sickness itself is relative. What, after all, is a disease?

Society has further assumed that a cure is both necessary and desirable.

I have not been consulted. In view of this, I wish to state that I should have been consulted; it should have occurred to the doctors that I might not wish to be cured, and, that, in the long run, the desire of a human being to live or not to live, to be cured or to remain sick, is his prerogative and does not belong to society or to anyone else.

Not having had the choice presented to me, I have, nevertheless, found it impossible not to make a choice. I wish to and will die after writing this. There is however a reason for writing this before I die.

If society insists that it does have a responsibility to cure illness, it must then also accept other responsibilities: such as (1) its own part in bringing about the illness, and (2) the reliability of its methods for curing the disease. A mental illness is not the result of one man's problems with *himself,* but of his problems with the world in which he lives; similarly, he should at least be consulted about his cure, since it is his life which is being "given back to him." I do not want mine.

Finally, if society can take upon itself the rejection of a human being in the form of locking him up, it should obviously follow that the release and return to society of such a person should not only be the choice of society, but of the individual. It may well have been that the force which originally brought an individual to a mental hospital was, of itself, a rejection of the world in which he lives. To successfully reject, then, the world into which he has been driven can only be done if there is something, some better world for him to go into. A world in which one human being can, for any reason, be restrained, arrested, and confined, is not one in which I would voluntarily choose to live. The values of such a social organization are automatically suspect. The fact that I was not asked whether or not I wished to be removed from society does not, I am afraid, preclude the possibility that I might wish to be consulted on whether or not I wish to return. I can only say here that my firm hope is that someday the "madness" of the so-called normal world will be apparent to all the so-called "normal" members. I feel certain, and my only basis for certainty is the statistics concerning admissions to mental hospitals, that this will be proven only when the so-called *mad* take the normal world over. The only thing a madman attacks instinctively is the *presence* of fear. A "normal" man attacks the *thing* he fears. There is a difference.

I signed my letter and read it over. It seemed satisfactory. I pictured the attendants finding my blood-soaked body in the morning and the resultant hue and cry. The fact of death, my own death, and their consequent feelings about it, gave me no particular satisfaction. The only thing I did not want to miss, or that I would regret not seeing, would be the look on the face of the doctor when he read my letter. There seemed to be no way for me to witness that. And then, suddenly,

I had a mental picture of an attendant reading the letter and disposing of it. Nothing would then be known of my reasons, nothing would be done about them. The only thing I would have achieved would have been my own death. That would be, in a way, good enough; but to die because one did not want to live was less satisfactory than to die to prove a point. Perhaps my only basic motive, my real reason, was to justify to myself the taking of my own life. I would have to think some more.

Just before time for my O.T. period, my name was called and, to my surprise, I was handed a letter. I did not recognize the handwriting on the envelope (which had been opened and resealed with brown tape) and I opened it, curious and interested. Who would be writing to me here? The very fact of getting a letter made me nervous, bringing me for the first time in several days close to at least a kind of feeling. It was like something reaching out to me from a world which I had, in my own turn, rejected; only the final blow remained to be taken against it. I opened it carefully and read:

Dear David Mitchell:

You may not remember me, but we met at the Erdmans' last March. When I saw them last night they told me that you were in the hospital and we all spoke of you with esteem, if you'll let me use that old-fashioned expression.

I will write you again—and more fully—if you'd like me to, but perhaps you would let me know if there are restrictions about receiving mail. When I was at Crossville, it was made very difficult for us, God knows.

Please telephone me when you are out on a visit or when you leave the hospital. It will be a great pleasure to see you again.

I hope that you are getting along well.

All good wishes from

Mary L. Anderson

Unaccountably, as I read the letter, my knees began to tremble, and still more mysterious and frightening, like a pulse beating me back into life in spite of myself, I felt feeling coming back into me, and with it a terrible active wish (not an acceptance, not a choice) to die. Somewhere in me I knew what had happened, and only from a stranger would this have been possible. This was the offer I had asked for. Once more I looked at the letter and read over that one sentence: "When I was at Crossville, it was made very difficult for us, God knows." Not only was it an invitation, a hand from the outside world, but from someone who had made the journey here and back. Funny, I had completely forgotten this woman, forgotten that I had ever met such a person... and yet now I could see her quite clearly: a hat with a veil, making her face vaguely indistinct so that she was a person I had sensed and felt rather than seen. And I had been told that she had been in a hospital. I did not remember if I had liked or not liked her. I only knew that now, by writing to me, she had grasped my hand and was pulling me as I could not have been pulled by anything else; setting my course back towards a recovery which I dreaded and hated. "...it was made very difficult for us, God knows."

Not only God.

FOURTEEN

THE WALL OF THE WORLD, a wall which I had broken and pierced, re-erected itself around me. When I awakened on the morning after I had received the letter, I was first of all conscious of awakening to pain. Like a sick man coming out of an anesthetic after a serious operation, my nerves began to reverberate to the well of pain inside me. I closed my eyes tightly, as if to shut it out, but it continued to lie inside me, spreading. When my head began to throb with it, I opened my eyes again. There was a dense fog outside the window, so dense that wisps of it, smokelike and curling, drifted in through the windows. The other men in the room were still asleep; it was not yet time to get up.

There seemed to me to be a terrible and impossible irony in my situation. As far as I had been able, I had cut myself off from my family, only to find that all other exits were also closed firmly against me. The events of my illness hung over my bed, pressing down against me, allowing no outlet for the physical pain which had spread over my entire body. If I had, up to now, resisted living in some way (perhaps, after all, I had never really faced living in the world) that was certainly no longer possible. I had thought of this as being a choice, and yet there were no alternatives in it, none that were acceptable. I could not find, search as I might, any justification for suicide; I was convinced that it was an act against nature, not against society. If I could have believed that to kill myself would have been a logical revenge, a real attack against society, the hospital, my parents, it would have been easy for me, but I could not. And at the same time, alongside the absolute inner denial of suicide as a possible solution, lay the fact of my enormous desire for death. My desire to get out of the hospital had vanished: what difference could it possibly make to me now to get out of the hospital, since I would only be releasing myself into a world that was essentially, if unconsciously, hostile. The unconsciousness of man's hostility to man was what frightened and saddened me most. It almost seemed as if there was some cosmic law, some power which we could not recognize consciously, which drove us to a life of inhumanity against our own kind. There was no conceivable explanation or excuse for war, and yet it was an accepted manifestation of humankind. But on what basis? How was it possible? How was it possible after what I had seen of war myself to accept it and to talk about something else, or talk calmly enough about the next war? And war, as a manifestation, seemed to me unceasing. It was waged, on a personal level, unceasingly. Only when it rose (as if it was a conflagration resulting from millions of individual sparks) to the social, organized level, did it become a first or second World War, a shooting war, a killing war, instead of a wounding and maiming war. True enough, it was not especially common for the average human being to physically wound or murder his neighbors, but emotionally, mentally...what crimes did we not perpetrate upon ourselves?

I got out of bed and looked out the window. The fog had settled itself over the hospital, hanging a few feet from the earth, obscuring all but the grounds and the lower edges of the buildings; it seemed to me an indication of the sadness of the world, an attempt to obscure this place which could not be anything other than a blot. Consciously, even man himself tried to hide these places. From the main road, it looked like rather a pleasant place: a school perhaps, or a well-organized factory. Landscaped and beautified for the comfort of the inhabitants: students or workers, one might think. And yet, on closer examination, one could find the metal fencing, obscured by bushes and trees, pretending self-consciously that it was not there at all.

After breakfast, unaware of the self-protective restlessness inside me, I wandered around the ward, looking into the faces of the other patients, staring at the attendants. I stopped suddenly, startled and frightened. I had joined the group of men walking in circles round and round the center tables...so this was what happened, on some level, to them? I withdrew hastily from the group and walked over to the door. I wondered how long it would be before Occupational Therapy...or even shock. Was this the day for my shock treatment? Anything to quiet this restlessness, this driving sensation, which I could not control and which cried out inside me for some physical expression. From here I watched them...the men walking around the tables...terrified that I had unconsciously joined them in that never-ending circle, a simple and direct physical expression of *the* vicious circle.

"Anybody want to help make some beds?"

I looked up. It was one of the attendants who had spoken.

"I will."

He looked at me. "Don't you have O.T. this morning?"

"I'm not sure," I said evenly...after all I had to face the fact that I wasn't sure. For all I knew this was Saturday or Sunday. Too late it occurred to me that he would not have asked me if it had been. Anyway, he didn't seem to notice the slip.

"Well, all right," he said. "It won't be for a while yet anyway."

Rows and rows and rows of beds. "Here, you two work together." Hospital corners, same as Army corners. I did not know the man working with me, but we glanced at each other from time to time in a silent agreeable reassurance. As we progressed from bed to bed, I felt a small sense of pleasure flowing through me. We worked well and easily together, establishing a rhythm in our movements, in the lifting of mattresses in a mutual understanding gesture, making the corners, tucking in the sheets, moving rapidly and silently from one bed to the next. Something inside me, something connected with the sensation of pleasure produced by this activity, seemed to be hammering against the wall of my consciousness, as if to give me a message. I felt that some solution was presenting itself to me now, but I did not know what it was.

Solution meant release. There was no other possible solution than the immediate one of being out of the hospital, and that was no solution. I could find no assurance in myself that the fact of being out of here would now guarantee that I would remain out. If my family did not send me back of their own accord, for reasons of their own, would I not perhaps drive myself back in? I recognized now that my delusions (and the very word had a peculiar savor on my tongue) were perhaps the absolute manifestation of escape, release, freedom from the world in which I had lived. They presented themselves to me, beckoning. Offering me a place in which to hide. If I had been able somehow to clothe myself in them again, to find in them a place in which to hide and to forget, I would have done so willingly, happily. But it was as if I no longer had the key, or could not find the door through which I had once entered into that other world.

When we had finished the beds in the large wardroom, the other patient was led back to the ward and I was told to wait. The attendant returned and examined me, as if questioning himself about me, making some important judgment. Finally, after eyeing me silently from a distance, he came up to me and said slowly: "Do you want to make some more beds?"

"All right." I was tired, I had already made a lot of beds, but I was reluctant to stop. I kept seeing the picture of myself in the circle of men around the table.

As if with misgivings, for he continued to look at me doubtfully over his shoulder, he led me down the hall. We stopped in front of a door which I recognized immediately as the room where the electric shock treatments were given, and he gestured to me to wait while he opened the door to look in. I looked in over his shoulder. I could see several unmade beds on one side of the room, and several people in a group on the opposite side. As the door closed, I heard a frightful cry ringing out through the silence of the halls.

"What was that?"

He looked at me, still doubtful. "They haven't quite finished giving shock," he said. "We'll have to wait a few minutes."

We waited for what seemed a long time. Finally two attendants came out of the door, holding a patient between them. His eyes were closed—he seemed to be walking in his sleep. Now I had seen it all and heard it, as well. I had seen myself go onto one of those beds, watched the preparation being made on me, and now I had heard the cry (had I myself made such an outcry?). Finally here was a man...myself even... staggering out after treatment, held up by the attendants. I watched them lead him to the alcove, deposit him on the bench, handing him over to the care of a gray lady, who smiled at once, and busied herself, getting ready for the moment when she would offer him an egg. It seemed a thing at which to marvel, an act of rather special wonder, that upon his re-awakening into the world, the first thing he would encounter would be this ugly—she was fascinatingly repulsive now that I looked at her—gray lady who would manufacture a smile as she offered him a sandwich, an egg, a cup of coffee.

"Well, Mitchell. What are you doing here?"

The attendant looked with me...it was Dr. Russell. Before I could speak, the attendant said: "He's a star bed-maker. I brought him down to help out in here."

The doctor frowned and then smiled. "How are you feeling this morning?"

I laughed. How long could I possibly go on with what seemed to me the ridiculous pretense of that question and its possible answers. I shrugged my shoulders. "Oh, Dr. Russell," I said, trying to smile, "are you seriously asking me that question? What possible answer is there in a place like this?"

He frowned again, looking embarrassed.

"Well," he began, and then faltered, waiting for me to say something more.

"Don't bother, Dr. Russell," I said, "but that is a silly question. I'll feel all right when this is all over with, at least I hope I will." I turned back to look at the patient sitting on the bench, still unconscious. "At least I learn more about what goes on here every day. I knew what it was like to go into shock, now I know what it's like coming out, too." I turned back to Dr. Russell. "If you want to ask someone how he feels, why don't you ask him? Do you know how he feels? What has happened to him since he was led into the shock room? Does he feel better, has he been improved? Are you positive in your heart of hearts that you've done the best thing for that man, or..." I smiled "...tell me something, Dr. Russell: is it possible that I know what really happens in shock as well as you do—or better? Maybe I know the terror of waking up out of it as you will never know it, as you couldn't know it, or have you had shock treatment recently? I wonder if you know what it is like to come out of it and not to know...not to know anything? I think you don't. Have you ever asked yourself what you have done to that man...or to me, for instance? What have you put out of my mind that will never come back into it? I don't know what irreparable harm you have done to me, I'll never know, perhaps. And that's the worst of it really. If you cut off my arm, or my leg, I'd know it, I could see it. But it's the not-knowing that is terrifying. I don't know even what it is that I no longer know."

He looked at me silently, his head not quite straight.

The man was coming out now, blinking his eyes dully at the woman seated in front of him. I pointed to him. "Look at him, Dr. Russell, take a good look. I don't know his name, but he doesn't either, so it doesn't matter. But don't look at *him*, look at me...even more than that, look at yourself. That's a man, not a 'him' or just a patient in a hospital. He's you and me or anyone...a male human being, and something essential has just been blitzed out of him, or may have been. In any case, he doesn't know if it has or not. He will *never* know. Think of it the next time you put somebody on one of those beds."

He shook his head slowly. "You're very bitter, aren't you?"

I shrugged my shoulders. "Am I? I don't think so. Just realistic, perhaps. But not bitter."

"I'd like to see you when you're through in there," he said. He turned to the attendant. "Bring him to my office when you're through with the beds."

This time the attendant made the beds with me. All clean sheets, clean pillowcases. Remnants of the shock treatment were distributed over the room, on the beds, on the floor next to them. The things that they stuck into your mouth—I supposed to keep you from biting your tongue or something—lay used and bloody here and there, to be picked up and tossed into a wastebasket.

When we had made the twenty-six beds, I was led into Dr. Bowles's office. Dr. Russell was seated at Dr. Bowles's desk. He stood up when I came in and indicated a chair next to the desk. "Sit down, Mitchell."

He hesitated after he had sat down again, tapping his fingers lightly on the green blotter on the desk and staring at them. Then he looked at me.

"I think I'm going to take you off shock treatment," he said.

"Why?"

His hands opened and closed and then opened again. "I don't think it's doing you any good."

"Oh?"

He nodded. "You resist it too much."

I did not say anything and since he remained silent, I stood up. "Was that all you wanted?"

"No, sit down," he said. "I want to tell you something."

"What?"

"Just that I think your discharge from here is up to you from now on. You're your own doctor."

I laughed. "Not exactly," I said. "If I was, I'd prescribe an immediate discharge."

He shook his head. "I'm not so sure you would, David."

"Don't tell me that we doctors disagree on this patient," I said, laughing again.

"Do you want to go home to your family?"

I shrugged my shoulders. "You might call it a choice of evils. I'm probably as normal now as I'm likely to get. After all, my family is at least used to my...my eccentricities, whatever they may be. They won't necessarily think of me as nuts...you might."

"Perhaps. Anyway you can't be discharged at once. Even if I wanted to discharge you today, I couldn't. You'll have to wait until Dr. Bowles comes back, and certainly until you've had a chance to see your family again."

Something occurred to me suddenly. "Perhaps you're right about that," I said, "but while I'm here I'd like to ask your permission to see Mr. Beckwith in the claims office this afternoon."

"What about?"

"A claim, obviously."

He hesitated again. "All right," he said. "I can't think of any reason why you shouldn't."

"Good. Thanks. Now was there anything more?"

"Only that..." he looked into my face again, directly. "Look, David, I think you're getting along very well. I suppose it is asking too much to ask you to try and look at this whole experience with less anger, less bitterness. But I would like you to try. You will have to be here a little longer, whatever happens. You're an intelligent person, you're not a dumbbell. I think you want to get well. I think you should try to use your time here to your own advantage. Keep yourself occupied, try not to think too much, and try not to think too harshly, for your own sake. Don't wrap yourself up in bitterness and hatred. It can't do you any good in the long run."

I smiled. "Behold a transformation. I'm all sweetness and light from now on. I love the hospital, the attendants, the doctors, you. You'll have to drive me out of here when the time comes."

He smiled slowly and shook his head. "Well, think over what I've said anyway." He extended his hand to me. "Whatever happens, I certainly wish you luck, David."

In spite of myself, I liked the man. Against my own feelings I took his hand, and as I did so, the pain shot up inside me again, crashing through whatever protective mechanism seemed to have formed itself in me to alleviate the pain. I stood up quickly and walked away from him without speaking.

By the time I went outside that afternoon, the fog had lifted. The grass was still sparkling with diamond drops of wetness, but the sun was high and the sky was cloudless. The feeling that had beaten its way back into me when I had shaken Dr. Russell's hand was still with me, pounding inside. I was hot, in the way I had been when I had had my radar beam so easily at hand, and because of the sharpness of my feelings, I felt continuously on the edge of tears. Yet with it, I had a sense of beginning acceptance. Some of Dr. Russell's words came back to me, fitting in with my own thoughts and questions. It was up to me. I was sure he was right about that, and yet it was not a thing I could accept or to which I could agree easily. I did not know about my discharge being *up to me* in any literal sense of those words, but another kind of discharge, some release from the bondage in which I had placed myself in relation to people, the world, was certainly up to me. Instinctively, unquestionably, I knew that it was up to me to *forgive.* Forgive who or what, and for what? In a sense, to forgive whoever and whatever besides myself had brought me to where I was...

"In my beginning is my end. In succession..."

Where had I read that, what was it? It came suddenly and brilliantly to my mind. *East Coker...T. S. Eliot.* I had memorized it all once. I struggled for it in my mind...one particular part I wanted:

> *...In order to arrive there,*
> *To arrive where you are, to get from where you are not,*
> *You must go by a way wherein there is no ecstasy.*
> *In order to arrive at what you do not know*
> *You must go by a way which is the way of ignorance.*
> *In order to possess what you do not possess*
> *You must go by the way of dispossession.*
> *In order to arrive at what you are not*
> *You must go through the way in which you are not.*
> *And what you do not know is the only thing you know*
> *And what you own is what you do not own*
> *And where you are is where you are not.*

In order to arrive there...a way wherein there is no ecstasy.

There was none, surely, in this way. And yet already I could feel a kind of quiet inside me, a deep sure striking of some melancholy note in my heart. Perhaps there were no words for it, but it was a thing which left no cloak of bitterness, and from which, I knew, even the sadness would some day disappear...or was it only that I would get used to it?

As I walked I looked around me at the physical world of the hospital, the buildings, the roads...and the lawns, fields, and trees. The world, even this limited world, seemed to me very beautiful, more beautiful than we conceivably deserved. What I could not ask of people I could easily ask of nature: of the sun, of trees, plants, flowers, lakes, rivers, grass, simply *to be*...to be openly and naturally what they were.

Near the main building there was a wooden bench, and when I came to it, I sat down. Whatever pressure or idea was driving me to attack Mr. Beckwith and the claim business had momentarily subsided. I felt as if I was gripping something, some intangible truth which I did not fully recognize and which I did not want to lose.

I sat there, with my eyes upon the ground, the warmth of the sun on my back, and in that moment there was nothing for which I wanted to ask. I felt no need, no human need; I had no ax on my own grindstone, no desire to attack or repel, only a great and deep wish to accept...not with my mind, but to accept the flow into myself of the world around me.

This painful happiness and peace was suddenly interrupted by two feet in black shoes appearing in my line of vision on the walk before the bench. I lifted my eyes slowly into the over-red face of...what was his name? Dr. Perrin! My jaw fell open of its own accord. We had recognized each other at once, and in that moment a great horde of different feelings whirled across his face: anger, doubt, fear, self-consciousness, embarrassment...

"Well, hello there!" he manufactured unctuously, like an announcer on the radio slipping into an accustomed and necessary routine..."How are you this fine morning?"

"Afternoon," I said automatically, and he repeated it after me. "Afternoon...yes, so it is. So it is."

I looked at him then, without saying anything more. As if he had said it openly, I could see the conflict within him resolving itself into a course of action that was both difficult and wearing to him...repugnant even. He braced himself to forgive...not me...but the poor sinner who sat before him on the bench; the man who had committed God knows what horrors and was now to be forgiven, provided he should repent.

"I'm Dr. Perrin," he said.

I cocked my head at him. Was he trying to pretend to himself or to me that we did not know each other...even well? "I know that," I said.

"May I sit with you a moment?"

"Yes. Sure." I moved my body on the bench, although there was plenty of room on either side of me.

He sat down, clenching his hands, and when he spoke again, there was confusion and embarrassment in his voice. "Well, well," he said, "it certainly does my heart good to see you out here. You've come along splendidly. Splendidly."

I looked at him. "If you could forget where you last saw me," I said, "it might be easier for you."

He looked startled, as if I had attacked him unexpectedly. "Oh, of course, my boy, of course. Naturally that's all forgotten."

I laughed. "Naturally it is not all forgotten," I amended. "And it will not be forgotten for a long time, either. Let's not kid ourselves about that."

He smiled uneasily. "Well, not literally of course, my boy. But we won't think about it, will we?" He said this as if he was speaking to a five-year-old moron.

I looked impatiently into his face. "Doctor, that is such a ridiculous thing to say, really. I will certainly think about it and I will certainly not suppress it." I began to warm to the conversation. "I think the attitude of the church is incredible. You should have seen your face when you recognized me. It was extraordinary to watch the mixture of feelings in you. You were furious, ashamed...God knows what you weren't, and then you sit down and calmly pretend that I don't know you, and that all of that is something to forget. We might at least try to be honest with each other if we're going to talk. Otherwise why bother? What did you sit down for? Why didn't you simply nod and pass me by?"

His face reddened slightly. "Well, we like to keep in touch with all our boys here," he said.

"Oh for God's sake. Now what do you mean by that?"

He tightened his lips and looked away from me. "How long have you been out of the pack room," he hesitated and added, "David?"

"Two or three weeks...maybe more. Why?"

"Have you come to services?"

I could not believe this. Surely not the old standard approach. "No, I haven't."

"Don't you belong to the church?"

"No."

"You mean you've never been a member of any church?"

"No."

"Why not, David?"

"Why should I be?"

"Well..." He hesitated again, but this time I could see his mind searching pleasantly for the proper answer. He was on ground that seemed safe and usual to him. "Well," he repeated, "you believe in God, don't you?"

"No," I said pleasantly. "I don't think so."

"But why not?"

I shrugged my shoulders. "I've had this conversation a great many times," I said. "Why should I? I have no proof of his existence."

"Have you no faith then?"

"What's that got to do with it? Does having faith automatically presuppose that I believe in God? Maybe I have faith in the sun, or the stars, or the growth of the grass. Where does God come in?"

"But it is God who creates all those things. It was God Who created you!"

I shook my head. "Do you really believe that? How can you deny evolution? As for creating me, my parents had sexual intercourse, Doctor, and here I am. I'm perfectly content with that. Who appointed you to tell me that I should or should not believe in God? You believe in him, I don't. You're happy in your way and I in mine. If you want to have a delusion about God, I won't try and destroy it, but for *God's* sake don't try and pass your delusion off on me."

He smiled and then turned fully to me. "I can remember when you thought you were Jesus Christ," he said. "You must certainly have some feeling about religion."

I was surprised and taken off my balance momentarily when he said this. I had not forgotten any of that, but I had not thought much about it either. "Well, Jesus Christ was not God," I said. "He was a man."

"He was the Son of God."

"Don't hand me that Immaculate Conception routine. He was the son of Joseph and Mary, and you know it as well as I do."

He shook his head again. "If you identified yourself with Jesus Christ, it was certainly not because you thought He was an ordinary human being."

"He wasn't an ordinary human being. But he wasn't divine, either. At least not in the sense that he came to the earth by some mysterious process. He was an extraordinary human being, granted, but so might any of us be. Since we're going back to that, remember also that you had no proof that I was *not* Jesus Christ, but you didn't find me in a manger, remember?"

"I certainly didn't think you were Jesus Christ!"

"Are you *positive* that I'm not?"

"Do you think you are?"

"No, I don't think so. But I'm not sure. I'll never be sure. What if you had believed me, for instance? The way Joan of Arc was believed for a while? What might have happened then? Given the chance, I might have proved to be the real saint of this year. How will you ever know? The fact that I'm not doesn't prove anything. If they'd shut either Jesus Christ or Joan of Arc up in a nut house as soon as they'd heard about them, the whole course of history might have been different. The trouble with you—with the church—is that you don't have any real faith. In the olden days there were miracles simply because people believed in them, not because they were really miracles. But now it's people like you who prevent miracles. Look at you...What really do you believe in? What can you prove to the sheep that do go to your churches? After all, Joan of Arc said she was going to save France and she did because she was given the opportunity. And why was she allowed to do it? Because people believed her. You may never know what you missed in not believing in me. Did you ever think of that?"

"If you had really been Jesus Christ, I would have known it. It would have been communicated to me."

I laughed again. I was beginning to enjoy this talk. "Really? Isn't that after all rather presumptuous of you? What makes you think you are so enlightened?"

"I have faith. I would have known."

I stared at him. "Tell me something. If you have so much faith, how do you accept the world? How do you feel about war, for instance?"

"War, my boy," he said slowly, "is the great curse of mankind. If everyone believed in the Lord, in the power of Love and Goodness, there would be no wars."

"I think I agree with that...at least in part. But is it enough just to believe, do you think?"

He shook his head. "No. One must act in accordance with one's belief."

"Do you?"

"To the best of my ability. I live according to the dictates of the Lord as they are communicated to me."

"That isn't what I asked you. That makes it dependent on your ability. But do you really?"

He looked at me sadly: "Where is the man who is without sin?"

"The man who does not compromise," I said evenly.

Dr. Perrin seemed to be wearying of the conversation.

"You put all of these things in such simple terms," he said. "As if faith, belief, the recognition of God were easily and simply proven. It should be as easy for you to recognize God as it is for a child to learn the recognition of a color. After all you accept that red is red without demanding proof, do you not?"

"I can see a color," I said. "I have proof of its existence, and it does not matter what name I give it."

"The life of man," he continued, "is far more complicated. Who has yet fathomed all its mysteries and complexities? No one, and yet here you are demanding proof. The very fact that it cannot be proven should be enough to make you believe in the power of the Lord."

"It makes me believe in some cosmic force," I said, "but I certainly do not limit that power or that force to an idiotic image of mankind. That form of limiting is presumptuous and egotistical. Why should we assume that we are created in the form of God, or the image of God? What preposterous vanity has led us to assume that?"

He shook his head again. "I do not wish to argue with you. Also, you must come to a more adult acceptance of the world around you before it is possible to discuss these things intelligently. You must recognize the conditions of the world as they are, accept them, and deal with them. You cannot change the world nor can you demand that it live up to certain principles and ideals. It is necessary to compromise if you are to continue to live in the world." He smiled tolerantly at me. "Maybe it is only a question of growing up."

I smiled back at him. "Growing up? Maturing into an adulthood that consists largely in taking for granted the very sins and evils which you are theoretically against? It seems to me that the clergy and the church are nothing but the final wonderful hypocrisy in an essentially rotten world. You hold up before us the ideal of Good, of Love, of Brotherhood, the principles of Jesus Christ, and then, with them, your wonderful magic hypocritical secret: that they are basically unattainable and impossible. Whoever invented religion was a clever man. He knew that only the unattainable, the impossible, was something to which we could always aspire. Once attained, what could we do but spit on it? Well I spit on it now, but I certainly hand it to the inventor! Condone, forgive, repent, pity, love...but do not change! What would happen to religion if we all changed? What would you do if there was no more incest, no more war, no more murders? You'd go out of business! And adultery, original sin? What Machiavellian guy invented the idea that reproduction of one's kind...the process of sex...was sinful? That was really smart. Hang a conscience and a sense of guilt on us because of our origins. Original sin! The only way we'll ever wipe that out is to commit mass suicide, and self-preservation is a pretty good guarantee against that." I laughed. "You know, Doctor, I have an idea. I think I will grow up in the way that you have suggested. I'll grow up so that I can sit comfortably in an overstuffed chair and pronounce platitudes about the ills of the world. I will grow up so that I, too, can accept the conditions and supposed ills of the world as natural and part and parcel of man's inheritance. War? So what? Send a package to a refugee when it's over, so that my conscience will be clear? Kill a man? Sure, I did it to protect my family, and my country. It was a crusade for democracy, fully approved by the church and the pope... but you aren't Catholic, are you? No, I thought not. And then when I've really grown up, you know what I'll do? I'll build an institution of my own, but not your kind. I'll build an institution inside which anything will be all right. A haven for pimps, whores, statesmen, churchmen, businessmen...anyone. And there, we'll have everything to delight human nature. And, Doctor, do you know what I think? I think I'll do all right. When I pass the hat, people will fall over each other throwing money into it. I won't promise them salvation, but I'll give them what they really want. For ten dollars all the supreme pleasures will be available to mankind. Yep. I think I'll make money in an adult way." I stood up and smiled at him. "And now, Dr. Perrin, if you don't mind, I'll be on my way. It was nice to have seen you on this best of all possible days in this best of all possible worlds. But I will not see you in church."

I made a mock bow to him and walked away, his eyes still on me. I looked now at the grass, the trees, the walks, but I had no sense of openness towards them anymore.

Inside the main building, I made my way directly to the contact section and walked into Mr. Beckwith's office and sat down beside his desk before he had a chance to speak to me.

Again he was embarrassed and frightened at the sight of me. "Good morning," he said nervously.

"Good afternoon," I corrected him. "No one seems to know the time of day today. I've come to see you about my claim."

"Why yes," he said. "Let's see...I don't think there's been any change. We haven't heard anything from the..."

"Not that," I interrupted. "I want to make a claim for limited disability."

He stared at me. "But as I explained to you, if you make a claim for limited disability now, the claim which is already filed will be..."

"I know, I know. I did not come here for advice, Mr. Beckwith. I came to make an application for limited disability compensation or whatever you call it."

"Yes, I understand, but as I explained..."

I cut him short again. "Mr. Beckwith, I don't know how you see your job, but, as I understand it, you are here as a sort of servant of the people in their dealings with the government. Whatever your interpretation of my case, or your personal feelings about it, all I want from you is to make an application for me. I understand what I am doing."

"Well, if you're sure..." He looked at me doubtfully and took a form from one of the drawers in his desk. "Does the doctor know that you're here?"

I nodded. "Yes he does. I got permission from Dr. Russell this morning."

"All right then. Now, let's see...your name is David Mitchell, is that right?"

"You know it is," I said. "Don't you have a copy of the other claim here?"

"Yes."

"Doesn't it have all the necessary information on it?"

"Yes."

"Good. Then give me that one, I'll sign it, and you can fill it out from the other one. That way we both save time."

"Well, if you're sure..."

"I'm sure." I took the paper from him. "May I use your pen?"

He nodded and handed it to me.

"Is this the only place?"

"Yes."

"Good." I signed it and gave it back to him. "Is that all that I have to do?"

"Yes. But are you sure you know what you're doing?"

"Perfectly. All I want to know is how soon this will go through."

"Right away. We'll send it out today."

"Fine."

"I hope you're not going to regret this," he said.

"Not a chance. And don't you worry about it. Just send it out."

"All right. It's your funeral."

"Could be," I said, smiling.

◦⟳◦

When I returned to Building 8, Dr. Russell was in his office and looked up at me. I paused at the door. "May I see you for a moment?"

"Certainly, come in."

"I've been thinking over what you said this morning," I said. "I think maybe you're right. Perhaps it wouldn't be the best thing in the world for me to go home right away."

He smiled. "I thought you might come to that conclusion. Tell me, how did you happen to come to it so quickly?"

I hesitated. "Was it so fast after all? It occurred to me that much of my trouble, the reasons for my being here, might quite possibly be connected with my family, certainly with my mother. And, while it's quite true that I will have to learn to deal with my family, it might not be wise for me to rush things. I'm not sure that my mother is the best person in the world for me to be with just now."

He seemed genuinely pleased. "I'm awfully glad to hear you say that, David. It would have been hard for me to say it to you. Both Dr. Bowles and I feel that your mother is...well, shall we say, very tense? Under the circumstances it might be very bad for you to be in any continuous contact with her. Your trial visit didn't work out very well, either."

"No, it certainly didn't." I laughed again. "It must put you in rather a difficult position," I said, "having to deal with patients on the one hand and families on the other."

He laughed too. "Well, confidentially," he said, "we often have much more trouble with the families than we do with the patients. If we could send the patients to some environment other than their families, we would be able to discharge many patients much earlier. Parents are very often the real causes of confinement."

I stood up. "I can certainly imagine they would be," I said. "I just wanted to let you know how I felt, that's all."

He stood up too. "While you're here, David, how about visits? Your mother will probably want to visit you. How do you feel about it? Do you want to see her now?"

I hesitated. "I think so. The sooner the better. Even if I'm not going to go home right away, I might as well get used to it. That is, unless you think it's a bad idea."

"Not at all." He looked embarrassed then. "David," he said slowly, "I'd like you to know how I feel about this. It makes me feel much better about you, really. I think you've made a surprisingly rapid recovery...I did think it was too rapid...but now I don't anymore. It's done me good to have you come here and tell me how you feel. When I get that kind of co-operation and understanding from a patient, it makes all the difference in the world to me. I hope you know that."

When he said that I felt like a traitor. I did not know exactly why, except that I knew that I was not being quite honest with him. I had an undeclared motive which was not clear, as if I was operating for reasons which were not entirely disclosed even to me. And yet, I knew that I was right, I trusted whatever instinct was forcing me to an action which I did not fully understand, as if it was an unexpected, unconscious ability to deal with this situation. I stifled the impulse to tell him that I felt a certain treachery in myself and said instead:

"Dr. Russell, don't thank me. I know it must be a satisfaction to you, but on the other hand there is no other doctor around here with whom a patient could be frank. I want you to know that I appreciate everything you've done for me, too. If all the doctors here were like you, this would be a different kind of place."

He smiled and his face grew red. "Well, David. It's nice of you to put it that way."

We both laughed. "So long, Doc. I'll see you."

"Goodbye, David. And...thanks."

FIFTEEN

THE NEXT VISITING DAY, I had waited and waited, but there had been no call for me, no one came to see me. Was my mother now taking me at my word? Was she going to make me pay for the way in which I had rejected her? Whatever it was, I instinctively warned myself against expectancy or alarm. Sooner or later she would come. Meanwhile, I had developed a satisfactory and busy routine. Bed-making (I was considered the best bed-maker on the ward) almost all morning, then O.T. and then after lunch, sweeping the halls, working with Mr. Sweetwater, and then supper. The evenings were the only times I still feared, but even they seemed to pass quickly enough for I was allowed to go out onto the grounds. Dave had also been given a pass and we walked along the roads, exploring the hospital grounds.

This afternoon, I had not left the ward, but as the day wore on I knew that no one would be coming for me, so I went out to sit in front of the building on one of three metal garden chairs which had been placed at the edge of the lawn near the road. Some of the patients were still outside, the ones who had both passes and visitors from home, sitting on the grass, walking along the road. For some curious reason, none of them deigned to sit on the chairs. In one group near me I recognized Joseph. Joseph and a rather young man and woman with him. The young man was obviously his brother, the woman... perhaps a girlfriend, or his brother's wife? As I watched them, they stood up from where they had been sitting on the grass, shook hands, and the two of them, the man and woman, walked away from him. As he watched them walking down the road in the direction of the main building, his body seemed to slump towards them in a kind of silent cry for their return. He straightened suddenly and turned away from them and started up the walk. As he passed my chair, he glanced at me and then came to a stop just beyond it.

"Hello, David," he said uncertainly.

"Hello. Why don't you sit down? It's not time to go in yet." Without saying anything, he sat in the chair next to mine and then stared down the road again at the retreating figures. He blinked his eyes slowly, as if he was going to cry.

"What's the matter with you?"

He turned to me, unrecognizing, and then his face lit up slowly and painfully. "You didn't have any visitors, did you?"

"No."

"Lucky you."

"Why? What do you mean?"

He shrugged. "Oh well, what the hell."

"What the hell, what?"

He jerked his head in their direction. "I'll never get out of here, I guess."

I looked at his face. It seemed to have diminished in size and increased in sadness.

"Why not?"

"Them. All they ever come here for is to get me to sign my compensation checks."

"Did you sign one today?"

He nodded.

"But why? Why don't you just refuse to sign them?"

He smiled at me. "And then what? If I don't sign them they'll just get mad at me and not come back to see me at all. If I can't stay on good terms with them, God knows when I'll get out of here."

I looked in the direction in which they had gone, but they were no longer in sight. Then I looked back at him, noticing for the first time the paper bag lying on his lap.

"What did they bring you?"

"Oh." He started suddenly. Then he opened the bag. "Cigarettes and candy." He put his hand in the bag and took out a package of cigarettes. "Here. I've smoked a lot of yours."

"Gee, thanks." I opened the pack and offered it to him, but he shook his head. "They didn't give you matches, too, did they?"

He reached in the bag again. "Yeah, here."

I took the book of matches from him and lighted a cigarette, then put the pack into the pocket of my jacket. I inhaled deeply, glad for the taste of the smoke deep in my lungs. I took the package out of my pocket and looked at it. Gift from a stranger, via Joseph, to me. I turned again in the direction they had gone, feeling a sudden, violent, and inexplicable fury rising up in me against these visitors, against the presumptuous and disdainful way in which they came in here with their little trophies of the outside world: cigarettes, candy, chewing gum (which was forbidden on the ward). Dropping little brown paper packages into the laps of the condemned and confined, getting a signature on a check, and then leaving with a promise of another visit, more candy, more cigarettes, and another check. Through the rising anger, I could feel the little knot of satisfaction about my claim. At least there wouldn't be very much to collect from me. Limited disability was not so high in figures. Perhaps it wouldn't be worth the effort, if, as and when the checks began to come in.

"They only come once a month," Joseph said, interrupting my thoughts. "They always come on the visiting day after the check gets here."

"The dirty, lousy, stinking sons-of-bitches!" I said angrily. With the outburst in words, I could feel something snapping inside of me, as if my own feeling had cracked the glaze of non-feeling with which I had covered myself, as if I had put a false and removable coat of paint on my own insides. Whatever the reasonability of people who were outside of this place, it was…no matter how you looked at it…a hell of a world. Joseph, whatever was wrong with him, was now a sicker man than before they had come here with their checks and cigarettes. If they had determined some objective course by which to keep him imprisoned in this place; if they had desired specifically (and did they perhaps?) to plunge him into the self-imprisonment which was the real confinement of this place, they could not have dreamed of a more effective means. I seized his hand suddenly in mine. "Don't let them do it. Don't let them. Next time, no matter what happens, don't sign the check. They'll come back, don't worry. They'll even let you out if that's the only way they can get the money. Even if they're convinced you're nuts, they'll get you out so you can sign those goddammed checks for them. Don't do it, Joe, don't do it. Next time, spit in their eye, but don't sign the checks!"

He looked at me, shocked and startled, and yet inside the shock there was a kind of mounting pleasure which I could feel from him. "Do you think so, David? Do you think if I don't sign them they won't keep me here?"

"I'm sure of it. I'm positive. Promise me you won't sign anymore. Promise me!"

He hesitated and then breathed deeply. "Okay, David. I promise." I trembled at the sound of his voice. It was like a declaration of marriage in its solemnity. The effect on me was to raise still further the level of fury inside me. I looked up fiercely at the sunlight and then at the sun itself, climbing down into the western sky. Well it might hide itself from the sights it must have seen this day. Even through the force of my feelings, I recognized that I was looking directly into the face of the sun, that I was not blinking at it, but looking wide-eyed and furious into it. I had not forgotten that I had been able to look at the sun fully before, but I simply had not done it for quite a while. That, then, had been true. And what else? Was it not possible that the entire delusion, the whole business, sun and Jesus Christ, the board of judges, all of it, every single bit of it, had a kind of reality which had been rejected and frightened away simply because it did not seem completely logical? And even Dr. Perrin the day before had not completely denied the possibility that I was still Jesus Christ or that I had been. I put my hands hard against my chest, feeling once more that warm pounding spot between my ribs. Radar, atomic power, whatever it was, it was back again. Maybe I had rediscovered whatever door it was I had once found accidentally. I struck my chest and glared fully and angrily at the face of the sun. With my anger, I felt a growing sense of enormous, violent power, as if I could obliterate the sun itself. And even as I looked, the clouds converged on the sun from every direction, as if to protect it from the force of my eyes. I watched and watched and sure enough, the clouds came together in front of it, erasing its face from the sky, leaving only the ruffled gray-brown billows of cloud and mist before my eyes.

I stood up, suddenly victorious and satisfied. This was a new and wonderful sensation. I was in no delusion now. I knew who and where I was, I knew Joseph, knew the time of day, knew what had just happened. Smiling widely, I said to Joseph: "Let's go in, it's almost time for supper."

Through supper, I continued to glare from time to time at the evening sky. The clouds had settled over the sun now, masking it completely. When I was back in the ward, I went to the porch and looked out. In every direction there was a layer of gray clouds, rising from the horizon and deepening in color. And, curiously, above the hospital grounds, and seemingly only above them, in the shape of a great umbrella, was a concentrated mass of black clouds, as if the central point of a storm was focusing itself upon the hospital, and no other part of the countryside. Instinctively, I distrusted my own vision for a moment and looked away. But there was no doubt about it. There was a black umbrella directly over these buildings and grounds, ending suddenly as if it had been inked into the clouds in an almost perfect circle.

As suddenly as the sun had disappeared into the clouds earlier, the rain began to fall. The other patients withdrew slowly from the porch, leaving me alone. A voice from the door called my name.

"Yes?" It was Mr. Harris the attendant, standing in the doorway.

"Don't you want to come in?"

I stepped back from the grillwork. "No. It's not getting onto the porch. I'll come in if it does."

How reasonable and easy it all was now. Little did he know. He had smiled and shrugged his shoulders. After all, how could he worry about me? The best bed-maker on the ward, the only perfectly reasonable patient. And then he had closed the door and smiled through it at me. Wonderful!

By keeping close to the grillwork of the porch, I could feel the rain hitting against my warm face. For some unknown reason, I struck my shoe against the cement floor, the nails in my heel grinding against the stone causing a spark. Immediately there was a crackling split of lightning in the sky, followed by a great crescendo of thunder. I waited, unbelieving, and struck my heel against the floor again. Same thing! How I had underestimated myself!

I repeated the process perhaps fifteen times, always with the same result. The rain was coming down violently now, and I had to move away from the screening to keep from getting entirely wet. I looked in at the lighted wardroom and saw Dave's face peering out at me. I dropped my hands to my sides and looked up at the sky again through the screening on my left. Still the same black circle above us, the rest of the sky still light. Whatever I was proving to myself, I was also not going to give myself away this time. No more pack room for me. I took one long last breath of the cool, damp air and opened the door. Dave came up to me as soon as I came in, giving me a curious, scrutinizing look.

"What were you doing out there, Mitch?"

I looked fully into his eyes, smiling at him. "Nothing. It's nice out there. Cool. I like storms."

"You do?"

I nodded. "Yep."

We sat down together on a bench, and I had an impulse to tell him about the rediscovery of my powers and the fact that I could now use them consciously. Could I really? Was there some other way to test myself? What about stopping the storm I had created? I smiled, and could feel my face relaxing, the muscles around my eyes and forehead becoming limp and easy again, the heat from my face subsiding into my chest. Then I waited. Once more the response was quick. As quickly as it had begun, the storm came to its end. The sky lightened, the rain almost ceased to fall, there was no more lightning. Would the sun still be up? I turned in my seat to look out of the window into the spot in the sky where I knew the sun should be. And sure enough (one had only to believe, after all!) the clouds became lighter and lighter, finally revealing specks of blue here and there, and then majestically, again like the opening chords of music, a ray of sun burst through the clouds and at last the sun itself. I turned to Dave, radiant and happy, and burst into sudden, wild laughter.

"What the hell has got into you?" he asked me.

I stopped laughing abruptly. "Nothing," I said soberly. "I just love to see the sun come out."

"I thought you liked storms."

"I do. I like nature. Storms, sun, rain...all of it. I love it all." It was on the tip of my tongue to say...*and I control it all.*

"Yeah, I guess I love nature, too," he said reflectively. "It's a lot more trustworthy than people."

I looked at him and then back at the sky. The black umbrella of clouds had drifted away from the hospital, dispersing and vanishing, like a troop of dismissed soldiers. On the edge of black I could see a stray piece of blackness, separated from the whole, vaguely the shape of a man. I caught Dave's arm with my hand. "Look at that…"

As if guided by my instinct, or some force from me, he saw what I meant at once. "Looks like a man," he said, and then laughed. "What are you laughing at?"

He stopped laughing but fixed me with a vague, not quite sure smile. "You'll think it's funny," he ventured.

"No, Dave. You know I won't."

He looked back at the sky, lowering his voice as he spoke. "It's like us, that cloud. Don't know if other people see it that way, but the way that cloud's broken loose from the rest of the black is like one of us… breaking through the edge of the world…going out into space, into the unknown." He turned to me, smiling confidently now. "I think I've got something there," he said, beaming. "That's what we are, really. Pioneers. Pioneers of the mind and the unknown. Pioneers of the only thing left. Before, they had to fight snow and rain and Indians to get to the West, now we have to fight doctors and wars and mental hospitals to get to another world." The smile disappeared from his face. "Did you ever think, Mitch, that maybe we were never nuts at all? That in some ways it was a wonderful place…at least where I was for a while. I don't know how it was with you."

I looked away from him. "It was a wonderful place, Dave. And it is a kind of pioneering…but…I sometimes don't know if I have the courage to come back again, all the way. I don't want to come back."

"I know." He paused and then looked up at me, into my eyes. His hand moved over to mine and covered it, and his lips trembled when he spoke. "David," he said (and he had always called me Mitch), "I want to say something to you. I have to say it. I'll never be able to say it to anybody else or at any other time, but I know you'll know what I mean."

"What is it, Dave?"

"I..." He turned away and shook his head. "Don't know if I can say it. Maybe it doesn't need saying, but..." he looked back at me. "...Dave, you *know*. And I *know* too. The rest of them don't know, or they forget, but I can't forget it and you can't either. And I don't want to. Out there..." he looked at the sky again "...out there I found something. I don't know what it was, maybe I'll never know really, but I can see it in your eyes, so I know it wasn't just me. If I know you'll never forget that, that you'll always remember that you've been there, too, then I'll be all right, I'll know that it was not *madness*...that it was finding something, and something that was...good. I'm different now than I was when I came here. I'm not all tied up inside anymore, and I don't hate. Almost as if what I found out there was something to do with love."

I nodded, and once again the embarrassment crawled onto his face. He gripped my hand more firmly and then took it away. "What I wanted to tell you," he said, "was..."

"What?"

He smiled. "I love you...because..." He spread out his hands. "Because you know...because you make it all right having been there."

I looked away from him and then back at him again. "I'll never forget, Dave. I couldn't anyway."

"Okay if I call you Dave from now on, instead of Mitch?"

"Sure."

"Thanks."

SIXTEEN

PIONEERS OF THE MIND...I HAD not realized that I was anything other than alone, until Dave had talked to me, and it now seemed to me curious that I should have divorced myself so completely from any identification with the other patients in the hospital. I had never believed or realized that their experience could have been in any way like my own. The knowledge that my experience was shared did not level it out, flatten it, but gave it instead a special and new importance to me. Whatever the doctors, attendants, families...the outside world might think of us, however they might judge us, we were a special company and had traveled to a special place. If now I could succeed in my efforts to get out of the hospital, to re-assume a place in the so-called usual and normal world and at the same time retain the knowledge of the other world into which I had made my way...if I could accomplish that, it would give me a special stature and, somehow, a means with which to combat what I was sure the average world would thrust upon me, or upon any of us who had been in this place: the slur, the raised eyebrow, the reservation, the excuse, the mark of having been a patient. Experience was the real teacher; surely no experience could be entirely bad; it did not seem to me possible that there was nothing to gain from having been here. And if I could retain the power which I seemed to have acquired with my stay here, I might then indeed find myself a special human being, an endowed creature.

Now a man with his own special secret, I began to enjoy my daily hospital routine. Not only was I the trusted bed-maker and hall-sweeper of the ward, but also Mr. Sweetwater had suggested that he might find a real job for me in the hospital. They were very short of clerks. Minor as such successes had seemed to me at first, with them I gained a special position, a particular triumph over the hospital personnel, the other patients, and over myself. It seemed to me important to be able to simulate a usual normal behavior and, at the same time, to conserve the special abilities which I felt I had acquired as a result of my delusions. No longer did the inner heat which I could call upon at will seem to me a manifestation of illness; rather, it was a definite indication of my ability to roam through two worlds simultaneously, arming me with special weapons, invisible and powerful. I determined to make little or no use of them while I remained in confinement, but the eventual possibilities upon my discharge seemed to me infinite. Should I wish, once I was free, I could have whatever revenge I might desire against the world, the hospital, society in general. My entire focus now was upon the special aim of getting, in a sense surreptitiously, out of the hospital. Like a criminal with the knowledge that an arsenal will be at his disposal upon his release from prison, I was content to wait whatever short time was necessary before my discharge now. I had no absolute assurance that the time would be short, but I did have a conviction that my instinctive behavior would lead me directly to my own freedom. I even had some proof that it was so. Already I had managed to alter the claim situation to such an extent that the problem of my family in relation to the claim was entirely different. After all, now there was little to be gained in keeping me incarcerated. Limited disability compensation was not continuing and indefinite, would not be paid after the period of actual illness was over, and already the doctors were more and more convinced of my progress, my return to normality.

And further, even Dr. Russell had gone so far as to commit himself against my family. *Your mother is...shall we say...very tense.* I sensed, although I did not know quite why, that there was some hidden resource in that statement; but even without knowing just what it was, I felt certain that when the time came to use it, I would know how.

The promised job as a clerk on a ward came unexpectedly quickly. When I reported to Mr. Sweetwater's office one afternoon, he led me immediately to Ward 10, the building in back of 8, and introduced me to the head nurse, a Miss Dunlap. On the way to the ward, he explained what the job would be, what I would have to do, and the conversation made me aware of the ground I had gained, the, in a sense, esteem in which I was now held by some of the personnel.

"I want to warn you," said Mr. Sweetwater, "that this is the first time any patient from an acute ward has been given work outside of the Vocational Rehabilitation buildings. I have had to get special permission in order to place you here, but I am fully confident that you will do a good job, and I am counting on you."

Pleased and surprised, for this was more than I had expected from him, I looked at the man. He did believe in me, he did have confidence in my ability and in my trustworthiness.

"You can count on me," I said easily, and then: "What kind of a ward is Ward 10?"

"It's called a leave ward, actually," he said. "Most patients from the acute wards are transferred to 10 for a month or so before they actually go home on a ninety-day trial visit. They give them more responsibility there and it is usually assumed that they require less medical attention or observation. They are pretty much on their own on 10. They make their own beds, wear their own clothes instead of a uniform. I think that once Miss Dunlap has seen you, she will request that you be transferred there, so not only will you be doing us a good turn, but you'll be that much closer to your ninety-day trial visit."

I frowned then. I had no intention of spending a month on any other ward, although I did not immediately see any way to circumvent it. Keeping my thoughts, my special secrets to myself, I did not mention this to Mr. Sweetwater, saying only: "That's fine."

As soon as I had met Miss Dunlap, I understood the full meaning of Mr. Sweetwater's warning. After looking me over carefully, as if I were an object which might explode in her face, she placed me at a desk on which there was a typewriter and paper. After asking me to wait for a moment, she left the office and then returned with an attendant. She smiled at me.

"David," she said, rather carefully, I thought, "this is Mr. Sedgwick, the ward clerk. He will tell you what to do and will be in here in case you need any help, or if there is anything that you do not understand."

I nodded and looked at him. "How do you do?"

"How do you do," he said, looking at me, with particular attention to my blue uniform. None of the people in the halls were wearing blues. They were all clothed in "civilian" clothing. I felt specially marked, and as he watched me I could feel the disturbance in him. This was probably his first contact with a patient from "8" ...with one of the violent boys.

Miss Dunlap, after a smile and a tentative reassuring pat on my shoulder, left us alone. Elaborately casual, I said: "What would you like me to do?"

Enunciating carefully, he explained to me in minute detail that I was to type a roster of all of the patients on Ward 10. "Double space, three copies, an original and two carbons. That will probably take you all afternoon."

I did not think so...it wasn't very long.

"Now..." He leaned over me without looking into my face. "Do you think you understand it all right?"

"Yes."

"That's fine. I'll sit right here in case you have any trouble."

I found it difficult to type at first, for though Mr. Sedgwick sat at some distance from me, reading a newspaper, I could feel him observing me, almost as if he had been looking over my shoulder. I braced my back and determined not only to disregard him, but to change his apprehension to admiration if possible. I did not try to type too fast at first, but gradually my speed increased until finally I was absorbed in the list, forgetting him completely.

When I was about halfway through the roster, he stood up suddenly, flashed a glance at me and walked out of the room. When he came back, he was accompanied by Miss Dunlap and another nurse.

"How are you getting along, David?" asked Miss Dunlap, putting her hand on my shoulder again, and then without waiting for a reply, she turned to the other nurse. "This is David," she said to her, as if I had no other name in the world, "and Mr. Sweetwater has sent him over here to help us out." She did not introduce us.

She picked up the finished work lying by the typewriter and showed it to the other nurse, looking at it herself as she did so. She shook her head as if amazed. "This is just wonderful, David," she said, smiling at me. "Just wonderful. You are certainly going to be a help to us."

As if at a signal, the other nurse and Mr. Sedgwick left the office and Miss Dunlap leaned over me confidentially. "David, how would you like to be transferred over here? You'll probably have to come to this ward before you are actually sent on your trial visit, and this would make it so much quicker. If you'd like, I'll speak to your ward doctor about it today and perhaps you can be transferred over here tomorrow. What do you say?"

Some inner doubt warned me against immediate acceptance of this offer, although I had been prepared for it beforehand. "I'd like to think it over for a day or so, Miss Dunlap," I said reasonably. "That is, if it won't make any difference to you."

She hesitated, disappointed.

"Would it be all right if I let you know the day after tomorrow? Or perhaps even tomorrow afternoon? You see, tomorrow is visiting day and I probably won't be back here until Thursday."

"Oh. Do you think you might be going home on a two-week pass?"

I shook my head. "I don't think so, but you never can tell. I'd rather wait until after visiting day."

She smiled again. "Of course, David, of course. And..." she hesitated, "well there's no reason why I shouldn't tell you this. You know I was quite worried when I knew you were from an acute ward, because we've never had anyone from 8 before, but, David, I'm really amazed. You've more than lived up to Mr. Sweetwater's praises of you. I'm awfully glad you came over to work here."

I smiled. "So am I, Miss Dunlap. And now, I'd better finish this."

When I finished the roster, I took it into Miss Dunlap's office since Mr. Sedgwick had not reappeared. Apparently I was now a trusted member of the hospital office force, a fact that more than pleased me. Of itself, this acceptance was a kind of special revenge upon the hospital and the personnel. When I gave her the roster, Miss Dunlap again put her hand on my shoulder. "Thank you so much, David," she said, and then impulsively squeezed my shoulder in her fingers. *"Such a nice boy,"* she said, and smiled.

I looked at her. With the squeeze and the faint embarrassment in her words, I had felt a sudden, shocking, unexpected sexual drive towards this woman, and I was sure that it had not originated with me. If I was actually transferred to Ward 10, would I end up sleeping with Miss Dunlap? I had to set the muscles of my face to keep from bursting into laughter. What a victory that would be! With what vindictive pleasure would I take on this woman!

Carefully sober, for I was feeling almost drunk at the moment, I looked into her eyes and said: "Miss Dunlap, it's been a real pleasure for me, too, and..." I lowered my eyes and then let them flicker back into hers "...I must say it's a pleasure to meet such a nice nurse."

She giggled faintly and withdrew her hand, and I moved slowly away from her. In a low voice, I said: "I'll let you know tomorrow, Miss Dunlap."

⌢

Visiting day again. In spite of my determination to be calm, I felt a disturbing, uncontrollable excitement. I had a sure sense that my mother would come to see me, and the prospect of the encounter made me a little apprehensive. I stayed on the porch, my eyes glued to the road, waiting.

She was the second visitor to arrive, and this time as she came near the building, she looked up to the porch. She did not see me at once and after her eyes had swept over the men looking out through the screening, they crossed slowly back again, finally coming to rest on my face. I smiled and waved and she waved back at me. I moved to the side of the porch to watch her coming up the path to the entrance of the building, and she waved again as she walked through the door.

I waited impatiently during the period in which she must have been talking to the doctor, and finally my name was called and I hurried out to the hall. In some way, it was a strange meeting. We advanced towards each other in the hall, tentatively, rather like lovers meeting after a quarrel, hesitant, unsure, and yet with their thoughts firmly tied to the prospect of a joyful making-up.

After she had kissed me, we drew apart. She laughed and said: "I've got a surprise for you, David."

"What is it?"

"I've brought Sarah Rogers with me. She's waiting in the car."

"Sarah Rogers!" My family didn't even know her. "How on earth did you two get together?" It was a surprise and I was not sure how I felt about it. I had had, and the memory embarrassed me now, a minor, fairly violent affair with her and had never introduced her to my family. It had been so long ago. How could she have known that I was in the hospital?

"She wrote you a letter, and I opened it. So I got in touch with her."

I felt a flash of anger at this intrusion into a life of my own, not necessarily a secret life, but at least a life that I had never revealed. I wondered if there was any special motive in this. Something made me hold back the anger. I smiled again. "Gee, that's swell. Where is she?"

"She's waiting in the car now. And since you have a pass, I brought a picnic lunch along and we can all go out on the lawn and eat. We haven't had lunch yet."

"I have."

"Oh, I know, but perhaps you can eat something. Can't you? I brought all your favorite things along."

I forced myself to smile again. "Swell. Let's go."

We walked to the car park near the main building. On the way we talked, defensively still, touching on nothing that was important. How was John? How well I had been doing in the last few weeks. No mention was made of my visit home, or my refusal to see her the last time she had visited me.

Sarah Rogers. Twenty-seven years old, almost beautiful, almost a lot of things. I looked at her through the open door of the car, at the disarrangement of her hair, the uncertain, confused smile altering her face and twisting her lips. When she spoke it was more a breaking of sound from her throat, husky and timid: "Hello there, David."

I took her hand in mine. "Hello, Sarah."

From behind me came my mother's voice. "Let's drive down the road near the main gate. There's a lovely place for a picnic there. You know, by those woods."

"Okay. Fine."

We got in on opposite sides of the car, pressing Sarah against each other, and straining away from her at the same time. Feeling her next to me, her body reluctantly, it seemed, wedged next to mine, the memory of physical possession came sharply not to my mind but to my body, embarrassing and strange now. Simultaneously I wanted and did not want to look at her. Her presence was not only a reminder of a shared past, but a reminder of the celibacy of the hospital, disturbing and irritating. I was glad when the car came to a stop and we got out, relieving the physical pressure of our bodies, busying ourselves with the lunch basket, the thermos, the rugs, even a tablecloth.

Although I had eaten lunch only an hour or so before, I was hungry. And the food was something we never saw at all at the hospital: crackers and cheese, beer (!), fresh fruit, deviled ham, peanut butter, chocolate. As if avoiding some subject which we all knew in our different ways was bound to have to come up, we talked in violently general terms about any impersonal subject. John's work, Sarah's job, her apartment in New York, my job in the hospital, the possibility of war with Russia, the Palestine question, and both my mother and I started, suddenly shocked, when Sarah, after looking around the grounds, seeming to breathe in the very beautiful day which I had only just noticed, said:

"This is really a lovely place. I shouldn't think you would mind staying here." Then she turned to look at me.

A deep silence fell over the three of us as I looked at her. The sun slanted across her face, and a mild wind blew her hair, softening the outlines of her face on which there was a sad, vaguely reminiscent smile now. Her eyelids opened and closed slowly and then her full gaze was directed at me, open, forgiving (although I did not know for what) and even desiring. I do not know in what way she felt she was presenting herself to me at that moment, but I saw her face as a target. The words had bitten into me, damning her, and my only wish now was to strike back into this face, this creature that sat here before me, forbidden and out of reach, cruelly open to me now.

I laughed a short laugh. "The beauties of confinement, Sarah, are manifold. Since I am a committed patient, I expect to be able to enjoy this loveliness for quite some time."

My aim was accurate. The silence descended further upon us, and I opened another bottle of beer.

"Mother?" I asked, offering it to her.

She shook her head.

"Sarah?" My voice was even, friendly, not-quite triumphant.

She shook her head, looking away from me. "No thanks."

"Well, here's how."

I drank from the bottle and then set it down, licking my lips.

"Do you have any cigarettes?"

Simultaneously, they reached in their purses, Sarah bringing out Chesterfields, and my mother offering Pall Malls. I reached over Sarah, "I don't like Chesterfields," I said, and took a Pall Mall.

The silence remained with us. Whatever reserve we had had about what we were not saying had now been broken; there was nothing more to say until we touched on what we were all afraid to come to. It was my mother, finally, who broke the stillness between us. Standing up and straightening her dress, not quite looking at me, she said:

"Why don't you two just stay here? I'm supposed to see Mr. Beckwith in the claims office."

Slowly, quietly and vaguely insolent, I looked up at her. "There won't be any news about the claim."

"Why?"

"I've applied for limited disability. That cancels the other application automatically."

She stared at me, doubt and anger playing across her face.

"What?"

I nodded without speaking.

As if controlling some inner violence, she said steadily: "Well, I said I'd be in to see him, so perhaps I had better anyway. I'll see you two later."

As she walked away from us, I watched her angry back until she got into the car, and then smiled. Whatever I was doing, and I was still not entirely sure, it seemed to be working out all right, at least it felt as if it was. I turned back to Sarah and stared at her.

She smoked silently and then crushed her cigarette in the grass. Still without looking at me, she said: "It's been a long time, hasn't it, David?"

I shrugged my shoulders. "Yes."

She rolled over on the grass, lying on her stomach, picking at the grass with her fingers. "David, do you remember something?"

"What?"

She looked at me briefly and then away again. "Do you remember when you asked me to marry you?"

I was shocked, as if the breath had been taken out of me. My face reddened, I remembered. "Yes," I said carefully, and then: "It *has* been a long time."

"Long enough for me to..."

"To what?"

She looked full into my face.

"I'd marry you tomorrow," she said quietly.

"You would?"

"Yes."

I laughed. "I'm not so sure that would be a good idea," I said. "Married to an ex-nut? Are you sure you'd like that?"

Her face twisted again and then straightened itself. "You know I'd never feel that way, David."

I laughed again, silently. "Nobody knows anything, Sarah. That's all I know."

"In other words, you mean that you don't feel that way? Is that it?"

I hesitated. "You could put it that way, if you want."

"Oh." She looked at me again. "Did you want to in the first place?"

I shrugged my shoulders again. "Why go on about it? I suppose I did or I wouldn't have asked you. But too much has happened since then."

She shook her head. "No it hasn't, Dave. I was a fool."

I was suddenly angry with her. "You've made your offer," I said. "You don't have to go on and on about it."

"David!"

"Nuts! 'And the greatest of these is Charity,'" I quoted to her. "Thanks just the same, I'm not having any."

"Oh, David!" She rolled over on the grass again, lying on her back now. Looking down on her face I could see that her eyes had tears in them. "I suppose," she said, her lips trembling, "that you have every reason to be bitter, but…"

"But what?"

"I didn't mean it that way, David. Really I didn't. When we were… when we were together…Oh, David, you know I loved you."

I nodded. "Yes…loved. That's all over now. You can't get that back." I was sorry now that I had struck at her so hard. "Sarah, you have to understand. I couldn't now. It's not the same anymore. I don't know what I want now. I've been…I've been someplace, Sarah, someplace you don't know anything about. I'm not back now. I don't know that I'll ever be back really. I…"

"What, Dave?"

"I don't know that I want to come back. I don't *want* to come back to where I was before. Out of here, yes, but not back to what I was. It's all changed. I'm not what I was, that's all. What I was…is finished."

She was serious. "I'm sorry. But one thing, Dave. Promise me one thing, no matter how you feel?"

"What?"

"Come to see me when you're out. Will you?"

I hesitated. Why not? "All right. I'll promise. I'll come." She lay back again. "Good, Dave. Thanks."

"Oh, that's all right."

She stood over us, flushed, excited, almost angry, but still controlling it. "David! I simply don't understand you at all. Simply giving away all that money. You might actually have had an income for life." She shook her head. "Don't you think it's ridiculous of him, Sarah?"

Sarah's answer was careful. "I don't know. I think people have to make up their own minds about these things."

I stood up. "Look, Mother, there's no point in getting excited about it now. It's done and it's irrevocable. The only way it could be changed would be to prove that I was not of sound mind when I made the second application, and that's impossible. In fact, Dr. Russell would testify, if necessary, that I was of much sounder mind when I signed the second one than when I signed the first application that you made. So it's done, and it will stay that way. But while we're on all this, there is something I want to know."

"What's that?" Her anger was disappearing reluctantly, bowing to the finality of what I had said.

"What about this commitment? Why was I committed?"

She hesitated, blushing. "Didn't they tell you about that? Dr. Bowles said I would have to commit you or else they would commit you themselves."

I shook my head. "But they can't do it themselves."

"Yes, they can, David. No matter what anyone has told you, they can. I didn't want to commit you, but when I was at the County Court on Monday, they told me that the hospital could commit you if the doctors advised it, and they definitely did."

"On Monday. What Monday?"

"Monday of this week."

"This week? What did you have to go back for?"

"I didn't have to go back. You were only committed on Monday of this week."

I glared at her. "Look, I saw the files. Dr. Palmer showed them to me. I was committed on June 12th."

She opened her hands in a gesture of helplessness. "David, I *know*. I went to the court Monday of this week, and that is the day of the commitment. I don't know who has told you what, but they have not been telling you the truth."

Did anyone know—or tell—the truth?

I laughed angrily. "Well, I'm not the only one they've been deceiving then," I said. "I'm not so sure they are working hand in glove with you, either."

"What do you mean?"

"Some of the doctors think that it would be much better for me to stay here. As a matter of fact they implied that they advised the commitment in order to keep me away from you, because they think you aren't good for me just now. What they called you was 'a very tense woman.' How do you like that one?"

"David, are you sure you know what you're saying?"

I nodded. "Sure I am. Ask Dr. Russell and see if he denies it. In fact, I'll go with you and then he won't be able to deny it."

"Well, I'll be damned!" She was angry again now, but not at me this time. "They told me that it was for your own protection, and that was the only reason." She looked at me, doubting and observing. "I'm not so sure that I wouldn't like to show them, and just sign you out right now."

Was it music, what could it be? The blood surged, rising and falling in my veins. "But could you now?"

"I certainly could. I went over the whole thing with the clerk of the court, or whatever he was. I can sign you out at any time as long as there is no hospital commitment...I mean, as long as I was the one who committed you. It only means that I'm responsible for you and that I'll see that you get whatever treatment the hospital advises for you." She paused, looking away from me, thinking. "That Bowles!" she exclaimed suddenly. "I never did like him anyway. I should have known there was some kind of dirty work going on. Imagine telling you that you were committed! It must have been a terrible shock to you!" She looked at me, her face filled with concern and tenderness. "You poor darling. Was that why you didn't want to see me that day?"

Was it? I wasn't exactly sure, but it seemed now a wonderful reason. I smiled at her. "Of course," I said. "What on earth did you think?"

She looked at me wide-eyed, I wondered if she was going to cry.

"Why, darling, I don't know what I thought. I thought maybe you hated me, I didn't know what to think…"

"Well," I said reassuringly, "it doesn't matter now. I feel so much better now that I know the whole story. I knew somehow that you couldn't do a thing like that without letting me know about it first." I paused then, watching her. "Boy," I shook my head slowly, "they certainly know how to play one hand against the other around here, don't they?"

She tossed her head. "Well! I'll show them. I've a mind to go right over to that building and tell them what I think of them. In fact, I think I will!"

Take it easy, take it easy, kept flashing through my mind. "Now don't get all hot and bothered about this, Mother," I said calmly. "They may have thought they had perfectly good reasons for doing this. Besides, I'm only beginning to rest well now, and I think if I stayed here a while longer, it might do me good, actually. We can go back now if you want, but I think we should just tell Dr. Russell that you think I'm getting along well and that maybe I could have another trial visit. After all," I took a deep breath…amazed at my own cleverness and skill…"remember my last visit home. We don't want any recurrence of that, do we? Let's say that I'll stay here for another week and then see if you can get me home on a two weeks' trial visit, or if by that time you really think I'm all right, then perhaps they'll let me go home on a three months' trial. In any case, I don't think we should antagonize them. They may have ways of making things much more difficult for us."

"Well, I'm so mad…"

Sarah's voice interrupted her, and we both looked down at her in surprise; I had forgotten she was there. "I think that is the most reasonable and sensible attitude any one could possibly have," she said to my mother, and then looked at me questioningly, examining me as if for some hidden motive.

"Sarah's right, Mother. Really she is. Now why don't you go over and see Dr. Russell. Tell him that you think I'm doing well...that is, if you think I am..."

"Ha!" she snorted, "if I think you are. Why you're as sane as I am!"

I smiled. "Good. Just tell him that and tell him what I said. I'm sure he'll feel that this is perfectly reasonable, too. He's an awfully nice doctor, anyway. You know him, don't you?"

"Yes, I do. And you're right. I thought he was kind of a young whippersnapper before, but if he'd been in charge here all along, I'll bet things would have been different." She thought a moment. "Was he the one who said I was...I was 'tense'?"

I nodded slowly. "As a matter of fact, he was. But actually he said that it was Bowles who had said it. I don't know that it means that he agrees with Bowles."

"Oh. Well, anyway, I still think he's a nice man. But, David, are you sure that you don't want me to do something about it at once? I'm perfectly willing to take you out of here right now."

I shook my head. "Really, Mother. My way is best. You know it is. Not only will it be better for me, but it will actually seem more sensible to the doctor, and that is what counts in the long run."

She looked at me then for a long time, and gradually the tears came into her eyes. "I'm so proud of you," she said. "Here you're the one who's been confined in this place and now you're having to tell me how to behave sensibly. I'm just a stupid impulsive fool, and if you didn't have so much sense, I'd probably be spoiling things for you now." She took my hand in her two hands. "Forgive me, darling, please. Forgive me."

It was not, somehow, the triumph I had wanted or expected, but it was even more than that...it was a whole vindication now. I felt cramped and speechless, in an overwhelming emotional exhaustion which came over me rapidly, almost like letting the air out of a tire. I wondered idly if I was going to collapse. I didn't.

Whatever sure instinct had guided me through what now seemed to me a tricky and dangerous path towards my release was something for which I then thanked God. Had I been the planner, the conscious developer of these events, I could not have done it so well. Something, in whatever journey I had made, had been added to whatever I had been, and in that moment, standing with my mother and with Sarah still sitting at our feet, I felt a life-giving surge of wholeness inside me. I had come through a fire and had not been burned. I knew that I was going to leave here at last, and further, I knew that I would never have to come back. Never. I stared at my hands. The scars were still there, and yet the one on my left hand...was it the light or what? ...seemed almost to have disappeared. It seemed right that only the scar on my right hand, my forward hand, the first to feel the fire, should be the one to wear—probably forever—the badge. Whatever it was, it was not a blotch, but in a sense a campaign medal. Easily, then, without vengeance, justification, anger, or self-consciousness, I looked not at the grass, the trees, the sun, Sarah or my mother; I looked instead, and from some distant place it seemed, at David Mitchell. Whatever he might be to someone else, whatever he might represent, however people might feel about him...however I felt myself about his being *me*...as I stared at him, easily enough I could love him. I was happy and relieved; something had been lifted from me. I came back to myself to look across the lawn, and there was no clouding of my vision, I had no difficulty with my eyes. I took off my glasses to look at the buildings, the flagpole, the long stretch of grass between them and me. It was almost from this place that I had first seen these buildings, this monster institution, so carefully disguising its real nature. I felt my body with my hands: the vehicle, the instrument, the machine that I had driven through such perilous spaces. It was a good machine; I'd have to start taking care of it now.

SEVENTEEN

AFTER THAT VISIT, THE DAYS themselves took on a special time of their own for me. Neither fast, nor slow, but almost frighteningly clear, so that I could watch the inevitable passing of the minutes taking me surely towards a destination at which I had confidently and accurately aimed the arrow of my self.

Doctor Russell had made no definite statement to me, and yet the fact of my imminent discharge was shown to me in many small ways. He had eyed me suspiciously, as if I had tricked him unexpectedly in a way which he could not help but admire. His only revenge was not to commit himself. Miss Dunlap was less reserved. Simply and obviously dismayed, she said: "Well, David! I hear we're going to lose you! Isn't that always the way? Just when we get someone good in here, they're snatched away from us. Well, good luck to you!"

Mr. Sweetwater and Mr. Saunders had both congratulated me, and had both gone further. Far enough to explain that my discharge was a real triumph for them. They hinted at secret battles with the doctors on my behalf and rather mysterious steps forward for them in their work. It was Mr. Sweetwater who announced triumphantly that I would be the first person ever to receive a final discharge from an acute ward. Even the attendants seemed pleased with me, as if I had become rather unexpectedly an asset instead of just one more liability. They felt, in some way, that they had stumbled across a hidden gold mine, a gold nugget that was a tribute to their treatment or behavior. Even Dr. Palmer, who had never seemed open or friendly to me, had taken it upon himself to stop me in the hall as I was sweeping, and asked me to come into his office and smoke a cigarette with him. He had looked me over carefully, his eyes coming finally to rest on my hands.

"Do you think you'll ever do anything like that again, David?"

"I don't think so," I said carefully.

"Do you know now why you did it?"

I shrugged my shoulders. "It is possible," I said, "that you are searching for a nonexistent motive, Doctor. After all, I stated originally that I did it to get my hands out of the cuffs, and I succeeded in doing that. Actually what other means would have had so spectacularly successful a result? I don't really think there was anything more to it than that."

"Well, perhaps you're right." He inhaled on his cigarette and looked at me again. "You know, we're all mighty pleased with you. This is going to mean a lot to us."

"Why?"

"Because we've been fighting to get permission to discharge patients directly from this ward. I'll admit that I was rather skeptical at first, but we did get special permission in your case, you know."

"You did? How come?"

"Dr. Russell did," he said. "He has a theory that acute cases are not likely to be chronic and that in the long run the worst thing that can happen to them is to keep them confined. I must say that I think he's right in your case. Anyway it's exciting to us if you turn out well for us...it's like discovering a new method of treatment. It opens up a whole new light on this kind of illness."

I laughed. "You're making me feel like quite a guy," I said, "but I think I'd better go back and finish sweeping the hall."

He looked at me rather solemnly then, shaking his head. "I guess you will do all right for us, David. Go ahead."

"Before I go, there is something I would like to know."

"Yes?"

Without raising my voice, I said: "Why did you tell me I was committed on June 12th?"

A denial swept across his eyes. He did not answer at once, and finally, looking at his hands, he said slowly: "It was not my idea, David."

I smiled. "It doesn't matter now. I just wanted you to know I knew. You can guess how I felt about that."

He looked at me and then down at the table. "I'm sorry."

"Don't lose any sleep over it, Doc," I said, and then held my hand out to him.

He shook it slowly.

⌒

One week after Sarah's visit with my mother, one week to the day, I was summoned into the presence of Dr. Bowles. When I reached his office, Dr. Russell was standing by his desk and they both offered me a chair.

Dr. Bowles looked at me for a long time before he said anything. At last, as if he had just turned from viewing a sunset, his eyes cleared. "Well, David." He said the two words and paused. "This is quite something, isn't it?"

It did not seem to be a question that I could answer, so I remained silent.

"We've decided to give you a two weeks' trial visit," he said then.

Two weeks! I was suddenly deflated.

It must have shown on my face, for a look of concern came over Dr. Russell's face, and he said quickly: "That's not all, David. That's not all."

"David," Dr. Bowles continued slowly, "if at the end of two weeks, your mother thinks you are all right, we will extend it to a three months' trial visit...you won't have to come back to the hospital at all then. So you see," he said, "a lot depends on those weeks at home. I want you to know how much this is going to mean, not only to you, but also to us, and even to others, David. Yes, it is going to mean a great deal to those men, the men in here with you. If we are able to prove successfully in your case that discharges from this ward can be good for the patients, we are going to be able to revise our whole system of treatment."

"Gee, that's fine," I said. "You won't have to worry. I won't be coming back this time."

Dr. Bowles nodded. "No, David, I don't think you will either. But," he hesitated and glanced at Dr. Russell, "there is one thing I want to warn you against."

"What?"

He sat back in his chair, readying himself for a lengthy speech. "David," he began, "when I was twenty-five...that was some time ago, of course...I used to smoke all the time. Two or three packages of cigarettes a day." He eyed me to see if I had taken this in fully.

"Yes?"

"Well, my boy, I began to realize that I was doing an injury to myself. It cut down my breath, tired me out...in fact, it was a thoroughly bad habit."

"Yes."

"David, I realized one day..." he leaned over, pointing his finger at me, "well, that I'd simply have to stop it. And, my boy, I did. Not by cutting down, not by taking a cigarette now and then. But by *stopping*. I have never smoked...never, David...a single cigarette since that day. No need to tell you that it's done me a world of good. I'm over fifty now, and look at me...healthy, full of energy. If I'd gone on smoking, I wouldn't be the same man."

"Do you want me to stop smoking?"

He shook his head. "No, David, I'm not going to ask you that." He looked at Dr. Russell, smoking a cigarette. "It seems to be a universal habit these days, and I could hardly advise it with Dr. Russell smoking at my elbow, now could I?"

"Well, you *could*..."

They both laughed.

"David," he went on, "it's not smoking that worries me. But something else. And I want you to promise me something."

I raised my eyebrows. "What is it?"

"Drinking." He paused heavily on the word, dropping it and holding it in the otherwise silent room.

"Drinking?"

He nodded slowly. "It can be the worst thing in the world, particularly for someone like you. Don't fool around with it, my boy. Just make up your mind once and for all never to drink again. Nothing. No beer, no wine. Nothing at all. It's the only sure cure."

"Sure cure? You talk as if I was an alcoholic!"

He smiled slowly. "Well? Well, perhaps not that, David...I don't say you're an alcoholic, that isn't what I mean, but remember the very first night you were in here, the one thing you wanted was a drink. Remember that?"

I nodded. It seemed pointless and silly to try and explain anything to him now. "Well, Dr. Bowles," I said, still laughing, "I don't think you'll have to worry about that, really I don't. After all, if I'd been a confirmed alcoholic, I'd have been screaming for the stuff all the time. Anyway, whatever you think, I'll guarantee that you don't have to worry about me and liquor."

"No, David. I want your solemn promise. It is very important."

"Okay." I said firmly. "I promise you I won't drink ever again."

"Do you mean it seriously?"

"Yep. Word of honor."

"Good. Fine." He stood up in his chair. "Your mother is coming for you this afternoon, and I may not see you again. In fact I hope I never see you again, for your sake." He looked at Dr. Russell. "Not only for your sake, but for my own. You've been more damned trouble to me than any other patient has ever been. I hardly slept nights when you were first here." He smiled at me again. "Anyway, that's all over now, isn't it?"

"Yes, it sure is."

He held out his hand. "Good luck, David. All the luck in the world. And don't ever come back here."

I shook his hand. "Don't worry. I won't."

"Good. Now I have to be off, but I think Dr. Russell wants to talk to you."

He made a sort of mock salute to us both and walked out of the office, leaving us alone. Dr. Russell walked around the desk and lowered himself slowly into Dr. Bowles's chair. He drummed his fingers on the green blotter...it seemed to be a mannerism of his...and then looked at me.

"Well, David," he said. "So you've come to the end of your journey."

I smiled. "Looks that way, doesn't it?"

His face colored. "You've rather taken things into your own hands recently, haven't you?"

I looked away from him, embarrassed. "I guess I have. But remember, it was you who said I was my own doctor. Maybe we didn't quite agree on the consultation."

"However it came out," he said slowly, "it's come out your way. I hope," his voice was very low and serious now, "that it doesn't seem too much of a victory to you."

I shook my head. "No," I said, "it doesn't. I had thought of it that way, at least I did until it suddenly happened, and then it wasn't so much a triumph—although I had expected it to be—but more just the logical way in which it should have worked out. It's right...that's all."

"Well, perhaps it is. You're as good a judge of that as I am, I think. But there is one thing...if you don't mind talking about it...one thing I would like to know."

"What is it?"

"How do you feel about it? What has it meant to you?"

I hesitated. I was not sure I knew the answer to the question, nor did I know how much I could express to him of my own feelings.

"I'm not sure I can tell you that, Dr. Russell. I'd like to, though." He offered me a cigarette and I took one, and he handed me the matches. When I had lighted it, I thought for a moment and then said: "If there is any law of life in which I believe, I think it would be that experience…simply in the general nature of things…cannot be harmful as such, unless you are determined to make it so. I've had an experience, Doctor. The simplest way I can put it is that it is up to me to make it a valuable experience, valuable for me. In some way already, this has been something that has increased my sense of my own wholeness. I don't know quite how to judge myself, but I am surely more of a human being today than on May 11th. If you can understand that."

He nodded. "Yes, I think I can easily understand it. One more thing, David."

"What?"

"What was the purpose of your illness?"

I was taken suddenly aback. "Purpose?" I echoed.

He nodded. "Yes. For any such tremendous action, any action of such obliterating violence, there must have been a purpose."

I had never thought of that, certainly. Evasively, I said: "Well, of course I was trying to escape…"

He shook his head. "That's too general, David. Much too general. And you know it. Anyway, you needn't answer it now. But think about it. The day you can answer that yourself, and you'll know, then you will reap your own reward from all of this."

"I guess you're right."

He nodded again. "I think so. I think that you will begin to reap a reward at once. But when you answer that question, then you will really have made this count. You are—as it were—aiming in the right direction. You'll get there."

I looked at him openly. "I think I will. I really think I will."

He stood up. "Well, David, that's all I have to say, I guess...that is, except goodbye."

"I'd like to say something too, Dr. Russell. I'd like to thank you again for all you've done. However much I've been my own doctor recently, none of it would have been possible without your help. I do know that, and I want you to know I know that."

"Nonsense," he said. "I only did what any well-intentioned blundering doctor would have done. You can take the credit for this discharge. You earned it yourself, don't ever let anyone tell you otherwise. *You earned it.*"

I looked away from him. "Yes, I guess I did."

He held out his hand and I took it in mine. "Thanks, anyway."

He smiled. "A couple of months from now," he said, "we're all going to be thanking you. Don't forget you're taking a responsibility along with you."

"I won't, Doctor. I won't."

I started out the door and he called to me. "Oh, by the way, one more thing."

"Yes?"

"You're pretty good friends with a boy named David Everett, aren't you?"

Dave! I'd almost forgotten him in the last few days. "Yes, why?"

"He's going to be the first to follow you, I hope."

"Gosh, that's wonderful. That's swell, Doctor."

"I thought you'd be glad to hear it. Particularly, David, since you've helped him out."

"I have? How?"

He laughed. "He's carrying the torch for you. He was in here this morning raising hell with Dr. Bowles. I know he'll get out now." He laughed again and looked at me conspiratorially. "If a few more of the patients knew how to upset Dr. Bowles, we'd have a lot more discharges around here."

We both laughed then. "Gee," I said, "I'm awfully glad about that."

"I know you are. And now if you'll wait out there in the hall, I'll send for your clothes."

"Okay. Oh, but, Doctor, could I go back on the ward for just a minute?"

"Sure, what for?"

"I wanted to say goodbye to Dave," I said.

"Sure thing."

He walked down to the ward with me and let me in with his key.

I said goodbye to several of the other patients that I had known, to Monty, even to Jerry. Finally, on the porch, I found Dave. Sitting by the wire screening, looking out.

"Hello, Dave."

"Hi."

"I'm leaving, Dave."

"What? No kidding! When?"

"Today. Right now!"

He jumped to his feet. "Gosh, Dave, that's wonderful. Wonderful!"

Our hands reached for each other automatically. We both smiled but we could not seem to say anything. At last, the words bubbling through his smile, "Boy, I'm glad for you. I'm glad for you."

"It won't be long for you either, Dave. Dr. Russell said it wouldn't."

He was embarrassed. "Hell, I won't stay here now that you're going. Who'd I talk to?"

Again we both laughed. "Dammit," I said, "I'm going to miss you."

"Aw, bull shit, kid." He gripped my hand tightly and let it go. "You get the hell out of here while the going's good. Go on."

He turned me around and gave me a shove. "Beat it."

I looked over my shoulder at him. "So long, Dave. I won't forget. Honest. Never."

He nodded his head quickly and then looked away from me.

The wait, and then the clothing man, and then the last of the minutes were ticking themselves out inexorably on the wall clock. I walked over to the door, looking out on the grass, the walk, the corner of the building, and then up the building to the porch. Even from here I could see the dark-blue clothing, and Dave's black head resting in the corner of the porch. I looked at him, unable to tear my eyes from his face, and then gradually my eyes dropped back from the porch to the road. A car came into view from behind the corner of the building, stopping in the small parking space near the sign "Doctors only." The door opened and my mother got out of the car and crossed the road. I looked away from her, first at the clock, into Dr. Bowles's empty office, then into the other office where an unfamiliar nurse was sitting at the desk. She smiled up at me and then returned to her work. I turned around to look at the door of the shock room, directly behind me. I hadn't made the beds in there today. Well...

"David." Was it my own voice, or had someone spoken to me? "David," it said, "what *was* the purpose?" I turned around quickly, but there was no one there.

My mother had started up the walk and I opened the door, not looking at her directly, and walked through it, hearing it close behind me. Any experience—who had said that?—any experience can be valuable. The world that I had penetrated, even though I had left it, belonged to me now. What I had touched was mine. That world up there—I looked up and then down at the scars on my hands—where I am not, but where I have been. Mental hospital, asylum, sanctuary. Dave and Dr. Russell. My hand, of itself, reached for the knob. The door was locked.

As my mother approached, her eyes upon me, I looked up at the sun. I forced my eyes open to it, but they blinked in pain. I could not look at it anymore. I could not go back.

AFTERWORD

By Alexandra Carbone, Managing Editor of
The Fritz Peters Collection

Documentarian of *Unapologetically Fritz*

WHY FRITZ? WHY NOW?

Because stories are not book reports. They are concentrated potions of experience. A quality story induces catharsis and understanding—a way to get more life out of life, to gain a wider view. Like Fritz Peters' *Boyhood with Gurdjieff,* our point of departure.

When we read the memoir years ago, we wanted to see Fritz mow lawns and make trouble on the big screen. Seeking out his other works, we discovered deeply personal stories about compelling times and places. The complex characters and paradoxical truths jump off the page and walk with the reader. We found classics – ahead of their time and falling out of print – so we embarked on a mission at Hirsch Giovanni to republish Fritz Peters' books, to make a documentary about him, and to adapt his books into movies. What you hold in your hands is the first step.

Life And Work

The themes seem disparate, but they coalesce in one person. Mental illness. Homosexuality. Spirituality. Military service. Death drive.

Nonconformism. The war of the sexes. The self and society. Work. Fritz wrote about them because he knew them; in fact, could not escape them, had something he had to say about them, something to get off his chest. The books are highly personal, highly autobiographical. Multiple friends of his reported that "He only wrote when he had a book in him," and when he did the writing would come out in a mad rush, "sometimes in only a couple weeks."

Fritz lived from 1913-1979. Born in Wisconsin, he spent much of his turbulent youth in France, interacting with remarkable people operating at a frontier of human experience. People like his mentor and father figure, G.I. Gurdjieff, and his aunt, Margaret Anderson— plus the gaggle of avant-garde greats in her milieu. Fritz learned that words and thoughts were a path to social standing and self-respect. "He was brilliant, talented. He hung out with e.e. cummings and D.H. Lawrence. He enjoyed the fame he got, but I think he wanted to be a big star," said his daughter, Katharine Rivers.

It is difficult to define a person, even in hindsight, since people are developing stories. But by midlife, Fritz's best writing was behind him. His memoirs *Boyhood with Gurdjieff (1964)*, and *Gurdjieff Remembered (1965)*, are the exception. His literary career after *The Descent (1952)* mostly amounted to rejected manuscripts and burned bridges. In the mid-1960s, a reader at Farrar Straus scrawled, "I doubt that the manuscript will get anywhere—it is so obviously [close to/or] psychotic. The poor bastard has had (and has given others) an awful life. I am not hopeful that anything will result."

Succumbing To His Demons

"He had a death wish, he was drinking himself to death," said Fritz's friend, psychologist Barbara Vacarr, of his last decade of life. Cirrhosis was noted on his death certificate. At the close of World War II, his mentor, mystic and healer G. I. Gurdjieff, recognized the delica-cy of Fritz's condition and recommended that he drink, but "con-sciously"...

> He insisted that I had such a need, but that it was periodic, and predicted that if I gauged the need properly I would go through periods where I would drink—or would need to drink—a good deal, and also sometimes through long periods when I would not need to drink at all; in fact, at such times, I would find that liquor might even be harmful for me.[1]

Gurdjieff implies that alcohol was a way to modulate Fritz's erratic moods, and probably anesthetize painful memories, but finding the prescribed balance proved perilous.

Mental illness has a nature and nurture component, both at play in Fritz's development. His childhood amounted to mitigated orphan-hood due to his parents' divorce and his mother's nervous break-downs. His mother remarried multiple times, selecting husbands who were not safe or did not want Fritz and his brother Tom present. Fritz preferred the care of Margaret Anderson, his maternal aunt, and her partner Jane Heap—largely so he could live at Gurdjieff's Institute. However, there were skeletons in that closet. This graphic episode that Fritz recounted in 1978 occurred when he was 11 years old. His disconnected, almost blasé attitude about it makes one wonder what other horrors he experienced:

> The final so-called disaster occurred when Jane [Heap], in a fit of anger...struck me with a board from a crate with nails in it.

1 Fritz Peters, *Gurdjieff Remembered* (Los Angeles: Hirsch Giovanni Publishing, 2021), 88.

Jane lost that one (or I won it, depending on how you look at it) because although the nails went all the way into my back and I was bleeding, I did not break down, cry, or otherwise participate in the scene. Jane was more than contrite, fell to her knees, hugged me, and begged for my forgiveness. I think that was the first time that my born 'rage to live' turned into active hatred. I told her that I would not only not forgive her—it was 'not my province' was one of the things that I said—but I told her that I would get even. I regret, in the long run, to have to admit that I did. On the same compulsive, unconscious, dreary level.[2]

His first novel, *The World Next Door (1949)*, shows how "succumbing to one's demons" in this manner, can be an oversimplification. As the novel unfolds in vivid stream-of-consciousness, we see that severe mental illness is not a sick spell that occurs in the context of a healthy mind, akin to a head cold. Instead, it is a state of confusion that overtakes a person who is a tenuous arrangement of wholeness; so, wholeness cannot be maintained over an extended stretch of life, with all its inherent hardships. Fritz explores the connection between alcohol and mental illness in this striking passage:

Only the liquor, a thin hot stream inside me, dripped like fuel to the last ember of warmth and light between my ribs, and fought the darkness. But there is another light beginning now: a light that does not warm, but reveals and distorts. In this light, pallor becomes sickness, and sickness, death. As the darkness itself had spread like the moving blotch of blood upon bright cloth, so this light penetrated the darkness.[3]

2 Fritz Peters, *Balanced Man* (London: Wildwood House, 1978), 62.

3 Fritz Peters, *The World Next Door* (Los Angeles: Hirsch Giovanni Publishing, 2021), 10.

When Fritz lost control of his mental state, on an extreme of what was then called manic depression, there would be no "Fritz" there to manage the alcohol, or moods, or work, or parenting, or other relationships. He would not know he was so compromised, and often neither would those closest to him. *Fig. 1* summarizes the periods of instability during Fritz's most productive decade of writing, much of which became fuel for his fiction. He recuperated in a mental hospital after his breakdown in 1958, during which he stared into the sun and claimed to be the second coming, just like the protagonist in *The World Next Door (see Fig 2)*. Forced to admit Fritz would never be a safe caretaker to their children, Jean Peters initiated divorce proceedings.

Fritz's ability to inhabit healthy and imbalanced states and communicate them to readers is one of his most illuminating transmissions—one for which he paid dearly. It would be an understatement to say that Fritz was a difficult person to live with and love. Though he was rarely single, his relationships were volatile and tended to end in explosions, if not mental breakdowns. This is perhaps why relationships—the ways in which they are doomed and the reasons they are inevitable—are what Fritz found most inspiring to write about. He distilled relationships into the heartbreaking truth that is the lifeblood of literature.

The World Next Door

The World Next Door is about a mental patient's relationship with himself, his medical staff, and his family. It examines everyone's interests and self-interest, as they scrap for dominance in the bureaucracy of a VA mental ward. Though highly autobiographical, it would be naive to take David Mitchell's words entirely at face value—he was, after all, suffering from paranoid delusions. Conversely, David Mitchell did not leave the VA Hospital against medical advice, whereas Fritz's former wife reports that he did *(see Fig. 1)*. Still, the novel speaks unflinchingly about how it feels to go through electro-shock and other crude techniques of early psychiatry, about cruelty from overburdened attendants, about a post-war government insti-tution that cared for some of its veterans (white, straight) better than others (black, gay).

In *The World Next Door,* the protagonist is conflicted about his homosexual inclinations. He claims not to prefer the company of men—he does not, therefore, identify as homosexual. However, he asserts the naturalness of his homosexual relationship: "I was in love with him, that's all."[4] Societal context makes this stance understand-able, yet revolutionary. This is because mental illness, discrimination, and homosexuality were linked in the context of a VA mental ward in the late 40s, much more deeply than today's reader might expect.

At the dawn of World War II, the U.S. military planned to cull any recruits at high risk for mental illness—prone to "shellshock," and costly disability payments. Psychiatry as a discipline was in its infan-cy, so the military added rounds of psychiatric testing to the phys-ical screening process. After World War I, "The U.S. Government spent more than a billion dollars to treat mental casualties, and it was widely recognized that the government had a responsibility to avoid a huge loss of men and money in the next war."[5]

In 1941, the category of "Homosexual proclivities" was specifical-ly identified as a form of mental illness incompatible with military

---

4 Peters, *The World Next Door*, 190.

5 Naoko Wake, "The Military, Psychiatry, and 'Unfit' Soldiers, 1939-1942," Journal of the History of Medicine and Allied Sciences 62, no. 4 (January 4, 2007): 466, https://doi.org/10.1093/jhmas/jrm002.

Fig. 1

His periods of disturbance (or, as we referred to them, his "manic" periods) are repetitive and cyclic. As far as I have been able to determine, after talking to his mother,(his former wife and a very close friend of his, the following disturbed periods occurred:

1945 two hospitalizations in Army hospital in France

1947 committed to Lyons VA Hospital in N.J. for 3 months, released "against medical advice".

1950 suicide attempt and subsequent hospitalization in Clinton, N.Y., after manic period of 3-4 months.

1953 automobile accident and hospitalizationfollowing manic period lasting from February to October.

1954 severe automobile accident after manic period of 1-2 months, around early summer.

1955 beginning period in May that decreased following our marriage in June.

1956 brief, but intense period following birth of our daughter in April, and another brief and not too intense period in August-September.

1957 June to November period, very intense in August then in October.

1958 December to February 9th commitment. Acute.

Fig. 2

Then, on January 17th, we moved. That morning he was completely irrational and unreasonable. Any differing of even trivial opinion caused a violent reaction from him. He took off his glasses and "looked into the sun"---which is indicative of the degree of his disturbance. (As described in World Next Door, in fact this was just like the book). His talking was incessant and highly erratic, but, as always, maintaining a certain logic, i.e., he would, after many and lengthy digressions, always return to his original point. During this time he spoke of his being the second coming of Christ, or going to the sun, etc.

Excerpts From a letter from Fritz's wife, Jean R. Peters to his Psychologist, Dr. St. Pierre, at the VA Hospital in Topeka Kansas, in 1958

(Fig. 1) We see how Fritz struggled with instability even in his most successful decade of writing. Elements from his novels are present, such as the suicide attempt in *Finistère (1951)*, and the car crash in *The Descent (1952)*.

(Fig. 2) *The World Next Door (1949)* is more directly autobiographical, as his wife Jean attested in further notes about his 1958 breakdown.

service by the advisory board to the military psychiatrists running the screening process. Homosexual behavior was deemed a form of sexual deviancy and a pre-psychotic state.[6] Many recruits with homosexual proclivities desired to join the war effort, however, and managed to avoid detection.

At the end of World War II, the U.S. Military hunted down and dishonorably discharged these homosexual soldiers. Gay servicemen found guilty of sodomy were incarcerated, as it was illegal, and lesbian soldiers were also targeted. A dishonorable discharge rendered these soldiers ineligible for benefits, and they suffered sometimes serious indignities in the process. At worst, they were held in impromptu brigs, in prisoner-of-war conditions, possibly sexually assaulted, even, by their own captors.[7] This phenomenon is echoed in *The World Next Door* when David Mitchell has an experience of being sexually coerced by an attendant in the VA hospital. For those homosexual soldiers lucky enough to be stationed where the U.S. Army ejected them under less inhumane conditions, the outcome was still damaging. A diagnosis would be placed on the gay soldier's discharge papers which could out them as homosexual.

If a diagnosis was listed on the discharge papers, the soldiers would be associated with a mental illness that sounded severe. "Psychotic personality" was one such label.[8] Anyone looking at their records could see the reason for their discharge—such as potential employers who requested military records for job applications. Homosexuals who managed to be hired were not secure in their offices, either.

---

6 Wake, "The Military, Psychiatry, and 'Unfit' Soldiers, 1939-1942," 476.

7 For first-hand accounts of this see *Coming Out Under Fire*, directed by Arthur Dong (1994; New York: Deep Focus Productions, Inc).

8 Wake, "The Military, Psychiatry, and 'Unfit' Soldiers, 1939-1942," 485.

Thousands of homosexual employees were purged from Federal positions during the Lavender Scare of McCarthyism, under discriminatory practices which persisted in the following decades.[9]

It is difficult to know how these policies affected Fritz during his short stint in the military, since he was justifiably mentally ill enough to be hospitalized and was honorably discharged. This context explains, however, why the medical staff was aware of David Mitchell's gay relationship in *The World Next Door*, and why the flirtation with the gay General was such a delicate matter. It explains why it was so difficult for Fritz and doctors to separate his sexuality from his mental illness. It also explains the stakes of going straight, and how confusing the situation must have been for a man with homosexual leanings, and manic depression, who was also attracted to women. A post-war reader would know this background, and perceive the hidden currents it creates in the storyline.

On the psychiatric side, as Fritz describes in *The World Next Door*, homosexuals tended to be well-behaved patients and many doctors treated them sympathetically; doctors had bigger problems on a mental ward. However, sympathy has its limits in the context of the pathologization of one's sexuality. Homosexuals of the time had difficulty navigating their mental health problems, especially if they refused to renounce their sexuality. Ed Field had such an experience with a doctor "who immediately decided that my homosexuality was at the root of all my miseries, and set out to change me."[10]

9 Suyin Haynes, "You've Probably Heard of the Red Scare, but the Lesser-Known, Anti-Gay 'Lavender Scare' Is Rarely Taught in Schools," *TIME* magazine, December 22, 2020, https://time.com/5922679/lavender-scare-history/.

10 Edward Field, afterword to *Finistère*, by Fritz Peters (Vancouver: Arsenal Pulp Press, 2006), 333-34.

Homosexuality would not be completely de-pathologized, removed from the Diagnostic Statistician's Manual (along with any loophole that enabled billing insurance for conversion therapy), until "ego-dystonic homosexuality" was removed in 1987.[11] This was after years of gay activism and vitriolic national debates. It would be three more decades before homosexuals earned an uncloseted place in the military, in 2011. Accordingly, Fritz's first-hand account of attitudes towards homosexuality, and the realities of homosexual soldiers on the VA mental ward, in post-war America, is compelling reportage relevant to both U.S. and Queer history.

The World Next Door impressed the medical community in 1949 and was carried in psychiatric libraries. They valued it because it was a unique first-hand account of what a severely ill patient experiences on a mental ward. Timely and bold, it also struck a nerve with post-war readers. "Not so much composed as forced out of the writer by the need to put down a terrible experience while still raw and quivering from its impact," wrote Antonia White, in *New Statesman*. With its experimental treatment of such gritty subject matter, Peters' autobiographical novel was critically well-received on the literary front and Fritz was lauded as a young writer to watch.

Finistère

"I loved *Finistère* because it was a beautiful love story. It showed Fritz's tenderness and the connection at the place where you could see his soul," said Barbara Vacarr.

Finistère, published only two years after *The World Next Door*, is a

11 Jack Drescher, "Out of DSM: Depathologizing Homosexuality," *Behavioral Sciences (Basel)* 5, no. 4 (December 4, 2015), Page 565, https://www.ncbi.nlm.nih.gov/pmc/articles/PMC4695779/.

coming-of-age, coming-out story about a teen's love affair with the tennis coach at his French boarding school. It is Fritz Peter's most successful book, by far. Hirsch Giovanni chose to adapt *Finistère* for screen first, not because of its popularity, but because of its zeitgeist as a landmark novel of queer literature. So much ground has been won for queer rights over the past century, and so many aspects of gender have been redefined, that the current mood is to be reflective about the past while envisioning the future. *Finistère*'s themes of confusion, isolation, and self-destruction in the face of intolerance are, sadly, still applicable to queer teens today. But *Finistère* also celebrates love's ability to blossom where it is required, and it portrays love as an instinctive tropism toward healing and hope. It is thus a pioneering gay paean as much as it is a classic romance relevant to anyone who loves.

Finistère would not be art if it did not ask difficult questions and reveal uncomfortable truths. Today's readers are, hopefully, dismayed that the lovers in *Finistère* are so far apart in age. Michel is in his late 20s, and Matthew is only a teen. Upon opening the book to read, this writer was concerned the material might be handled inappropriately. Closing the book, those concerns were allayed. *Finistère*, with all its controversial aspects, provides valuable insight into the field of human experience.

It is perhaps unavoidable to compare *Finistère* to Nabokov's *Lolita*. *Lolita* is also a classic, adapted to film amid controversy. Readers find its age gap scandalous. However, Humbert Humbert, the narrator of *Lolita*, has a predilection for young ladies and premeditatively targets girls without remorse. He marries Lolita's mother to get closer to the object of his desire. Humbert is, simply put, a pedophile. On the contrary, Michel is a gay man who is uncomfortable with older/younger affairs, even though they were accepted by his peers in 1920s

Paris. Michel broke with his long-term lover when the latter engaged in an encounter with an adolescent, the last straw after multiple infidelities. Heartbroken and disgusted, Michel accepts a teaching position that his father arranges. Michel is relieved to escape the excesses of Paris and has abandoned all hope for love. Suppressing his sexual impulses entirely—"vows of chastity, purity, reform"[12]—seems the best course of action. Matthew, though younger, initiates and directs the affair. Such details mitigate Michel's questionable behavior as much as possible. Many readers will likely react with moral disgust anyway, condemning Michel, opining that as the superior, Michel should have drawn a line—should not have engaged in any physical encounter with a student. Michel could have waited, they might say, if the two really loved each other. That perspective is valid.

However, relationships like Matthew and Michel's happen, and they happen for a reason. *Finistère* faces this reality. Why did it happen in this case? Why was it doomed? Does that mean such relationships are always doomed? Would Matthew have survived to adulthood with nobody to love him? If Michel had loved Matthew better, would their affair still have ended in tragedy? Was it possible for Michel to love Matthew better? What family and societal contexts contributed to the outcome? How would you feel if you read it as a teenager? Would you feel differently if you read it as a parent? Have you ever done anything unwise for love? Saying Michel should have drawn a line is like saying Othello should have ignored Iago. Pondering controversial situations in stories develops wisdom and compassion, fostering better decisions in the real world. That has always been the utility of tragedy.

Finistère feels too closely observed to be invented, but due to the covert nature of the relationship, it is unclear to whom it refers. Even

---

12 Fritz Peters, *Finistère*, (Los Angeles: Hirsch Giovanni Publishing, 2021), 146.

the dedication to the novel is an enigma: "For A.P.S. and L.S.B.S 1900-1950." Enigma invites conjecture. It is the only dedication Fritz writes that does not use full names. A person born in 1900 would be thirteen years older than Fritz (born Arthur Peters), roughly the age gap in the novel. A person who died in 1950 would have passed while Fritz was writing *Finistère*. Fritz attended boarding school in France for short periods of time, though he never graduated high school nor worked as a teacher.

When Fritz wrote *Finistère* he was in his late thirties and married to *Harper's Bazaar* fiction editor, Mary Lou Aswell. Fritz dedicated *The World Next Door* to Mary Lou, "without whom this book would not have been written." Aswell also had an interest in mental illness; she edited a book titled *The World Within (1947)*, shortly before meeting Fritz, which is a collection of "fiction illuminating the neuroses of our time." She fostered the careers of many homosexual writers in Bazaar's pages, including Truman Capote. Ed Field, (Fritz's friend, gay poet and World War II veteran) reported that what Fritz wrote depended on the relationship he was in at the time, so it seems that Mary Lou was Fritz's most effective muse.

Aswell would go on to partner with sculptor Agnes Sims, her first same-sex lover, and Fritz dedicated his next novel, *The Descent*, to Agnes. The two women moved to Santa Fe, where their household was openly possible. One of the most affecting dynamics in *Finistère* is the impossibility for same-sex relationships to endure in a culture that is so intolerant of them. Although the current fashion bends toward feel-good LGBTQ stories, it is also important to understand the necessity of societal support to provide a framework for lasting relationships. In *Finistère* the "problem" was not the homosexuality, it was the intolerance. It is this perspective that made *Finistère* so pioneering. Threatened by Matthew's naivete, Michel remarks, "I suppose there's no reason why you should be able to understand that your happiness is something the world would think of as ugly and horrible and unnatural. But they do and I guess you'll learn soon enough."[13]

The *New York Times* review echoed this sentiment, saying "So far as this reviewer recalls, this is the best novel he has ever read on the theme of homosexuality (Proust excepted) and its tragic consequences in a world made up of 'selfish, ruthless, cruel, egocentric people.'"[14] Ed Field agreed: "*Finistère* is a marvelous book. It was the first gay novel I read, the rest were pulp."

The Descent

During the breakup of his marriage to Mary Lou, at the close of 1950, Fritz stood on the side of the highway interviewing motorists in upstate New York. He was working on his next novel, *The Descent*. If *Finistère* is a novel about why homosexual relationships cannot work, *The Descent* is a novel about why heterosexual relationships cannot work. We see couples poisoned by gender norms; the desire to dominate and be dominated poisoning Henry and Mabel, the cycle of lust and shame poisoning Caroline and Tom, the projections of male inadequacy poisoning Richard and Dorothy.

At the time Fritz operated in society as a heterosexual, but he always had male lovers. Fritz writes female characters remarkably well for a male writer, inhabiting them in a manner that only someone who has been an object of male desire can. He has an objective, almost anthropological eye to gender relations. Doris Hart, the hospital admin

13 Peters, *Finistère*, 155.

14 Herbert F. West, "Deep Water — And Black," *New York Times*, February 18, 1951, https://www.nytimes.com/1951/02/18/archives/deep-water-and-black.html.

from *The Descent*, exemplifies this when she casts off the desire for validation from her patronizing, patriarchal psychologist. "What was it that Dr. Cramwell had written? 'Psychological problems?' 'Primeval female sexual manifestations?' It was all a lot of nonsense. And why was she spending ten hard-earned dollars an hour to go to him?"[15]

Doris Hart's reverie continues on a slightly different track, "She thought of her husband with curious unexpected tenderness. If she stopped going to Dr. Cramwell, he'd be able to afford a new suit. And she might, eventually, be able to afford a television set." *The Descent* is also a portrait of post-war America and its hyperactive consumer-conformism, playing out in intimate relationships. This conformism was itself a veneer over societal divisions and war trauma—exemplified by the character of Jim Curran, the troubled war veteran. How can veterans relate to those who stayed home, and vice versa? How can men and women bridge the gender gap? Another return to normalcy. Do we all realize how normal it is to feel unfulfilled? What is the American Dream's answer to that? Where are we all going, so fast?

A tightly written suspense novel with a *Twilight Zone* feel, *The Descent* was well-received. However, Fritz could not know the turn his life was about to take. He would not publish again for twelve years. After finishing *The Descent*, Fritz fell into a long-term relationship with a man for the first time, Santa Fe-based painter Cady Wells. Fritz thought Cady was "the one," but it ended in volatile fights:

> Although Cady was enraptured with Fritz, his friends found
> Peters threatening and hateful, and he was a deeply disturbed

---

15 Fritz Peters, *The Descent* (Los Angeles: Hirsch Giovanni Publishing, 2021), 255.

man (he apparently once tried to kill Cady with a knife). Another of Peters' lovers, the painter William Brown, explained that each time Peters had a homosexual love affair he would rebound from it by marrying.[16]

Cady died soon after their split, of a heart attack, and Fritz headed into family life, marrying Jean. As *The Descent* foretold, and as already discussed, family life was not a good fit. After their divorce, Fritz moved to New York and finally found a stable relationship, by Fritz's standards, with painter Lloyd Goff. He seemed more at peace living as a gay man, according to his daughter. He sent money home for the children and kept in contact via frequent letters, phone calls, gifts, and occasional visits. He finally attempted writing again. His U.K. publisher, Victor Gollancz, encouraged him to write memoirs. Fritz published *Boyhood with Gurdjieff* in 1964, for which Henry Miller wrote the preface, saying "I regard it as something on a par with *Alice in Wonderland*, a real treasure of our literature."[17] Although it was a critical success followed by a sequel, *Gurdjieff Remembered* (1965), in terms of sales the memoirs found only a niche. *The World Next Door* was recorded for French radio and there were references, in Fritz's letters to Farrar Straus, to film deals that never solidified. He attempted writing novels again, and the rejections hit hard. He harangued Farrar Straus to republish his earlier novels or else revert the rights to him. Fritz was soon short on cash, began drinking more and more heavily and took on a seedy appearance. At the start of the 70s, Fritz headed back to Santa Fe, began a new novel, and published

16 Lois P. Rudnick, "Under the Skin of New Mexico: The Life, Times, and Art of Cady Wells," in *Cady Wells and Southwestern Modernism*, ed. Lois P. Rudnick (Santa Fe: Museum of New Mexico Press, 2009), 71.

17 Henry Miller, preface to *Boyhood with Gurdjieff*, by Fritz Peters (Santa Barbara: Capra Press, 1980), Page ii.

a final essay about Gurdjieff. Although Gurdjieff had died some 30 years earlier, Fritz spent his last days remembering the man and what they had meant to each other.

Gurdjieff — Father Figure And Guru

Gurdjieff had a powerful personality and a magnetic aura; it was easy for him to attract seekers to learn the esoteric wisdom he had accumulated. A mainstay of the philosophy at his *Institute for the Harmonious Development of Man* was that people go through life "asleep," so precious few develop themselves anywhere near their capacity. This is due to a failure to "do the work"—people lack the knowledge and focus to develop their various "centers." The "centers" are the Intellectual, Emotional, and Physical modes of being. These centers operate individually and together, creating new processes, requiring many types of "work" to exercise them all. Gurdjieff even called his teachings, "The Work." Confronting the real world, and all the obstacles one must overcome to finish a job, was one way to "wake up." This was chop-wood-carry-water spirituality, involving tasks like cooking, gardening, roofing, lawnmowing. Music and dance held a special role in the curriculum. Gurdjieff also employed flamboyant tricks, like pranks, to incite friction between people, launching them headfirst into healing crises. Dealing with the "unpleasant manifestations of others" leads to self-awareness and growth. Therefore, Gurdjieff appreciated Fritz's diligence, as much as his aptitude for mischief:

> Gurdjieff laughed, "What you not understand," he said, "is that not everyone can be troublemaker, like you. This important in life—is ingredient, like yeast for making bread. Without trouble, conflict, life become dead. People live in status quo, live only by habit, automatically, and without conscience. You good for Miss Madison. You irritate Miss Madison all time—more than

anyone else, which is why you get most reward. Without you, possibility for Miss Madison's conscience fall asleep.[18]

Putting Gurdjieff's practices in parable form is what Fritz achieves in *Boyhood with Gurdjeff*, in the direct style of Gurdjieff's teaching. As Gurdjieff's personal assistant, Fritz had an intimate view of the goings-on in the Institute. Gurdjieff appreciated Fritz's interest in philosophy and psychology, saying that Fritz was a "trash can" for Gurdjieff to "dump" his teaching into. What probably made Fritz so empty is that he had been abandoned by his family. He needed a trustworthy adult who could direct his curiosity and his stubborn streak. Fritz would never shake Gurdjieff's influence and would always work to digest it – Gurdjieff's ideas pervade Fritz's writing. Though Fritz read voraciously, he never finished high school nor attended college. Gurdjieff's Institute was his education, the stories he walked with and measured against. Michael Vacarr, Fritz's friend explained:

> Fritz said Gurdjieff saved his life. He was the only adult who made sense to him. Could Gurdjieff have saved his brother's life? I don't know. There was something Fritz brought to the situation with Gurdjieff that allowed Fritz to benefit from it. And Gurdjieff didn't let Fritz get lost in feeling sorry for himself.

Shortly before his death in 1949, Gurdjieff enacted an impactful prank-teaching, when he made an announcement at a gathering of students that Fritz attended. As Fritz recounts it, Gurdjieff said:

18 Fritz Peters, *Boyhood with Gurdjieff* (Los Angeles: Hirsch Giovanni Publishing, 2021), 170.

'In life is only necessary for man to find one person to whom can give accumulation of learning in life. When find such receptacle, then is possible die.' He smiled, benevolently, and went on: 'So now two good things happen for me. I finish work and I also find one person to whom can give results my life's work.' He raised his arm again, started to move it, this time with a finger extended and pointing, around the room, and then stopped when his finger was pointing directly at me. There was an enormous silence in the room and Gurdjieff and I looked at each other fixedly, but, even so, I was aware that one or two of the others had turned to look in my direction. The tension in the atmosphere did not lessen until Gurdjieff dropped his arm, turned, and left the room.[19]

Fritz would struggle with the mantle of chosen successor for the rest of his life. Gurdieff's motivations for announcing this were mysterious, and Fritz thought of a few explanations. First, it might be "actually true." Second, it might be intended to "expose" Fritz's "massive ego" to himself—this was the preferred explanation of many Gurdjieff followers. Third, perhaps it was "a huge joke on the devout followers."

There is a special irony in selecting a person with a Messiah Complex to be one's "true successor." It is even possible Gurdjieff was making a joke at his own expense. Whatever the case, Fritz was "moved, confused, and perplexed" by the event.[20] Fritz would spend the rest of his days causing fuss and friction at Gurdjieff meetings and claiming to be the true successor, whether he truly believed it or not.

~~~~~~~~~

19 Peters, *Gurdjieff Remembered*, 90-91.

20 Peters, *Gurdjieff Remembered*, 93.

Why Fritz?

Fritz was more human than most. With internal and external experiences so extreme, he encountered the range of human experience in a way most people do not. There has always been a link between manic depression and creativity, perhaps because it is difficult to communicate peak experiences without resorting to art. In person Fritz could be charming, present, helpful, and funny—also irascible, inappropriate, inebriated, and exhausting. All of that is in his writing.

Given Fritz's extreme states, it is surprising that the real power of his writing is its startling clarity; the bullseyes of emotional truth he finds. "The shadows are the first to go," is the first line of *The World Next Door*—Fritz claimed e. e. cummings said it was "the best first sentence in the history of the English language."[21] Fritz's writing is true, and clear, and evocative; also, readable. Fritz desired "always to be known as a readable writer rather than a great artist."[22] There is something of Gurdjieff's teachings and character in the pragmatism, the immediacy, the uncompromising search for truth and self, that is at the heart of it.

But the biggest tragedy of mental instability, which Fritz captures in *The World Next Door*, is being unable to understand, or control, the way one hurts people. "Seeing ourselves how others see us," as Gurdjieff would put it—is a challenge for everyone, but especially for those with a tenuous grasp on "self." Even in his healthiest and happiest moments, Fritz spent his life in this exile. He wrote to us from the electroshock table, from the queer underground, from

21 Jane Madeline Gold, *Down from Above, Up from Below* (Rhinebeck: Epigraph Books, 2021), 25.

22 Richard H. Costa, "Author Pens Tale of Route 20," *Utica Observer-Dispatch*, December 10, 1950.

puberty, from the side of the road, from a marriage on its last leg, from the rubble of World War II, from Gurdjieff's intentional community. Fritz went there and reported back—that was his gift.

VETERANS ADMINISTRATION

Lyons, New Jersey

October 25, 1950

YOUR FILE REFERENCE:

IN REPLY REFER TO: 5110HP10PD

Farrar, Straus & Co., Inc.,
53 E. 34th Street,
New York 16, New York

Attn: Mr. Roger W. Straus Jr.

Gentlemen:

As publishers of Fritz Peters' book, entitled "The World Next Door", 1949, you will be interested in knowing that we at this hospital have been tremendously interested in the contents of this publication. You may be aware of the fact that Mr. Peters was at one time a patient at this hospital and that the story he describes actually deals with the problems and events which took place at this establishment.

The book is of tremendous interest and it can be considered not only as an artistic product of the highest calibre, but also a a psychiatric revelation of immeasurable importance and significance. There is hardly any publication in world literature which can be compared with the depths of penetration and with the uncanny insight of the author in putting into words his experiences while undergoing the psychiatric process.

We considered the book so valuable that we have held many seminars discussing the book's implications with our psychiatric residents and other professional personnel who were anxious and eager to get a first-hand bit of information of a patient's experiences as reflected through the artistry of a creative personality.

We intend to elaborate many features of the book psychiatrically and to lecture about it in psychiatric organizations, and to publish some aspects of it in scientific Psychiatric Journals. However, in order to do that we would like to have your permission to quote from the book and to give full credit to its sources. Would it be possible to secure such permission?

One of the undersigned is Director of Professional Education, in charge of training and education of psychiatric residents, staff and other professional personnel; the other, has been in close contact with Mr. Peters while he was hospitalized at this hospital. His interest is not only scientific, but personal, and

An inquiry by or concerning an ex-service man or woman should, if possible, give veteran's name and file number, whether C, XC, K, N, or V. If such file number is unknown, service or serial number should be given.

A letter from the Veterans Administration hospital where Fritz Peters was previously admitted, to Roger Straus, founding publisher at Farrar, Straus and Co. Ironically, this was written after *The New York Times* published a negative review of *The World Next Door* from a bestselling author, so as not to upset the VA. The fear was that the book's controversial content and tremendous first-hand account of the patient experience would expose them, but it went on to be carried in psychiatric libraries. This was pulled from the New York Public Library archives.

he considers himself privileged to have been associated with such
an unusual personality as Mr. Peters.

Thank you in advance for your courtesies.

Very truly yours,

Leslie Freeman
LESLIE FREEMAN, M. D.

Arpad Pauncz
ARPAD PAUNCZ, M. D.
Director, Professional Education

FRITZ PETERS
1913 – 1979

Born in Madison, Wisconsin, Arthur Anderson "Fritz" Peters was the author of both novels and memoirs, which touched on themes of spirituality, mental illness, homosexuality, self and society, always through the lens of an unrelenting individuality and nonconformism.

Peters' most successful novel was *Finistère*, published in 1951, which sold over 350,000 copies and was an influential and unapologetic work of early gay literature. Due to instability in his family life, Peters spent his childhood between Europe and the United States, often nurtured by those adults who were able and willing to assist.

Central to his upbringing was his aunt Margaret Anderson and her partner Jane Heap, creators of *The Little Review* literary magazine, along with other members of their circle, such as Gertrude Stein. Most notably, the esoteric teacher Georges Gurdjieff interacted closely with Fritz from an early age and was hugely influential in Peters' life and literature. *Boyhood with Gurdjieff*, Peters' most popular memoir, paints these figures and their projects in a thoughtful and intimate light.

About The Publisher

Hirsch Giovanni Entertainment is an LA-based independent production company founded by Hollywood industry veteran, David M. Hirsch and Giovanni J. Guidotti, CEO of Giovanni Eco Chic Beauty in 2019. The intersection of books and films led to the establishment of Hirsch Giovanni Publishing in 2022. The two divisions form a connected effort to usher compelling narratives into the world.